"The tale overall is incredibly charming, the writing dramatic, and the characters bold."

—*Romance Reader*

"Absolutely delightful." —*Fresh Fiction*

"A sexy, quirky, altogether fun read, Valerie Bowman's *Secrets of a Runaway Bride* is everything a romance should be. Block out a few hours for this one...once you start reading, you won't be able to stop!"

—Sarah MacLean,
*New York Times* bestselling author

"Valerie Bowman pens fabulous, sexy tales—it's no secret she's a Regency author to watch!"

—*USA Today* bestselling author Kieran Kramer

## SECRETS OF A WEDDING NIGHT

"The most charming and clever debut I've read in years! With her sparkling dialogue, vivid characters, and self-assured writing style, Valerie Bowman has instantly established herself as a romance author with widespread appeal. This engaging and sweetly romantic story is just too delightful to miss."

—*New York Times* bestselling author Lisa Kleypas

"Clever, fun, and fantastic!"
—Suzanne Enoch, *New York Times* bestselling author

ALSO BY VALERIE BOWMAN

*Secrets of a Wedding Night*
*Secrets of a Runaway Bride*
*Secrets of a Scandalous Marriage*

# The Unexpected Duchess

## VALERIE BOWMAN

St. Martin's Paperbacks

This is a work of fiction. All of the characters, organizations, and events portrayed in this novel are either products of the author's imagination or are used fictitiously.

THE UNEXPECTED DUCHESS

For information address St. Martin's Press, 175 Fifth Avenue, New York, NY 10010.

ISBN: 978-1-250-04207-1

Printed in the United States of America

St. Martin's Paperbacks edition / May 2014

St. Martin's Paperbacks are published by St. Martin's Press, 175 Fifth Avenue, New York, NY 10010.

10  9  8  7  6  5  4  3  2  1

*For my sister, Janet Culkin,*
*who has to explain to the IT guys at work why*
*she has book covers with half-naked men on*
*them hanging in her office.*

*I love you, Janny.*

## ❧ CHAPTER ONE ❧
### *London, Late June 1815*

Lady Lucy Upton blew a leaf away from her lips. A twig in her eye and a mouthful of foliage were the unfortunate by-products of having her head lodged in a hedgerow. Not to mention, it was a bit chilly outside tonight. But this had been her idea, after all, and she intended to see it through.

Lucy was secure in her position behind the bushes in the Chamberses' garden just steps away from her dearest friend, Cassandra Monroe. There might be a ball going on inside the stylish town house, but out here they were quite alone . . . for the moment. Lucy pushed her head through the branches as far as she could and craned her neck to see Cass.

Cass stood on the other side of the hedgerow, rubbing her shaking hands up and down her pale, trembling arms. "What if I cannot hear you, Lucy?" she whispered.

"Don't be nervous, Cass. I'll be right here."

Cass gulped and nodded.

"See, you heard that, didn't you?" Lucy asked.

Another shaky nod from Cass.

"Excellent," Lucy called out.

The light from the candles that had been sprinkled throughout the gardens cast a warm glow on the pebble-strewn path where Cass stood. "What if he doesn't come?" Cass asked, tugging on her gloves, a sure sign she was nervous.

"He'll come. He said he would, didn't he? And Jane agreed to remain inside and keep an eye on things. Your mother, specifically."

"Yes, he said he would come. Though heaven knows I want to die of embarrassment. And if Mother discovers I'm out here meeting a man in the gardens, she'll disown me."

Lucy grunted. "Not if the man in question is the Duke of Claringdon."

"Mama will be so angry if she learns that I'm discouraging him." Cass bit her lip.

Lucy readjusted her position behind the hedge. "That's just it. We must ensure she doesn't find out."

More tugging on the gloves. "What if the duke guesses you're back there and becomes angry?"

"Must you always worry, Cass? He won't know. And even if he does, he has no business becoming angry. While I give the man credit for his bravery in war, it hardly ensures he'd make a good husband."

"I'm certain he'll make someone a perfectly fine husband, it's just . . ." Cass glanced away.

Lucy knew. Her heart wrenched for her friend. Unrequited love was an awful thing. "He's not Julian."

Cass bowed her head. "Cousin Penelope says Julian should be home any day now but . . . I just can't . . ."

"You don't have to explain it, Cass. I understand. Well, I don't understand love, having never been in it myself, but don't worry. First we'll see to dispatching the duke, and then I intend to ensure you are given your chance with Julian."

Cass rubbed her arms with renewed vigor. "I'm being ridiculous, I know. Julian is supposed to marry Penelope."

"It doesn't matter," Lucy replied. "The fact is you do *not* want to marry the Duke of Claringdon and you shall not. Regardless of what your mother might want. Not if I have anything to say about it. I cannot countenance anyone being bullied and I certainly shall not allow you to be. By either your mother or the duke. Besides, you can never go wrong if you're honest and follow your heart."

"Oh, Lucy, that's what you always say. And I love you for it, I truly do. I've no idea how you think you'll be able to give me a chance with Julian, but I do adore your optimism."

"First things first. And at present our problem is the duke."

Both young women were silenced when a shadow blocked the lights from the French doors leading to the house. The sound of gravel crunching beneath boots met their ears.

"It's him," Cass whispered, her voice wavering.

"Do not be intimidated, Cass. Courage, my friend. Be bold!"

In the next instant, the little clearing in which Cass stood was overpowered by the presence of the Duke of Claringdon. The moment he saw Cass, he stopped. From her vantage point, Lucy could only see him from the chest down. The impossibly broad chest down. She swallowed.

"Lady Cassandra," the duke intoned, bowing.

Cass gave a little squeak and curtsied. "Thank you for meeting me, Your Grace." Her voice was high and frightened. Lucy wished she could reach through the branches and give Cass's hand a warm, encouraging squeeze. *Courage, Cass. Courage.*

"I must admit, I was a bit surprised that you asked to meet me here," the duke said.

"I did not mean to surprise you, Your Grace, I merely wanted to . . . I merely wanted to . . ."

Lucy snapped from her thoughts. This was it. Time to begin. Cass was already floundering for words. Lucy cleared her throat. "I hoped we could speak privately, my lord," she whispered loudly.

Cass repeated the words in a shaking voice.

"I see" came the duke's response. He took a step forward, and Lucy sucked in her breath.

"Please, Your Grace, come no closer. I wouldn't want anyone happening upon us to consider our meeting here an impropriety," Lucy offered, in a voice low enough she was certain the duke couldn't hear.

Cass repeated the words.

The duke laughed. "You do not find it an impropriety, Lady Cassandra, to be alone with me in the garden?"

Lucy frowned. Well, if he was going to quibble over details. "I only ask for a moment of your time, to make my wishes clear."

Cass said the words quickly.

"Very well. Go ahead," said the duke.

Lucy took a deep breath. "While I am certain there are many young ladies who would be flattered by your attention, Your Grace, I must admit I am not one."

Lucy could almost feel Cass cringe as she repeated the words. She frantically tugged on her gloves as she spoke.

Lucy moved her head to catch the duke's reaction. She swallowed. Oh, she shouldn't have looked. Just as she'd discovered earlier in the ballroom, the man was handsome. Too handsome.

"I see, Lady Cassandra. And may I ask exactly why *you* feel this way?"

Lucy pulled up her shoulders. Uh-oh. He was demanding a reason. What? He couldn't conceive of a lady who would not welcome his advances? A moment ago she'd felt a bit sorry for the duke, but her protective instinct for Cass overpowered her thoughts. Now she wanted to cut him to the quick with her words. Which just happened to be her specialty.

"You may have yet to discover a woman who was not enamored of you, my lord. But I assure you, they do exist," Lucy whispered to Cass, narrowing her eyes on the tall man.

Another small squeak escaped from Cass's mouth. She turned her head sharply to the side. "Lucy, I cannot say that." The words rushed out in a tiny whisper.

Lucy nearly fell through the bush. This entire charade was dependent on Cass maintaining their façade. *Just repeat the words*, she mentally begged her friend, repeating her sentence in a rush.

Cass's eyes darted to the side and Lucy held her breath, waiting for her friend to say the withering sentence.

"I cannot say, my lord," Cass replied instead. "It's just that I . . ."

Lucy groaned. Cass wasn't going to say it. Ooh, if only Lucy could say it herself. A silly vision flashed before her eyes. One of her snatching Cass off her feet, pulling her behind the hedgerow, and rushing out to stand in her stead. Yes, silly. And unlikely to work. A pity. Very well. Lucy would be forced to tone down her words if she was going to help Cass. And she could tone down her words . . . if she . . . thought about it for a moment. She took a deep breath.

"Very well. Let me be clear. I am singularly uninterested in becoming the future Duchess of Claringdon,"

Lucy provided. "Especially when the duke is so obviously arrogant and overbearing."

Cass gasped. "Lucy!"

The duke's eyes narrowed on the hedgerow then. Lucy instinctively drew back her head just before he marched forward, reached around the bush, and pulled her sharply into the clearing. She came flying out, twigs lodged in her dismantled coiffure and several leaves trailing into her décolletage. A twig had scratched her cheek. She rubbed it, glaring at him.

The duke eyed her with an arrogant inclination of his head. "I thought you had an echo, Lady Cassandra. Now I see your serpent's tongue has a name. Good evening, Miss Upton."

# CHAPTER TWO

Derek Hunt narrowed his eyes on the young woman he'd plucked from the bushes. He could see enough of her in the light from the candles scattered about the gardens. She had bouncy black hair and bright blue eyes—wait, one of her eyes was blue, the other was hazel—and a decidedly unhappy look on her upturned face. Her chest was heaving with what was no doubt indignation, and if looks could cause bodily harm he'd be a heap in the mulch right now.

Lady Lucy Upton.

He'd noticed her earlier in the ballroom. All the men had noticed her. She was stunning. Even with leaves stuck in her hair and a twig hanging from one dark curl. He'd heard a rumor about something unusual in her appearance but he'd not been able to discern it before. Must be the eyes. Regardless of their odd colors, she was a beauty.

He'd questioned Lord Chambers about her.

"Firmly on the shelf," Chambers had replied. "No suitors."

"Why's that?" Derek had asked nonchalantly. "She's certainly pretty enough."

Apparently, the lady had a rapier for a tongue. She jabbed with nouns, riposted with verbs. And she delivered adjectives with a particular flourish. By all accounts, she was a master. One who could rip an overzealous beau to shreds in mere seconds. According to Lord Chambers, it didn't take long for the eligible bachelors of the *ton*, those who were not otherwise occupied with war, to disentangle themselves from any association with Lady Lucy.

Derek eyed the dark-haired beauty closely. He had recently turned thirty. He had just returned from the war. He'd spent years being shot at and had nearly died half a dozen times on battlefields across the Continent. Now he was looking for peace.

Lady Cassandra had been recommended to him. She was considered quiet and demure. "The perfect choice for a wife," Swift had said. The perfect choice for a man seeking a peaceful life. An obedient wife.

Lady Lucy Upton was the exact opposite.

"Your Grace," Lady Cassandra began, obviously fumbling to explain the highly unusual situation. "We were just . . ."

Derek crossed his arms over his chest and watched the two young women. Obviously Lady Cassandra was mortified. Her lovely face was bright pink, and she looked as if she wanted to flee from this entire debacle. Lady Lucy, on the other hand, looked as if she was merely getting started.

"I think I know what you were doing," he replied, staring down his nose at the two of them. "If I don't mistake my guess, Miss Upton here was behind the bushes, offering you guidance in the form of things to say to me." His eyes were riveted on Lady Lucy, who clearly wanted to slap him. "Am I right, Miss Upton? Do words escape Lady Cassandra?"

The beautiful termagant opened her mouth to speak. She was shaking with antagonism toward him. Oh, he couldn't *wait* to hear this.

"Why don't you choose someone to provoke who is worthy of your skill?" Lady Lucy shot back at him.

He arched a brow. "Like you?"

Her eyes blazed fire at him. "Exactly like me. I may not match you in height, weight, or arrogance, but I assure you that I am not intimidated by you. And while we're chastising each other, *Your Grace*, you might be reminded that I am the daughter of an earl and am *Lady* Lucy, not Miss Upton."

Derek had to bite the inside of his cheek to keep from smiling at the reprimand. He'd known perfectly well he was speaking to a lady. But there was nothing the peers of the realm hated more than anyone misquoting their precious titles. He himself had been born the first of three sons of a soldier. A complete nobody who rose to his rank purely on his own military merit. Yes, he was a duke now—rewarded by the Crown for his exceptional decision-making skill in battle, or so they'd told him—and everyone was eager to make his acquaintance. It sickened him. And he refused to play. Though interestingly enough, Lady Cassandra and Lady Lucy didn't seem to care a bit about his illustrious title at the moment, did they?

Derek watched Lucy Upton. He had spent the last few years barking orders. He was a man used to having those orders carried out immediately, and here was a slip of a young woman who not only refused to snap to attention but also seemed to enjoy antagonizing him. He had to reluctantly admit, it fascinated him.

The solider in him admired her penchant for forthrightness. He also reluctantly admired her for standing up for her friend and being loyal. But Lady Lucy was not about to dissuade him from his goal.

"My apologies, *my lady*," he said with a mocking bow. He didn't miss her haughty look of disapproval.

"We're ever so sorry for deceiving you, Your Grace," Lady Cassandra said, her voice still quavering. She shuffled her slippers through the gravel, looking as if she'd just confessed to the greatest sin imaginable.

"No, we're not!" Lady Lucy nearly shouted, her arms crossed, her fingertips tapping near her elbows.

Lady Cassandra's angelic blue eyes went wide. "Lucy!"

Derek held up a hand. "No. No. Lady Cassandra. Please allow *Lady* Lucy to speak. I'm quite looking forward to her explanation."

Lady Lucy propped her fists on her hips and took two steps forward. She moved a hand up to her hair and plucked out the errant twig. "We do not owe you an explanation, *Your Grace*. But the truth is that Lady Cassandra is not interested in your suit. It's that simple."

"Is it?" he asked, solidly planting a smirk on his face.

"Yes."

"And is that *your* opinion, Lady Lucy, or Lady Cassandra's opinion?"

He could tell she was grinding her teeth. "Ask her," Lady Lucy replied.

"I would, *my lady*, but I'm afraid you would answer for her." He gave her a false smile.

Lady Cassandra made a noise that sounded as if she were being suffocated. "I suggest we all go back indoors and—"

Lady Lucy continued speaking to Derek as if Lady Cassandra hadn't even spoken. "How dare you question the actions of a lady?"

Derek stared serenely back at her. "How dare you answer for Lady Cassandra?"

Lady Lucy's eyes seemed to be changing colors with her mood, the one turning deep sapphire and the other mossy green. "If you were a gentleman, *Your Grace*, you wouldn't question Lady Cassandra and her disinterest in your advances."

His gaze remained on Lady Lucy's face. "Lady Cassandra, are you currently betrothed to another?"

"N . . . no." Lady Cassandra gulped.

"Then there is still hope for me," he replied, continuing to watch Lady Lucy.

She gave him a withering glare. "You're not listening, *Your Grace*," she managed through clenched teeth.

"On the contrary. I believe I've understood you perfectly. But I've fought many a losing battle in my day, fought them and won. I don't give up easily."

Derek had no idea why he was even still speaking with them. He didn't know how to woo a lady. It was hardly something he'd been trained for in the military. But something about the way they both wanted to dismiss him brought out his competitive nature. That, and the fact he intended to master this particular skill before it was all over. True, Lady Cassandra had apparently been out for five seasons already, but he actually preferred that. Marrying a young girl held little appeal to him. And there was the added benefit that his interest in Lady Cassandra appeared to have Lady Lucy near to an apoplectic fit. That was just fun. And then there was his promise to Swift.

"But Cass is not interested," Lady Lucy continued. "I thought I'd made myself clear."

"You did make yourself clear, my lady, and I'm sorry," he said, staring down his nose at her again.

Looking a bit mollified, she pushed up her chin and plucked an errant leaf from a curl near her forehead. "Sorry for bothering Lady Cassandra?"

He widened his grin. "No, sorry you've mistaken me for someone who gives a toss what you think, Miss Upton."

# ❧ CHAPTER THREE ❧
*Two hours earlier*

Derek Hunt scanned the crowded ballroom brimming with sparkling ladies wearing the latest fashions and their gallant escorts wearing high-necked cravats. Laughter, champagne, dancing, and revelry filled the large room. Derek straightened his own cravat and slid a hand into his pocket. He swallowed hard. Had it really only been a fortnight since he'd laid his hand on his dying friend's shoulder on a blood-soaked battlefield outside Brussels? Swift hadn't died. Not yet. But he expected the news at any moment. And here Derek was. He'd returned to London, been granted a dukedom by the Crown, and was even now in the market for a proper wife. The future mother of his future son. Swift had insisted he go. And Derek had had no choice. He'd had his orders from the War Office, but still, he disgusted himself.

A fortnight ago, Derek hadn't known whether he'd be alive tonight. Now he was lifting a champagne flute from the gleaming silver tray of a footman bedecked in the finest livery. As if Derek had never stepped foot on the battlefield, never watched as his countrymen were sliced down in front of him, never heard the agonizing screams of his dying friends. In London, the parades and parties given in honor of Napoleon's defeat were all the rage. And here he was tonight, the celebrated hero, enjoying the victory along with everyone else. As if he'd never seen the real horror of war.

And he was a duke? A bloody duke? It still didn't feel real to him. Why had he been made a duke above all the other officers? They'd all risked their lives, done their duty, fought honorably. Many had died.

Derek had cut around the outer defense of Napoleon's ranks. Seeing the opportunity, he'd made the decision in an instant and ordered his soldiers to take the opening. That decision had been a fortuitous one, a turning point in the battle. The Duke of Decisive they were calling him as soon as the reports of the battle floated back to London. Decisive, he was. He'd been made that way, after all.

Derek drew the champagne flute to his lips and took a long swallow. Good stuff, that. French. He smiled at the irony just before narrowing his eyes and scanning the room again. He was no longer in battle, but he still had a goal.

There she was. Lady Cassandra Monroe. Derek's investiture was dependent on him choosing a wife of whom the Crown approved, and Lady Cassandra Monroe's reputation and connections were impeccable. She also just happened to be tall, blond, and beautiful. And quiet and demure if Captain Swift had been correct about her temperament. The perfect wife for a man who'd just spent his last years in the upheaval of battlefields. Lady Cassandra Monroe was exactly the type of woman who would ensure that Derek lived his remaining days in peace and quiet. Precisely what he wanted.

But most important, he'd promised Swift. As he'd

watched his friend grit his teeth and writhe in pain on the packed earth outside Waterloo, Derek had promised he would find Lady Cassandra and marry her.

And Derek Hunt, whether lieutenant general or duke, *never* went back on a promise to a friend.

❧

Lady Lucy Upton stood on the sidelines of the ballroom tapping her slipper in time to the music. It wasn't as much of a lark as being at the theater—few things were—but she did love music and she adored dancing. She sighed. She hadn't been asked to dance in an age, but that didn't keep her from enjoying the tune.

"Why do you think he's staring at me that way?" Cass glanced skittishly in the direction of the newly minted Duke of Claringdon.

Lucy stopped tapping her foot and followed her friend's gaze. "I'm not certain, exactly. But he does seem to be pinning you with his eyes. Not exactly a gentleman, the duke."

Cass dared another glance. "I must admit he is handsome. But he doesn't have Julian's blond hair." She sighed.

Lucy glanced over at the duke. He was standing by the Grecian column in the middle of the crowded ballroom. She narrowed her eyes. Very well. Cass was right. The Duke of Claringdon was handsome. More than handsome, actually. Spectacularly handsome. He was also huge. Soaring and muscled, he looked like the god of war come down from Olympus. He was well over six feet tall, had midnight-black hair and jade-green eyes, wide shoulders that tapered to a flat abdomen, and muscles from top to toe. A war hero to boot. A lieutenant general known for his decisiveness. He'd won a variety of battles over the last few years and had been sent to meet Wellington in Brussels just before Waterloo. The Duke of Decisive, they called him now.

He was also arrogant and commanding, they said. Which, Lucy was certain, was quite an asset on the field of war, but his way, at the moment, involved making her friend nervous.

And for that, Lucy would not stand. Lucy, bold, blunt, completely without a demure bone in her body, had only two friends in this world—well, three if you counted Garrett—and Cass was one of them. Elegant, modest Cass who was too friendly and kind to rebuff anyone. Yes, Cass had always been quietly loyal to Lucy, and Lucy was nothing if not loyal back. If Cass wanted to avoid the attentions of the Duke of Claringdon, well, Lucy would assist her in any way she was able.

"How do you suppose he managed to have such a golden glow to his skin?" Cass asked, stealing another surreptitious glance at the duke.

Lucy wrinkled her nose and shrugged. "I heard he was on holiday in Italy just before he was called back to battle. Apparently his last mistress was Italian." She stole another glance herself.

Yes, the duke was powerful and more handsome than he had a right to be. And the whole war-hero bit didn't diminish his appeal, but he came from a completely unknown family—and most important, Lucy wasn't about to allow him to bully Cass. And something told her that the duke had set his sights on her friend.

Lucy didn't exactly blame him. Who wouldn't love Cass? Why, she'd had more offers than you could count. And she'd refused them all. Yes. Cass had managed to remain unattached for the last five seasons, waiting for her precious Julian to return from the war. Which *would* have been a splendid idea. The only problem was that Julian was all but betrothed to Cass's cousin Penelope. As soon as Julian returned from the Continent, he and Penelope planned to formally announce their engagement and marry.

"Lady Chambers introduced me to him earlier," Cass said, referring to their hostess. "She told Mama the duke had specifically asked to meet me."

Lucy raised both brows. "What did he say to you when you were introduced?"

"Nothing out of the ordinary," Cass replied. "It was just the way he *looked* at me. As if he was examining me. I didn't like it. I told Mama so."

Lucy snorted and then clapped her hand over her mouth to stifle the unladylike noise. "And what did your mama say?"

"She said I should be flattered." Cass bit her lip.

Lucy rolled her eyes and tapped her foot in time to the music again. "Of course she did. He's a duke. An incomparable catch as far as your mother is concerned, no matter who his family is. His just glancing in your direction has probably got her planning your wedding trousseau."

"He frightens me," Cass whispered. "He's just so big and he looks as if he could kill a man with his bare hands."

Lucy patted Cass's shoulder. "I know, dear." She glanced back at the duke. She didn't want to make things worse by suggesting to Cass that he probably *had* killed men, a great many of them, with his bare hands. Lucy had no doubts. But he didn't scare her. Not one bit.

Cass tugged on her gloves. "When he looks at me, I want to shrink back against the wall."

Lucy had just opened her mouth to offer some additional comforting words when their third friend, Jane, came hurrying up. Jane had chestnut-brown hair, wide brown eyes that were framed by a pair of silver-rimmed spectacles, and a lovely face that she usually kept buried in a book. Despite Jane's desire to remain unattached, Jane's mother dutifully dressed her up and trotted her out at every ball every Season, hoping her bookish bluestocking of a daughter would eventually catch some gentleman's eye. She never did. Which is precisely how Jane liked it.

Jane reluctantly spent her time at these affairs badly pretending to enjoy herself, famously scribbling notes for her future books, and biding the time until she grew old enough that her mother would give up and allow her to remain at home in peace.

And that was why, at the ripe old age of twenty-three, Cass, Lucy, and Jane were all solidly on the shelf.

"What's happening?" Jane asked, slipping into line beside the two of them.

Still tapping her foot, Lucy shrugged. "I'm enjoying the music, and Cass here is hiding from a duke."

Jane's head snapped to the side. "A duke?"

"The Duke of Claringdon," Cass replied in a hushed whisper. "He's watching me."

Jane snuck a glance at the duke. "Ooh, he *is* watching you. Who knew he'd be so large? And handsome? I expected him to have scars, perhaps be missing an ear or something."

Cass slapped at Jane's light blue sleeve. "Good heavens, that's positively morbid. You and your writerly imagination."

Lucy eyed the duke, arms crossed over her chest. "He doesn't look as if he's missing anything to me." She shook herself. "But that's not the point. If Cass isn't interested, she isn't interested."

"Do not worry," Jane replied, addressing her remarks to Cass. "Simply tell him so. He's certain to immediately retreat. Men like him usually have enormous overconfidence that is easily deflated."

Lucy glanced over at the duke, who was still eyeing Cass like a prize horse. "Something tells me it won't be that simple. The man seems to be quite used to getting his way."

Cass was busily smoothing her skirts, her eyes downcast. "Lucy's right. But even if I wanted to, I couldn't tell him I'm not interested. I'm not like you, Lucy. When I'm frightened, words completely leave my head. I wish I had a bit of your gift for witty repartee."

Lucy snorted again. Oh, she might as well completely give up attempting to be ladylike. It just wasn't in her. "And I wish I had your ability to keep my mouth shut when I ought."

"It's easy, truly. You simply have to— Oh good heavens, he's coming over." Cass's voice reached a high note Lucy had never heard before.

"He surely will ask you to dance," Lucy said, watching the duke's inexorable advance.

"Just thank him and tell him you're not in the mood for dancing at present. That should be that," Jane added with a resolute nod.

"Be bold." Lucy whispered her most famous bit of advice.

"Easy for you to say," Cass squeaked.

Lucy squeezed Cass's shoulder lightly. "We'll be right here." She and Jane moved quietly back toward the wall.

Cass took two brave, if shaky, steps forward to meet the duke. Lucy and Jane watched as the two spoke for a few moments—and the next thing Lucy knew, the duke led Cass onto the dance floor. *Oh Cass, no.* Lucy threw up her hands and turned to Jane. "She really does have a problem saying no to anyone."

Lucy watched Cass and the duke whirl around the dance floor, Cass with her pretty honey-blond hair and the duke with his striking dark features.

"Poor Cass," Jane whispered. "If she wasn't so in love with Julian, she and the duke might make a beautiful couple actually."

"She'd be miserable with Claringdon," Lucy replied matter-of-factly. "Besides, I for one say she may well have a chance with Julian when he returns from the Continent."

Jane arched a brow, giving her a highly skeptical look. "There are plenty of men to choose from. I've never understood why Cass is so set on that particular one."

"She loves him, and I intend to assist Cass in remaining completely unengaged this Season until she can have her chance with Julian at last," Lucy replied, twisting her mouth into a half smile.

"Why, Luce, I never realized what a romantic you are." Jane sarcastically batted her eyelashes at her friend.

"Not romantic, merely determined," Lucy replied with a resolute nod.

Minutes later, when Cass returned from the dance alone, Lucy snatched her into the corner with the two of them.

"What did he say?" Lucy's own voice took on a high note this time.

Cass's face was bright pink. She shook her head. "He paid me lovely compliments and said he should like very much to call upon me tomorrow. Oh, what am I going to do? I want to discourage him, but the words just will not come out of my mouth. I simper like a fool when he speaks to me. Not to mention that Mama has insisted that I encourage him. She's been watching the entire time."

Lucy and Cass turned their heads simultaneously to see Cass's mother, Lady Moreland, eyeing them approvingly with a pleasant smile on her plump face. Clearly, the woman had visions of a dukedom dancing in her head.

Jane had pulled a book out of her reticule and was busily reading it, obviously no longer that interested in her friends' antics. She pushed her spectacles up on her nose and nodded absently toward Lucy and Cass. "It's too bad you two cannot switch bodies for the evening. I've every confidence that Lucy could set the duke back upon his heels in mere seconds."

Lucy clapped her hands and Jane's head snapped up from the book.

"That's it!" Lucy cried.

"What's it?" Cass asked, her eyes wide.

Lucy rubbed her gloved hands together with glee. "Jane's perfectly right. Each of us is good at something different, correct?"

Jane eyed Lucy curiously. "I'm not entirely certain I follow."

Lucy grabbed her friends' hands. "I'm adept at speaking my mind and being quite blunt. It's a curse, I know. I've never been able to curb my tongue. Mama's told me often enough. And then of course there was the incident with the queen at my come-out."

Cass bit her lip. "Yes, that was unfortunate."

"A memory I rarely dwell upon, I assure you. But I long ago made peace with my reputation and my penchant for forthrightness."

"Yes, you're quite good at speaking your mind," Cass agreed with a nod.

"And *you* are good at attracting gentlemen and looking stunning and befriending everyone you meet, Cass," Lucy said.

Cass smiled at that. "I suppose I am."

Lucy continued, "And Jane is good at—"

"Oh, this I simply cannot *wait* to hear," Jane replied with something of a smirk on her face.

"Stop it," Lucy replied. "You're good at being exceedingly clever and knowing things none of the rest of us know. Why, if you were allowed to be in Parliament you would have negotiated the peace years ago and would have the taxes set to rights while you were at it."

"Please tell that to my mother," Jane said with a laugh. "She doesn't quite see the merit in all my reading and writing."

"I still don't understand, Lucy," Cass replied, her blue eyes cloudy with confusion.

"Don't you see?" Lucy said. "We all must help one another. Help one another to get what we want. We'll each do the thing the others cannot do and assist one another."

"What do you mean?" Jane asked, looking more interested by the moment.

Lucy smiled brightly. "I want to marry well. I don't need love or any of that nonsense, but I'm expected to make a decent match, if I can ever find a gentleman whom I can stand that is—" She drew in a breath. "To date, I've been a spectacular failure. I frighten gentlemen away. Cass can help me be more, ahem, attractive to men. Or at least not send them running."

"Go on," Cass prompted, blinking rapidly.

"And Janie, you want to remain entirely unattached, do you not?" Lucy asked.

"Absolutely!" Jane replied. "Entirely and forever."

"Repelling gentlemen is my specialty. I can help you immensely." Lucy laughed.

Jane smiled at that. "I need you to convince my mother that she can stop making me attend these odious social evenings."

"I'll help," Lucy agreed.

"And Cass?" Jane asked.

Lucy pulled them both closer. "I already have a plan. Cass wants to have her chance with Julian, correct? True love and all that. But you can't do it if your mother is encouraging the Duke of Claringdon and insisting that you accept his suit. I'll be your voice, Cass. I'll tell you exactly what words to use to dissuade the duke from pursuing you."

"You will?" Cass's eyes were round.

"Yes," Lucy replied. "I shall help you with the duke. Now you must send him a note. We must get him out of this ballroom and away from your mother's prying eyes." Another quick glance at Lady Moreland assured them that her eyes were indeed, still prying. "Ask him to meet you outside tonight, beside the hedgerow in the gardens. I'll hide behind the bushes and whisper what you need to say and you'll repeat it."

A wide grin spread across Jane's face. "You know, that plan is just mad enough that it may work. It'll be just like Horner in *The Country Wife*. Only less risqué." Jane was forever mentioning her favorite plays.

Cass shook her head, a worried look flashing across her pretty face. "No. No. It won't work at all. He's sure to hear you, Lucy."

"We'll just make certain he's several paces away," Lucy replied. "You'll tell him not to come any closer. For propriety's sake, of course. It's perfect."

Cass's wide blue eyes turned to Jane. "Janie, what do you think?"

Her forgotten book shoved back into her reticule, Jane crossed her arms over her chest. "I think I shall be out in the garden hiding behind the hedgerow with Lucy so I don't miss a moment of this."

Cass wrung her hands. "But what if it *doesn't* work?"

Jane patted her friend's shoulder. "What does Lucy always say? Be bold? At this point, you've nothing to lose. And if anyone can manage this feat, it's our Lady Lucy here."

Cass gulped. She eyed both her friends warily and took a moment to speak. "Very well. If you're certain, I suppose I'll try it."

Lucy smiled an enormous smile and clasped her hands together. "Excellent. Leave everything to me. It'll be just like one of the romp plays we love so much. I'll set the arrogant duke back on his heels. We have an appointment in the hedgerow."

# ❧ CHAPTER FOUR ❧

The next morning Lucy spent an inordinate amount of time in the breakfast room of her cousin's town house mentally compiling a list of crushing things to say to the Duke of Claringdon when they next met. Why, the man was a complete boor. How dare he call her Miss Upton? How dare he question Cass's wishes? How dare he tell her he didn't give a toss what she thought? The Crown may have bestowed a title upon him, but it obviously could not bestow the good breeding and manners that should come along with it.

She'd already cataloged an entire plethora of things to say to bring the duke to his knees when a footman arrived to announce that her friends were waiting in the drawing room to see her.

By choice, Lucy lived with her aunt and her cousin Garrett. Garrett had been her closest childhood friend. Lucy's own parents would never forgive her for not being a boy. They'd essentially disowned her. Well, completely ignored her for the most part. And while her parents preferred to remain in the country, Lucy adored Garrett's mother, Aunt Mary, who acted as her chaperone while she was in town.

Lucy hastily made her way to the drawing room. If Jane and Cass were there, surely Garrett had made his way to the drawing room as well. Garrett seemed to appear wherever Cass was lately. Lucy suspected he had an infatuation with her beautiful blond friend.

Lucy pushed open the double doors to the drawing room and marched inside.

"Ah, Your Grace, lovely of you to join us," Garrett said in his usual sarcastic tone. Lucy hid her smile. Yes. Garrett was here. The honorific he'd called her by was a jest between the two of them. He'd begun calling her that soon after her come-out, after all the eligible suitors had fallen away. Lucy had heard one of them say that he wasn't interested because of her wasp's tongue and high airs.

"You'd think she was a duchess the way she carries herself," Lord Widmere had said. It had stung Lucy, but only that first time. She refused to allow anyone to see her hurt and her shame. She'd spent her life trying to be the son her parents didn't have, shunning all things ladylike and girlish. Was it her fault she spoke her mind and refused to suffer fools? Her penchant for unvarnished honesty had earned her the reputation of having a shrew's tongue. But if it helped in situations like Cass's debacle with the overbearing Duke of Claringdon last night, she'd take her so-called waspish tongue over being a demure little miss any day. And as for her supposed duchesslike airs, well, those had been an unfortunate by-product of her refusal to show anyone that their rejection hurt. She pushed up her chin, squared her shoulders, and told herself she didn't need the approval of the *ton*. What did it matter to her what they thought?

So she'd shared Lord Widmere's words with Garrett, and they'd made a jest of them. A jest that nettled her still a bit, but she absolutely adored her cousin, even if her father detested him. Perhaps because her father detested him. Father couldn't stand Garrett for the simple reason that Garrett would inherit his title and estates one day and he was not Father's very own son. Ah, what a loving family.

Lucy returned Garrett's smile and fell into a deep curtsy. "At your service," she said with a smile.

Garrett was sitting next to Cass—he was always sitting next to Cass—his longish dark hair brushing his collar, his hazel eyes, the same color as one of Lucy's, flashing in merriment.

"We didn't wake you, did we?" Garrett asked.

"Absolutely not." Lucy swept up her violet skirts with one hand and made her way over to the settee to sit between Cass and Garrett. She flourished the piece of parchment in her hand. "I was up with the sun this morning writing a list of things for Cass to say to the Duke of Claringdon when he calls on her."

Jane sat on a chair across from them steadfastly reading a book.

"How is Cassandra supposed to read off a list with the duke standing there?" Garret asked.

"I suppose you have a better idea, Upton." Jane calmly pushed up her spectacles and turned the page.

Garrett opened his mouth to issue a no-doubt-scathing retort. Garrett and Jane had disliked each other upon sight. They'd met at a play they'd all attended five years ago, and the two had fallen into a continual war of words.

Lucy had long ago learned it was best if she cut their wordplay off at the start.

"As a matter of fact—" Garrett began.

"She'll just have to memorize them, that's all," Lucy interrupted.

Cass pressed her hands to her cheeks. "Memorize them? Oh, no. I'm afraid I cannot." She took the parchment from Lucy's grasp and eyed the first few lines. "Lucy, I'll never be able to remember all this—and even if I did, I'd be too shy to say it."

Garrett gave Lucy an I-told-you-so stare. "There, you see. You cannot go putting words in Cassandra's mouth."

Lucy plucked the paper back. "What's wrong with this?" She cleared her throat, reading the first paragraph. "'While I'm certain there are scores of ninnies who would fall all over themselves at the slightest crook of your ducal finger, I do not happen to be one of them. I believe I've made myself exceedingly clear on the point and must wonder what they taught you in your military schools because it appears understanding the King's English isn't among your varied talents, whatever *those* may be.'"

Garrett gave Lucy a long-suffering stare. "Honestly? *Must* I tell you what's wrong with that?"

"I quite like it," Jane added, not taking her eyes from the page she was reading. "Perhaps a bit too long for my taste but clear enough."

Garrett narrowed his eyes at Jane. "Of course *you* like it. If provided a quill you'd most likely write something far worse."

Jane snorted. "Something far worse? What's that supposed to mean?"

"I mean you like it because I don't. I swear if I claimed

the world was round you'd say it was flat merely to be contrary," Garrett replied.

"You give yourself *far* too much credit, Upton. It makes me question—"

Garrett opened his mouth to speak. This time Cass stopped him.

"Oh, Lucy, you must know I couldn't possibly say that to the duke," Cass said, her cheeks bright pink.

"Why not?" Lucy asked.

"For one thing, it's terribly rude," Cass replied.

"Not to mention I doubt the duke would believe that Cassandra came up with that on her own, even if she could memorize all of it," Garrett added.

"And I know I'll never be able to memorize all of *that*." Cass gestured to the paper.

"I don't see why not," Lucy replied. "Just think of it like one of our beloved plays. Pretend you're an actress."

Cass's eyes went wide. "An actress! Why, Mama would lock me in my bedchamber for a week if she knew what we're up to."

Lucy tossed a frustrated hand in the air. "Who cares what your mama—?"

"Read another, Lucy," Jane requested. "Perhaps a shorter one, easier to remember."

"Very well." Lucy sat up straight and scanned the page. She flipped to the next. "How about this? 'Sir Duke, I regret to inform you that I am otherwise occupied tomorrow and the next day and the next. I am engaged every day upon which you might inquire as to my availability. In fact I am feeling a trifle under the weather at present and hope you will retrieve your hat and gloves with all due haste and remove yourself and your equine companion from this address.'" She finished with a firm nod of her head.

Jane arched a dark brow. "*That* was shorter?"

"It was every bit as rude," Garrett added, shaking his head.

"Lucy, I would never say something like *that*." Cass tugged on her gloves. "It's just too mean."

Lucy tossed a hand in the air again. "Mean? Mean? Cass, the man is trying to court you and refuses to take no for an answer and you're worried about being mean?"

Garrett gazed at Lucy skeptically. "How do you know Claringdon won't take no for an answer? I knew him several years ago in the army, long before he was a lieutenant general, of course. He seemed a reasonable chap to me."

Lucy turned to her cousin and gave him an exasperated look. "You weren't there last night, Garrett. Tell him, Cass."

Cass swallowed and peered around Lucy to address Garrett. "He did seem quite determined."

Jane nodded. "I agree with Lucy. He was rather unwilling to hear the word *no*. You may just have to be a bit more forceful, Cass."

Garrett gave Jane a smug smile. "Oh, and I suppose you would memorize such a speech and have no trouble rattling it off."

Jane turned her attention back to her book. "I don't need to memorize anything. I've become quite proficient telling off pesky gentlemen from dealing with *you* through the years, Upton."

Before Garrett had a chance to reply to that barb, Cass grabbed Lucy's hand. "Oh, Lucy. I cannot memorize those words."

"Of course you can, Cass," Lucy said.

Cass bit her lip. Her eyes were wide as inkpots as she stared at Lucy. "Promise me you'll come over this afternoon and be there when he pays his call."

Lucy crossed her arms over her chest and tapped her slipper on the carpet. "Oh, I'll be there all right. Whether the duke likes it or not."

## ❧ CHAPTER FIVE ❧

Derek scrubbed his hands through his hair, pushed back his chair, and stood up from the large oak desk in the study of his new town house. He paced over to the large windows that overlooked the street and braced one hand against the wall. Damn it. The reports delivered from the War Office this morning didn't look good. Not good at all.

Not only was there no news of Swift's condition—the last Derek had heard, Swift had been taken to a makeshift hospital outside Brussels—but there was no news of Donald or Rafe, either. Donald, Swift's older brother, was the Earl of Swifdon. He was also a spy for the Crown and had been in Brussels just before the last battle. He and Rafe, Captain Rafferty Cavendish, had been assigned to a highly secret and highly dangerous mission to spy on the French line as it advanced toward Brussels. Neither man had been heard from since. According to this morning's reports, they were both presumed dead.

Derek clenched his fist against the wall. Damn. Damn. Damn. He was completely bloody useless here, standing in an overly decorated town house in Mayfair. He belonged on the trail on the Continent, searching for his friends, seeing to Swift, helping ease his friend's last days on earth however he could. But his orders had been clear. Return to London immediately and play the part of the victorious new nobleman. The country needed a celebration, apparently, and Derek's presence in the ballrooms of London was meant to give them their hero.

And he hated every moment of it. This town house. This life. It wasn't for him. He'd never aspired to be a duke. And he'd had no preparation for it. *Return to London, you're a duke now* had been about the extent of Wellington's orders.

He might be stuck in London, but he would use his prized decisiveness to do what he could to help his friends. He sat back down at his desk, pulled out a sheaf of parchment, and plucked a quill from the inkpot. He had some ideas. Places where Swifdon and Rafe may be holed up if they'd been injured or forced to hide. Derek had to get someone from the War Office to listen.

He had to find Swifdon and Rafe. That much was certain. If Swift was dying, Derek couldn't allow Donald and Rafe to die, too. No. He wouldn't allow it.

He finished writing his list for the War Office and signed and sanded the parchment, then heated his new ducal wax seal over a nearby candle and sealed the paper closed. He rang for a footman to bring the missive round to the War Office posthaste.

He'd done all he could do for his friends for now. In the meantime, he would continue with his pursuit of Lady Cassandra. That was something he could do for Swift. Compared with the horror of war and the torture of not knowing the fate of his friends, how difficult could a bit of courtship be?

## ❦ CHAPTER SIX ❦

When Derek was ushered into Lady Cassandra's drawing room, he got the distinct impression that the entire household had lost its collective mind. The butler stammered, the housemaids ran into each other, and the two footmen nearly tripped him in the corridor. Apparently, a duke received a much different level of service than a lieutenant general did. If he was still becoming accustomed to his new title himself, it certainly didn't help matters to have an entire household staff scurrying about as if the prince regent himself were paying them a visit.

"His Grace, the Duke of Claringdon," the butler intoned, ushering Derek into the drawing room.

Derek grimaced. How long would it be until he heard that title and actually thought of himself?

"What is your name, my good man?" Derek asked the butler.

"Shakespierre," the man replied with a completely straight face.

Derek did a double take. "Shakespeare?"

"No, Shakespierre, Your Grace. It's French."

The butler took his leave, and Derek shook his head. That wasn't French. Yes, he was in a strange house to be certain. He turned his attention back to the room at large.

Lady Cassandra sat perched upon a cream-colored settee like a pretty doll. Her blond hair was piled atop her head, and she wore a pink gown that complemented her bright blue eyes. Eyes that watched him carefully, almost fearfully. Good God, the chit was frightened of him. He'd have to overcome that before he asked for her hand.

A sharp movement across the room caught his eye, and a flash of pale yellow skirts revealed . . . Lady Lucy Upton.

"Your Grace," Lady Lucy said before he'd even had a chance to greet Lady Cassandra. "To what do we owe the pleasure of your company?"

Her voice dripped with sarcasm. Derek eyed the beauty up and down. A pity she was such a harridan, because the woman had a lush exotic look to her tilted eyes, dark shiny hair, high cheekbones, and full lips that nearly begged for a man to kiss them. Only he'd no doubt draw away bloody and bitten, he thought with a wry smile. Why Lady Cassandra insisted upon keeping Lady Lucy by her side, he would never understand, but apparently Lady Lucy was the price Derek must pay for Lady Cassandra's company. So be it. If he couldn't handle one little spoiled Society miss, he wasn't worth his salt.

"I came to pay a visit to *Lady Cassandra*," he replied with a tight smile.

"Please, have a seat." Lady Lucy gestured to the chairs across the room and blinked her long, sooty eyelashes at him.

"Y . . . yes," Lady Cassandra echoed softly. The poor young woman looked as if she were about to bolt at any moment, like a soldier caught stealing rations.

Derek strode over to a chair near the settee where Lady Cassandra perched. He waited for the prim Lady Lucy to flounce over and take a seat before he took one himself. Ah, the aristocracy and their tiny fancy chairs. A man his size was likely to break it to bits. He shifted uncomfortably and pointedly ignored Lady Lucy.

"I trust you are well today, Lady Cassandra," he said.

Lady Cassandra nodded. "Oh, yes. I'm quite well. How are you"—she cleared her throat—"Your Grace?"

"Excellent. And how are your mother and your father?"

"Both quite well also, thank you. Mother is out paying afternoon calls and Father is at his club."

Derek nodded. Lady Lucy was sitting at an angle behind him where he couldn't see her face but he got the distinct impression, from the many times Lady Cassandra's eyes flitted over to look at her friend, that she was somehow feeding her information. She was like a bloody spy from the War Office, that woman.

"Not too tired from the festivities last evening, I presume?" he asked.

Lady Cassandra's eyes flitted over to Lady Lucy. "No. Not at all."

Derek gritted his teeth and shifted in his ridiculously small seat. "What are your plans for this afternoon?"

Another quick glance toward Lady Lucy. "Oh, I . . . um. That is to say, we . . ."

"We're having a look at the shops," Lady Lucy announced from behind him. "Quite busy today. Quite."

Lady Cassandra looked a bit relieved to have been spared the need to answer the question.

"And what about tomorrow afternoon?" he asked Lady Cassandra, but his entire attention was attuned to the little minx behind him.

Again, Lady Cassandra looked to Lady Lucy for her cue. "I . . . we . . ."

"Quite busy tomorrow afternoon as well," Lady Lucy interjected.

That did it. Derek stood, lifted his chair with ease, and placed it at an angle where he could see both of them properly. "Seems I'm addressing my remarks to the wrong lady."

Lady Cassandra's hand flew to her throat. Lady Lucy's unusual eyes lit with fire, and she stared down her haughty little nose at him. "I don't know what you mean." She blinked innocently.

"Don't you?" He arched a brow at her.

Lady Lucy shrugged. "You've asked after our plans and we've told you."

He gritted his teeth. "I asked after *Lady Cassandra's* plans and you've answered for her."

Lady Lucy crossed her arms over her chest and stared him down. "I'm Lady Cassandra's chaperone."

"Oh, really? An unmarried female acting as a chaperone?" he retorted.

"Yes. I'm eminently qualified," Lady Lucy replied.

"That I doubt." Another tight smile from him.

Lady Lucy nearly came out of her chair. "How dare you?"

"Oh, I dare quite easily, my lady. What I don't understand is why you insist upon acting as if—"

A small, ladylike throat-clearing interrupted them. Lady Cassandra's attempt to get the two of them to stop arguing, no doubt. He turned his head to face her. "My apologies, my lady."

"What are your plans for the afternoon, Your Grace?" Lady Cassandra ventured.

"Seeing as how you're already occupied, I may ride out to Huntingdon and see the new estate."

"The estate that was endowed upon you with your title?" Lady Cassandra asked.

"Yes, seems I'm a landowner now," Derek replied.

"You might want to get under way as soon as possible," Lady Lucy offered. "It's quite a journey from here, is it not?"

"Ready for me to take my leave, my lady?" He eyed her with suspicion.

She innocently batted her long lashes at him again. "I meant no such thing. That would be *rude*."

"Ah, yes, and you've no experience in that quarter, do you?" he replied tersely.

Lady Cassandra gasped quietly and Lady Lucy gave him a withering glare. "Seems you do, Your *Grace*."

Derek blew a frustrated breath between his teeth. "Lady Lucy, perhaps you and I have words better said to each other in private."

Lucy raised a brow. "The two of *us*?"

"Yes."

"In private?"

"Yes."

"Would you prefer it if I left?" Lady Cassandra offered, looking quite relieved at the prospect, actually.

Derek shook his head. "No. I'm willing to have a short private conversation in the corridor with Lady Lucy if she is willing."

Lady Lucy immediately stood up and gestured toward the door. "By all means."

Lady Cassandra watched them, her mouth a wide O, her lovely blue eyes blinking rapidly. Derek offered his hand to Lady Lucy, who promptly refused it with a tight smile and stalked ahead of him out the door of the drawing room. He followed her and closed the door behind them.

Lady Lucy swung around to look at him, her arms still crossed resolutely. "Yes, Your Grace?" A fake smile was plastered to her face—and there went those distracting eyelashes again. Bat. Bat. Bat.

He cleared his throat. "My lady, it seems you and I have got off on the wrong foot. I'd like for us to start over."

She dropped her arms to her sides. "Very well. Do you intend to desist in your courtship of Cass?"

"Absolutely not."

"Then I'm afraid we cannot start over."

He inhaled a deep breath through his nostrils. "Why exactly do you find me so objectionable?"

"For one thing you're overbearing, for another, you're arrogant." She pointed toward the drawing room door. "Cass is a sweet soul. She wouldn't hurt a bee and she's friendly to everyone. She needs someone to look out for her best interests."

He arched a brow. "And that someone is you? Not her father?"

Lady Lucy shot daggers at him with her eyes. "In this case, yes."

He poked out his cheek with his tongue. "So there can be no truce between us?"

She folded her arms over her chest again. "Not as long as you insist upon courting Cass."

He nodded. "So be it."

Lady Lucy placed her hand on the door handle, ready to open it and return to Lady Cassandra. "You'd do well to take my advice and leave her alone. You're only wasting your time."

He narrowed his eyes on her certain little back. "And you'd do well to stop interfering. You're only wasting yours."

She turned her head slightly to face him and gave him a once-over. "I'm not about to stop, Your Grace."

He inclined his head. "Neither am I, my lady."

This time she arched a brow, giving him a challenging stare. "Very well. Then, may the best opponent win."

# ❧ CHAPTER SEVEN ❧

The Miltons' ball was quite an affair. It usually marked the end of the Season and was held just days before everyone left London for their country houses or holiday towns.

Cass wore a stunning peach-colored ball gown. Her hair was swept up on her head, and emeralds sparkled on her neck. Lucy glanced down at her own ensemble. Next to shining Cass, she looked colorless in her silver embroidered gown with diamond bobs at her ears. Jane wore her favorite blue. Jane was always beautiful, though she never thought so. Tonight her mother had confiscated her book when she saw it peeking out of Jane's reticule, resulting in Jane being both far more involved than usual and far more irritable.

"Garrett will be here later," Lucy explained as the three of them piled out of Jane's parents' coach. Jane's mother was their chaperone for the evening. Her father had been knighted for his intellect and because the man had no son, his daughter had become as academic as her sire, much to Jane's mother's dismay.

"I like Mr. Upton a great deal," Mrs. Lowndes said.

Jane leaned over and whispered in Lucy's ear. "She means she likes the fact that when your father dies, Upton will be an earl." Jane rolled her eyes.

"Yes, cousin Garrett is such a sport," Lucy responded to Jane's mother, elbowing Jane. "To accompany us all summer no less."

Cass readily agreed, nodding. "Oh, I do adore Garrett. It's ever so kind of him."

Lucy nearly winced. She hoped Cass didn't repeat that in Garrett's presence. She already could tell she'd have to have a talk with Garrett sooner rather than later. His hope that Cass would someday feel anything more than friendly toward him was a futile one. Garrett well knew that Cass loved Julian. She supposed Garrett was just incapable of not falling in love with beautiful Cass. Apparently just like the Duke of Claringdon.

And speaking of the Duke of Claringdon, would *he* be at the ball tonight? And why did the prospect excite her a bit? Another opportunity to match wits.

Thank heavens Cass's mother hadn't been home yesterday when the duke paid his call. If that worthy lady had been a witness to Lucy's shocking behavior toward the duke, she wouldn't let her see Cass ever again. Lucy was certain of it. Lady Moreland had never much cared for Lucy. The only reason she allowed Cass to remain her friend was because she was the well-connected daughter of an earl and they were country neighbors. But if Lady Moreland suspected Lucy was up to something, surely she'd never allow Cass to see Lucy again.

Over two hours later, when the Duke of Claringdon was finally announced in the Miltons' ballroom, all three friends turned to stare.

Cass winced and tugged at her gloves.

"Not to worry," Lucy replied.

"He's certain to leave you alone after the incident in the hedgerow," Jane offered. "Don't you think?"

"Not after what he said to Lucy in the corridor," Cass replied.

"What did he say to Lucy in the corridor?" Jane wanted to know, but they were unable to share the story with her before the duke found his way unerringly to their little group.

"Lady Cassandra," he said in his smooth, deep voice, bowing over the hand she offered. "A pleasure. Would you care to dance?"

Lucy opened her mouth to issue a scathing denial just as Cass's mother swept up to them. "Your Grace, so good to see you this evening." Lady Moreland curtsied.

The duke bowed to the matron. "I assure you, the pleasure is entirely mine. I was just asking Lady Cassandra if she would care to dance." He gave Lucy a smug look over Lady Moreland's blond curls.

"Why, of course she would," Lady Moreland answered, nudging Cass toward the duke.

Cass gave Lucy a fleeting glance before settling her hand on the duke's arm and allowing him to escort her to the floor.

Her work done, Lady Moreland flitted away into the crowd, while Lucy and Jane watched the dancing from the sidelines. This time, Lucy tapped her slipper a bit angrily to the music. "I so wish I could be Cass's voice," Lucy grumbled.

"It didn't seem to have an effect last time," Jane remarked.

Lucy crossed her arms over her chest, letting out a huff of air. "Cass gave me away by refusing to repeat what I said. She finds it so difficult to be the least bit curt with anyone. But the duke is a man who doesn't understand anything but bluntness."

"A pity he's not attempting to woo you," Jane replied, raising her brows.

"If only I could speak *for* her, though."

Jane pursed her lips. "Lucy? What are you thinking?"

Lucy tapped her fingertip to her cheek. "You know . . . it just might work."

"How would you ever manage it?" Jane asked.

Lucy smiled widely and pointed a finger straight up in the air. "I'll find a way. Don't I always say, 'Be bold'?"

Jane was just about to reply when Garrett strolled up to them, his hands pushed into his pockets. "I'd say you're not doing so well on the Cassandra-and-the-duke front if the two of them are dancing." He nodded toward the couple.

Lucy slapped at his sleeve. "Shh. I'm trying to hear what they're saying when they dance by."

Garrett laughed at that. "Why don't you dance with me and we'll go listen?"

"I'll dance with you," Jane piped up.

Lucy and Garrett exchanged expressions of complete surprise.

"What?" Jane asked with a shrug. "Mother took my book. I'm rather bored. Just don't step on my feet, Upton."

"*Such* a compelling offer," Garrett said with a snort. "But by all means, Miss Lowndes, let's dance."

The two spun onto the floor while Lucy waited on the sidelines trying to get a glimpse of all four of them and tapping her foot in time to the music as usual. Typical. The first good offer she'd got to dance in an age and it had been from her cousin. And that hadn't even materialized.

Several moments later, the music stopped and Garrett and Jane returned to where Lucy stood.

"We couldn't hear much," Garrett reported.

"Yes, a pity," Jane said, pulling up her gloves. "I have a brilliant idea, however."

"What?" Lucy asked hopefully.

Jane leaned forward as if she were about to impart a huge secret. "Why don't we *ask* Cass what he said to her?"

They all turned to face Cass, who had just returned from the dance floor herself. She stared at the floor and shuffled her slippers beneath her gown.

"What is it, Cass?" Lucy asked. "What did he say?"

"He asked if I would go out onto the terrace with him and have a refreshment," Cass replied.

The Miltons had set up their refreshment table outside under the stars, and a steady stream of partygoers came in and out of the open French doors that led to the terrace.

"And you said yes?" Lucy gave her friend a disapproving stare.

Cass nodded guiltily. "I didn't want to be rude. Besides, Mother was glaring at me. She makes me so nervous."

Lucy tossed a hand in the air. "Cassandra Monroe. I don't understand you at all. You've turned down more suitors than I can shake a stick at yet this one seems to be too much for you."

Cass covered her face with her hands. "I know. I know. But I've always turned down everyone quite politely. The duke doesn't seem to accept that."

Lucy nodded. "He refuses to take no for an answer. He may be a duke but he's no gentleman."

"You cannot blame the chap for trying," Garrett added with a smile in Cass's direction, one that made her turn a lovely shade of pink.

"Don't worry, Lucy. You've done quite enough to help me already. I won't ask you to come with me this time," Cass said. "I shall do my best on my own."

Lucy shook her head. "I'll come with you all right. I'll come with you and give him a piece of my mind. In fact, I have an idea." She grabbed Cass's hand and stalked off.

Garrett and Jane watched them go.

"Do be gentle with the poor man. He's only a war hero, Luce, he may not be used to your ruthless tactics," Jane called after her.

Lucy turned back to face her friend and winked at her over her shoulder.

❧

Lucy tapped a finger against her cheek as she stared out the French doors to the Miltons' terrace. There he was. The Duke of Claringdon. Waiting for Cass and looking deuced handsome.

"Aren't we going out?" Cass asked, paused at her side.

"Not yet," Lucy replied, still tapping her cheek.

"Why not?" Cass wrinkled her brow.

"Because . . . I'm thinking . . ."

Cass's eyes widened. "Oh, no. Lucy? What do you intend to do?"

Lucy paced back and forth in front of the doors. "Cass. Last night it was obvious that you cannot repeat my words. You're too . . . too . . . nice for your own good."

Cass nodded. "I know. And I hate myself for it."

"Don't worry. I'll help. But if we're going to truly dissuade the duke, we need to be more forceful with him. Blunt. Honest. Forthright." Lucy nodded.

"I know that, Lucy, and I intend to try, truly, but I—"

Lucy swung around, her silver skirts brushing her ankles. "Here's what I propose. There's a balcony above the terrace over to the side above the garden. We'll go up there. I'll hide behind you where he cannot see and I'll speak for you this time."

Cass shook her head. "Speak for me? I don't understand."

"You'll be there. He'll think it's you speaking, but it will truly be me."

The color drained from Cass's face. "Oh, no, Lucy. I don't think—"

"Don't worry, Cass. I can imitate your voice perfectly." She demonstrated, raising her voice and speaking in a softer, more demure tone.

Cass giggled and pressed her fingers against her lips. "I have to admit, you do sound like me, but what if he knows? After what happened the other night, I'd be mortified if he discovered we were up to something like that again."

Lucy peered at the window. "He won't find out. And if he does, it may just make him angry enough to change his mind about courting you."

"Do you really think so?" Hope lit her features but quickly faded. "But what if Mama—?"

Lucy turned back to face her friend. "Cass, do you or don't you want to rid yourself of the duke once and for all so that when Julian comes home you'll be free?"

Cass nodded. "I know being free isn't going to make a difference when Julian comes home, but yes, that's what I want."

"Then allow me to try this. I can say the things you cannot say. Please, Cass, let me help you. I'll go up to the balcony and be your voice."

Cass bit her lip and glanced out the window to where the duke stood with his back to them. "I suppose you know how to get up there?" she asked with a sigh.

"Not yet, but I'm about to find out," Lucy answered with a grin.

# ❧ CHAPTER EIGHT ❧

"Your Grace." Lady Cassandra's soft voice came floating out of the air.

Derek stood alone on the terrace. He turned. No one was there.

"Your Grace," came the voice again. This time Derek followed it around the corner to a small private part of the Miltons' garden. Roses twined prettily up a trellis and ended in a bright cluster under a small balcony. There, atop the balcony, stood Lady Cassandra looking as lovely as one of the flowers at her feet.

"Lady Cassandra," he called. "What are you doing up there? I was hoping you would agree to go for a walk with me in the gardens." He gestured toward the garden path in invitation. The candlelight wasn't as strong in this part of the garden and while he could make out Lady Cassandra's form, she was cloaked in shadows for the most part, including her face.

"Your Grace, I prefer to remain here, and there's something I wanted to say to you." Her voice was steady and sure. More steady and sure than he'd ever heard it, actually.

He nodded. "Yes?"

"Stop courting me."

He furrowed his brow. "Pardon?"

"You're wasting your time."

Heat rushed to Derek's face. Wasting his time? Those were Lucy's words, not Lady Cassandra's. Now he understood. The waning candlelight, the balcony, the fact that her voice was a bit different. Lady Lucy was behind this. Literally. She was standing behind Lady Cassandra and speaking for her. He might not be able to see her, but he knew without a doubt she was there. He should be furious. Instead he found himself more than a little amused.

"I am?" he asked, smothering his smile. "I'm sorry to hear that."

"Yes, I want you to go away. For good."

Derek twisted his lips. His amusement faded. He'd had just about enough of these antics. He'd made a promise to Swift, damn it. He was a decent catch. He knew that much. And he knew deep down that if Lady Cassandra had a chance to get away from her bossy friend, she might be persuaded to give him a chance. Instead, he found himself in the idiotic position of having to prove to this young lady that a duke was actually someone she might want to consider marrying. Utterly ridiculous. If he hadn't promised Swift, he might readily walk away from this entire situation, but he *had* promised Swift. Damn inconvenient, that, and Derek refused to be dissuaded by the likes of Lucy Upton. With that thought riding high in his mind, he called back to Lady Cassandra. "What if I refuse?"

That should do it. The feisty Lady Lucy didn't like it when anyone questioned her.

The voice became a bit more piqued. "Why would you refuse?"

He folded his hands together behind his back. "Because I intend to change your mind."

This time the voice was decidedly disgruntled. "Your Grace. I don't mean to be rude, but—"

"Don't you?" he countered.

"Of course not. What an utterly stupid question."

"Lucy!" This obviously from the real Lady Cassandra.

"Cass, stop it," came Lady Lucy's hushed whisper.

"I don't *enjoy* being rude," the fake Lady Cassandra's voice amended. "But you leave me little choice as you're completely insufferable."

"Lucy!" came Lady Cassandra's half-strangled voice in reply.

Derek unabashedly grinned up at them. "Let's stop this, shall we? Lady Lucy, if you have something, rude or otherwise, to say to me, I suggest you say it directly."

Lady Cassandra squeaked and fell back into the shadows and Lady Lucy's defiant, pretty little face appeared. She leaned over the balcony and blinked at him, shooting daggers with her unusual eyes. She braced both hands against the balustrade and leaned down to challenge him head-on. "Fine, *Your Grace*. Let me be quite clear. Cass isn't available. Leave her alone."

Beside her, Lady Cassandra hung her head.

Derek glanced at Lady Cassandra. "Is that right, my lady? You're not available? When I asked you yesterday you said you were not betrothed to another."

"I'm . . . not," she breathed, tugging on her gloves and looking extremely uncomfortable.

"Then I don't understand," he replied.

Lady Lucy hunched her shoulders and glared at him. "You don't have to understand. I'm telling you."

Ignoring Lady Lucy's reddening face, he turned his gaze to the other lady again. "Is this true, Lady Cassandra?"

"Yes," Lady Cassandra said in a shaky voice. "And you frighten me a bit, Your Grace."

"I understand, Lady Cassandra," Derek replied as tenderly as he could. "I hope to have the opportunity to change your mind. If you get to know me a bit better, perhaps—"

Lady Lucy nearly leaped from the balcony. He could just imagine her lithe form tangled in his arms. Truthfully, he wouldn't put it past her to jump on him. "Good heavens, can you not take no for an answer?" she asked.

Derek arched a brow at her. "Seems not. While I can understand Lady Cassandra's reluctance, I'm confident that once she comes to know me a bit more, she will think better of me."

Lucy glared at him, her chin raised, her eyes flashing, defiant. "That is your problem. You're far too confident."

Cass slunk back into the shadows.

"Confidence wins battles," he countered, with a grin.

"This is not a battle," Lucy shot back.

Another eyebrow raised. "Isn't it?"

She glared at him, her nostrils flaring. Some of her adorable little curls had sprung free from her coiffure and were bobbing jauntily along her cheeks. "I've found that often the things in life most worth winning are those worth fighting for, my lady."

Lady Lucy clenched her fists. "Cass is not a prize to be won."

Now she was angering him. Who exactly couldn't take no for an answer here? "No, she's a lady who has the full faculty of her tongue and can make her own decisions without her friend chasing off all her suitors."

Lucy gasped. She straightened to her full height, which was all of nearly five and a half feet. "You don't know what you're talking about. I would never presume to insert myself in Cass's affairs. Cass *asked* me to help her." She clenched her jaw. Without looking behind her, she addressed her friend. "Cass, will you please tell *His Grace* that you asked me to be here?"

Lady Cassandra cleared her throat. Her voice came, thin, shaky. "I did. That is true."

"And that you want me to help you?" Lady Lucy continued.

"Yes," Lady Cassandra added.

Derek turned his attention back to Cass. "I can appreciate that you don't know me, my lady. And that I can be . . . intimidating. But I assure you, I have only your best interests at heart and I would like very much to get to know you better."

"She doesn't *want* to get to know you better," Lady Lucy nearly shouted. "She's in love with another man."

Derek's head snapped up. "Is that true, Lady Cassandra?"

Even in the waning light he could tell Lady Cassandra's face was bright red. "Y . . . yes." She nodded slowly.

Derek furrowed his brow. "And has this other man asked you to be his wife?"

"No, no." She shook her head vigorously.

"But you expect him to?" he asked.

"No. Actually, Your Grace, I do not expect him to at all."

A smile spread across Derek's lips. "Well, then. Competition is my specialty."

Lady Lucy snorted. "What is the matter with you? Why do you insist upon pursuing a lady who is clearly not interested?"

Derek shrugged. "I just heard her say that she does not expect an offer from this other man. Who is this fool, by the way?"

"That's none of your affair!" Lucy shouted.

The two faced off, glaring at each other like Napoleon and Wellington. Derek had to admit, with no small amount of surprise, he was enjoying it.

"Look, Lady Lucy, I'm more than a bit tired of having this same conversation with you time and again. I have just one thing to say and Lady Cassandra might as well hear it—" He took two steps back to see her but couldn't. "Lady Cassandra?"

Lady Lucy glanced around, too. "Cass?"

Lady Lucy turned in a circle. "She's gone."

# ❧ CHAPTER NINE ❧

Lucy couldn't sleep. She slid the coverlet from her legs, draped her robe over her shoulders, and slowly paced in front of the open window. A slight summer breeze blew in, and crickets chirped in the garden behind the house. She could think of one thing and only one: Derek Hunt, Duke of Claringdon. In all of her years she'd never met anyone so . . . so . . . provocative.

She pressed a hand to her throat. That look he'd given her when she leaned down over the balcony. She felt exposed, as if she'd just been seen without her clothing. The duke's bold gaze was that assessing. It was challenging, probing, and a bit too perceptive for her comfort. It was as if he could read her thoughts and knew she was up to something. Which of course she was. Hmm. Perhaps the duke was a more formidable opponent than she'd allowed.

Who was this man, the Duke of Claringdon? He seemed astute. She'd give him that. And he seemed to know when she was mocking him, something most men of her acquaintance never quite picked up on. Oh, they knew when she sliced them to bits with her tongue. That was certain.

But most of them didn't know, didn't really know, that her disdain was more about their inability to match wits with her.

The duke, however, had known. It was as if he'd seen right through her. Knew what she was about. She wasn't used to the gentlemen she encountered being as clever as she was, frankly. She breathed deeply. Why did he spark her temper so easily? She was angry at him, true, but she was also angry at herself. Where had her intellect fled when that man had accused her of inserting herself into Cass's affairs?

"You don't know what you're talking about," she'd countered lamely. That hadn't been like her at all. Where was her infamous wit? Her biting words? They failed her when she needed them most.

Lucy had opened her mouth to issue a scathing retort. But nothing had happened. She'd never been so incensed in her life. Usually when she delivered withering words to men of the *ton*, they slunk off and kept their distance forevermore. Derek Hunt, however, seemed to enjoy it and return for another dose. Absolutely infuriating.

That man was completely, irrevocably convinced that he was right. He was too sure of himself by half, and it didn't help his arrogance that he just so happened to be maddeningly handsome. Why was he so intent on courting Cass when she clearly had no interest in him? Cass was beautiful and sweet and clever and lovely, of course. Very well. No wonder he was intent on courting Cass. She was demure and quiet and an excellent choice for a bride. The whole thing might just be perfect, actually, if Cass were interested in the duke. But Cass had been hopelessly in love with Julian since she was a girl.

No one knew that better than Lucy. She'd spent countless hours hearing about how handsome and strong and noble Julian was. Cass adored a man she might never have. It was sad, to be sure, but it was true. And even if Lucy didn't bring it up often to keep from hurting poor Garrett's feelings, it was plain to anyone who'd heard Cass speak about Julian that she still held out some sort of hope that fate would intervene and make him hers. And Lucy intended to facilitate such an event. Only at present it seemed as if she was in a standoff with the Duke of Stubborn. Cass would just have to speak up and tell him there was no hope of changing her mind, no matter how long he waited. That was all there was to it.

Unless . . .

Lucy swallowed hard. What if Cass actually *had* changed her mind? The man was handsome and heroic and a duke, wasn't he? And even if the idea of Cass loving that arrogant, assuming blowhard— No. No. That was not helpful. It did no good to call him names. Especially when he wasn't present to hear them.

Lucy paced back over to her bed and sat with her foot curled beneath her. She and Cass hadn't actually spoken about it since that first night, had they? Perhaps Cass *had* changed her mind. She wasn't coming out and telling him to leave her alone outright, was she? And tonight she'd even told Lucy she didn't need her help in the garden. Was it possible that Cass had reconsidered her feelings toward the Duke of Claringdon?

Lucy wrinkled her nose. Why did that thought make her so uneasy? She shook her head. There was only one way to discover the truth. She must ask Cass. Ask her outright if she did indeed enjoy Claringdon's attentions, and if Cass said yes—oh, she couldn't possibly say yes, could she? At any rate, if she did say yes, then Lucy would step aside. Step entirely aside. And leave them to their courtship. It was that simple. She pulled off her robe and snuggled under her covers again. She'd fall fast asleep now that she had such a reasonable plan of action.

But one hour later she was still tossing about and plumping the pillows. If the plan was so simple, why couldn't she sleep?

❧

Derek tossed the quill against the ledger. Why he was up in the middle of the bloody night counting the same row of figures for the eighth time, he would never know. He'd been unable to sleep, and coming down to his study had seemed like a good idea an hour ago. Now, however, he realized he was wholly unable to accomplish anything. His mind raced with thoughts of his frustrating experience at the ball tonight. Specifically with Lady Frustrating herself, Lucy Upton.

What was wrong with that woman? She refused to give him a moment's peace. She turned up like a shadow whenever he had the slightest opportunity to be alone with Lady Cassandra. She appeared to be doing it out of some misguided sense of friendship. Derek understood all about friendship, after all. Apparently, Lady Lucy believed she was being a bosom friend to Lady Cassandra, but if the bossy little baggage would only stop for one moment and actually think about what she was doing, she might realize that preventing her friend from being courted by a young, healthy, eligible duke—who wasn't hard on the eyes if he did say so himself—was not perhaps in Lady Cassandra's best interest. But Lady Lucy seemed so damn stubborn and sure of herself. He doubted she was interested in seeing things in any sort of a different light. It was maddening.

Derek had even considered approaching Lady Cassandra's parents and informing them of Lady Lucy's interference. Surely the earl and countess wouldn't welcome Lucy's plans to ensure their daughter did not marry a duke. But that didn't sit well with him, either. He had the thought for the one hundredth time: If he couldn't even handle one little spoiled Society miss, was he worth his title?

Perhaps it was true that Lady Cassandra was indeed in love with another man as they'd told him this evening, but that didn't bother him. If the sop didn't even have the wherewithal to court her, he stood little chance of winning her. No, it was Lady Lucy who posed the more dire threat. Derek stood, crossed to the sideboard, and poured himself two fingers of whiskey.

And to make it even more frustrating, Lady Lucy was too beautiful. The entire thing would be much easier to deal with if she had a plain face or a giant wart on her nose. Instead, when he verbally jousted with her, he was having thoughts that had nothing to do with wanting her to go away. Instead, they were more like thoughts about rolling around naked with her in his big bed. And that was altogether distracting. Not to mention inappropriate. Damn it.

He tossed back the whiskey. Tossed it back and allowed it to sink to his belly exactly as he'd done on countless freezing-cold nights sleeping outside a battlefield in a tent. He'd lived through war. One that had killed thousands of his countrymen. He'd led men through that war safely. No, it was not possible that he would be stopped by a stubborn little slip of a miss. Not possible at all. Regardless of the way she heated his blood.

If Derek knew anything it was military strategy. When waging war, you've got to know as much about your enemy as possible. He needed to discern what it was about him that Lady Lucy so objected to. He'd play her game on her terms for now, then turn the stakes against her. Obviously, he had to get past Lady Lucy to win Lady Cassandra.

And he knew just how he would do it.

# ❧ CHAPTER TEN ❧

Lucy made her way downstairs the next day to meet Cass and Jane in the drawing room. When she paused in front of the door, she couldn't help but overhear a bit of her friends' conversation.

"Please, Janie, you must help me," Cass said.

"I don't think it will work at all," Jane replied.

"But I cannot possibly do it alone. I'm already forced to pretend that I'm a complete ninny."

Jane snorted. "Yes. You're even beginning to convince me."

"I'm not certain how long I can continue to—"

Lucy pushed open the doors and strode inside. "Continue to what, Cass?"

Cass blushed and started at the sound of Lucy's voice. Jane glanced away.

"Oh, Lucy, there you are." Cass tugged on her gloves.

"What's wrong?" Lucy asked. "You're talking about the duke, aren't you?"

"You could say that," Jane offered, staring out the

window as if the most interesting thing in the world were happening in the street beyond.

Cass gave Jane a stern look before turning back to look at Lucy. "Yes, we were talking about the duke. You'll never believe what's happened."

Lucy crossed over to the chair to hug her friend. As usual, Cass was perfectly put together. She was dressed in a simple pale blue day dress with a matching pelisse, a white bonnet atop her head, and white kid gloves. "What is it, Cass? What has you so upset?"

Cass pressed her gloved hands against her pale cheeks, making solid impressions of pink. "I don't know what to do. Truly, I don't."

Jane rolled her eyes.

Lucy sat across from Cass and patted her hand. "Calm down. Calm down. Now, what's happened?"

Cass dropped her hands into her lap, bit her lip, and stared out the window.

"It cannot be all that bad. What is it?" Lucy prompted.

Cass squeezed her pretty blue eyes shut and then the words tumbled from her mouth in a tangled rush. "Mama told the duke that I'd go riding in the park with him this afternoon."

Lucy snatched her hand away. "She did what?"

Cass tugged at her gloves. "I know. I know. He came to call and he was speaking so quickly and Mama was so enamored by him and . . . Oh, Lucy, all I know is by the time he left we'd all agreed that he would fetch me and a footman at six o'clock. What am I to do?"

Jane fluttered her eyelashes at Cass. "I suggest you tell him—"

"Shh," Cass said, giving Jane another disgruntled look. "I need Lucy's help."

Jane huffed and pulled a book from her reticule. "Fine. If you say so."

Lucy folded her arms across her chest and tapped her fingers along her arms, considering the duke's latest play. This news shouldn't surprise her. The man was determined, and so was Lady Moreland. But the duke had taken advantage of the situation, ensuring Lucy was not there when he next asked Cass to accompany him somewhere.

A reluctant grin spread across Lucy's face. Hmm. She had to admit it was well played of him. He'd already learned from experience, hadn't he? If Lucy or Cass had had any idea that he was planning to pay Cass another visit, Lucy would have been sitting right there next to her friend waiting to do battle. He'd warned her, hadn't he? She'd let down her guard, been too lax when she should have been prepared. But now that she knew just how cunning her opponent was, she would not make the same mistake again.

First, however, she had to find out how Cass truly felt. She leaned forward and braced her hands on her knees, facing her friend. "I must ask you a question."

Cass blinked at her, her own knee bobbing up and down rapidly. "Yes, Lucy?"

Lucy stared her directly in the eye. "Have you changed your mind at all? About the duke, I mean?"

Another set of blinks. "I'm not certain I follow."

Lucy flourished one hand. "I only wonder if you've decided you might be interested in the duke's attentions after all. And if so, that's perfectly—"

The look of pure shock mixed with a bit of horror in Cass's eyes gave Lucy her answer. "Oh, Lucy, no. I never know what to say in front of the duke and he's just so, so . . ."

"Overbearing?" Lucy offered.

"So . . ."

"Arrogant," Lucy said.

"So . . ."

"Frustratingly sure of himself?" Now she was ticking off his faults on her fingers. She could keep going all day.

"So big!" Cass finally finished.

Jane rolled her eyes again at that. Lucy wrinkled her nose and made a harrumphing noise. "I suppose so. A big ox if you ask me."

A shudder went through Cass, but she didn't meet Lucy's eyes. "I've no doubt his opponents were fearful just seeing him on the battlefield. Why, his arms are like scythes and his chest is so wide and his shoulders so broad—"

Lucy plucked at her collar. It was far too hot in the drawing room this morning. Where was the maid to open the windows? "Yes, he's a giant. A giant lout if you ask me," she grumbled.

Cass leaned forward and grasped Lucy's hand. "I've no idea how you're brave enough to say some of the things you've said to him, Lucy. How do you do it?"

"Yes, Lucy, how do you do it?" Jane propped her elbow on the arm of her chair and rested her chin upon it. Cass glared at her.

Lucy waved a hand in the air. "I've no idea how he's had the nerve to say some of the things he's said to *me*. Believe me, I've got quite a lot more to say."

"Oh, Luce, that's why I love you so. You're never afraid to speak your mind." Cass bit her lip. "But what'll I do? He expects me to ride in the park with him."

Lucy sat up straight. "The duke accused me of sticking my nose in your affairs last night. I do not want to do that."

"No. No. Not at all. I need you to help me, Lucy," Cass assured her.

A harrumping noise came from Jane this time.

Lucy nodded. "Very well. I had to make certain that you still wanted my help. But now that you've reassured me that you do, indeed, need—no, want—my help, I am perfectly resolved." The Duke of Claringdon and his arrogance would not overpower her sweet friend. "Don't worry, Cass. We'll handle it."

"Oh, Lucy, I do so want your help." Cass wrinkled her nose. "What shall we do?"

Lucy folded her hands in her lap. "I'll come with you. That's all. You need a chaperone, do you not?"

"The perfect solution," Jane said.

Cass ignored Jane. "But Lucy, as the duke pointed out yesterday, you're not a proper chaperone."

Lucy shrugged. "That's not about to stop me. And at any rate, we'll be accompanied by your footman. Your mother isn't planning to attend, is she?"

Cass shook her head jerkily. "No. I rather think she's happy to see us go off alone. Shameless, really."

Lucy crossed her arms over her chest and smiled to herself. "*His Grace* didn't seem particularly interested in listening to what I had to say last time. This time I'll give him no choice. If he intends to outlast me in this game of ours, he doesn't know with whom he is dealing."

Jane raised an eyebrow. "Are you both quite certain this is wise? I doubt the duke will like it very much if you're there, Lucy."

Lucy allowed a wide smile to spread across her face like summer jam on bread. "I know the duke won't like it. That is the very best part."

# ❦ CHAPTER ELEVEN ❦

When Collin Hunt came strolling into Derek's study, Derek immediately saw the hint of a smile on the younger man's face.

"Your Grace," he intoned, bowing.

Derek stood, rolling his eyes. "Enough of that."

"What, did you think I wouldn't show the proper respect due your new illustrious title?" Collin laughed.

Derek took two long strides over to him and clapped his brother on the shoulder. "For someone who used to share a tiny bedchamber with me and another person, I think we can leave off with the formalities."

Collin's grin widened. "If you say so, Your Grace."

Derek shook his head. "I do."

Derek offered him a seat, and Collin made his way over to the leather chairs in front of the desk and sat down. His face turned sober. "I have some bad news, Derek."

Derek returned to his seat behind the desk. His gaze snapped to his brother's face. "What is it?"

"It's Adam."

Derek folded his hands on the desk in front of him. "What about him?"

"He was with them, Derek."

Derek narrowed his eyes. "With them?"

"Yes, on the mission. It was his first."

Derek slammed his fist against the desk. "Who the hell authorized that?"

"Apparently, General Markham thought it was a fine idea. Thought Rafe and Swifdon needed backup."

"That's ridiculous."

"I can't say I disagree, but you know how persuasive Adam can be."

Yes, they both knew how persuasive their youngest brother could be. Adam had never taken no for an answer in his life. He'd been training to become a spy, but in Derek's well-known opinion, he hadn't been ready yet to be tested in the field. Apparently, Markham had believed otherwise, or had been convinced of it by Adam.

"They're all missing. All three of them? Is that it?" Derek asked.

"Yes. They had orders to spy on Napoleon's base. They haven't been seen since before the battle. I'm leaving tomorrow to search for them."

Derek clenched his jaw and nodded. "I cannot tell you how much I want to go with you."

Collin nodded back. "I know you do, Derek. But you have your orders."

"I bloody well nearly begged Wellington to let me go."

"I don't think he wants our entire family in danger. You know it would crush Mother."

Derek nodded solemnly. "Take care of yourself, Collin."

"I intend to, and I intend to bring Adam back with me. For Mother."

"Thank you," Derek said softly.

Collin shook his head and changed the subject. "Speaking of Mother, seems you're about to make her a very happy woman indeed. What's this I hear about you courting a lady? Marriage and children in your future?"

Derek laughed a humorless laugh and turned to face the windows. "Ah, yes, my courtship. It's going about as well as the search for Swifdon and Rafe, I'm afraid."

Collin arched a brow. "Really? Courtship is not your strong suit, Your Grace?"

Derek gave his brother a warning look. "Don't call me that."

Collin barked a laugh. "I'd have thought that gaining such an illustrious title might have helped you attract a bride."

Derek pushed back in his seat and breathed a long sigh. "I'd have thought the same thing . . . until I met Lady Lucy."

"Lucy? I thought her name was Cassandra, something."

"Oh, the lady I'm courting is named Cassandra. The lady who's causing me no end of trouble over it is named Lucy."

Collin poked his tongue into his cheek. "Lucy, eh? Careful, Your Grace, you sound as if you just might be enjoying the trouble."

## ❧ CHAPTER TWELVE ❧

Lucy had been relegated to the back of the carriage like an unwanted maiden aunt chaperoning on May Day. She jostled along as the conveyance bounced through Hyde Park, giving the footman, who was clinging to the back of the thing, a commiserating smile every once in a while. Cass had given her strict orders. "Please don't say anything too, too rude. I shall attempt to make my intentions clear myself this time." Cass had given a firm nod.

Lucy had reassured her friend. "I'll try, truly. I'll do my best. And I have complete confidence in your ability to handle the duke."

"It may be best if you remain silent." Cass bit her lip. "If he invites me to do anything else with him, I'll be firm."

Lucy nodded. "Understood."

Cass gave her friend a bright smile and a tight hug. "Oh, Luce. What *would* I do without you?"

"You'd probably end up married to a duke."

They'd both laughed, but their laughter had been cut short by the arrival of the duke himself. He'd entered the drawing room, as handsome as usual, and managed to keep a smile on his face even when Cass announced, "I would feel ever so much better if Lucy joined us."

For her part, Lucy managed to keep a perfectly innocent look on her face. The duke accepted the pronouncement with as much grace as His Grace could muster. "As you wish."

Lucy and the duke exchanged fake smiles before Lucy took her place in the second seat of the phaeton. The groom jumped up into his position and they were off before Lucy had a chance to finish tying the wide bow of her bonnet beneath her chin.

As the conveyance bumped along the dirt road toward the park, the duke and Cass talked about the weather, the Season, Society, and the latest amusements at Vauxhall Gardens. Lucy kept her mouth tightly clamped the entire time, not particularly interested in the conversation, until the talk turned to the war.

"Did you lose many friends in battle?" Cass tentatively asked the duke as the coach made its way through the impressive iron gates of Hyde Park. Lucy turned her head to listen, precariously perched on the seat behind them.

He replied with one nod. "I did. Too many."

"The man I . . . have feelings for. He was there," Cass admitted.

Lucy's heart wrenched for Cass.

"I'm sorry to hear that," the duke continued. "Did he make it home safely?"

Cass shook her head. "Not yet. I haven't heard from him. I expect to any day now."

"War is a hideous business." The duke's voice was solemn.

Lucy wrinkled her brow. She considered his answer

for a moment. Of course she'd always thought war was hideous—but a seasoned soldier, a lieutenant general, thinking the same thing? She assumed they relished the battles. Looked forward to them even. Didn't it provide them with their chance at honor, valor, victory?

"It's a necessary evil to defend the country," he added. "But I do not relish war."

Lucy tilted her head to the side. Surprising that he would say such a thing.

Cass raised her voice as loud as Lucy had ever heard it. "I hate war. It's kept my friend away for so many years."

The duke's voice was low. "It's kept many of us away for many years, I'm afraid, Lady Cassandra. I'm glad it's over."

Cass nodded.

"Tell me, why don't you think your friend will propose to you when he returns?" the duke asked.

Cass hung her head. "He won't. He . . . he can't."

"Is he married?"

"Something like that."

"Unrequited love is painful," he said.

Lucy's head snapped up. Unrequited love? The duke was discussing unrequited love? Why, she hadn't known he was capable of such tender emotions.

"What do you know about unrequited love?" The words flew from her throat before she had a chance to stop them.

"Lucy!" Cass's voice held a note of rebuke.

The duke turned his head toward her. "No. It's all right, Lady Cassandra. Frankly, I've been surprised Lady Lucy here has remained silent as long as she has."

Lucy glared at him. "Well?"

"Love, I've found, is a messy business. Marriage is another matter entirely," he said.

"Spoken like a poet," Lucy retorted.

"Lucy, please," Cass begged.

The duke arched a brow at Lucy. "Something tells me a poet would be made short shrift in your world, my lady."

Lucy narrowed her eyes on him. "What is that supposed to mean?"

"It means any man who isn't willing to dodge your gibes is quickly gone, is he not? I suspect that's why you've taken such a dislike to me. I don't run away at your slightest barb."

Lucy squeezed her hands in the folds of her skirts. How did that man manage to get to the heart of things so easily? It was as if he had a window into her personality. And was it true that she disliked him so vehemently because he refused to leave? She bit her tongue. No use giving him more ammunition to lob back at her. Why, oh why, did he make her so insane? "Perhaps you should."

"You seem to know a lot about affairs of the heart, my lady," he said. "What about the war? Do you know anyone who won't be coming back?"

Lucy jerked back as if he'd struck her. He was questioning whether she'd been hurt in life. Seen painful things. Lost someone she loved. "I've lost someone. Someone quite dear to me."

A combination of surprise and regret passed over his face. "A man?"

Lucy looked away. "Yes."

The rest of the journey continued in silence. When the phaeton finally rolled to a stop in front of Cass's parents' town house, the duke alighted and helped Cass down. He left the footman to help Lucy.

"Will I see you tomorrow evening at the Havertys' dinner party, Lady Cassandra?" he asked.

Cass nodded. "Yes, I'll be there, but—"

This was the moment. Cass would tell him she didn't want to see him again. And if that happened and he finally took no for an answer, then—

The duke's arrogance and assuming manner had left Lucy wanting more, another chance to put him in his place. She brushed past him, pulling Cass into the house with her. "*We'll* see you there, Your Grace."

"I look forward to it," he replied.

"I'll wager you do."

"You're not about to scare me off with your sharp tongue, my lady," he said.

"We'll see about that, Your *Grace*," Lucy replied.

She had nearly shut the door behind them when the duke's strong, sure voice rang out behind them. "That sounds like a challenge to me."

Lucy didn't look back. "Oh, Your Grace, if I were challenging you, you'd know it."

"Very well," he said. "While we're on the subject of wagers and sharp tongues, I'd like to challenge *you* to one, Lady Lucy."

She froze, standing as still as a statue. Then she slowly turned to face him, her eyes narrowed on his features.

She tilted her head to the side. "To what? A wager?"

"Yes," he replied with a smile on his face.

"A wager?" Cass gulped.

"What sort of wager?" Lucy asked. She had to admit, she was intrigued. Quite intrigued, actually.

"I challenge you to a battle of words. Tomorrow night, at the Havertys' party."

"A word challenge?" she scoffed. "You challenge *me*?"

Cass pointed a finger in the air. "Um, Your Grace, I'm not certain if you understand exactly . . ."

The duke waved away the warning. "Oh, I understand,

perfectly. Lady Lucy here is known for her way with words. Correct?"

Cass nodded.

He grinned. "And I intend to show her up."

Lucy picked up her skirts and crossed the threshold into the house. She didn't let him see the small smile that had popped to her lips. It had been an age since anyone had challenged her. "You'd best get plenty of sleep tonight, Your Grace. You'll need it."

## 🌸 CHAPTER THIRTEEN 🌸

"The betting book at White's has seen no rest in the last twenty-four hours." Garrett slapped his gloves against his knee as the four friends bounced along in his carriage to the Havertys' party the next evening. "Everyone in town is speculating about your challenge with the duke."

Lucy straightened her shoulders and eyed her cousin. "First of all, how has everyone in town found out about it? Second, I didn't think you were a member at White's."

Garrett laughed. "I'm not. But everyone at Brooks's has been talking about it nonstop as well. You wouldn't believe how high some of the bets are up to."

"You didn't answer the first question," Lucy pointed out.

Garrett shrugged. "Very well, I *may* have mentioned it to a few chaps."

"Dissolute gambler," Jane mumbled, pulling the book away from her nose. She eyed Garrett over the top of it. "And out of curiosity, exactly how high are the bets?"

Garrett whistled. "High enough to buy a new carriage. And I'll ignore the fact that you just called me dissolute."

Jane smirked at him.

Cass worried her hands. "I think it is disastrous, simply disastrous."

Lucy reached over and patted Cass's knee. "Don't worry, Cass. I'm certain to win."

"I know that, Lucy. I'm just worried that it'll harm your reputation and . . . Making a bet with a duke, the Duke of Claringdon of all people, cannot be good for your reputation. I'm certain of it."

"Reputations are highly overrated if you ask me," Jane said from behind her book.

Garrett's eyebrow shot up. "Really?" he asked, his voice dripping sarcasm.

Jane pulled the book down to the tip of her nose and eyed him over its edge. "Yes, are you surprised I think that, Upton?"

Garrett shrugged. "No. Not particularly. Perhaps I'm only surprised that you admitted it."

"I'm a bluestocking, Upton. If I gave a toss about my own reputation, I'd study far less and spend far more time worrying about things like hair ribbons and frocks."

He blinked at her innocently. "Bluestockings don't wear hair ribbons, Miss Lowndes?"

Jane pushed up the book to hide her face again. "We wear them, Upton. We just don't *care* about them."

"I'm truly worried for Lucy tonight," Cass continued, interrupting them.

Jane dropped her book again. "I'm not worried. I'm looking forward to it, actually. I can see tomorrow's headline in the *Times*, 'Lady Lucy Crushes Claringdon.'"

Lucy raised her chin and smiled. "Thank you for your faith in me, Janie."

"And I, for one, want a front-row seat tonight," Jane added with a sly smile.

Cass waved her hand. "I'm worried. What if the headline ends up being, 'Duke of Claringdon Wins Yet Another Battle'?"

"Do you really think our Lucy will let him win?" Garrett asked.

"Thank you, Garrett," Lucy replied.

"I just think the duke is quite clever, and he's seen a lot of the world," Cass said. "I would hate for you to be humiliated, Lucy."

Lucy regarded her friend closely. "Don't worry, Cass. I'll be fine. Have some faith." Truth be told, she'd had her own moment of doubt in the middle of last night. Confronting the duke in public? Why, she wouldn't be human if she didn't have a moment's doubt, would she? Would the arrogant duke consider for a moment if he would lose to her? She'd quickly got over it, however.

Lucy had few talents. Charming people, dancing, playing the pianoforte—those skills had eluded her for her entire life, but cutting people to shreds with her tongue? That was a gift the universe had seen fit to bestow upon her and she never doubted it. Well, perhaps for one brief little minute last night, but in the end, she knew she'd win. She had to.

When Lucy's little group entered the ballroom, tension crackled in the air. It was as if one hundred pairs of eyes turned immediately to watch them.

"I wonder if the duke is here already," Cass whispered from her right.

The answer to that question quickly materialized in the form of their hostess, Lady Haverty. The woman glided up to them with a sly smile on her face. "Lady Lucy, good to see you. The Duke of Claringdon has yet to arrive."

Lucy let out her breath. Why did that reprieve give her a bit of peace?

"Thank you so much for your kind invitation this

evening," Lucy replied. Her friends also greeted their hostess warmly.

"My pleasure," Lady Haverty said. Lucy got the distinct impression that that lady was ever so glad to be the hostess of what was sure to be one of the most talked-about dinner parties of the Season.

"Yes, well, be certain to let me know when the duke arrives," Lucy said in what she hoped was a casual voice.

She did not have long to wait. It seemed mere minutes later that a commotion at the door caused everyone to glance up while the butler intoned the name of the Duke of Claringdon.

"This is it," Garrett said under his breath, giving Lucy a warning glance laced with an encouraging smile.

Lucy shrugged. "I'm perfectly ready whenever he is."

Within a matter of minutes, the riotous crowd had jostled the two of them together toward the middle of the ballroom and Lucy looked up into the daring, handsome face of the Duke of Claringdon.

She curtsied. "Your Grace."

"My lady." He bowed and brushed his lips across the knuckles on her gloved hand. She shuddered. Not fair. She snatched her hand away as if it had been burned.

The crowd quickly filled in around them.

"Seems we've garnered quite an audience," he said, shoving his hands in his pockets and circling her. "What shall we discuss?" He arched a brow in a challenge.

She gave him her best false smile. "You're so clever, Your Grace. I defer to your expertise in picking a subject."

He eyed her warily. "Sarcasm becomes you, my lady."

She smirked. "So I've been told."

"Why don't you dance with me first and we can think about it?" he offered.

She nearly snorted. "Dance with you? No. Thank you."

One brow shot up. "Ah, now *that's* surprising."

She regarded him down the length of her nose. "What is?"

"Why, with your reputation for wordplay, I'd have thought you'd find something infinitely more clever to say in response to a gentleman with whom you do not wish to dance than, 'No. Thank you'."

He was mocking her. Her face heated. Her ears were no doubt turning red. "You think you can do better?"

He inclined his head in acceptance, a devilish smile on his firmly molded lips. "I *know* I can."

She crossed her arms over her chest and glared at him.

He grinned and raised his voice so the audience would hear him. "This shall be the wager then. I shall come up with a plethora of more inventive ways to turn down a dance than 'No, thank you.'"

"How many?" she asked, still trying to quell the riotous emotions in her middle.

The duke turned and called out to their audience. "Does anyone have a pack of cards?"

"I do!" Lady Haverty offered, calling to a footman to bring cards posthaste.

The wait was not long. The footman hurried back with the cards while the entire ballroom appeared to converge upon their little enclave. In the meantime, Cass and Jane gave Lucy encouraging smiles and then faded into the crowd with everyone else.

The duke took the cards from the footman and presented them to Lucy with a flourish. "My lady, pick one, if you please."

"What for?" Lucy asked, valiantly attempting to keep the rising panic from her voice. What was he up to?

"Whatever card you draw will be the number of responses I invent."

Lucy arched a brow. "And what if I draw a royal?"

"Twenty," he answered simply, as if he did this sort of thing on a regular basis.

She eyed him warily but hovered her hand over the stack and plucked a card from the center. She flipped it over. "The King of Hearts," she announced with a satisfied smile.

A muffled *ooh* made its way through the crowd.

"You wouldn't be interested in the best two of three, would you?" he asked with a jaunty grin.

Lucy shook her head and smiled back at him. "Twenty sounds perfect to me."

He winked at her. "How did I know you would say that?"

She shrugged. "Lucky guess?"

"Very well," he agreed. "I shall come up with twenty better ways to refuse a dance with a gentleman than your 'No, thank you.'"

Lucy tapped her slipper against the parquet floor. She had no choice. He'd made the challenge and she must see it through. Wise of him actually, to keep her from being the one to use her tongue. Quite wise indeed. "Very well. I accept. Let's hear them."

"Ah, wait. First, we must decide. What shall be the forfeit?" he asked, plucking nonchalantly at his ivory cuff.

Lucy arched a brow. "Forfeit?"

"Yes. What shall the winner win?"

She wrinkled her nose at him, then stepped forward to whisper so their audience would not hear. "When I win, you agree to leave Cass alone."

He appeared to consider it for a moment. "Agreed," he whispered back. "Only because I know I will win."

"And what do you intend to win?" she replied.

He bowed again. "Why, the coveted dance with you,

my lady." This, he said loud enough for the entire audience to hear.

Lucy had to concentrate to keep from allowing her jaw to fall open. As if that rogue truly wanted a dance with her. It was ludicrous, of course, but not much of a threat. She had every intention of winning.

"Very well, Your Grace. Let's get this over with, shall we?"

The crowd seemed to lean forward collectively, eager to watch the proceedings. "This is almost better than the theater," she heard Jane say from somewhere in the large mass of people.

"You sound confident that I will fail, Lady Lucy," the duke said.

"I *am* confident, Your Grace." Lucy couldn't help the little thrill that shot through her at the prospect of the challenge. My, but it had been an age since anyone had asked her to dance and even longer since anyone had challenged her, truly challenged her. She was used to slicing potential suitors to bits with her tongue and continuing about her affairs. But this man—oh, not that he was *her* suitor, no, he was Cass's suitor—at least he challenged her. Didn't hang his head and slink away like a wounded animal. Oh, yes, she was looking forward to this, a bit too much actually.

The duke folded his hands behind his back and began to pace around the cleared circle. "I shall begin with the obvious. 'Dancing with a man of your charm might make me swoon, my lord.'"

Lucy rolled her eyes.

"'I could not in good conscience accept your offer to dance when there are so many other ladies here with dance cards just begging to be filled by someone as prestigious as yourself.'"

A little smirk popped to her lips. He circled around her.

" 'It would be rude of me to dance with you, knowing my skill would only serve to cast you in a less-than-flattering light.' "

"I like that one," she admitted.

" 'I wouldn't dare be so presumptuous as to accompany his lordship onto the dance floor knowing the color of my gown would clash with my lord's dashing evening attire.' "

"Preposterous," she said, pretending to study her slipper.

" 'I'm sorry, my lord, but my maid laced my stays too tightly to possibly consider the exertion.' "

"That one's just silly," she replied. "Besides, I wager you've heard all those and more."

"A few," he admitted with a grin.

"I confess myself disappointed," she said. "I thought you had more imagination than that, Your Grace." The crowd was watching her but instead of feeling self-conscious or shy, Lucy found she relished the attention. It had been an age since anyone in the *ton* took any notice of her. And here was the dashing Duke of Claringdon challenging her to a verbal duel. The best part was that it seemed to be *enhancing* her reputation instead of shredding it to bits as Cass had feared. Everyone's gaze was trained on her with a mixture of awe and envy.

"I'm not done yet," the duke continued. " 'I'm sorry, my lord, but I cannot possibly dance with you, as I'm having my wig washed.' "

She snorted at that. "I do *not* wear a wig."

"Not the point," he added with a grin. "Where was I?"

"Number six," someone called helpfully from the crowd.

"Quite right. Let's see. Political. 'I'm sorry my lord,

but I must decline as I've taken a vow of no dancing until the Importation Act is defeated.' "

"As if," Lucy scoffed.

He didn't stop to take a breath. " 'I'm sorry, my lord, but there isn't time as I'm to be a stowaway on a ship bound for the Americas tonight.' "

"That one doesn't even make sense." But she couldn't help but smile.

"Yes, but it's interesting, is it not?" he asked with a roguish grin.

The crowd cheered in appreciation. Lucy shrugged.

" 'Being so close to a gentleman of your esteemed stature is likely to fluster me so much I shall tread upon your feet,' " he offered.

"Hardly," she snorted.

" 'If I were to dance with you, my lord, I'd jeopardize my prestigious position as head wallflower.' "

Jane materialized from the crowd, pointing a finger in the air. "To be precise, Your Grace, *I* happen to be the current holder of the prestigious position as head wallflower."

"Duly noted," the duke said with a grin.

Lucy shook her head at her friend. Jane nodded and blended back into the crowd.

The duke was playing to the audience now, smiling outright and clearly enjoying himself. " 'I'd rather be shooting at Napoleon than dancing with you.' "

Lucy inclined her head. "I'm not a half bad shot."

" 'I cannot dance because I have to look for my smelling salts.' "

Lucy afforded him a long-suffering stare. "Not likely."

" 'I'd rather be eating army rations,' " he added. And then, " 'I'd rather be buying a turban.' "

"A turban?" She gave him an incredulous look.

" 'It's far too warm to dance,' " he continued.

She sighed. "That one's probably true."

He tugged at his lapels. " 'Dancing is against my morals.' "

She giggled at that.

" 'Aww, I would dance with you but I don't want to make you look inept.' "

"Far too similar to an earlier reply," she scoffed.

"That was number eighteen!" someone called from the sidelines. Lucy could have sworn it was Garrett.

She gave the duke a challenging stare. "Only two more. Can you manage, Your Grace?"

He straightened his already straight cravat. " 'I would not care to fend off the hordes of other ladies vying for a dance with you this evening.' "

"Number nineteen!" the crowd shouted.

Lucy drew in a deep breath. One more. Only one more. He was going to do it. He was going to win. And that meant . . . she would have to dance with him.

The duke cleared his throat. "I've saved the best for last." He gave her a wicked smile. " 'I'm afraid, my lord, that if I were to dance with you, I'd be entirely too charmed and end up falling hopelessly, madly in love with you.' "

"Number twenty!" someone shouted. Cheers went up just before the crowd became silent. Tension filled the room. Lucy held her breath. Everyone was watching her. By God, the man had done it. He'd come up with twenty things to say that were better than her simple "No, thank you." He'd shown her up. She should be embarrassed. Humiliated. Instead all she could think of was the fact that she'd promised him a dance.

The duke took his time. He strolled to the end of the open space and strolled back. He gave her an arch grin. "I have one more. An extra reply, if you will. One to replace the questionable number eighteen."

More cheers from the crowd. Lucy eyed him carefully. "One more?"

"Yes," he replied.

"I'm on tenterhooks." She tried to sound bored and hoped her voice didn't shake.

He cleared his throat. "'Why, Your Grace, I'd be delighted to be your partner for the next dance.'"

She smothered her smile behind her glove.

"Don't you think that's infinitely better than, 'No, thank you'?" he asked. "I do."

The crowd erupted into cheers once again.

Lucy pushed up her head and swallowed. She had to give it to him. He had won. As if on cue, a waltz began to play.

He strolled over to her and offered her his hand. "My lady, I believe you owe me this dance."

## ❧ CHAPTER FOURTEEN ❧

Lucy tried to quell the riotous nerves swirling around in her belly the moment the duke offered her his hand. Never let it be said that she was anything but a gracious loser. She curtsied to him and placed her gloved hand on his.

The crowd melted away as others paired up for the waltz, but a steady buzz of whispers kept up and Lucy had no doubts they were all talking about them. She should muster some sort of outrage, but she had to be fair. "No. thank you." It hadn't been her most shining example of wit. He'd seen his opening and taken it. Well done of him, actually.

He may have won, but she didn't have to enjoy dancing with him. When she thought about it reasonably, the waltz wasn't the bad part. No, Lucy was more upset that he hadn't failed because it meant he wouldn't stop pursuing Cass. But even as Lucy told herself that, she knew it wasn't why she was disappointed. There had been little hope that he would stop trying to court Cass. The wager had been lost before it had begun. She'd told herself she'd really only hoped he'd make a fool of himself, but the truth was that the reason she was truly disappointed was because she knew the duke *would* still be pursuing Cass. He might be dancing with her at the moment—and he was a lovely dancer—but he would be back at Cass's side sooner rather than later. Why did the thought make Lucy so melancholy?

"You're angry," he said as he spun her.

Out of the corner of her eye, Lucy spotted Garrett, Jane, and Cass watching them. "No." She shook her head. "I'm not, actually."

"Why am I not convinced?" he replied.

She shrugged. "You won. I lost. It's simple."

His grin was devilish. "Do you regret having to dance with me?"

She smiled at that. "Reluctantly, I must admit, you're an accomplished dancer, Your Grace."

He laughed. "Does that surprise you?"

She pursed her lips. "I pictured you more of a skilled soldier."

"Believe me, I'm much better on a battlefield than in a ballroom."

"Then you must be quite good on the battlefield." Ooh, she shouldn't have said that. Her cheeks heated.

His eyes were hooded. "You're quite pretty when you blush."

She shook her head and glanced away. "I forget myself. I mustn't add to your legendary arrogance by complimenting you."

He squeezed her hands and a little thrill shot through Lucy's body. "I think I can take a few compliments."

She had to laugh at that. Why, was he trying to charm her? If she didn't know any better she'd think so. And it had been an age since anyone other than her father's old friends who had gout and felt sorry for her had asked her to dance. Well, her father's old friends or Garrett. Either way they were pity dances. But to take to the floor with this handsome, dashing young partner, to feel pretty, to feel as if she were actually being courted. Oh, it was too much. It made her long for things she knew weren't for her. And she wasn't being courted. She wasn't. She must remember that. This man was Cass's beau, whether Cass wanted him or not. Lucy had to remember that. Had to. She and Cass and Jane had agreed. First they'd see Cass free of the duke, then they'd concentrate on convincing Jane's mother to leave her alone to be a bluestocking, and *then* they'd concentrate on finding a husband for Lucy. Not a love, certainly, but a husband. A good man who wouldn't be scared of her and who would treat her decently. Surely that wasn't too much to ask. Cass would help her. Cass was so good at charming people.

And speaking of Cass, Lucy would do well to at least attempt to convince the duke of the futility of his efforts there . . . for the umpteenth time. It was a more industrious use of her time than indulging in useless fantasies.

She took a deep breath. "I know I didn't win the bet, but I do have to say I think you should really listen to me when I tell you that your courting Cass is a waste of time."

He shook his head. A bit of the shine faded from his eyes. His voice was solemn. "Lucy, that's not going to happen."

The use of her Christian name made Lucy suck in her breath sharply. "I don't think you understand how committed she is to the man she loves."

"The man who refuses to offer for her?"

"It's complicated."

"No doubt. But the fact is that I made a promise, and I—"

Lucy shook her head. "Promise? What are you talking about?"

"It doesn't matter. I've made up my mind. And when I make up my mind, I don't change it. They don't call me the Duke of Decisive for nothing."

Lucy wanted to jerk herself out of his arms. There it was again, his insane arrogance. "We're talking about a woman's life here. Not a move made in battle."

"I know exactly what we're talking about. It's my life, too. If Lady Cassandra had told me she was betrothed to another, or even that she intends to be, I'd be more inclined to stop my pursuit of her. But she's told me herself on more than one occasion that that is not the case."

Lucy gritted her teeth. "But she hopes to be betrothed. She *wishes* to be."

"Wishes and hopes are quite different from reality," he said simply.

Lucy stopped dancing. She tugged her hands out of his grasp. "You think I don't know that?" Then she turned in a swirl of green skirts and strode away.

❧

Derek watched her go. He supposed he deserved to be left alone on the floor after he'd won the wager and embarrassed her in front of the occupants of the ballroom. He'd been astonished actually when she hadn't seemed incensed at the beginning of their dance. It was as if she admired him for his little show. No doubt she found it brave of any man to take her on. She was different tonight. As if something had changed between them. In fact, if he didn't know any better, he'd swear he'd seen tears in her eyes just before she'd walked away.

God, Lucy Upton was a conundrum. He had to grudgingly admit that he'd been surprised that she hadn't acted petulant and angry after he'd won the bet. She'd taken her defeat quite easily, actually. Why had he expected less of her? She was a worthy opponent, Lady Lucy. Not one to act anything other than gracious when fairly defeated. He couldn't help but admire that about her.

"You won. I lost. It's simple." She'd said it so matter-of-factly, without the hint of trying to garner sympathy or a shred of self-pity. He liked that about her. Liked it a lot.

Dancing with her, talking with her, verbally sparring with her even, had been the most enjoyment he'd had since he'd come back to London. She was challenging and interesting. He looked forward to spending time in her company if he was being honest. But it didn't change the fact that he intended to marry Lady Cassandra. He'd spent his life making the right decisions, the first time. He wasn't about to second-guess this one. It had actually dimmed his enthusiasm for the conversation with Lucy when she had changed the subject and brought up Lady Cassandra. Cassandra was an entirely different issue. It was like discussing one's landholdings versus one's moves on the battlefield. It was almost as if the two shouldn't meet.

Lucy seemed intent on convincing him that Lady Cassandra was in love with another man. He understood that. And it didn't bother him. Whoever this chap was, he was either unable or unwilling to offer for the girl—and so much the better for Derek. Marriage, like any other major life decision, was best made with facts and a rational head. All love did was complicate things. Cassandra might believe she was in love with this man, but he obviously wasn't a viable marriage partner. And as long as Cassandra did her duty after their marriage and provided Derek with a legitimate son, he didn't much care whom she chose to spend time with. As long as she was discreet, of course.

Why was Lucy so invested in her friend's marriage prospects? Perhaps it was because Cassandra had asked her to help. Cassandra didn't seem as if she had much of a stomach for being forthright. He'd thought that's what he wanted in a mate but he had to admit it was a bit frustrating. Lucy, on the other hand, was as forthright as she could be. Or perhaps she merely enjoyed ripping her friend's suitors to shreds with her daggerlike tongue. Regardless of her reasons or her intentions, Derek wasn't about to let Lucy dissuade him. He'd received a letter today from Swift informing him that his condition was worsening. Derek had wanted to punch his fist through a wall when he'd had to write back to his dying friend and say that he wasn't yet betrothed to Cassandra.

He wasn't. Yet. But he would be.

## ❧ CHAPTER FIFTEEN ❧

Derek ripped open the letter that sat on the top of the stack of correspondence the butler had just delivered on a silver tray. A silver tray? Really? Would Derek ever get used to having his mail delivered that way? Wellington himself had given him the referral for the butler. Hughes was his name. The man had been nothing but exceedingly proper since Derek had hired him. The butler had seen to the hiring of the rest of the household staff and the furnishing of the fine town house, all in an effort to make the residence fit for a duke. Yes, everything was quite proper and in order. Only Derek felt like a counterfeit.

He sliced open the letter with the opener and ripped out the sheaves. Collin had only been gone a few days but he'd already sent a letter. Derek could only hope it contained good news.

*Your Grace,*

*I hope this letter finds you well. I've got quite a good lead on the last known location of our group.*

*It's a small town in France. I'll be traveling there over the next few days and hope to send good news once I find them. I visited Swift in Brussels. He's not good, Derek. Not at all. He asked if you've become betrothed to Lady Cassandra yet. I told him you are in the process of doing just that. I didn't tell him that Swifdon, Rafe, and Adam are missing. No use upsetting the man on his deathbed. Look for another letter soon.*

*Yours,*

*Collin*

Derek crumpled the letter in his fist. He'd written Wellington and once again nearly begged the man to allow him to leave and help search for the others. The result had been the same as before. A decidedly pleasant yet solid no. Derek was needed here, should find a wife, settle down. Wasn't Lady Cassandra Monroe a fine choice?

He'd nearly groaned in frustration, but orders were orders. Every military man knew that. All Derek could do was sit here and wait for Collin's news. His brother would keep him informed. He could count on him.

# ❧ CHAPTER SIXTEEN ❧

Despite the impropriety, Lucy hurried straight into Cass's bedchamber the next morning. Lucy hadn't even stopped to remove her gloves or her bonnet, just made her way directly up the staircase and into her friend's room. She flew over to the bed and stroked Cass's hair. "What is it, dear? What's happened?"

Cass was lying prostrate on the bed, one arm flung over her eyes, tears streaming down the sides of her face, sobbing as if her heart were broken.

Lucy had no clue what was wrong. She'd only received a note from Cass's mother an hour ago saying she must come immediately, that Cass was inconsolable.

Lucy sat next to her friend and rubbed Cass's arms. "The duke, he didn't say anything or do anything—?"

Cass turned toward her and blinked at her. Her pretty blue eyes were bloodshot and overflowing with tears. She blew intermittently into a handkerchief that was wadded up in her fist. She shook her head. "No, no. It's nothing to do with the duke."

Lucy expelled her breath. She should have known better. The duke wouldn't be the one to make Cass cry like this. It made no sense. Lucy had been too preoccupied with the duke lately to remember the usual source of Cass's distress.

She put a hand on Cass's shoulder and searched her face. "It's not . . . Oh, heavens, Cass." Lucy's breath caught in her throat. Pure terror streaked through her chest. "It's Julian, isn't it?"

Cass's sad little nod and accompanying sob confirmed what Lucy already knew. It *was* Julian.

"Is he . . . ?" Lucy swallowed the painful lump in her throat. She couldn't force the word *dead* past her lips.

Cass shook her head rapidly this time. "No. He's alive. For now. But he's—" She sobbed again and pressed the handkerchief to her eyes. "Oh, Lucy, he's dying."

"No," Lucy whispered.

Cass nodded, the handkerchief now pressed to her nose. "I received a letter from cousin Penelope today. Julian is in a makeshift Belgian hospital. He was gravely wounded in battle."

Lucy closed her eyes, desperately searching for the words that would serve to comfort her friend. The news wasn't quite as dire as she'd expected. Julian was still alive. That was something, but the fact that he was about to die was barely better. "Oh, Cass. I'm so sorry."

Cass hung her head. "I just cannot stand to think about him dying all alone."

Tears filled Lucy's eyes. "He's not alone. He's got doctors and I'm certain there are women there, tending to him as if he were their own."

"But he doesn't have anyone who loves him," Cass sobbed.

Lucy swallowed back her own tears. Crying would not help Cass a bit and might just make her more sad. No, Lucy had to be strong. "What about Penelope? Did she say she might try to get there before . . . the end?"

Cass shook her head rapidly. "No. Nothing like that. I do not think she means to go."

"What exactly did she say?"

Cass looked a bit embarrassed. "She said, 'Whom shall I marry now? I've been waiting for Julian for years. I'm on the shelf.'"

Lucy furrowed her brow. Now, *that* was poor form indeed. Though it was in keeping with what she knew of Penelope. Cass's cousin did seem the sort who would be more interested in her own marital prospects or lack thereof than the death of her poor betrothed.

"Oh, Lucy, Julian is so brave and wonderful. He didn't deserve this. And I . . . I never had a chance to tell him . . ." Her voice trailed off into a series of tiny sobs. Lucy put her arm around her.

"Cass." Lucy squeezed her friend's shoulder. "You must try. He may still be alive. Write to Julian immediately. Tell him how you feel about him. How much you love him. Let him go to his grave knowing how much he means to you."

Cass dabbed at her dripping eyes. "I want to, Lucy. Heavens knows I do. I cannot tell you how much. But I . . ." She sucked in her breath and shook her head again. "I don't know."

Lucy kept her tight grip on her friend's shoulder. "Why not, Cass? What harm will it do now? You cannot want him to die without knowing how you feel."

Cass blew daintily into the kerchief. Lucy smiled slightly. Even in the depths of her sorrow, her friend was demure and lovely. Lucy would look like a drowned cat if she cried that hard and would be blowing her nose with a Christmas goose's honk.

Cass drew a deep breath. "For one thing I've no idea how bad he is. Apparently, he told Pen that he doesn't expect to live, but the doctors have no way of knowing how long it will be. Oh, Lucy, what if he's already dead?"

Lucy pulled her arm away and turned to face Cass, sitting up on her knees and facing her imploringly. "You don't know that. Not yet. He may be dead but he may well be alive and live for some time, long enough to receive your letter. Don't you see? You must try."

Cass trembled. Her face fell. She appeared to consider it for a moment. "Do you truly think he would want to hear this on his deathbed?"

Lucy pulled her hands back and rubbed them distractedly up and down her arms, trying to think of some way to convince Cass of the importance of this decision. "He may, Cass. He may love you as much as you love him. He's written to you for years, has he not?"

Cass plucked at the handkerchief that now rested in her lap. "There never has been any talk of love in our letters. And I haven't received a letter from him myself in some time, not since before the battle. He wrote to Pen, not me. That says something."

Lucy searched her friend's face. "There may not have been talk of love between you, yet. But what if he's thinking the same thing you are, Cass? You *must* tell him. Take it from me. I never got to say good-bye to the one person who meant the most to me before he died."

Cass bit her lip. She was obviously considering it. Lucy seized the moment to spring from the bed and rush over to the writing table, where she plucked up two sheets of parchment and a quill. She hurried back over to Cass, but not before scooping up a large book to use as a writing surface. "Here, use this. Write to him. Tell him."

Cass opened her mouth, obviously to protest.

Lucy pressed the quill into her friend's hand. "No, Cass. No excuses. Do it. You must."

## ❧ CHAPTER SEVENTEEN ❧

The Mountebanks' dinner party was abuzz with music, laughter, and talking. Course after course of fine fare was served *à la russe*, and Lucy found herself making awkward conversation with Lord Kramer to her right and Lord Pembroke to her left while giving Jane and Garrett long-suffering looks. Those two were seated next to each other and appeared to be happily engaged in their usual playful ribbing. Lucy envied them. Even the sharp barbs and verbal jabs they were no doubt trading would be preferable to the excruciatingly dull conversation about the weather that she was trapped in with Lord Pembroke. Just how many words might one use to adequately describe fog? Surely they were coming to the end of a finite list?

After dinner, the ladies played cards in one of the Mountebanks' salons while waiting for the gentlemen to join them.

"I'm worried about Cass," Lucy whispered to Jane, who'd joined her in the middle of the room during a break in the play.

"I am, too," Jane whispered back. "She refused to come with you tonight?"

"Yes. All she can think about is Julian. She's distraught."

"It's just so terribly sad," Jane replied. "And Penelope's hideous behavior can't have been easy for her to bear."

"You know Cass. She thinks the best of everyone. She excused Penelope's behavior saying she must be in shock or denial."

"Or Penelope is just awful," Jane replied, waggling her eyebrows over her spectacles.

Lady Mountebank called for the ladies to take their seats for the next round of cards.

Jane's gaze darted to the doorway. "Now's my chance. You don't happen to know where Lord Mountebank's library is, do you?"

Lucy arched a brow. Jane took off in search of the library at every event they attended.

"What?" Jane asked with an innocent shrug. "Even if the supply is rubbish, it's bound to be more fun picking through Lord Mountebank's moldering books than trying to explain to Lady Horton why she must always follow suit in whist."

Lucy laughed. "There I cannot argue." She kept her eyes trained on the ladies seated around her own game of whist and the swift hand of Lady Crandall, who had been known to slip an extra ace from her reticule and blame it on her old age and senility.

As if reading Lucy's mind, Jane tilted her head toward Lady Crandall. "I, for one, cannot wait until I can act as batty as Lady C without the whole of London thinking I'm too young for it. I'd put a turban on my head and bump people with my cane now if I thought for a moment I could get away with it. Why, I might even consider acquiring a parrot."

Lucy snorted. She opened her mouth to say something equally saucy just as the doors to the salon opened and the gentlemen strolled in.

"Ooh, I must go." Jane scooted toward the doors. The gentlemen's entrance caused just the distraction she needed to slip unnoticed from the room.

The men spread through the room, and Lucy was all too aware of the Duke of Claringdon's presence. He sauntered in wearing a claret-colored dinner jacket, dark gray trousers, and a perfectly tied white cravat. He looked good. Too good. Garrett wasn't far behind him.

As her cousin strolled up, he and Jane exchanged exasperated glances. When he reached Lucy, he turned around, watching Jane leave. "She's off to the library, isn't she?" He sighed.

"But of course," Lucy replied with a laugh.

Garrett shook his head. "Predictable."

"I wish you and Jane would stop your constant bickering. You might consider giving her a chance. She's been an excellent friend to me."

Garrett's face reflected his skepticism as he shoved his hands into his pockets. "I'm not the one who's not giving someone a chance. She's been rude to me from the moment we met. And I don't particularly care for being treated like an idiot. You're famous for your sharp tongue but as far as I'm concerned, the sharpness of your tongue doesn't compare to the scimitar behind Miss Lowndes's teeth."

"Jane's really quite nice once you're on her good side."

Garrett wrinkled his brow. "Good side? I've seen no evidence that such a side exists. And if it does, it wouldn't appear until after she finishes lecturing you on the proper care and feeding of thoroughbreds and then telling you the exact dimensions of Stonehenge and then enumerating the many virtues of repealing the Corn Laws."

Lucy shrugged. "She's intelligent and well read. That shouldn't intimidate you in the least."

"Intimidate me, nothing," Garrett shot back. "I simply prefer my conversations to be with ladies who don't insist upon ripping me to pieces with their tongues."

"Hasn't stopped you from being *my* friend." Lucy grinned.

Garrett smiled at her. "Compared with Jane, your tones are dulcet, dear cousin. You choose to flay others with your wit, leaving only the nicest sentiments for me."

Lucy laughed out loud at that and then clapped a hand over her mouth when she noticed the ladies at the nearest card table giving her disapproving looks. "I'm only nice to you because you're going to inherit all of Father's holdings one day and I don't want you to toss me onto the streets."

Garrett grinned back. "I know."

Lucy couldn't help but smile. She loved her cousin without reservation, and the two had exchanged this sort of silly banter for years. She knew without a doubt that Garrett would do anything for her and she him. Neither would ever want to see the other hurt.

And that's why she had to ask him her next question.

Lucy took a deep breath. It was time. She might not have this opportunity again. "So would it be fair to say that you prefer a lady more like Cass than Jane?"

Lucy held her breath. It was the first time she had ever mentioned Cass to Garrett in such a manner. But she had to know. Did Garrett love Cass or not?

"Cassandra." Garrett's face immediately turned sober. "How is she? Did you speak with her today?"

Lucy let out her pent-up breath. Her cousin had managed to change the subject. But they were both worried about Cass. "She's so upset, Garrett. I didn't know how to comfort her."

Garrett nodded grimly.

Lucy turned her head slightly and nearly gasped. The duke was standing only a few paces away. He was speaking with Lord Mountebank, laughing at something the viscount had said. Distracting, his laugh. Deep and rich and—

"I can't imagine what she must be going through," Garrett said, pulling Lucy from her wayward thoughts.

Lucy cleared her throat, doing her best to ignore the duke's proximity. "Jane paid Cass a visit as well. She told me about it earlier. Nothing helped." Had the duke taken a step closer?

Garrett cursed lightly under his breath. "And I suppose nothing will help. A broken heart is a difficult thing to mend. I suspect only time will help."

Lucy couldn't help but think that Garrett, while clearly worried for Cass, might just be hoping that given time and space, Cass could fall in love with him after Julian was gone. It was lovely to contemplate her cousin and her best friend together—but Lucy had to be truthful with Garrett; she always had been. She took a deep breath, willing away the unwanted thoughts of the duke behind her. "Garrett, I must tell you something."

Garrett nodded, narrowing his eyes. "What is it?"

"I told Cass she must write to Julian and tell him the truth."

Garrett turned his head slightly, eyeing her warily. "What do you mean?"

Lucy held out her hand in a supplicating gesture. "I mean she cannot just allow Julian to die without knowing how much she loves him."

Garrett ran a hand over his face. "Are you jesting? What good could come of telling the man something like that on his deathbed?"

Lucy blinked at him. She lowered her voice to a hoarse whisper. "I cannot believe you're saying this. Don't you think he should know how she feels? And more important, don't you think Cass shouldn't have to live the rest of her life knowing she never told him?"

Garrett settled his hands on his hips. "Frankly, no, Lucy. I don't think so. I think it's a phenomenally bad idea actually."

Lucy nearly growled in frustration. How could Garrett think that way? She wasn't particularly known for her romantic notions, but even she could tell that if you loved someone as desperately as Cass loved Julian, you should never allow him to go to his grave without telling him. "You can never go wrong if you're honest and follow your heart," she murmured.

"And that's supposed to fix everything?" Garrett replied, a muscle ticking in his jaw.

"If you were about to die, wouldn't you want to know that someone loves you?" Lucy immediately clapped her hand over her mouth. They both knew that Garrett had been about to die once. In a desert in Spain. He'd been shot in the chest. Nearly bled to death. But she and her fun-loving cousin rarely spoke of such a time. And certainly they never spoke of how he lived with the guilt that he should have been the one who died just as she lived with that same guilt. But for an entirely different reason. No. That would have been a subject they would never broach. But it was never far from their minds and they both knew it.

Garrett cleared his throat. His voice was solemn. "I can

say with all honesty that if I could do nothing about it, I wouldn't want to know."

Lucy searched his face. "You cannot mean that—"

"Lady Lucy, come and make a fourth for our hand," Lady Crandall called, gesturing her over toward their card table. Now that the men had sufficiently settled into the room, the ladies were back at their intention for another round of cards. And Lucy's popularity had somehow increased exponentially ever since her challenge with the duke. The *ton* was so odd.

Lucy fought her wince. She didn't know if she could take another round of Lady Crandall's loose fingers.

"Go ahead," Garrett said, nodding toward Lady Crandall. "I'm going in search of Lord Mountebank's study and a glass of brandy if I can find one."

Lucy sighed. "You're abandoning me? Very well then. Cards it is." She lifted her skirts and made a move to proceed to Lady Crandall's table when the Duke of Claringdon stepped in her path.

"Lady Lucy," he said. "May I have a word?"

Lucy instinctively took a step back. Somehow being that close to him made her feel a bit off-balance. Even after having spent time in his immediate company the last couple of days, she was still struck by his stunning good looks and the maddeningly intoxicating scent of him, like spice and soap.

"Just a word, Your Grace. I'm wanted as a fourth." She nodded toward the card table.

The duke glanced over his shoulder to acknowledge Lady Crandall. That lady gave him a positively leering stare. He turned back to face Lucy, his eyebrow arched in a skeptical semblance as if to say, *Yes, I'm quite certain you're dying to play whist with Lady Crandall.*

Lucy pursed her lips. "Your Grace?" The last time she'd seen him she'd escaped from his presence like a frightened, angry child. She would not allow him to rile her like that again. She must act as if she were completely unaffected by him.

His eyebrow settled back into place. "Where is Lady Cassandra this evening?"

Lucy gave him a tight smile. "Not here."

His face became a stone mask. "I can see that."

Another tight smile. "Then perhaps you didn't need to ask the question after all."

He set his jaw. "You don't care to tell me why Lady Cassandra didn't accompany you this evening?"

Lucy plucked up her skirts again and moved around him. "Not particularly, Your Grace."

She glided over to her chair, sat down, and scooped up the hand of cards she'd been dealt. Lucy plastered a smile on her face, despite her inward cringe at her own behavior. She hadn't even wished him good evening. Even for her that was unbelievably rude.

Why did that man bring out the very worst in her? She could have easily told him that Cass was having a bad night. That Cass had discovered that her good friend— the man she loved—was dying. But something about the duke's smug demand that Lucy tell him made her intent on keeping it to herself. He was just too . . . too . . . arrogant. Sure of himself. Handsome. She glanced over at him. He was already in conversation with Lord Mountebank again and didn't appear to give another thought to Cass. Why did he have to act as if he cared? Cass was just another notch in his belt, another win on the battlefield for him. He'd admitted it himself. He saw winning Cass as a challenge, a competition. And Lucy would not let her friend be treated so cavalierly.

"Count me in, Lady Crandall." Lucy eyed the cards in her hand and grinned over their tops. "I look forward to soundly beating you ladies."

❧

Exactly one hour later, Derek waited in the corridor outside the salon where the ladies were playing cards. He'd done his duty and made the rounds chatting with his host and the other gentlemen. He'd even searched for Jane Lowndes. But he'd been unable to find that lady. It had been his last resort to ask Lucy where Lady Cassandra was, but there'd been no help for it. He didn't enjoy Society dinner parties. Especially when all anyone wanted to ask him about was how horrific Waterloo had been. They wanted all the gory details, all the juicy bits, but had they an inkling in hell what they were asking about, they wouldn't even mention it. They'd put it as far from their minds as possible. Yes. Men who had truly seen war had no desire to remember. He'd come here tonight for one reason and one reason only, to see Lady Cassandra. Further their acquaintance. Get closer to fulfilling his promise to Swift. And she wasn't even here. It was frustrating to think he'd wasted his time. But he couldn't very well stalk out the door. He had to keep up the semblance of giving a damn. Even more frustrating was that little hellcat Lady Lucy.

She was driving him mad. He'd met generals in battle who gave him more to go on than this young lady. Damn it. He'd faced down the enemy, he'd taken battlefields, he'd hoisted the Union Jack over bloody fields and tossed dirt over the bodies of his friends. But he could not, for the life of him, crack the armor of this one spitfire. He clenched his jaw. What was he to do with her?

The door to the salon opened and Lucy came strolling out. Ah, just as expected. He'd known she wouldn't be able to sit and play cards all evening. She'd pretended to be interested, but he could see in her eyes, the way her knee bounced up and down impatiently the entire time she'd been playing, that the game held little interest for her. No doubt she'd been biding time the same way he had and would go in search of her friends Jane and Garrett as soon as possible to take her leave.

And that was why Derek had been waiting in the corridor for her. Waiting for his chance.

The moment she passed him, he stepped from the shadows directly into her path. "My lady."

To her credit, she didn't scream. Didn't even seem as if she noticed him other than the fact that he'd caused her to stop. Instead, she touched one hand lightly to the base of her throat and had the temerity to eye him up and down. "Your Grace. Hiding in corners again?"

He fought the urge to grind his teeth. He was still getting used to people calling him "Your Grace," but not the way she made the honorific sound, like someone crunching glass between their teeth.

"Lady Lucy, I was hoping to have another word with you in here." Instead of allowing her to say no, he shot out his hand, captured her wrist, and dragged her into the drawing room on the other side of the corridor. That was how one had to deal with the likes of Lady Lucy. Give no quarter.

He tugged her into the room behind him, shut the door after them, and turned to face her. She did not look amused. The light from a brace of candles across the room illuminated her unusual eyes.

"Where is Lady Cassandra this evening?" he asked.

Lucy gave a long-suffering sigh. "I told you. She's not here. I thought you could gather as much from her absence." There was that eternal sarcasm.

He spoke through clenched teeth. "I'm asking you where she is."

Lucy crossed her arms over her chest and gave him a narrowed-eyed stare. "And what if I said I don't intend to tell you?"

Derek closed his eyes briefly and poked his tongue into the side of his cheek, biting against the words that rushed to his lips. The ones he wanted to say. The ones he shouldn't say.

"Allow me to attempt this in another manner, my lady. Why are you so intent upon meddling with my affairs?"

Lucy's mouth dropped open. "Meddling with your—? Oh, that's funny. You might have fooled me. I was under the impression that you just accosted me in the corridor and pulled me in here for questioning as if I were a French spy. But apparently, I'm meddling with *your* affairs." The look she gave him was entirely ironic, complete with batting her long, sooty lashes. Derek longed to wipe it from her face. Mostly because he could smell the tantalizing scent of her soap, and it was a shock to his groin.

He set his jaw, trying to keep on task. "Do you deny that you've been interfering with my courtship of Lady Cassandra?"

A half smirk popped to her lips. "Absolutely not."

Her color was rising and she looked even more beautiful than usual. Derek paced away from her. "And I'm asking why? Why do you insist upon interfering?"

"Why do you think for a moment I owe you an explanation? Your arrogance is beyond bounds, even for a war-hero duke."

"Is that so?" he thundered.

"Yes. It's so. Now, if you'll excuse me, I'm leaving." She attempted to step around him, but he blocked her path.

She plunked both hands on her hips and tilted her head up to face him, shooting sparks at him with her eyes. "Using your size and your strength to intimidate me, Your Grace? You might frighten Cass but you don't frighten me."

He shuddered with frustration. He wanted to reach out and shake her. Why was this woman so bloody difficult? He'd known opposing generals who'd made him less angry and given him more to go on when trying to decipher the best course of action to win the battle. His hands were on his hips, too. He eyed her, breathing heavily through both nostrils.

She taunted him with her next words. "At a loss for words, Your Grace? That's a first."

She battled those gorgeous lashes at him again. His pulse jumped with each look. That was it. She'd batted them one time too many.

"As a matter of fact, yes," he growled just before he tugged her into his arms and brought his lips down to claim hers.

# ❧ CHAPTER EIGHTEEN ❧

Lucy's mind floundered in circles when the duke's mouth met hers. Stunned. That's what she was. Her breath caught in her throat, and her mind raced at a speed she was quite certain was not healthy. He was kissing her. The Duke of Claringdon, the war hero, the man who'd heretofore been attempting to court Cass, was kissing *her*. Her mind might be floundering, but her body, as if by a will of its own, molded to his.

She should push him away. That thought rode her brain like a horse winning at the Ascot, but all she could do was feel the hot wetness of his mouth on hers, recall the little dimple in his cheek that she'd seen just before his lips claimed hers, and feel the beating of his heart that happened just below his Adam's apple. Her heart slammed into her rib cage again and again. It was almost painful. But when the duke turned her in his arms and pulled her against him roughly, his tongue pushing between her lips and ravaging her mouth, she ceased thinking entirely.

He tasted like brandy. She'd snuck a sip or two from Papa's stash in the study on special occasions and yes, the duke was exactly what brandy tasted like. But better, because along with it was the passionate force of this man whom she had to admit she was wildly attracted to. True, she didn't like him one bit, but gorgeous and rugged and handsome and muscled . . . Ooh, she shuddered. Against her will, not to mention her better judgment, her hands moved up to twine around his neck. He was so tall she was forced to stand on tiptoe even though he was bending down to her. He groaned in the back of his throat and pulled her even more tightly against him. His tongue was hot and wet and skillful, demanding, taking but also giving, and Lucy was rocketed with a barrage of sensations and emotions she'd never known existed.

She became vaguely aware of a moan. It must have been her own. It jolted her back into consciousness. She pressed with all her might against his broad shoulders. He pulled back and stepped away, panting a little and staring at her with those hooded green eyes as if she were some mythical creature come to life and not a flesh-and-blood woman standing in front of him her lips no doubt red and swollen from his potent kiss.

She stood there dumbly, breathing heavily, her hand pressed against her middle. Her stays had never felt so tight. Her body had never felt so hot. Her mind had never been more confused. What the devil had that been about? She pressed the back of her hand against her lips. They were scorching as if he'd burned her. She placed her other hand against the back of the sofa to steady herself, breathe.

What had she just done?

Kissed the abominable Duke of Claringdon, that's what.

It was improper. It was indecent. It was wrong for half

a score of reasons. She didn't even *like* him. Not like that. Not like *any* way.

And why was *he* kissing *her* while they were on the subject? It made no sense.

She took two deep breaths, sucking air back into her lungs. Searching her mind for a coherent thought. Thankfully, the duke had turned away from her and was pacing in front of the windows. It helped that he was not staring her down while she tried to make sense of the nonsensical.

First things first. She squared her shoulders. She could handle this. She could. She'd just think about it rationally. Logically. First, and most important, what would she tell Cass? Could she tell her? Should she? Oh, no. She couldn't tell Cass. Even if she could somehow manage to explain that he had kissed *her*. Cass was grieving. The last thing she needed was a betrayal from her closest friend. But was it a betrayal? Cass didn't care for the duke, but . . . No. No. No. Telling Cass was out of the question. Too complicated.

She eyed the duke's broad shoulders. The man knew how to fill out a dinner jacket. She'd give him that. A dinner jacket that just happened to accentuate the flatness of his abdomen and— Oh, for heaven's sake. She should be ashamed of herself. For the barest hint of a moment, she smiled softly, touching her still-scorched lips. Oh, very well. She shouldn't have kissed the Duke of Claringdon, but it had been enjoyable. It had been quite, quite enjoyable. As much as she hated to admit it, the man knew what he was doing on and off the battlefield, it seemed. And besides, she couldn't take it back now. The damage was well and thoroughly done.

She pushed up her chin as he turned to face her.

❦

Derek turned toward Lucy, opened his mouth, shut it, and then quickly turned on his heel toward the windows again. Damn it all to hell. He'd thought he'd known what he would say but seeing her with her hair a bit mussed and her lips swollen from his kisses made every thought in his head scatter. And at the moment, an even more immediate problem was the stark evidence of how her kiss had affected him, readily apparent with a glance at his trousers. No, facing her had not been a good idea. Not at all.

He scrubbed his hand through his hair and tried to think of something awful to cool his ardor.

Lady Crandall's hideous laugh.

The Earl of Westwood's abhorrent teeth.

*Swift dying.*

That did it.

What the hell had come over him? Why had he kissed her? Very well. She was beautiful and frustrating and challenging and clever. But he didn't even like her. Did he? No, of course he didn't. And yet . . . she was beguiling in her own stubborn way. Damn it. Not only had he gone and kissed a woman he didn't like, but he also had kissed the closest friend of the lady he'd been actively attempting to court for the past several days. Bad, bad form. What if Lady Lucy told Lady Cassandra about this? And of course she would tell Lady Cassandra about this. Women told each other everything, didn't they? Yes, it had only been one kiss but when dealing with young unmarried females, a kiss had quite an import. He wouldn't blame Lady Cassandra if she never spoke to him again.

He sucked in and blew out three deep breaths. A trick

he'd learned long ago in the army. It cleared one's head. Good for one's decision-making ability.

Very well. The deed was done. It did no good to have recriminations. He'd made his choice and it was over. All he could hope to do would be to reassure Lady Lucy that it had been merely a moment's indiscretion, an impulsive response to the tension in the room. Not a promise or anything else. Simply a response to a stimulus. He must somehow convince her to remain quiet. To keep her mouth shut. Her mouth. Shut. It hadn't been. A moment ago. When his tongue had been inside it. Oh, bloody hell he was getting hard again. Damn. Damn. Damn. Why did it have to be so good, too? Couldn't she have had cold thin lips or hideous breath or something? It would have made the entire affair that much easier. Instead she'd melted like butter in the sun at the insistent pressure of his mouth, and he'd been halfway to melting himself.

That was it. It had simply been far too long since he'd kissed a woman if Lucy Upton was affecting him like this. Fine. It had been a—ahem—moving kiss. Blast it. And that look of pure shock upon her face when he'd pulled her into his arms. That, that one moment, might have made it all worth it. Or even better, the fact that she'd kissed him back, with passion. And they both knew it. Let the little oh-so-sure-of-herself miss stew on *that*.

❧

When the duke turned to face her this time, Lucy had plastered a calm (and self-righteous, thank you very much) look upon her face. She crossed her arms over her chest and pushed up her nose in the air just a tad in an attempt to seem above it all. She hoped it would be convincing. It didn't feel convincing.

He cleared his throat. "That was . . . only a kiss. A mistake. We'll pretend as if it never happened."

Lucy tilted her head to the side, incredulous. "No apology, Your Grace?"

He tilted his head to the opposite side. "Do you want one?"

"Ever the gentleman." She rolled her eyes.

He ran his fingers through his hair. "It meant nothing."

"Of course it meant nothing, to *you*," she agreed, a bit stung by his words though she'd die before she admitted it, "but how do you plan to explain this to *Cass*?"

A challenge rested in his green eyes. "We're not going to tell Lady Cassandra."

"You might not plan on it, but I certainly—"

He narrowed his eyes on her. "You're not going to tell her, either."

She tossed a hand in the air. "How do you expect that to be the case?" she scoffed. "I cannot wait to hear this."

"Because if you tell her, you'll have to explain why you kissed me back."

Lucy narrowed her eyes on him. Just what sort of a game was he playing? "So what? Do you intend upon taking liberties with all of Cass's friends? Is Jane next?" Cass would most likely swoon if he kissed her the way he'd just kissed Lucy.

He looked skeptical. "Don't be absurd. Believe me, I can control myself around all of you."

"Because you've done a smashing job of it so far." Eyes still narrowed, Lucy considered him for a moment. She tapped her foot along the carpet. "Would you care to explain to me why you are so set on courting Cass? You've made it quite clear that you have no intention of desisting in your pursuit of her, yet you've never exactly explained why you're so interested in a woman who isn't the least bit interested back. Especially given that you're here at this dinner party tonight taking liberties with *me*."

He paced away from her and cursed under his breath. "Lady Cassandra was . . ."

She blinked at him innocently. "Yes?"

He growled. "Let's just say she was recommended to me."

Lucy took a step back, pressing her hand to the exposed skin above her décolletage. "Recommended to you? What the devil is that supposed to mean?"

The duke slashed his hand through the air. "It makes no difference. I didn't intend to kiss you. I had a momentary lapse of judgment. If you'd like an apology, I'll give it, but there's no need to make more of this than it was."

She pushed up her nose again. "It'll be a cold day in hell, *Your Grace*, before I ask for your apology. If you were a gentleman, you would have offered without my having to ask."

He pushed his hands inside his pockets and looked at her through heavy-lidded eyes, the slow spread of a smile on his lips. "If I were a gentleman, my lady, I wouldn't have kissed you like that."

Lucy fought the urge to childishly stamp her foot. He had her there. Which only served to confuse her more. Why *had* he kissed her? She eyed him carefully. And why was he so blasted handsome? Hmm. Again, that particular thought was not helpful. Not in the least.

Very well. Cass didn't need to know about this embarrassing little incident. Especially when it would make no difference to her and she was in the midst of such sadness for Julian. No. Lucy would not bother Cass with this news.

Besides, if Lucy did her duty as a friend and did what she'd promised Cass, she would get rid of the overbearing duke, so what did it matter?

Lucy took a deep breath. "Very well, I won't tell Cass about this incident on two conditions."

The duke placed his hands on his hips and tilted his head to the side again. "Only two?"

She smiled at him sweetly. "I can add more if you'd like."

He narrowed his eyes at her. "What are the two?"

"First, you must promise never to take such a liberty again—"

"Done!" The relief on his face was irritating.

The swiftness of his reply caused Lucy to grit her teeth. He didn't need to seem so blasted happy about that one. "Second, you must finally agree to leave off courting Cass."

He dropped his hands to the side. "No, I cannot promise that."

She slashed an arm through the air. "Why not?"

"Because I fully intend to take Lady Cassandra to wife regardless of this minor accident here tonight. Rest assured it will not happen again."

"How can I possibly know that?"

Skepticism etched across his face. "While I'm certain you're quite used to men being unable to control themselves around you, Miss Upton, I am perfectly capable."

"Stop calling me Miss Upton and you didn't seem so controlled a few moments ago." She crossed her arms over her chest and tapped her fingers along her elbows.

"I told you, it was a momentary lapse in judgment."

"And how do I know you won't have another inconvenient so-called momentary lapse in judgment with the next young miss you find in a library?" she shot back.

He let out a long, deep breath. "You drive me mad, do you know that?"

She snorted. "The feeling is entirely mutual."

He turned, strode past Lucy, and opened the door to the drawing room. "Enough. Since you refuse to tell me why she didn't attend tonight, I intend to call upon Lady Cassandra tomorrow and see for myself."

## ❧ CHAPTER NINETEEN ❧

"I'll make all the arrangements," Garrett announced the next afternoon at Cass's parents' town house. The four friends were enjoying a lavish tea prepared by the Monroes' cook in an attempt to lure Cass into eating something.

Cass had reluctantly come down to the drawing room to greet her friends, but she seemed entirely uninterested in anything on her plate. Cass's parents had gone out to make some social calls and so the four of them were alone in the house with the servants.

Cass sighed. "I'm not certain it's such a good idea." Resting her chin in her hand, elbow propped upon the table, she pushed her biscuits and teacakes around her plate. She'd been doing so all afternoon and had yet to take a bite.

"Oh, but it is. I think it's a brilliant idea. Don't you, Jane?" Lucy kicked Jane, who sat next to her on the settee.

Jane barely glanced up from the newspaper she'd been reading. "Pardon? Yes. Yes. Brilliant!" She pushed up her spectacles on her nose and took a large bite of her own biscuit.

Lucy nodded. "See there, dear, everyone's in agreement."

Cass turned soulful blue eyes to Garrett. "It's ever so nice of you to offer your house in Bath to us for the remainder of the summer, but I just don't know that I should leave London right now. If Penelope receives another letter from Julian, I want to be here in town so I can learn the news right away. And there's always the chance that he may write to me himself."

Lucy patted Cass on the back. "But dear, you said yourself that Penelope and her mother are retiring to their country house for the rest of the summer soon. No one stays in London in August. We must go. The post will make it to Bath just as surely as it will make it to London. It's even a bit closer to Penelope's country house, is it not?"

Cass's eyes brightened a bit. "I suppose that's true."

"It's absolutely true," Lucy said with a nod. Garrett quickly agreed.

"I, for one, am all for it. Any excuse to get away from my mother's watchful eye," Jane said. "I consider this the start to Lucy's experiment to help me dissuade my parents from forcing me to marry."

Garrett slapped a palm on the table. "The devil you say. Your parents are forcing you to marry? That's news."

"In theory," Jane replied. "Aren't all parents forcing their daughters to marry?"

"You make it sound as if you're off to the gallows," Garrett replied, rolling his eyes.

"It feels like it." She smiled at him sweetly.

"In your case, if they're forcing you, they obviously haven't done a very good job at it," Garrett added.

Jane closed her eyes and pushed up her nose. "That is because I have become quite adept at sidestepping their attempts. Well, that and the fact that no one wants to marry a bluestocking. That part is merely luck actually." Jane laughed at her own joke.

"I've never known anyone so proud of being a bluestocking," Garrett said, snapping his own bit of newspaper open in front of his face.

"And I've never known someone so proud of being a dissolute rake. Oh, and profligate gambler. Mustn't forget that."

Garrett allowed the edge of the paper to fold down so he could eye Jane over its top. "I gamble only upon occasion, and I'm hardly dissolute."

"If you say so." Jane went back to paying more attention to her teacake than to Garrett. "This trip to Bath is just what I need," she continued. "Besides, I cannot wait to go to the circulating library there. It's one of the best in the country."

Garrett leaned back in his chair and crossed his legs at the ankles. He let out a long breath. "Of course you can't wait. Take you to a holiday town and all you're interested in is the library."

Jane tapped the tip of her finger against the paper. "Careful, Upton, or I'll wonder at your quarrel with libraries. Though I suppose it does help one's attitude about such things if one is able to read."

Garrett shook his head slowly in a long-suffering manner. "I've been to the circulating library in Bath many times, Miss Lowndes. In fact, I'm one of its most devoted patrons."

This time Jane didn't even glance up. "Yes. I'm certain they're appreciative of your coming in to look up the remedy for a sick head after a night of too many cards and too much drinking."

Lucy gave them both a warning look. "Would you two stop? We're doing this for Cass, remember?"

"Yes, of course." Garrett turned back to face their friend. "Just say the word, Cassandra, and I'll make it happen."

"I suppose Mama will be all right with it," Cass said tentatively, taking a sip from her juice glass.

Lucy covered Cass's hand with her own. "She will be, dear. Aunt Mary will be there with us so it's all properly chaperoned. We'll drink the waters at the Pump Room, take tea, go for a daily stroll along the Upper Crescent. You'll see. You'll feel better in no time."

Cass gave her a weak smile.

"And the best part is," Lucy added, pressing her lips together tightly, "we'll be getting away from that odious Duke of Claringdon."

Jane raised a brow. "And here I thought you'd got over your intense dislike of the duke, Lucy."

"I don't know what you mean." Lucy's gaze fell to the tablecloth. She swallowed. She hadn't told Cass about the kiss she'd shared with the duke. But the more vexing question was—why hadn't she told Jane about it? Or Garrett? They all told one another everything. But something inside her, some inner hidden part, was embarrassed, shy even. And it was a singularly unpleasant and new experience. She'd never been shy a day in her life, and she certainly shouldn't be shy about anything involving that blowhard the Duke of Claringdon. So why hadn't she told them?

Very well. She would. Just as soon as they made it to Bath and safely away from that man. She would tell Jane and Garrett and they would all think of some way to dissuade him once and for all. Perhaps the time away in Bath would cool his ardor . . . for Cass. Surely, he would be leaving London soon for the lands and properties he'd been given as a part of his dukedom. Wouldn't he?

Cass bit her lip. "I know I should be flattered by the duke's attention but I just cannot be."

"Of course you don't have to be, dear." Lucy patted her hand. "If you don't like him, you don't like him." *And if you don't like him, why did you kiss him?*

Cass nudged her biscuit again. "It's not that I don't like him, it's just . . ."

They all knew what she wanted to say. He wasn't Julian. It always came back to that.

"Oh, Lucy. You said he mentioned last night at the party that he intended to pay me another call today, didn't you?" Cass asked.

Lucy swallowed. "Yes, that's right." Though she hadn't mentioned any of the rest of her conversation—among other things—with the duke.

"Promise me you'll stay with me today. When he comes to visit, I'll need you."

"Of course I promise, dear." She didn't relish the thought of being in the same room with him, but she couldn't leave Cass to fend for herself with the blackguard.

"And I promise to leave immediately and secure our travel plans to Bath." Garrett stood and made a sweeping bow in the general direction of all the ladies.

Lucy smiled brightly. "We're going to Bath!"

# ❧ CHAPTER TWENTY ❧

"We're going to Bath," Lucy announced with another bright smile on her face two hours later. This time she was speaking to the Duke of Claringdon, who sat in a chair across from Cass in the Monroes' drawing room.

He appeared to be avoiding all eye contact with Lucy, which only served to make her more relentlessly cheerful. Without bothering to look at her, he said, "Bath, eh?" He sat back in his chair and crossed his booted feet at the ankles.

"Yes, Bath." Lucy punctuated it this time with a resolute nod of her head. She'd assumed she'd find it a bit difficult to look at him, too, after the kiss they'd shared. But she was actually enjoying delivering this particular bit of news. And the more he refused to give her the satisfaction of looking at her, the farther she leaned forward in her seat and glared at him.

"Just decided to take a trip?" he pressed, tugging on his snowy white cuff as if he hadn't a care in the world.

Lucy braced both hands on her knees and eyed him. She'd foiled him and he didn't appear to like it one bit.

And of course he couldn't just allow them to share the news and wish them well; he had to pry for details. She wrinkled her nose. If he had an ounce of chivalry, he'd already realize that part of the reason they were fleeing west was to evade his unwelcome presence. He must suspect that. Ugh. No doubt that was why he was asking.

"Papa thinks the waters will be good for me," Cass added, offering a delicate teacup to the duke. Of course, she hadn't mentioned how her Mama had railed against the idea, convinced that any journey that took Cass away from the duke's company was quite a bad idea indeed. But Cass's papa had intervened and insisted she go. He knew how upset Cass had been at the news of Julian, and he thought the change of scenery would do her good. Thank goodness for Cass's papa.

The duke leaned forward to accept the teacup that Cass offered. Lucy watched their interchange with the hint of a smile playing around her lips. The man didn't drink tea and never would. She'd noticed that about him on the first day he'd visited, but Cass never seemed to pick up on this bit of information pertaining to their esteemed guest. She insisted upon presenting him with the drink as if he'd somehow change his mind (and personality) suddenly. Lucy lifted her own cup to her lips. Why, Cass would do better to offer him a brandy. He'd be more likely to drink it. Lucy hid her smile behind her own teacup.

"I've never been to Bath," the duke replied. He paused to set the unwanted drink on the side table before pushing out his legs again.

Lucy swallowed and tried to avert her eyes. Oh, my, but he did have long legs. Long and fit. And he was wearing dark gray breeches and an emerald-green waistcoat that brought out the color of his eyes. She glanced away.

His eyes? Now she was waxing poetic about his eyes? Oh, this had to stop and immediately. She set down her teacup and folded her hands in her lap. "Never been to Bath? I've never heard of such a thing."

His gaze barely flickered over her. "Yes, well, there's not much occasion to go to a holiday town when one is in the army, is there?" He gave her a tight smile, and Lucy tried to pretend that she wasn't remembering what it felt like to kiss him. She would not blush. By God. Would *not*. She was not a blusher!

"Oh, of course not, Your Grace," Cass rushed to assure him. "But Bath is an absolutely lovely town. All rolling hillsides and so green and pretty. And the Assembly Rooms and Pump Room and the Roman ruins. Why, it's quite breathtaking." Lucy's heart wrenched for her friend. Cass was doing so well pretending to be happy and cheerful in the duke's company. As if she hadn't spent the entire night sobbing. She looked as fresh as a flower, too. If Lucy had cried all night, she'd look like a puffed-up pigeon.

The door to the drawing room cracked open just then and Cass's mother came bustling inside. "Oh, forgive me, Your Grace, for being late for your visit but I only just learned you were here." She gave Lucy a narrowed-eyed glare that caused Lucy to wonder if the matron had somehow discovered that she'd bribed the footman to keep the news from Lady Moreland as long as possible. That blasted Shakespierre must have cracked.

After exchanging pleasantries with Lady Moreland, the duke resumed his seat. He always looked like a giant trying to fit into the tiny rosewood chairs of the Monroes' drawing room. "I was just telling your daughter that Bath sounds like a place I should visit," he said to Lady Moreland.

A warning bell tolled somewhere in the back of Lucy's

mind. She watched in silent, slowly dawning horror as Lady Moreland's mouth opened and the words came chirping out, "Oh, you should. It's an absolute must."

"It's settled then," the duke responded quickly without allowing Lucy or Cass to speak. "I'll visit Bath as well. See what all the fuss is about. I may even buy property there. Sounds like a splendid place."

Cass's mouth formed an O and she blinked in obvious surprise. Then she smiled at the duke and nodded before glancing away and taking a shaky sip of tea.

Lady Moreland's smile stretched from ear to ear. "Excellent. I'm certain you young people will have a splendid time."

Lucy set down her cup, plunked her hands on her hips, and narrowed her eyes at the duke. "You were not planning to go to Bath!"

He slowly turned to face her and gave her a long-suffering stare. "First of all, how could you possibly know that, Lady Lucy? And second, after Lady Cassandra here has just spent several minutes extolling the town's virtue, I am entirely certain that I do indeed want to visit the place."

"But you— But we—" Lucy couldn't form a thought. She was livid. How had that man managed to thwart her again in the span of a mere fifteen minutes? And while she'd been keeping vigil? Very close vigil. Why, he'd snuck in and made his move right in front of her even. They called him the Duke of Decisive. He should be called the Duke of Deviousness.

"Lady Lucy, please," Lady Moreland said, giving her a curt nod. "I believe the duke has made up his mind."

"Indeed I have, madam," he replied. "Do you have any objections, Lady Cassandra?"

Cass glanced at Lucy, then at her mother who gave her

a stern stare. "No, of course not, Your Grace," she said softly, tugging at the collar of her gown.

The next half an hour rattled by as the duke managed to wheedle every bit of relevant information out of a far-too-accommodating Lady Moreland. His questions rang out like a barrage, making Lucy shake with a combination of growing frustration and complete futility as Lady Moreland set about cheerfully answering them one by one. Where were they staying? With whom? What street did the house sit upon? How long did they intend to visit? It was utterly ridiculous. And every attempt Lucy made to circumvent the answers was met with a direct repeated question by the duke that either Cass or her mother somehow seemed compelled to answer.

By the end of the interview, Lucy was seething with anger. Cass's eyes were cloudy with confusion. And the duke and Lady Moreland looked like cats with bellies full of cream.

Finally the duke stood to take his leave. He made a sweeping bow. "I look forward to seeing you in Bath, Lady Cassandra."

Cass nodded weakly and attempted to manage nearly half a smile. "Yes, Your Grace." Lady Moreland smiled and patted her daughter's shoulder.

"You, too, Lady Lucy," the duke added with a devilish wink as he strolled out the door.

## ❧ CHAPTER TWENTY-ONE ❧

The journey to Bath was bumpy, hot, and a bit crowded to be honest, what with Jane, Lucy, Cass, Aunt Mary, and Garrett all squeezed into Garrett's coach. And while it was a superb vehicle, by the time the conveyance pulled to a stop in front of Garrett's fine town house in the upper streets, Lucy was rubbing bruises out of places she didn't know existed.

The door to the town house flung open and the servants came bustling down the steps to help them alight from the coach. Aunt Mary turned into a whirlwind of efficiency, ordering the servants about and directing everyone to their respective rooms. Lucy's aunt Mary, Garrett's mother, had never been accepted by her own mother. "Far too brash and friendly," Lucy's mother had said of her sister-in-law, a frown firmly on her lips. But that was just what Lucy adored about her aunt. Aunt Mary always had a smile on her face and treated everyone with warmth and enthusiasm.

The footmen shuffled to and fro, unloading the luggage from both the carriage they'd ridden in and the one that had followed them with the extra trunks. They all entered the grand house and were quickly ushered into one of the drawing rooms where they were served tea and refreshments.

"I'm so glad you all came on this trip with us," Aunt Mary said, her voice a high-pitched rush of excitement. "We shall have a grand time this summer. You'll see."

"Thank you for having us, Aunt," Lucy replied.

"Oh, it's Garrett's house now, not mine." The shadow of sorrow passed briefly over her face. Aunt Mary had been a widow for over two years, since Uncle Charles had passed away.

Garrett had just finished taking a sip of tea. "Mother, it's as much yours as mine."

Aunt Mary patted her son's hand. "Such a good boy. I'm lucky to have you."

Lucy smiled. How she wished she and her own mother could have a relationship like that. Or she and her father, for that matter. Her parents had long ago given up hope for her to make a decent match and mostly stayed in the countryside lamenting the fact that Garrett would one day inherit all their lands and Father's title. It was sad, really. When they might all be a big happy family. As if those existed.

Aunt Mary clapped her hands, calling Lucy's attention back to the drawing room. "There is to be a grand ball just two nights hence at the Upper Assembly Rooms. It's certain to be a great deal of fun."

"Excellent," Garrett said.

"Looking forward to it," Lucy replied.

"Me too," Jane offered, though no one truly believed her.

Cass seemed less than enthusiastic, but she managed a small smile when Aunt Mary insisted that she would go and have a grand time.

"And Mrs. Periwinkle told me that the Duke of Claringdon has just rented a house on Uphill Drive."

Cass's eyes looked a bit fearful. Lucy crossed her arms over her chest. "Yes, we heard he'd be coming, too."

"Ooh, how did you know, dear?" Aunt Mary asked, sitting on the edge of her seat as if the duke's comings and goings were of the utmost importance to her.

Lucy took a sip of her tea. "He told us himself."

Aunt Mary nearly toppled from her seat. "You spoke to the duke?"

"Yes," Lucy replied. "He's been attempting to court Cass."

Aunt Mary looked as if she was tempted to throw her teacup in the air. Her eyes were as wide as the saucer. She clutched at her chest. "The *Duke of Claringdon* is courting our Cassandra?"

Cass shook her head fervently. "Oh, not really. Not—"

"He's *attempting* to," Lucy repeated. "Cass, however, is not interested."

If Aunt Mary were the type to have an apoplectic fit, surely it would be well under way by now. She'd somehow managed to retrieve a fan from a wrinkle in her skirts and was fanning herself at a pace that made Lucy worry for her wrist; indeed, her entire arm. "What? Not interested in the Duke of Claringdon? How is that possible?" She stared at Cass as if she were a mythological creature who'd just flown through the window out of the pages of a storybook.

Cass's face flushed pink. "He's only paid a call or two."

"Don't forget you went riding in the park," Jane chimed in, stuffing her second tea biscuit in her mouth.

Cass nodded. "Yes. We also went riding in the park."

"We've been trying to rid ourselves of him, actually,"

Lucy added, unsuccessfully attempting to keep the pique from her voice. "But he insisted on following us to Bath."

"He's come here for you!" That was it. Aunt Mary might very well have an apoplectic fit after all. Lucy wondered if Cass traveled with smelling salts. A fainting spell seemed imminent.

"No. No. He wanted to see the town. He's never been," Cass assured her, squirming in her seat.

"Cassandra, you're being modest." Garrett's voice was quiet and calm. "The duke appears to be quite taken with you."

Cass plucked at the folds in her butter-colored gown. She wouldn't meet his eyes.

"You know what I think?" Jane piped up. She'd just finished her last tea biscuit and dabbed at her lips with the edge of her napkin.

"No, what?" Garrett asked, a smirk on his face.

Jane completely ignored him. "I think *Lucy* is better suited for the duke than Cass."

For the first time since they'd begun speaking of the duke, Cass had a happy look on her face. "Oh, I quite agree."

"Furthermore, I think she *may* actually be a bit interested in him," Jane added, a small smile on her lips.

Lucy went hot and cold. She snapped up her head and blinked at her friends. "The duke? Me? Interested in the duke? I most certainly am not."

Jane pursed her lips as if she were about to whistle and took a small sip of tea. "Are you quite certain?"

Cass nodded. "I have to admit, I've had the same thought a time or two."

Garrett crossed his arms over his chest and sat back in his chair. A bark of laughter followed. "Lucy and the duke. Now, there's a thought. How do you like that, Your Grace?"

Lucy set her teacup down with a clatter. She didn't know what to do with her hands. She settled for folding them in her lap. "You are all being absolutely ridiculous. There is no one I admire less than the Duke of Claringdon."

"Oh, yes, he's only a handsome, wealthy, war-hero duke," Jane said, fluttering a hand in the air. "What's to admire?"

Lucy narrowed her eyes at her friend. "If he's so magnificent, why don't you pursue him?"

Jane laughed at that. "An overbearing controlling soldier? Not my sort. He is, however, *your* sort."

Lucy's mouth dropped open. "Preposterous. I don't have a sort."

"Don't you? He's just like you," Garrett chimed in.

Lucy made a mental note to kick her cousin the next time they were out of eyesight from her darling aunt. In the meantime, she counted ten and picked up her teacup again. She refused to allow her friends to bait her any longer. They were just teasing her, after all, and she'd got a bit too ruffled about it. But as she sipped her tea she couldn't help but think of what Jane had said. The duke was just like her, was he? Gulp.

## ❧ CHAPTER TWENTY-TWO ❧

The Upper Assembly Rooms took Lucy's breath away. They always had. Since the first time she'd seen the magnificent ballroom when she was eighteen. So formal and grand with sweeping high ceilings, frescoed walls, and sparkling chandeliers. Bath was a place for holidays, and while some found it too sleepy for any true amusement, Lucy had always loved the quiet intimacy of the town. She and Garrett had spent many happy days here. Lolling about on the grass in the Upper Crescent, taking tea at the Pump Room, exploring the Roman ruins, and riding through the hilly countryside. Bath was lovely. And a ball at the Assembly Rooms was always delightful. Except, that was, when the Duke of Claringdon appeared.

Cass had accompanied them. They'd managed to cajole and convince her. She wasn't in mourning, strictly speaking. Julian was not related to her. Not to mention the fact that the man had not yet died to her knowledge, but she was heartbroken nonetheless. It took more than a bit of convincing to get her to agree to come with them. She knew she had to put on a happy face for Society and pretend to enjoy herself, but she turned down every dance—and that included the one that the duke requested.

Lucy wore a pretty sapphire-colored gown and a strand of pearls, while Jane wore a light-blue high-waisted gown and a matching gold pendant. Cass looked radiant as ever in a lavender-colored gown with diamonds around her neck and entwined through her hair.

"He's here," Jane whispered once they'd made the rounds at the ball and had a chance to see who was in attendance. She motioned with her chin over to the opposite side of the room where the duke stood apparently holding court with his latest set of admirers in a new town.

"I honestly didn't believe he'd do it until I saw him here tonight." Lucy shook her head.

"He told you he intended to come, didn't he?" Jane replied.

"Yes, but—" Lucy bit the tip of her finger. "The nerve of that man. It shouldn't surprise me, but it does."

Garrett took a sip of the drink he held in his hand. "I, for one, applaud him."

Lucy glared at her cousin. "You cannot possibly mean that."

Garrett smiled. "On the contrary, I do. He knows what he wants and is intent upon winning it."

Jane rolled her eyes. "You're talking about our Cass, not some trophy."

Garrett took another sip. "I simply mean that his tenacity is to be commended."

"I think it's positively dreadful," Lucy said. "His following her here is the last thing Cass needs. Especially so soon after the news about Julian."

"He's coming over," Jane whispered.

Lucy sighed. "Of course he is."

"Miss Lowndes, now might be the perfect time to ask

you to dance with me," Garrett said, handing off his empty glass to a passing footman.

"Are you asking or telling me you should ask?" Jane replied sweetly.

"It depends," Garrett replied.

"Upon what?"

"Upon whether you will say yes."

Jane cocked her head to the side. "I will, but only because I don't want to be standing here in the middle of the crossfire when Lucy and the duke go at it. Which is sure to happen any moment now."

"You flatter me," Garrett said, sarcasm dripping from his voice.

"You should be flattered. Besides, it was better than Lucy's response to the duke's offer to dance," Jane replied with a snort.

Lucy wrinkled her nose at them. The pair took off to dance just as the duke strolled up. A brandy in one hand, his other shoved negligently in his pocket, he looked nothing if not the debonair nobleman out for a night's amusement.

He stopped in front of Lucy and Cass. Cass had just finished talking to Aunt Mary, who stood impatiently by their side, clearly waiting for an introduction to the celebrated nobleman. He bowed gallantly to all three of them.

"Lady Cassandra. Lady Lucy." He straightened to his full height and took another sip. "And this must be your . . . sister?" He nodded toward Aunt Mary.

Lucy arched a brow in his direction. "This is my aunt, Mrs. Upton. Aunt Mary, the Duke of Claringdon."

"A pleasure, madam." The duke bowed over Aunt Mary's hand while she blushed a bright shade of pink.

"It's so lovely to meet you, Your Grace," Aunt Mary twittered.

Cass executed a perfect curtsy of her own but Lucy just glared at him. "Your Grace. I see you made it to Bath safely," she managed to choke out. And that only because she'd promised Cass she'd attempt to be civil.

"No doubt to your chagrin, Miss Upton," the duke replied in his usual haughty tone.

Lucy opened her mouth to issue a scathing retort but Cass elbowed her, so she managed to utter something useless and untrue about it being nice to see him.

"Lady Cassandra, would you do me the honor?" the duke asked, gesturing toward the dancing.

Cass shook her head. "I'm ever so sorry, but I find that I'm not quite up for dancing this evening, Your Grace."

"A pity." He inclined his head in acknowledgment and took another sip of brandy. "Are you certain you won't reconsider?"

Cass nodded this time. "I'm quite certain."

"If you change your mind—"

That was it. Lucy snapped. "She said she was not interested." Lucy was already incensed by the fact that the man had followed them to Bath; now he was here badgering Cass when she clearly didn't care to dance.

"Lucy!" Aunt Mary's tone was admonishing but Lucy couldn't help herself, not even for her beloved aunt.

The duke's mouth quirked up. "I don't suppose I could interest *you* in a dance, could I, Lady Lucy?"

He was taunting her. She could see it in the flash of his green eyes. But she would not allow him to rile her. She was just about to open her mouth to tell him no in the most inventive way she could possibly muster when the thought occurred to her that she did, indeed, have something to say to him and perhaps a dance would be the most opportune time to do so.

"I should be flattered," she said, in a tone that sounded

anything but. "I've washed my wig, and Jane's already claimed the title of Queen of the Wallflowers here tonight."

The duke didn't miss a beat. He bowed to Cass and Aunt Mary to excuse himself, discarded his brandy glass on a nearby table, and pulled Lucy onto the dance floor. The two ladies watched them go.

They had barely gone one turn when Lucy said, "How are you enjoying Bath, Your Grace? Decided upon buying property yet?"

"As a matter of fact, I have. I've found I'm quite taken with the town."

"Oh, wonderful, perhaps we can all have group holidays here in the future. That would be delightful, would it not? Given our history?" She innocently batted her eyelashes at him.

The duke stared Lucy straight in the eye. "Oh, no you don't. Look. I know you don't like me being here one bit, but what happened between us was a mistake and is in the past and we cannot change it. I—"

Lucy nearly tripped. Her jaw dropped open. "You honestly think I don't like you being here because of that kiss?" She lowered her voice so others wouldn't hear and glanced about. It appeared to be safe.

He arched a brow. "That's not why?"

"No, actually. It has nothing to do with it. I'd quite forgotten about that kiss." No she hadn't, but no sense feeding his arrogance with the fact that she couldn't seem to *stop* thinking about it.

"Then am I to assume your objection to me remains whatever your original objection was? Not that I ever knew *that* reasoning."

Lucy set her jaw. "Don't you see that Cass is upset?"

He looked at a loss for words. "Upset?"

"Yes. She's just received some very bad news. Her dear friend. A man. A soldier. A captain. He was injured in battle and has yet to return. She received word this week that he won't be coming back. He is the man she loves."

"He died?" The duke's voice was soft, respectful.

Lucy nodded, once. "He's dying. She expects to receive word any day now."

The duke's face was grim. "I know what it's like to lose men, good friends in battle. My own closest friend was gravely wounded over there. I'm sorry for her loss."

"Then you might consider being considerate of her feelings and leaving her alone."

"Regardless of what you may think of me, my lady, I don't particularly relish chasing about a woman who doesn't seem particularly interested in me."

Lucy didn't meet his eyes. "You might have fooled me."

"It's true," he ground out.

"Does that mean you intend to stop pursuing Cass then?"

"I certainly will if she wishes me to."

"Of course she wishes you to. She's madly in love with Julian and he's about to die. How can you possibly imagine that she wants to be courted by another man at the moment?"

The duke's brow drew up into an alarming frown. "Wait a minute. *Julian?* I thought Julian was engaged to her cousin."

# ❧ CHAPTER TWENTY-THREE ❧

Lucy's mouth fell straight open. She stared at the duke aghast. They stopped dancing and he quickly maneuvered them both to the sidelines of the room, his hand on Lucy's back.

"How do *you* know about Julian?" Lucy asked as soon as they were standing near the wall.

The duke glanced around the ballroom. "I believe this conversation is best had in private."

Woodenly, Lucy allowed him to escort her from the ballroom, through the long corridor, and out onto the stone-paved street. A few attendees were coming and going, but for the most part they were alone in the moonlight.

As soon as they reached a private spot, Lucy tugged her arm from his grasp and turned to face him. "I'll repeat my question, how do you know about Julian?"

The duke paced away. "Captain Julian Swift is my closest friend."

Lucy stood entirely still. She was frozen, couldn't believe it. She supposed it stood to reason that Julian and the duke could know each other. They'd both been in the army and were in Brussels, but closest friends? Truly? And if that was the case, then . . .

"Did Julian tell you about . . . ?" Oh, now all the pieces were falling into place. "You said Cass had been recommended to you as a potential wife. Julian recommended her?"

"The very same. And it's a bit more complicated than that. I promised Julian I'd marry her. When he was dying."

Lucy pressed both hands to her cheeks. "I don't know what to say." But she understood now. She finally understood. The duke had been chasing Cass around for days, unsuccessfully trying to court her, refusing to take no for an answer, putting up with all of Lucy's ill-tempered attempts to dissuade him—and he'd done it all for his friend, Julian. Julian who was dying. Julian who'd recommended Cass to him. No, made him *promise* to marry her. Made him promise a dead man he would marry her. Lucy shook her head. She wrapped her hands around her middle and paced back and forth, too.

"I had no idea she's in love with him," the duke continued. "From what he told me, he was all but engaged to her cousin, Penelope something."

Lucy paced away, feeling vaguely nauseated. "He is," she whispered. "They've had an understanding since they were quite young."

The duke braced a hand against the side of the building. "But you're telling me that Lady Cassandra loves Julian?"

"Yes. She's loved him since she was a girl."

"Does Julian know?"

"He might by now. She wrote to him as soon as she learned he was dying. But no, before that she never told him. What was the point?"

The duke snatched his palm away from the wall and ran his fingers through his hair while his other hand rested on his hip. "Blast it. I had no idea she was in love with him. Though I must say it explains quite a lot."

Lucy couldn't help her snort. "What? You cannot imagine a lady not being interested in you unless her heart is already taken?"

His shrug gave her his answer.

"You are unbelievably arrogant," she said. But for some reason she couldn't help her smile. It was all just too much. Here she'd been trying to chase him away like an angry bird protecting her chick and he'd sworn an oath to a dying man to succeed in his courtship. The same courtship she'd been desperately trying to thwart. If it wasn't all so sad, she would laugh.

When he spoke, his voice was soft. "Truly, Lucy, I didn't know she was in love with Julian."

He'd called her Lucy. It made her catch her breath a little. Oh, she *could* insist he not be so forward with her but at the moment she didn't want to argue any longer. They'd just had a breakthrough, the two of them. He finally understood that Cass loved another man. Not just any man, *Julian*. And she finally understood why he hadn't given up. Besides, he'd given her a kiss to nearly singe off her eyelashes the other night; allowing him to call her by her Christian name didn't seem half so scandalous. She might as well begin calling him Derek, too.

When he smiled at her, her heart forgot a beat.

"So you can understand now why you should leave Cass alone?" she said softly, but the words made her inexplicably sad. If he did go away and leave Cass alone, Lucy would never see him again, either. It's what she'd been telling herself she wanted. But did she?

"I can't do that," he said.

Lucy's head snapped up. "What do you mean? Why not?"

He turned to her and looked her in the eye. "I made a promise to my friend."

"But Cass doesn't love you."

He groaned. "Believe me, I understand. It's been no great fun chasing her around. But it sounds as if Cassandra won't love anyone but Julian. He holds her in the highest regard, I can tell you that. But even if Julian were to live, he'd come back here and marry her cousin. He planned to do that. I know he did. He told me as much. I promised Swift I'd marry Lady Cassandra and I intend to keep that promise. I'll be a good husband. She'll receive a generous allowance after she provides me with an heir, she can go anywhere, do anything. I won't stand in her way."

Lucy clenched her fist. She couldn't believe it. Even after what they'd just discussed, he didn't intend to stop his pursuit of Cass. This man was refusing to listen to reason. And he was being so cold . . . so calculating about the prospect of marriage. It shouldn't surprise her. Many *ton* marriages were based on much less but for some reason, coming from him, it made her angry. He wasn't from the *ton*, damn it. It wasn't his world. Or hadn't been, at least. Why did he have to be so matter-of-fact about a proposal?

Lucy nearly scratched her nails down her arms in frustration. "Why do you want a woman who doesn't want you?"

"You're wrong. I want to marry a woman who doesn't *love* me. That's quite different than whether she'll accept me. Don't confuse marriage with love."

Lucy's head rang as if she'd been slapped. *Don't con-*

*fuse marriage with love.* What a mad, mad thing to say. But wasn't it what she expected from her own marriage? If so, why was it making her so angry right now? It made no sense. She opened her mouth to speak but no words came out. *Me? Speechless? There's a first time for everything indeed.*

The duke nodded solemnly. "I plan to give Cassandra time to come to terms with all of this. But I will marry her."

### ❧ CHAPTER TWENTY-FOUR ❧

"My dear cousin, I have some good news for you," Garrett announced to Lucy two nights later, just as they were preparing to leave for yet another ball at the Assembly Rooms. They were walking down the stairway together.

Lucy eyed him askance. "Good news? Whatever do you mean?" She had spent the last two days, vowing, *vowing*, to keep her nose out of the affairs of her friends. Well, Cass's at least. After her last frustrating and disappointing interaction with the maddening Duke of Claringdon, she decided to remove herself from the entire situation. She'd done what she could. If Cass wanted him to stop, it was up to her now to say so. He wasn't listening to Lucy. He was on a blasted mission to honor a dying friend. No, the Duke of Claringdon had no intention of heeding Lucy's pleas. Never had and never would. She hated to admit defeat but it was time. Only a fool didn't know when to quit.

Garrett looked dashing in his black formal evening attire and snowy white cravat. "I just learned my friend

Berkeley is in town. He'll be at the ball tonight. He told me he's very much looking forward to meeting you."

Lucy wrinkled her brow, trying to remember her cousin's friend. "Berkeley? Berkeley? The name sounds familiar."

"We went up to Eton together. Capital fellow. A viscount, don't you know?" Garrett said. He handed Lucy down onto the landing and followed her off the steps.

Lucy cocked her head to the side. "Why have I never met him?"

"What she means to ask is, *Is he handsome?*" Jane added from the foyer where she was busily pulling on her pelisse.

"That is not what I meant," Lucy said, marching into the foyer to retrieve her own pelisse.

"If Lucy doesn't want to know, I do." Cass came quietly plodding down the stairs in a pretty green dress. She'd been doing her best the last two days to stop crying and remain brave in the face of the news about Julian. If the idea of a new gentleman's interest in Lucy kept her preoccupied from her grief, Lucy was more than happy to oblige.

Jane, her pretty silvery pelisse smartly fastened, turned to face them all. "I do, too."

Garrett arched his brow at all three of them. "Don't tell me you're all interested. He's only one man."

Jane rolled her eyes. "I'm not interested in *that* way. I simply want to know for Lucy's sake."

"Me too," Cass agreed.

Lucy pulled her cloak over her shoulders. "I find it quite suspect. In all these years, Garret, you've never introduced me to any of your friends. Trying to get rid of me finally?"

"I have a strict rule. I don't try to matchmake with my friends. I suspect it's one reason my friends are still my friends. I am making an exception in this case because Berkeley specifically mentioned to me that he wanted to meet you. I am now asking you if you're interested in meeting him. That is the extent of my involvement in this little affair."

Lucy snorted. "You never answered my question. Why have I never met him before?"

Garrett shrugged. "Because he lives in the North and rarely comes to town."

Lucy nodded sagely. "Ah, he must not have heard the rumors about me."

"He must have heard rumors that you are beautiful," Jane said. "That's why he wants to meet you, Lucy."

"Oh, how sweet of you, Janie. And here all this time, all I've needed to do was to wait for gentlemen who'd never come to London," Lucy replied. "It's been so simple, really."

"Or those back from the war," Jane said. Lucy and Jane exchanged a glance.

"He doesn't have a goiter on his neck or a clubfoot or anything, does he, Garret?" Jane asked.

Garrett pulled on his leather gloves. "No, why do you ask?"

"We merely want to ensure that Lucy may actually want to meet him," Jane pointed out.

Lucy sniffed. "I can't be such a chooser. A goiter and a clubfoot may end up being my fate what with my prospects. Neither sounds particularly bad at present."

"He has neither," Garrett replied, shaking his head. "Honestly, the way you ladies talk, I swear it's a wonder any matches are made in this country at all."

"You'll notice that no matches have been made for the three of us," Jane added with a laugh.

"Coincidence?" Garrett shot back.

Cass finished with her own pelisse. "No goiter and no clubfoot. Sounds entirely promising, Lucy."

"But how do we know our friend Lucy here won't chase the poor man off, as usual?" Jane said with a laugh.

"Because her cousin has recommended him. He cannot be objectionable, given that," Cass replied with a nod.

Lucy laughed. "I've no objection to meeting him, but let's not plan my wedding quite yet. And if I'm to curb my tongue, you must help me, Cass."

"My pleasure," Cass replied with a curtsy.

Lucy smiled at her cousin. "Come now, Garrett, there must be something wrong with your Lord Berkeley. What is it?"

"There is nothing wrong with him," Garrett insisted. "He's handsome, or so the ladies always say, he's dashing, fashionable, wealthy, well educated. He may be a bit . . . Oh, you'll see for yourself."

"A bit what?" Jane asked. "Gouty? Old? Smelly?"

Garrett rolled his eyes again. "None of those things. And I'm finished talking about this. I already wish I'd never brought it up."

"Who is gouty, old, and smelly?" Aunt Mary came hurrying out of her rooms to join them.

"No one, Mother," Garrett said, giving the other three a warning glare.

The three ladies exchanged laughing looks as the butler held open the door for them and they all trotted down the steps and climbed into Garrett's coach.

Once they arrived at the Assembly Rooms their little group seemed to scatter to the four winds. The Duke of

Claringdon was there, Lucy noted with some ire, but she refused, *refused*, to acknowledge him or to go anywhere near him—or Cass for that matter, if he was speaking to Cass. It was the first opportunity to test her self-imposed abstinence from the matter of Cass and the duke, and she meant to stand by her resolve.

Lucy was tapping her slipper in time to the music, drinking a glass of punch, and having a lovely conversation with Mrs. Periwinkle about the flowers in the gardens along the Upper Crescent when Garrett tapped her on the shoulder.

"Lucy."

She stopped tapping and turned at the sound of her cousin's voice. "Yes?"

Standing beside Garrett was a gentle man who could be described as nothing other than gorgeous. He had golden hair, crystal blue eyes, and a physique any man would admire. Tall and muscled with a bit of a cleft in his chin, when he smiled at her, his perfectly aligned white teeth twinkled in the firelight. Ooh, in addition to having neither a goiter nor a clubfoot, it seemed Lord Berkeley was, in fact, amazingly good looking. Lucy felt a bit light-headed.

"Lucy, may I introduce you to my friend, Christian, Lord Berkeley?" To Lord Berkeley he said, "Christian, this is my cousin, Lady Lucy Upton."

Lucy curtsied. A promising beginning, to be sure. Oh, she mustn't make a mess of this and say anything outlandish or rude. "A pleasure to meet you, my lord," she managed. That was well done, wasn't it? Neither outlandish nor rude. A good start, actually.

Lord Berkeley gallantly bowed over her hand. "My lady, the pleasure is entirely mine."

From across the room, she saw Cass and Jane avidly watching. When her eyes met theirs they fanned themselves rapidly to indicate that they approved wholeheartedly of the dashing Lord Berkeley. Lord Berkeley's gaze soon followed Lucy's. When he glanced toward her friends, Cass and Jane immediately looked up at the ceiling and around at the backs of their dresses, feigning interest in anything to keep from being caught staring.

Lord Berkeley returned his gaze to Lucy, who was trying her best to keep from laughing. A smile hovered on the viscount's face. "Friends of yours?"

"Yes," Lucy replied. "Though I'm a bit hesitant to claim them at the moment."

Lord Berkeley smiled at that. "W . . . Would you care to dance, Lady Lucy?"

Ah, a man who knew to call her Lady Lucy instead of Miss Upton, *what* a pleasant change of pace. But had that been a bit of hesitation in his voice? Was she not what he had expected after all? Surely someone as good looking and dashing as Lord Berkeley would be more interested in someone more like . . . Cass. Oh, she mustn't think such unhelpful thoughts. Instead she gave him a bright smile. "Why, yes, my lord, I would. Very much."

Lord Berkeley, she soon discovered, was a lovely dancer. Not much of a conversationalist, however, at least not during their dance. Perhaps he preferred to concentrate on the steps. And he was doing a marvelous job. The man swept her around the floor with an ease and grace that surprised her in someone so tall. Yes, the duke was tall and he was a lovely dancer, too, but— No. She *refused* to think about the duke. Not tonight. She firmly pushed him from her mind.

After their dance Lord Berkeley led her back toward

the refreshment table. "Tell me, Lady Lucy, how is it that we have not met before? I find it such a pity."

Ooh, perhaps this was when she would discover what Garrett had meant when he had said Lord Berkeley was a bit . . . She'd been studying the man throughout their dance and had found absolutely nothing lacking about him. She gave him a wide smile. "I was just asking Garrett that same thing earlier, my lord. He mentioned that you rarely come to town."

"It's true. I've been to a few functions here and there over the years but I much prefer the country. Don't you?"

Lucy thought about the question for a moment. The country meant her parents. No, she was not a devotee of the country. "I wouldn't say that I prefer it, my lord. I certainly do like holiday towns like Bath. Tell me, what brought you here?"

"My own cousin is getting married here this week," he said.

Married. The word caused Lucy to remember how she'd told her own friends not to begin planning her wedding quite yet, but she couldn't help but think what sort of a life she would lead were she and Lord Berkeley to be a match.

"Ah, best wishes to your cousin, then. Are you enjoying Bath?"

"Yes. Quite," he replied, giving her a dazzling smile.

Lucy smiled back. The viscount was tall and handsome and quite a good dancer. But she mustn't seem too eager. Besides, the more time she spent in his company, the greater chance she might say something outlandishly rude. She *must* watch her tongue. "Thank you for a lovely dance, Lord Berkeley."

"You're quite welcome, my lady."

Lucy opened her mouth to continue their conversation,

but another guest came up to pay his respects to Lord Berkeley. The viscount was forced to excuse himself. Lucy sighed and said good night.

Twenty minutes later, she and her friends were sitting in a small cluster of chairs along the sidelines of the dancing drinking ratafia and laughing. "I swear I don't know how in the world I've gone this long without Garrett introducing me to some of his handsome, dashing friends," Lucy said.

"Or more specifically Lord Berkeley," Jane added. "The man seems perfect to me."

"Why, if Lord Berkeley had been around the year of your come-out things might have been quite different for you, Lucy," Cass added.

Lucy had to smile at that. "You mean I might not be an on-the-shelf rapidly devolving into a spinster?" But even as she had the thought she wondered if it was really true. Would she have appreciated Lord Berkeley's good looks and good manners five years ago? She couldn't be certain. But tonight. Tonight she'd enjoyed them indeed. Lord Berkeley was exactly the sort of man she should be interested in. Impeccable manners and impeccable breeding. Quite different from a certain someone who knew little about the ways of the *ton* and Society even if he did happen to be a duke. Yes. Lord Berkeley was a perfect match. Though she couldn't help but glance over at Derek from time to time to see if he'd noticed her new companion.

Blast it. Why did she even care? Interestingly enough, Derek had kept his distance from Cass tonight. Was it because of the Julian connection? Had that caused him to rethink his pursuit despite his comments to the contrary the other night? Or was it because Lucy was otherwise occupied and not paying a whit of attention to Cass and him this evening? Now, *that* was an interesting question.

Was the duke only interested in Cass when Lucy was hovering around like a mama hen ready to pounce and peck him the first chance she got?

No. No. No. It didn't matter. The duke was not who she should be thinking about. Lord Berkeley was. She refused to look back in Derek's direction.

# ❧ CHAPTER TWENTY-FIVE ❧

"Dance with me?" The request sent a hot wave down Lucy's spine. The warm breath of the requestor made gooseflesh rise on her neck.

She turned her head but she already knew who it was. Derek. He was standing there in his black formal evening attire, one hand in his pocket, his other stretched in offer to her. And blast it all, he looked positively smashing.

Lucy wanted to say no. She wanted to refuse him. She glanced about. Lord Berkeley had gone off in search of more refreshments, and Derek had obviously used this opportunity to come looking for her.

She opened her mouth to deny him, but somehow the words wouldn't come out. And of course "No, thank you" was out of the question.

She turned to face him, arched a brow, and without saying a word, laid her hand on his outstretched one.

He led her to the dance floor, took her in his arms, and spun her around. "Berkeley, eh?"

She concentrated on keeping her face completely blank. "What do you mean by that?"

His face remained blank, too. She couldn't read a single thought. "Nothing."

"Then why did you ask?" she countered.

Derek spun her again. "I merely hadn't noticed you paying so much attention to him before tonight."

She inclined her head a bit. "That's because I just met him tonight."

"I see."

"And what about you? I've never seen you pay so little attention to Cass," Lucy countered.

"Been watching me, have you?"

Lucy gave him a narrow-eyed glare.

"I could say the same about you," he continued. "You haven't been paying much attention to Lady Cassandra, either."

"I've decided that you and Cass—" She cleared her throat. "That's not my battle to fight any longer. It never was actually." Was that a look of disappointment that crossed his face?

"I see. Giving up so easily?"

He was outrageously trying to bait her. She would not rise to it. "There's nothing to give up. Cass asked me to help her be blunt with you. I was. You refused to listen. That's all there is. Cass won't marry you. I know she won't. But I intend to leave it to her to handle from now on."

Derek didn't say a word. He merely watched her. Lord Berkeley had returned to where Lucy had been sitting and he stood, holding two glasses of champagne. He watched Lucy and Derek dance, an inscrutable expression on his face.

Derek nodded toward him. "Berkeley looks none too pleased that you're out here with me."

Lucy glanced over. "He asked if he might fetch me a refreshment. I should get back."

Derek arched a brow. "He has the monopoly on your time tonight, does he?"

"Not at all," she shot back. "I simply enjoy his company."

"Unlike mine?" His voice was a husky whisper that did something funny to her insides.

"I didn't say that, you did." Why was he making her flustered all of a sudden?

Derek narrowed his darkened eyes on her. "I don't understand you."

She nearly laughed out loud at that. "That makes two of us, Your Grace. I've never understood you. Though I suppose now that I know you and Julian are such close friends, everything you've done makes better sense to me."

"But you still don't believe Cassandra and I should marry?"

Lucy shook her head. She wanted to pull herself out of his arms and run far, far away. She didn't know why. "I don't know what I believe anymore."

Derek glanced back in Lord Berkeley's direction. "I'd better get you back. I'd hate to be called out by the likes of the viscount."

He was mocking the man. Given Derek's talent on the battlefield, he would make short work of a duel with Lord Berkeley. The viscount was obviously more of an intellectual type.

She felt the sudden need to defend the viscount. "You might take a lesson from Lord Berkeley in manners and comportment," she replied, hoping her barb struck home.

If it did, Derek didn't give her the satisfaction of knowing it. Instead, he led her back over to where Lord

Berkeley stood and handed her off. "Good evening, my lady," he said, kissing the back of her hand. Lucy's skin burned where his lips touched her.

Lord Berkeley acknowledged Derek and handed Lucy her champagne flute. She thanked him prettily. Derek drifted off in the crowd and Lucy couldn't help but watch him leave.

"A friend of yours?" Lord Berkeley asked.

"I wouldn't call him a friend," Lucy replied, taking a sip of her champagne. "More like someone I trade barbs with."

"I heard that you and he had a word challenge at a ball in London."

Lucy nearly choked on her drink. She wanted the floor to open up and swallow her. "Um, yes. He . . . fancies himself a wit."

"And you, my lady, you're quite adept with words as well, are you not?"

Lucy took another sip for good measure. She smiled at him. "I do my best, my lord."

Thankfully she was spared from more questions about Derek when Lord Berkeley asked her to dance again. Another trip around the floor with little conversation, but he was a lovely dancer just the same. And it was nice to have a break from having to spar with someone. For a bit.

❧

Derek knocked back his third brandy of the evening. He clunked the snifter down on the tray of a passing footman and resisted the urge to wipe the back of his hand across his mouth. He'd done that during his army days often enough, but in the ballrooms of Bath, that was not quite the social standard.

He eyed Lucy Upton across the floor. She was dancing with Berkeley, smiling, and seemingly having a wonderful time. What was it about her interaction with the viscount that was driving Derek mad? Normally at these things, he made an attempt to court Cassandra, Lucy came and fought with him about it, and all was right with the world. He nearly groaned. How wrong was that? Tonight, Lucy seemed as if she didn't have a care and Lady Cassandra was unoccupied most of the evening, yet Derek could not seem to bring himself to go to her and ask her to dance. Not tonight. Why? Was it because he'd learned that Cassandra was in love with Julian?

Derek wanted to believe that was the case, but he knew it wasn't true. He hadn't cared in the least the last two nights when he considered Cassandra's feelings for Julian. He didn't love Cassandra himself, so he didn't begrudge her her feelings for Swift. Damn it. Why couldn't he put one foot in front of the next and go ask Cassandra to dance? That was the next step in this courtship. To get her alone with him, away from the prying eyes and Lady Lucy's sharp tongue. And tonight was the perfect opportunity for that. Lucy was—he glanced over to see her dancing with Berkeley still—completely preoccupied. Why did that thought make his chest burn? Make him want to connect his fist to Berkeley's fine, aristocratic face?

Damn it. Berkeley was the sort of man whom Lady Lucy and Lady Cassandra belonged with. He came from an impeccable family with an impeccable name and a long lineage of service to the Crown. He knew all about proper titles, and proper manners, and proper everything. He was just the sort of man Derek would never, could never, be. But those men were everywhere he looked. They always would be. Why did he care so much that Berkeley in particular was spending time with Lucy?

Derek growled under his breath and called to a footman to bring him another brandy.

# ❦ CHAPTER TWENTY-SIX ❦

Lucy awoke to the startling sound of something hitting her window. A clatter, then silence, followed by another clatter.

"What in the world?" She rubbed the sleep from her eyes, tossed back the covers, and pulled on her robe just as another clatter hit the glass. She hurried over to the wall, pushed up the window, and leaned out.

Derek stood in the backyard holding a candle. She could barely make out his face in the soft glow. "What are you doing?" she called in a half shout, half whisper.

He staggered a bit. "Throwing pebbles at your window, what do you think?" he called out jovially, perhaps a bit too loudly.

She eyed him warily. "Well, for one thing, you've got the wrong window. Cass's chamber is in the front of the house."

"I know."

"Shh." Lucy waved her hand at him. "Do you want to wake the entire house?"

"No. No. No," he sort of sang back.

Lucy leaned farther out of the window so he might better hear her. "I won't even ask how you know where my window is, let alone Cass's. I don't want to know."

"I am extremely crafty, my lady," he announced, taking off an imaginary hat—just where was his hat?—and bowing once more.

Had he stumbled again?

Lucy narrowed her eyes on him. "Good heavens, you are foxed!"

"No!" he called back with a look she could only call disgruntled on his face.

"Yes, you are." She couldn't help the little smile that popped to her lips. "You are. You're drunk as a wheelbarrow."

He put his hands on his hips. "Come down here."

She laughed at that. "I don't think so. I'm wearing my night rail and a robe and it's the middle of the night. It's entirely indecent. What do you think you're doing here at this hour?"

"Come down here," he called again. "I want to see you in your night rail. Indecency doesn't bother me."

Had he just waggled his eyebrows at her? Oh, heavens, he really was drunk as a wheelbarrow. It was a sight, to be sure, an unexpected sight, to see the Duke of Claringdon foxed, slurring his words, and good Lord was he pulling off his cravat? She leaned against the window frame and watched him. It was a bit fascinating. He was quite a pleasant drunk, she thought with some irony. Why had she assumed he'd be cross? Not that she'd ever pictured him drunk. He burst into song just then, confirming her suspicions that he was quite jovial while in his cups indeed.

"Shh," she called down. "You'll wake Garrett and he'll probably call the night watch."

"No, he won't. He's a good chap, Upton. Knew him in Spain. Good chap. Good chap."

Lucy hid her smile behind her fingertips. "What are you doing out there? Why did you come here tonight?"

"Why? Do you wish I was Berkeley?"

Lucy sucked in her breath. It wasn't possible, was it, that Derek was jealous? Oh, my, this made things even more interesting. More interesting, indeed.

"For some reason I highly doubt Lord Berkeley would do such a thing," she offered.

"You're right, because he's dull," Derek said. "And he wouldn't want to muss his perfect proper hair." Derek had finally tugged his cravat from his neck and was busily wrapping it around his hand.

"What precisely is proper hair?" She squinted. "What are you doing with your cravat?"

"I'm using it as a tourniquet," he announced, "as I am in need of one."

Lucy gasped and leaned farther out the window in order to get a better look. "Are you hurt?"

He held the hand he'd been wrapping aloft. "My fist is bleeding."

"Why?"

"Punched a tree."

She furrowed her brow. "What? Why?"

He leered at her. "Come down here and I'll tell you."

She smothered another smile. He must not be hurt too badly if he continued to be so contrary. "Not possible."

"I'm coming up then!" He set something in the grass. Was it another drink?

Lucy stepped away from the window. "No!"

But he wasn't listening. He'd already begun scaling the tree in front of her window. He grabbed a low-hanging branch, levering himself up. His shirttails came out of his waistband, affording Lucy a dark but tempting view of his midsection. Six muscles stood out in sharp relief against his taut skin. She pressed her lips together. "Oh, I wish I hadn't seen that. I'm not going to be able to forget that," she whispered, shaking herself.

"You'll kill yourself," she called to him.

He'd already made it up to the second set of branches. "No, I won't. Believe me. If I didn't kill myself in the wars, I'm not about to let a blasted tree end my life."

She had to smile at that, too. And she had to admit, he did seem rather adept at climbing given the fact that he was drunk and injured.

He made it to the third set of branches and swung himself out to the farthest limb, the one closest to her window.

Lucy gasped. "Be careful!"

He grabbed the branch and swung himself into the opening, legs first. Lucy stepped back to allow him room and then lurched forward to grab him around the waist. She held tight, pulling him with all her force so he wouldn't be tugged back out by the momentum of his swing. Once he realized she had him, he let go of the branch and worked his way entirely through the window with Lucy's help.

As soon as Lucy ensured he was safe, she let go and stumbled back. She put her fingers to her lips and watched him sitting on her sill. He had a roguish grin on his face and looked like the cat who'd swallowed the canary.

"*That* was dangerous and stupid," she said. But she couldn't help but glance at the deep V of skin exposed from where his cravat had been. She swallowed. Hard.

"Nah, it was fun," he declared, still grinning. "If not *proper*." He slurred the last word and said it as if he hated it. What was his preoccupation with the word *proper* to-night?

"You could have died. You still might. Come away from that window," Lucy said.

He stood up and lurched toward her. "Your hair is down," he whispered in an awed voice.

Lucy self-consciously pushed a hand into her curls. Oh, this was inappropriate for about two dozen reasons.

"It's beautiful," he whispered next. Her stomach flipped. *Beautiful*? He lifted his fingers to touch her hair and Lucy's eyes riveted to the bright red on his hand, bleeding through the makeshift tourniquet. "Your hand. Let me see."

He turned away from her and took two steps toward the chair near her writing desk before he crumpled. She rushed forward and wrapped her arm around his waist. He leaned heavily against her and slipped his arm around her shoulder. He smelled like brandy and fresh grass and something else that made her want to bury her nose in his half-open shirt. Trying to rid her head of that unhelpful thought, she helped him over to the chair, where he nearly collapsed.

Lucy knelt on the floor in front of him and quickly unwrapped the cravat from his injured hand.

"Ouch." He winced. "That hurts."

"Come now, you big baby. How did you survive the war?" Lucy gasped when she pulled the bloodied cravat away and saw the extent of his injuries. "Oh, my! Your knuckles are scraped clean of skin and they are full of dirt."

"It's nothing. Just a flesh wound." He grinned at her.

"A flesh wound that may well become infected. Stay here. Don't move. And for heaven's sake, keep quiet."

She left him sitting haphazardly in the chair while

she rushed from the room, through the corridor, down two sets of stairs, and around to the kitchen pantry. She quickly gathered some clean bits of linen, a bowl that she filled with fresh water, and some spices and supplies to make a poultice. She hurried back up to her bedchamber.

When she entered the room, she let out her pent-up breath. Thankfully, Derek was asleep. He was slumped over in the chair. Snoring. Loudly.

At least it was better than him wandering around the upstairs of the household singing or telling bawdy jokes or something.

She hurried to his side and unwrapped his hand again. Apparently, he'd managed to wrap it back up while she'd been gone. The moment she immersed his fingers in the water bowl, he woke up and nearly howled. She clapped her palm over his mouth. The feel of his hot breath against her skin made her belly jerk. When she realized he remembered where he was and nodded, she removed her hand.

"I'm cleaning this out and making a poultice," she announced, already busily setting to work.

He raised his brows. "Didn't know a lady like you knew how to make a poultice."

"I know how to do a great many things," she responded. "I had several animals when I was a child. I took excellent care of them. I learned how to make this particular poultice for my horse."

"You're putting a horse poultice on me?" he nearly shouted.

She clamped her hand back over his mouth again. "Shh. And yes. It works for humans, too. I made it for Garrett once when he and the neighbor boy got into a fight."

Derek smiled against her palm and her belly fluttered again. She jerked her hand away. "Who won?" he asked.

"Who won?" She shook her head at him. "What does that matter? It was probably ten years ago."

"I bet Upton remembers who won."

She smiled at that. "You're *such* a male. Very well. I remember. Garrett won. But his hand was a mess for days. This poultice helped."

"Whatever you say, my lady." He leered at her.

Lucy made quick work of the poultice. She mixed the ingredients she'd brought with the remaining water in the bowl and stirred and packed it together until it made a fine paste. Then she grabbed Derek's wrist.

"This may hurt," she announced.

"I've been shot, I doubt—Owww!"

She pressed her lips together to keep from laughing. She'd always given her animals a bit of a relaxing balm before applying this poultice, but Derek deserved a bit of a sting for coming here tonight and making a scene, the drunken lout. Not to mention he'd scared her half to death by climbing that tree and swinging into her window. How would she have ever explained a duke's dead body in the backyard?

He clenched his teeth. "This had better work."

"Don't be so childish." She pressed the poultice against his hand a bit too firmly. "Now, do you care to tell me why you got into a fight with an inanimate object?"

Derek sucked in his breath through clenched teeth and winced. "I didn't *intend* to get into a fight with a tree."

She pressed her lips together. "Oh, of course. I'm certain no one does. Jumped out at you, did it? Frightened you?"

He gave her a long-suffering look. "No, actually. I thought it was a man."

"A man? What man?"

"Berkeley."

Lucy let his hand drop and put both of her fists on her hips. "What the devil are you talking about?"

"It's quite simple, really. On my way home, I was thinking about Berkeley, got angry, and punched a tree."

She sighed. "So you didn't actually believe the tree was Lord Berkeley?"

"No, but I wish it had been," he grumbled. "Would have punched him in his proper mouth."

She rolled her eyes. "I'll wager your fist would look a lot better if you had. Why did you want to punch Lord Berkeley?" She picked up Derek's hand again and pressed the poultice.

He looked away out the dark window. "Wouldn't you like to know?"

She wrinkled her nose and pressed tighter. He winced and she smiled. "Fine, don't tell me."

He rested his other elbow on his knee. "How long have you known Berkeley? I've never seen you with him before."

"I told you earlier, I met him tonight. Garrett introduced us. He seems quite enjoyable."

Derek made a harrumphing noise. "You looked as if you were enjoying him." He grumbled again. "I'll wager he's never done an honest day's work in his entire proper life. Couldn't shoot an elephant at ten paces. Couldn't—"

She squeezed the poultice again. "Are you quite through?"

He gave her a half-leering drunken grin. "Yes."

She arched a brow at him. "Why did you come to my window and not Cass's?"

"Because I wanted to see *you*." He tapped her on the nose with the tip of his finger to punctuate the last word.

Lucy tried to ignore the little thrill that shot through her at his words. "Why?"

"I don't know." He wrapped his hand around her neck and pulled her mouth to within an inch of his. "Perhaps I wanted to kiss you again. What would you say to that?"

Lucy's heart was beating so hard she was certain he could hear it, too. The warmth and pressure of his hand against the exposed skin on the back of her neck was making her feel a little drunk herself. All she could do was stare at his lips. Was he truly going to kiss her again?

Oh wait. He'd asked her.

She slowly traced her tongue over her own dry lips. "What would you say to that?" he'd asked. For the second time in her life, with the same man, Lucy found herself speechless.

*Be bold!* The words streaked through her brain. Derek was entirely foxed. It was more than probable that he wouldn't remember a thing that happened here between them tonight. Isn't that what Garrett had told her about his infrequent bouts of drunkenness? Be bold, indeed.

"I would say, kiss me," she breathed.

Derek obviously required no other inducement. His other hand came up to her shoulder and he pulled her against him as his mouth captured hers. The kiss was long and hot and wonderful. Lucy couldn't breathe. She couldn't think. She didn't want to.

His fingers filtered through her hair and then moved down her neck, past her shoulders, and to her hips. He grabbed her and pulled her onto his lap. He'd lifted her as if she weighed no more than a doll. He was so big. So big and yet so tender. His mouth moved over hers with an urgency and finesse that belied how inebriated he seemed to be. This was no sloppy kiss from a man too deep in his cups. Unfortunately Lucy had been on the receiving end of one or two of those—though of course she'd ended them with crushing verbal set-downs. This kiss, however—this one was going to end with her never being the same.

When Derek's lips finally moved away from hers, she gasped for breath and briefly rested her forehead against his. She was feeling things in all sorts of places she hadn't felt before. Hot, wet, warm places. Places that were aching. "You're a good kisser," she whispered against his mouth.

She glanced away self-consciously and pulled herself off his lap, then stood and dragged the other chair from the corner over to where Derek sat.

He tilted his head to the side and regarded her. "I'm a good kisser but earlier you told me I have your blessing to court Cassandra, finally, after all this time."

Lucy sucked in a breath and glanced away. "That's right."

He narrowed his eyes on her. "Does that decision have anything to do with Lord Berkeley?"

"What? No. Why?"

"Never mind. Is my hand fixed?"

"Just a minute." She gathered the clean linens from the desktop where she'd set them and wrapped them tightly around his wound, taking care to ensure that the poultice remained firmly in place. "There."

He pulled his hand from her grasp.

"You should see a doctor tomorrow. Have him look at it and make certain it's not infected."

"It'll be fine." He stood up and gestured toward the stairs. "Do you mind if I, um, leave through the front door?"

She smiled at that. "I think it would be best."

"Sorry to bother you this evening, my lady."

"Be careful getting home."

He made his way to the door of her bedchamber, opened it, and looked back at her. "Give your proper Lord Berkeley my best."

## ❧ CHAPTER TWENTY-SEVEN ❧

Lucy knocked lightly on the door to Cass's bedchamber. "May I come in?"

"Lucy, is that you?" her friend replied in an equally soft voice.

"Yes."

"Of course you may come in," Cass called.

Lucy shuffled inside. She was still wearing her night rail and summer robe of soft linen. She hadn't been able to sleep after the encounter with Derek. *Derek*. What about Derek? How did she feel about Derek? She didn't know. He was the most confusing man she'd ever met. What had he been thinking, swinging into her bedchamber in the middle of the night? In addition to breaking his own neck, he might have ruined her reputation, brought the whole house running to see what the commotion was, or all three. He'd been reckless tonight, out of control, and she'd never seen him be either. And if she didn't know any better, she'd say the man was severely jealous of Lord Berkeley. Not that there was anything to be jealous of. Why, Lord Berkeley had been the first man to pay attention to Lucy in an age. He was handsome and knew how to dance, but she'd only just met him. She had no idea what his true character was. She assumed that he must not be too odious since Garrett saw fit to befriend him, but that hardly meant she and he would make a good match. Still, it was promising, and she did intend to see him again. Before they'd left the ball, she'd agreed to allow him to call on her.

But for some reason she felt as if it was no coincidence that the same night she and Lord Berkeley had danced, Derek had come swinging through her window. Was it? Oh, why and when had everything got so out of control? That's why she'd come to visit Cass. She had to tell Cass that Derek knew Julian. Until tonight, she'd thought it might be too much for her friend, but now she realized Cass deserved to know everything.

She took a deep breath. Not only did she not know what to think about Derek, she didn't know what to say to Cass. And there was absolutely no way to explain why she had the man's bloody cravat folded up in the bottom drawer of her wardrobe . . . and she may have sniffed it—the non-bloodied part—a few times before she put it there.

She made her way over to Cass's bedside and sat on the edge of the mattress next to her friend. "I'm sorry I woke you."

Cass yawned and stretched her arms high above her head. "It's all right, Lucy. But what is it? What's wrong?" She snuggled her cheek against her pillow.

Lucy straightened the wrinkles out of her robe. "I'm sorry about the other night, Cass."

Cass's brow furrowed. "Sorry for what, Lucy?"

"Sorry I got into a fight with the duke in front of you at

the Assembly Rooms. I was just trying to help. For some reason he makes me so . . . so . . . angry. I don't know why."

Cass gave her a soft smile. "You've always had a temper, Luce. That's what makes you so fierce and strong. You're not a ninny like I am. It's what I've always admired about you."

"You're not a ninny, Cass."

"Aren't I?"

"No. You're lovely and friendly and think the best of everyone."

"Fat lot of good it's done me." Cass gave a wan smile.

"You're lovely, Cass. Derek . . . The duke is quite taken with you."

Cass yawned again and gave her a sleepy smile. "And Lord Berkeley seems quite taken with you."

Lucy looked down to where her fingers were intertwined in her lap, resting against her white robe. "That's why I came to your room, Cass."

"Why?"

"First, I want to tell you what the duke said to me two nights ago." She couldn't call him Derek, not in front of Cass.

Cass's blue eyes widened. "What is it?"

Lucy took a deep breath. "I hope you're not angry with me, but I told him you were heartbroken over Captain Julian Swift."

Cass looked wistfully out the dark window. "I'm not angry with you, Lucy. He may as well know. What does it matter if he knows his name?"

"Cass, the duke knows Julian. He's said they're close friends. He said Julian recommended he come back to England and court you."

Cass's face went pale. "He said that?"

Lucy nodded. "Yes. And he also said he doesn't intend to stop courting you, Cass."

Cass traced the pattern of the coverlet with a long tapered fingernail. "I've been thinking a lot about everything tonight." She closed her eyes. "I cannot argue that the duke doesn't have a point."

Lucy searched her face. "What do you mean?"

Cass's breath was long and drawn out. "The fact is that Julian will probably not make it home. And even if he does, he's still engaged to Pen." She looked up and met her friend's eyes. "I've decided I'm being foolish, Lucy."

Lucy couldn't breathe. The air had been sucked from the room. "Cass? What are you saying? Do you have feelings for Derek?"

# ❧ CHAPTER TWENTY-EIGHT ❧

Lucy couldn't concentrate on the banter of her friends at Lady Hoppington's Venetian breakfast. Normally Jane and Garrett's wordplay amused her, but tonight it just drowned into noise that she couldn't sort out in her head. She pressed her fingertips to her temples. All she could think about was her discussion with Cass last night.

Cass had answered the question, finally. She'd said that she didn't know how she felt and needed to think about everything. Understandable, given the riot of emotions she must have endured during the last sennight. But even though her friend's answer hadn't been the one Lucy had been dreading, she still felt uneasy about the situation. Should she tell Cass that she'd kissed her potential betrothed? Would that sway Cass's opinion? And if so, was that fair to Cass? Through his title alone, Derek was an extremely good catch, and if Cass did indeed have feelings for him or thought she could, it would be entirely selfish of Lucy to tell her that they'd kissed. Twice. Especially when she and Derek had both agreed that the kiss had meant nothing and wouldn't be repeated. At least they'd agreed to that the time they'd both been sober. The other time didn't count. Did it? And so what if the man had climbed through her bedchamber window last night? He'd been drunk and needed someone to treat his injured hand. She'd helped him. And very well, she'd kissed him once more, and perhaps that was not her best decision. Though the kissing had been extraordinary. She had to admit.

A headache throbbed in her skull. Oh, she was the worst friend in the entire world. The very worst. The situation was absolutely awful. Untenable, really. And now there was Lord Berkeley. He was the first decent potential suitor she'd had in years. She'd be a fool not to continue their acquaintance. She should spend her time with Lord Berkeley, get to know him better, see if they suited. Shouldn't she?

She needed to talk to Jane. Jane was always sensible. Always right. Always knew the answer. Yes. Jane. Where was Jane?

Lucy swung around, intending to find her friend, drag her into a corner somewhere, and confess all her sins. But the moment she turned, she ran straight into . . . Derek.

Gulp.

"Lucy?" He placed a hand at her elbow to steady her. "Are you all right?"

She couldn't look at him. She kept her eyes trained on her slippers. "Yes. I'm fine."

"You look as if you've just seen a ghost." His voice was smooth.

She cleared her throat, still watching her slippers. "No, truly I'm fine."

"Are you *certain* you're all right?" She dared a glance

up. His gaze was focused on her in that disconcerting way of his. The way that made her feel like he could see through her.

"Yes. Why?"

His brow was furrowed, and he was watching her with a funny look in his eye. "I don't know. You seem . . . different."

Lucy squared her shoulders. She needed to compose herself and quickly. He obviously didn't remember their kiss last night. For the better. Obviously. But if Derek could tell she was acting differently, no doubt Cass, who'd known her since childhood, would be able to tell Lucy was a mess within five minutes. She was merely discombobulated. The headache was getting to her. That was all. She would be quite all right.

"Lucy," Derek continued. "I wanted to say something to you."

She held her breath. "Wha . . . What?"

"I wanted to apologize."

She closed her eyes briefly and then stared at his shirtfront. "For what?"

"For my behavior last night." He glanced about to ensure they wouldn't be overheard, but no one else was standing anywhere near them.

She winced. "You remember . . . everything?"

"No, that's just it. I don't remember most of it. So if there's anything I need to apologize for—"

She let her shoulders drop and expelled a relieved breath. "Oh, no, no, no. No need to apologize for anything."

"Yes. There is. It was completely irrational and irresponsible of me. I promise it won't happen again."

"How is your hand?" she asked, desperate to turn the topic from his apology.

He glanced down to the bandaged appendage. "Healing nicely thanks to your tender ministrations."

She smiled but glanced away. Why was it that all she could think of were the glimpses she'd had of his bare stomach and the feel of his hot mouth against the palm of her hand when she'd tried to keep him from speaking last night? Not to mention the actual kissing. She swallowed hard.

She took a deep breath and hazarded another glance at his face. "May I ask you something, Derek?"

He smiled when she used his given name. "Of course."

"When you . . ." She swallowed again. "When you last saw Julian. Was he . . . ? Did you think he wouldn't survive it? Is he truly dying?"

Derek's face took on a somber hue. He put his hands on his hips and blew out a breath, staring out the window as if he was trying to remember. "It was bad, Lucy. Quite bad."

She nodded slightly. "So, you do think he will die?"

One awful word. "Yes."

Lucy stumbled backward, away from him. Away. He reached for her but she scrambled out of his reach. "I must go," she murmured, turning and picking up her skirts. She had to force herself not to run.

That settled it. Julian would die if he was not already dead. Cass deserved a secure future with a handsome nobleman who had sworn to protect her. It was true that Garrett might take offense, but Garrett, while wonderful, was merely in line to be an earl, not quite as eligible as a duke.

Lord Berkeley was perfectly nice. He was handsome and dashing and he wanted to see Lucy again. He wasn't chasing after her best friend, sworn to marry her by a promise to a dying man. Yes. Much less complicated.

She would still talk to Jane, come clean. Admit everything. Clear her conscience. She and Jane would think of a way to give Cass the little push she needed to actually accept Derek.

But Lucy already knew. She had to stop having feelings for Derek immediately and ensure the match between him and Cass.

# ❧ CHAPTER TWENTY-NINE ❧

Where in the world was Jane? Lucy had been searching for her throughout Lady Hoppington's house for the last half an hour. She'd checked all her usual haunts: the library, the children's study, every small nook and cranny she could find in which Jane might insert herself to read a book. Jane certainly wasn't making it easy for Lucy to confess. To make matters worse, Garrett was nowhere to be found, either.

And guilty as it made her, she'd been avoiding Cass tonight. She just couldn't bear to see her friend and know how horrendous she'd been. She turned the bend in Lady Hoppington's corridor and stopped short. There, behind a large cabinet, stood Derek.

And he was not alone.

Lucy froze. A woman's voice floated on the air. "I'm quite sorry, Your Grace, for the way I've behaved."

Lucy closed her eyes. It was Cass. Cass and Derek were having a private conversation and damn her to hell but Lucy could not, for the life of her, move her feet, turn away. She should not eavesdrop, especially not on this conversation, but she just couldn't make herself go. Instead she pressed her back against the wall and held her breath, listening intently for every word between them.

"Lucy told me that she explained to you that I . . . love Julian," Cass continued.

"Yes" came Derek's sure, strong reply.

"I've always loved him, I'm afraid. But I know he belongs to my cousin Penelope. That is, if he . . ." Cass's voice cracked, and Lucy's heart broke again for her friend.

Derek's voice was low. "If it helps to know it, Lady Cassandra, Captain Swift held . . . holds you in the very highest regard."

Lucy could hear the smile in Cass's reply. "Yes. As I do him. I've written to him every day while he's been in the army."

"He told me how much he looked forward to your letters."

Lucy's eyes filled with tears. This had to be excruciating for Cass to hear.

"Thank you, Your Grace, for telling me that," Cass murmured.

"Of course," Derek replied.

"I must admit something to you," Cass said.

Lucy held her breath. *Admit something? What? What?*

Cass's voice was soft. "When I first met you, I was frightened of you. Terribly frightened."

"I'm sorry if I frightened you," Derek said.

"No. No. It wasn't you, not you, yourself. It's just . . . that you're so . . ."

*Ridiculously handsome*, Lucy thought and then stepped on her own foot for her idiocy.

"It's complicated," Cass finished.

"I understand," Derek replied.

"I just wanted to tell you that I'm not frightened of you

anymore, Your Grace," Cass said. "As soon as I learned you were Julian's friend. Well, any friend of Julian's is my friend, too."

"I'm glad to hear that, Lady Cassandra. And I want you to know that I intend to give you all the time that you need. But I do hope that eventually, you'll believe that we might get to know each another a bit better."

"Thank you, Your Grace," came Cass's reply. "And if you'd still like to, you have my permission to court me. When I'm ready, of course."

Derek remained silent.

Lucy turned her head away and swallowed the painful lump that had formed in her throat.

## ❧ CHAPTER THIRTY ❧

This time the letter from Collin was even shorter. It had been scrawled on a bit of dirty parchment his brother had obviously scrounged up somewhere. Collin must be in a very rough place indeed.

> *I found Adam. He's hurt but will survive. Bringing him home. No sign of Rafe and Swifdon. They were captured by the French. Adam managed to escape. Derek, it doesn't look good for them.*

Derek slammed his open palm against his desk. Damn it all to hell. It seemed they would be having a double funeral for the Swift brothers. How would he ever tell Swift's mother? His sister, Daphne? God. That conversation would be one of the most difficult of his life. It didn't sound as if Penelope, Swift's intended, much cared, but Daphne and Louisa Swift would be devastated.

Adam was alive. That was the only comfort Derek had. Though it felt wrong to be glad over that news when the news for the Swift family was so dire. Not to mention Rafe. His relatives would need to be found and told as well. The lad had been a reckless hellion but a braver young man, Derek had never known. Wellington and the War Office would try to send a man to tell the families but Derek would stop them. He would make the journeys himself. He would be the one to tell Louisa and Daphne and Cavendish's family. They would not be informed by some nameless drone from the War Office.

Adam was safe. Derek closed his eyes and repeated that to himself. At least his mother would have the comfort of knowing her three boys were alive. She'd been so worried about Derek going to war—and when Adam and Collin had announced their intentions of working for the War Office, she'd been beside herself. But she knew she couldn't keep her adult sons for doing what they would. She'd resigned herself to praying for them and waiting for the mail to bring any news. Derek would write to her immediately. He could tell from the state of the missive Collin had sent that that his brother wasn't in a position to write to their mother in Brighton at their family home. He'd asked her to come to London and stay with him, but she'd insisted on staying near the shore until she heard the fate of her sons. Perhaps now she'd make the journey into town and live the life that would be afforded to her as the mother of a duke. That was some small comfort.

Derek rubbed the back of his neck and groaned. He had nothing to do for the moment but get back to the business of courting Lady Cassandra. And he should be pleased by his progress on that score. Last night she'd told him she would entertain his courtship. Finally. This is what he'd been waiting for. Why didn't it feel like a victory?

## ❧ CHAPTER THIRTY-ONE ❧

"Lucy, please, you must, for me." Cass was lying propped up against a large group of pillows in the middle of her bed.

"No, no, no. I couldn't. You know how the duke and I get along. Like oil and water. I think a housemaid would be much better to do it."

Cass sneezed into her handkerchief. "But I cannot send a housemaid to tell the duke how sick I am. He's certain to think I'm making it up to dodge him again. If you go, you'll be ever so much more convincing."

Lucy watched her poor friend. Cass's eyes were red, and her nose was running. She clutched a handkerchief in her fist and had a score of sneezes on her lips. Cass was ill. That was obvious. And no wonder. The poor young woman had been under severe strain for days. Lucy would do anything she could to help her friend. Bring soup. Read stories. Check her fever. Keep her company. But she drew the line at traveling to Derek's rented house on Up-hill Drive and informing him that Cass would not be able to see him today because she was ill.

First of all, Lucy didn't trust herself around Derek, and second—and perhaps more important—she feared Derek would doubt her. Given their history—passionate kisses notwithstanding—she was the very last person he would believe when told that Lady Cassandra didn't want to see him. The whole notion was ludicrous actually.

"Write him a note," Lucy pleaded. "You can be convincing."

"I'm rubbish at writing letters," Cass replied. "You're ever so much more convincing than I am. You know that."

"You're not rubbish at writing letters, Cass. You've written to Julian every day for years."

Cass waved the hand that held the handkerchief in the air. "That's different, that's Julian. I can say anything to Julian. The duke still intimidates me a bit."

Lucy snorted. "I don't see why."

"Oh, Lucy, please do it. You've such a way with words," Cass begged.

Lucy breathed deeply. "Such a way with *outlandish* words. When delivering a simple message, I'm no more adept than a housemaid would be."

"Please, Lucy?" Cass batted her eyelashes at her.

"Cass, no. Can't we ask Jane?"

Cass laughed, and it sent her into a coughing fit. When she recovered she said, "Jane would have her nose so far in a book, she'd bypass the duke's house."

"What about Garrett?" Lucy pleaded.

"That would just be strange. The duke knows you, Lucy. He likes you."

Lucy gulped. "Are you daft? He most certainly does not like me, and he only knows me because I've been inserting myself into your affairs for far too long. It's high time I remove myself from the entire situation. Besides, Lord Berkeley intends to pay me a call this afternoon."

Cass gave her puppy-dog eyes. "That won't be for hours yet. Please, Lucy? For me?"

In the end, Lucy should have known she was helpless to say no to Cass. First of all, if Lucy protested too vehemently Cass was certain to wonder why. And second, Lucy apparently couldn't resist the urge to see Derek once more. But she hated being a messenger for Cass. And Derek *would* think she was lying, there was no question about it.

She tied her bonnet under her chin, pulled on her gloves, and set out with a footman down the street, around the corner, and four streets over to Derek's rented house. She closed her eyes and said a prayer to the heavens. Perhaps he would not be home. That would be ever so convenient.

When they finally reached Derek's address, the footman rapped on the door. Lucy squared her shoulders and cleared her throat, ready to explain her presence to an overly arrogant butler and leave as quickly as possible.

The door swung open.

"Lady Lucy Upton to see his grace, the Duke of Claringdon," the footman pronounced.

"I have a message for His Grace," she added. "I'm happy to leave it and—"

"Just a moment," the butler intoned. She'd been correct. Overly arrogant. Just like his employer.

The butler ushered her into the foyer. The footman waited outside. Lucy glanced around. The house was decorated sparingly but tastefully.

With his head held high as if he were serving the king in the royal palace, the butler strode down the corridor. Lucy fidgeted, hoping he'd return as soon as possible and inform her that His Grace wasn't accepting any callers today.

No such luck.

When the servant returned two minutes later, he offered to take Lucy's pelisse, and then escorted her into a drawing room a few paces away. "His Grace shall be in momentarily," he intoned.

Lucy tried to manage a smile. Oh, of course *His Grace* was going to torture her with his company. And since he knew it was her, he'd probably make her wait. In fact, the minute he'd heard she was at his door, he no doubt set about taking his time.

Lucy made her way around the room, touching the bits of art and figurines that lay on the tabletops. Who had Derek rented this house from? She wasn't certain of the owners. But it was a grand home. Certainly fit for a duke. Would he purchase it? Live here? Would she return to this home in future years, the guest of the Duchess of Claringdon, her good friend Cass? The thought made her inexplicably melancholy.

The door behind her opened and she turned to see Derek standing there. He wore a light gray coat, a perfectly starched white cravat, and dark, superfine trousers. His broad shoulders filled out his coat, and Lucy momentarily shuddered. Why did that man have to be so good looking? Utterly unfair.

"Lady Lucy," he said, bowing to her. "Are you cold?"

She curtsied. "Pardon? No . . . I . . ."

"To what do I owe the pleasure?" he continued.

Lucy pushed up her chin. She intended to get this unwanted little visit over and done with as quickly as possible. "I've come on Cass's behalf."

"Oh? We spoke last night, you know. She indicated that she'd be willing to allow me to court her."

Lucy hesitated. "Yes. I . . . I know."

"Don't tell me she's already changed her mind." A half smile rested on his lips.

Lucy dropped her gaze to the floor. "No. No, she . . . she's taken ill and begged me come and tell you she cannot ride with you today."

His eyes narrowed. "She's ill?"

"Yes, truly." Oh, Lucy had known he wouldn't believe her. "She's quite eager to continue your acquaintance, however, she just wanted you to know that she's got an awful head cold and—"

He arched a brow. "Why do I find it difficult to believe that she's—how did you put it?—eager to continue our acquaintance?"

Lucy closed her eyes for a moment. He was not about to make this easy on her, was he? "She's trying. I think the strain of Julian's injury has made her weak. I'm not surprised that she's ill. I'm quite worried about her."

"And she chose *you* to come and tell me?"

"Yes, actually. She didn't think a housemaid would be sufficiently emphatic enough."

His mouth quirked. "Oh, she's right about that. You're known for your emphasis."

Lucy narrowed her eyes on him. Now he was making her angry. Mocking her and questioning Cass's illness. "Perhaps you'd like to pay a call and see for yourself?"

"No need," he replied. "I told her I'd give her time and that's exactly what I intend to do. If she needs time, says that she's ill—"

Lucy gritted her teeth. "She *is* ill."

He raised a hand in a conciliatory gesture. "Please, Lucy. Let's not argue today."

"Of all the pompous, overbearing . . . Why can't you think for one moment that I'm telling the truth? When have

I ever lied? Cass is willing to give you a chance, despite her broken heart, and yet you insist upon—"

He put one hand on his hip. "It doesn't matter why she doesn't want to see me, does it?"

"You're what? Annoyed that she's ill?" Lucy paced away from him, crossing her arms over her chest. She clenched her jaw. "It makes no sense. I don't get the impression that you have any great love for Cass and yet you insist upon courting her, marrying her, all because Julian recommended her to you?"

"I told you. I made a promise to my dying friend. And I intend to keep that promise."

"At any cost?" she tossed back at him. "Even Cass's happiness and health?"

"I don't expect you to understand. Captain Swift asked me to take care of the girl. I need a wife. I want children. It makes sense. I know Lady Cassandra doesn't love me. I don't love her, either, but one day I'm certain we'll learn to tolerate each other."

Lucy wanted to throttle him. "Tolerate? That's the word you choose? You have no heart. Cass deserves love, happiness, passion." As soon as that last word flew from her lips, she clamped her hand over her mouth. She hadn't meant to say *that*.

His brow shot up. "Passion?"

She glanced at her slippers, wanting to kick herself. But now that she'd said it, she wasn't about to back down. She pulled her hand away from her mouth and raised her chin. "Yes. The kind of passion that comes when two people truly love and respect each other."

His voice was husky. "I've found that passion can complicate a relationship, my lady."

She paced toward him and stood only a space away.

She glared up at him. "You're a menace. A menace to Cass. I don't know why she's giving you a chance but you don't deserve it. You're cold. You're heartless. You have no emotion."

He grabbed her upper arms. "No passion?"

She turned her head away from him. She couldn't drag the word *no* past her suddenly dry lips.

"I beg to differ, my lady." He pulled her into his arms and kissed her.

## ❧ CHAPTER THIRTY-TWO ❧

When Derek's lips met hers, Lucy had been coursing with anger. An anger that quickly turned into uncontrollable lust the moment he tugged her body against his. Damn him. She hated him. He was awful. But his insistent hot mouth was rubbing against hers, and his tongue was making her insane.

"Passion like this?" he whispered hotly against her cheek.

"Yes," she growled back, meeting his lips again with a fervor that matched his own.

He scooped her up into his arms and strode two long paces toward the settee, where he laid her down and quickly covered her with his body. His hands ravaged her coiffure. His lips were on her cheek, her ear, her neck.

Lucy was mindless. This was wrong for half a dozen reasons but at the moment she didn't care. She was entirely unable to conjure the strength of mind to push him away or even to protest. She wanted this. This passion between them. Whatever it was and whyever it existed, she wanted it. Needed it right now.

She would worry about the consequences later.

"Damn you. Why do you make me so insane?" he whispered against her hair, nuzzling her ear and making her eyes roll back in her head.

"Damn *you*. Why do you make me want to scream?"

His mouth trailed down to her décolletage. His fingers worked quickly at the buttons on the back of her gown. When the dress loosened, he quickly pulled down the fabric and stays. Then his hot mouth was on her breast. Lucy arched her back and gasped. She whimpered in the back of her throat. She'd never felt anything like it. *Passion*. She didn't want it to end. He bit her nipple lightly.

"I want to make you scream for a different reason," he murmured, just before his mouth captured the tip of her other breast. She wished she could tug him away but her hands tangled in his hair and held him to her. This was passion, the kind of soul-crushing passion that made no sense. This was the kind of thing that lovers experienced. The thought came out of nowhere. Lucy had read and heard enough to realize that. It wasn't the demure little chaste kisses that men and women who barely tolerated each other shared. This was the kind of thing you broke the rules for. The big rules. With big consequences.

His thigh was riding high between her legs, and Lucy moaned when he pressed against her. She was a swimming hot mass down there. She reached her hand down between the two of them to feel him through his trousers. He was hot and hard and reaching for her.

"I don't like you," she whispered between clenched teeth as she rubbed him up and down.

Derek's eyes were closed and his teeth were clenched. He groaned, looking as if he were in abject pain from the stroke of her hand.

"I don't like you, either," he ground out. "And perhaps your issue isn't that you don't like me but that I'm not your precious Lord Berkeley." He opened his eyes, and the emerald green of them stared into Lucy's soul.

She could deny it again. This time it would be true. He wasn't Lord Berkeley, but she was having difficulty recalling the man's face at the moment. Slowly, Derek pulled both of her hands up and easily pinned them over her head with one of his.

"Planning to show me how much you dislike me, Your Grace?" she whispered.

"No, right now, I want to show you how much I do like you."

She could have struggled against him, tried to pull her hands away, but it would have only been for show and of no use. The man was twice her size and powerful and rugged. Instead she pushed up her chin, offering him her neck. He kissed it then, bit her softly. She should scream at him, tell him to stop, but the truth was that him pinning her down like this made her melt. Blast it. This overbearing man knew *exactly* what he was doing.

His other hand traveled down to the bottom of her skirts and tugged up the fabric. Oh, God, what was that for? She desperately wanted to find out. Lucy shuddered. His hand traced a fiery hot path up her leg, over her silk stocking, up her bare thigh. He grasped her ankle and pulled it around his hip, bringing their intimate parts into closer contact. Lucy moaned and arched her back. Her aching breasts pressed against his hard chest. Derek's mouth dipped lower again to nuzzle her breast as his free hand moved slowly, inexorably between her legs. She bucked against him, wildly trying to free her hands but also desperately scared he would let go and stop. His lips returned to clash with hers.

She tore her mouth away. "What are you doing?" she whispered against his rough cheek.

His eyes bore into hers. "Giving you something you desperately need." His finger found her then, and her mouth fell open. She gasped. Her head rolled to the side.

His finger slid inside of her and Lucy's thighs clenched, her breathing hitched. She shut her eyes and moaned.

"Yes," he whispered hotly into her ear.

When his thumb touched the nub of pleasure between her legs and rubbed her in a rhythm that matched the slow slide of his finger in and out of her, Lucy went completely limp. She did not thrash, did not fight, she just spread her legs wider and let the overwhelming feelings course through her. He was playing her body like a finely tuned instrument, and she was helpless to resist.

He moved his head back down to her breast and the brush of his slight stubble against the soft skin there made her tremble.

He kept it up. The rough bite of his tongue against her nipple. The slow slide of his finger in and out of her. The masterful glide of his thumb over the most sensitive spot on her body. Lucy shuddered again. Her entire body tensed and she panted into his ear, breathing heavily, helpless to control the spasms that began in her most intimate spot and then spiraled out and up, making her entire body quake and shiver. She closed her eyes. Then her hands went limp in his embrace. He'd just given her the most incredible experience of her life and she'd wanted it.

"You're a good kisser, too," he whispered with a roguish grin against her lips.

## CHAPTER THIRTY-THREE

Lucy rolled over on her bed and jammed her pillow over her face. This was all Jane's fault. All right, very well, it was not Jane's fault. But if she'd had a chance to speak with Jane in the last day or two, she might not have got into this untenable position. Kissing the Duke of Claringdon? Passionately? At his house? In the middle of the day? Unthinkable. But true. And doing . . . more. *Much* more. That was the only word she could conjure to classify the other things that had happened between them. Just thinking about them made her hot and left her wanting. She couldn't help the little smile that popped to her lips.

Lucy tossed the pillow aside, scrubbed her hands over her face, and groaned. She stared at the ceiling. What was she to do? She was not only the worst friend in the entire world, she would die of guilt. That was all there was to it. She'd somehow managed to right her clothing and scramble out of Derek's drawing room earlier without much of a good-bye, hideously awkward though it had been. They'd barely spoken two words to each other. No apologies. No discussion about how their little interlude would affect Derek's courtship of Cass. No. Cass had not been mentioned and so much the better. What could they do to possibly make this right? There was no talking it away.

Lucy had faced the poor footman who'd been patiently waiting outside the whole time while she'd been tumbling around on the sofa with the duke. Thankfully, the servant didn't say a word about her mussed clothing and wild hair. She pulled her bonnet down tight over her messy coiffure and nearly ran through the streets to get back home as soon as possible, the footman trailing her. That had been hours ago and she was still hidden in her room, alone with her regrets. Were they regrets? Or just deliciously wicked memories?

How would she ever explain this to Cass? And explain she must. "Oh, Cass dear, just a moment. You know the man who's been courting you? The handsome duke? Yes, him. I just happened to do some unspeakably inappropriate things with him earlier. Have a happy marriage!"

Lucy couldn't even laugh about it. It was ludicrous. It was wrong. And even though she knew Cass didn't have deep feelings, or any really, for Derek, it still didn't make what had happened between them acceptable. It was wrong, wrong, wrong. Blast it. Why had she allowed Cass to talk her into going over to Derek's house? She'd known better. Truly known better. And at any rate she should have brought Janie with her. But instead, she'd pranced off knowing that she'd end up doing or saying something she shouldn't. And oh, she'd done both. Spectacularly.

Where *was* Jane? Jane needed to tell her what to do. Lucy clamped the pillow back over her face and groaned.

❦

After Lucy left his house, Derek made it his foremost duty to locate the boxing club in Bath and join immediately. He was already well into a bout with a chap who was little match for him. And yes, if truth be told, every punch he landed he pretended to be pummeling Berkeley. But despite having dealt some crushing blows, he still couldn't erase the memory of his afternoon interlude with Lucy Upton.

How had his plan gone so wrong? Derek was nothing if not decisive. He prided himself on it. Lived for it. Lived *because* of it. Being decisive had literally saved his life more than once. His father's words echoed in his brain: "A man is decisive. He makes decisions quickly, accurately. He doesn't hesitate."

Another punch.

And Derek's decisiveness had caused him to choose Lady Cassandra to take to wife. She might be a bit shy and her penchant for using her friend to speak for her wasn't her most endearing quality, but she was lovely, and sweet. Most important, she would be a steadfast wife. He could survive a bit of shyness while she was getting used to him.

What did he care if she thought she was in love with Julian? The stark truth was that Julian wouldn't be coming back from the Continent and even if by some miracle he did, he couldn't propose to Lady Cassandra. Besides, love didn't exist. The fact that Cassandra thought she loved Julian demonstrated how inexperienced she was. But that was still acceptable. Love wasn't part of the equation. Derek wanted a wife who would be true to him, of course, and he could tell that whatever unrequited love pulsed through her veins, Cassandra would not cuckold him. If Julian lived and married her cousin, Julian would never be so dishonorable as to be unfaithful, either. He knew his friend well enough to know that. Derek merely needed to convince Cassandra to give him a chance and see things from his perspective. They would make a fine match. They would have strong, healthy children. They would both go about their lives and their pursuits independently of each other as most of the couples of the *ton* did, and that was perfectly fine with him. His own parents might have enjoyed a very different marriage, but he inhabited a new world now. A successful union did not require the complication of passion.

*Passion.* He slammed another fist into the poor chap in front of him. The lad needed to learn to use his left with a bit more skill. He'd tell him as much after the match concluded.

Passion was what Derek had experienced with Lucy Upton this afternoon in his bloody rented drawing room of all places. Damn it. He hadn't felt that on fire for a woman in . . . perhaps forever. It made him angry. Why? Because he'd felt out of control with her. He was never out of control. In fact he prided himself on being completely in control at all times. Lucy Upton made him feel lacking in control. It had been as if a force had come over him. He'd been unable to keep his hands off her. And damn it, he knew why.

The woman drove him mad. She was bossy, strong, and controlling. She was too sure of herself by half and she refused to back down. Derek was completely unused to anyone who wouldn't retreat in the face of his will, especially that slip of a woman. Hell, he'd frightened seasoned generals in battle, but for some reason Lucy Upton was completely unintimidated by him. Her reputation preceded her. A wasp's tongue was what they said about her. *Wasp* was an apt description. He'd been stung by her more than once now. But instead of it making him want to stay away from her the way it appeared to affect his fellow peers, Derek was drawn to her like a moth to a flame. To his chagrin, he found that he actually looked forward to his interactions with her, and for more reasons than one. Why did she have to be so bloody beautiful on top of it all? She was a challenge. A female challenge the likes of which he had never encountered. And it intrigued him.

Derek threw another punch that connected solidly with his opponent. Damn it. He'd already made his decisions. He didn't want a challenge. He wanted peace. Another punch. And quiet. Another punch. No more fighting. A fourth punch. He'd had enough of fighting. Lucy Upton was the kind of woman who wouldn't give him a moment's peace. She could have her bloody Lord Berkeley. So why did Derek crave her?

The chap across from him was a bloodied mess and acknowledged defeat. Too bad he *wasn't* Berkeley. Derek apologized profusely for breaking his nose. Poorly done, that. He hadn't meant to hurt the lad. But his mind had been preoccupied with thoughts of Lucy Upton. Damn it.

Derek gathered his belongings and left the club. He took off on foot back to his town house. What about Lady Cassandra? He was supposed to keep courting her. Had promised Julian. But what sort of a scoundrel would he be, courting Cassandra after what he'd done with Lucy this afternoon? Damn it all, why had he done those things with Lucy? He was a highly trained military officer. He had no excuse for his loss of control around her. And the passion with which she'd responded to him—it made him hard again just thinking about it.

Blast it. What was he going to do? Things could not continue this way. That much was certain.

Apparently Lady Cassandra was ill. He believed that now. And though he didn't wish an illness on her, it did afford him time. Time to think. Time to decide what to do next. About both ladies.

# ❧ CHAPTER THIRTY-FOUR ❧

Later that afternoon, Jane and Lucy sat in chairs facing the bed in Cass's bedchamber. Jane was reading Wollstonecraft to their ill friend while Lucy pretended to embroider. In truth she was merely poking the needle through the material and picking the thread back out again. Over and over. She'd attempted the same stitch a dozen times. Oh, it was no use. Guilt rode her hard. She couldn't embroider. And the words Jane read weren't holding her interest, either.

What would Derek do now that *that* had happened between them? What would he say to her? What would he say to Cass? How would everything progress from here? Oh, she was a miserable human being for doing what she'd done today.

"Lucy, has Lord Berkeley come to call?" Cass asked with a sly smile moments after Jane stopped reading and shut the book.

Lucy looked up nervously from her stitching. Lord Berkeley. She hadn't even thought about him since her afternoon with Derek. Lord Berkeley had been the first decent suitor she'd had in years and now she'd gone and acted like a harlot with another man. Now, *that* was a pickle.

"What? Oh, yes. Yes, he came to call. Twice," she answered Cass.

"And what happened?" Cass asked. "I cannot believe we've been sitting here all this time and you haven't mentioned it."

"Yes, what happened, Lucy?" Jane asked, leaning forward.

"Oh, we had tea yesterday and it was . . . it was . . . nice."

Jane stuck out her tongue. "Ugh. Nice?"

"It was," Lucy insisted.

Cass scrunched up her nose. "Somehow 'nice' doesn't sound so nice."

"He's really quite a nice man," Lucy added. Oh, what was the use? Her friends knew her too well. The fact was that she and Lord Berkeley had exchanged barely more than a few words both times he'd come to call. She wasn't certain if it was because she had nothing to say or because he had nothing to say. But they'd both quietly sipped their tea and smiled at each other off and on and that was all there was to it. *Nice* was probably too effusive a word. Not to mention, the entire time Lord Berkeley had been sitting in the drawing room, Lucy had been having wayward thoughts about Derek. And *that* had not been helpful at all.

"There's that word again," Jane said, shaking her head. "Nice."

Cass took a deep breath. "Perhaps you should see him again. Find out if you get along better next time. That reminds me. You never told me, Lucy, what did the duke say when you told him I was ill?"

Lucy jumped. She pricked her finger with the needle.

"Ouch." She popped the appendage into her mouth to suck on it briefly before saying, "What? I told you."

Cass shook her head weakly. "You said he gave me his well wishes, but you never said if you thought he believed you about my illness."

Lucy sat up straight, dropping the detested embroidery into her lap. "I think he believed me."

Jane gave her a funny look. Lucy still hadn't had a chance to speak with Jane, and she desperately wanted to. She'd merely whispered to her earlier as they'd entered Cass's room that she wanted to have a private word at some point. Jane had nodded.

Cass looked hopeful. "Do you really think he did believe you?"

Lucy nodded. It was all she could do with Jane's assessing gaze on her.

"Did you fight with him again, Lucy?" Cass sighed.

Lucy wanted to sink through the floor. She couldn't look at Cass. She kept her eyes pinned to the embroidery circle. "No. I. We were quite . . . civil today." Heavens, lightning would strike her. She was a harlot. A lying harlot.

"I'm glad to hear that, Lucy," Cass continued. "Because I was hoping that you would keep him company while I'm ill."

Lucy's head snapped up. Her eyes went wide. "Keep him company? What?"

Jane almost hid her smile behind the edge of Wollstonecraft.

Lucy pointed at Jane. "Why can't Jane do it?"

Jane pulled the book away from her lips. "Don't look at me. You're the one who has history with the man. We can't confuse him by tossing a third lady into the equation."

Cass leaned back against her pillow and sneezed into her handkerchief. "Lucy, you know he's used to you."

Lucy gulped. *You could say that.*

"He's been around you as much as he's been around me," Cass continued.

*Uh, he's been a bit more around me, to be honest.*

"You two may not be friends, per se, but I think he'd appreciate you keeping him apprised of my condition. We'd talked about going on a picnic. Seeing the ruins. Things like that."

Lucy tapped on the embroidery frame. "And you can do all those things, Cass. Just as soon as you're feeling better."

Cass smoothed a hand over her bed-mussed hair. "It's most unfortunate that I've been taken ill. I feel horribly guilty about it."

Guilty? Lucy swallowed. She knew all about guilty. "What have you to feel guilty for, Cass?"

Cass shook her head. "The way I treated the duke up till now. I've been so rude."

Lucy leaned forward in her chair and rubbed her hands over her eyes. "No, I was the rude one."

"But only at my request." Cass sneezed daintily into her handkerchief.

"It doesn't matter, Cass. I'm certain he's pleased that you're willing to speak with him now," Lucy replied.

"But I'm worried that he'll become disinterested," Cass replied. "Find someone else to court if I'm ill for too long."

"If he finds someone else to court, he doesn't deserve you," Jane added. "Remember, Mary Wollstonecraft said, 'Women are systematically degraded by receiving the trivial attentions which men think it manly to pay to the sex, when, in fact, men are insultingly supporting their own superiority.'"

Lucy nodded. "Absolutely. Jane's right. Perhaps it's better if you let him go."

"I know. I know," Cass agreed. "But after the way I've

treated him, I'd feel so much better if you'd agree to keep him company, Lucy. Please? Besides, it can't hurt Lord Berkeley to believe he has a bit of competition."

Lucy glanced at Jane and gave her a pleading look. Lucy couldn't say yes to this. Couldn't put herself in the path of more temptation with the duke again. Could she? Was she strong enough?

Jane shrugged. "You might as well agree to it, Luce. Something tells me Cass doesn't intend to stop until you do."

"No," Cass agreed, a smile on her face. "I won't."

Lucy nearly whimpered. "Very well, Cass. I'll keep the duke company for you."

## ❧ CHAPTER THIRTY-FIVE ❧

Derek was sitting in the study going over ledgers. The accounts for the lands he'd been granted as part of his dukedom were a bloody mess. Someone with absolutely no head for figures had been handling them to date. Derek had already dismissed the steward and hired a new solicitor to help him run things, but he intended to work through every single figure himself. Damn noblemen and their damn unwillingness to manage their own affairs. Why, the last owner had been robbed half blind. But far be it from an aristocrat to actually see to his own business. Derek would see to it, and put it all to rights before he allowed anyone else to so much as touch a page of the ledger.

A knock at the door made him glance up. "Come in."

Hughes stood there, his back ramrod-straight as usual. "Your Grace, you have a visitor."

A visitor? Was it Lucy? Somehow he doubted it, but just the thought of having her in his house again made him shift uncomfortably in his suddenly too-tight breeches. "Who is it, Hughes?"

"A Lord Berkeley, Your Grace. He asks for a moment of your time."

Derek tossed his quill atop the ledger and sat back in his chair, clasping both hands behind his head. Berkeley? What the devil? That made no sense at all. "Is he alone, Hughes?"

"Yes, Your Grace."

"Show him in."

Derek narrowed his eyes on the far wall of his study. What could Berkeley possibly want with him?

Hughes returned in a mere minute with the man in question. After ushering him into the study, the butler pulled the door shut.

Berkeley bowed to Derek. "Your Grace, thank you for seeing me."

"Come in, Berkeley. Have a seat."

Berkeley made his way over to Derek's desk and sat in one of the two large leather chairs in front of it. "Thank you, Your Grace."

Derek stood and strolled over to the sideboard where he splashed a bit of brandy into a glass. "Care for a drink, Berkeley?"

"No, thank you, Your Grace. I don't consume spirits stronger than a bit of wine."

Derek arched a brow at the sideboard at that news. "You don't mind if I have a brandy, do you?"

"Not at all."

Good. He could tell he was going to need it. He swiped the glass from the tabletop, tossed a bit of wine into another glass for Berkeley, handed it to him, and crossed back over to his desk where he took a seat. "Tell me, Berkeley. What brings you here?"

Setting his wine glass aside, Lord Berkeley moved forward on the edge of the chair and placed his folded hands on top of the desk. "I wanted to . . . to ask you f . . . or a f . . . favor, Your Grace."

Derek took a drink. "A favor?"

"Yes, Your Grace. It's involving Lady Lucy Upton."

Derek breathed in deeply through both nostrils. "Lady Lucy? What about her?"

"Well, Your Grace." Berkeley straightened his cravat. "I am . . . you c . . . could say that I am quite interested in c . . . courting Lady Lucy."

Derek narrowed his eyes on him. Where exactly was he going with this? "Go on."

"I'd like v . . . very much to c . . . court her formally, Your Grace, and I . . . I n . . . need your help. If you're w . . . willing to give it, that is."

Derek downed the entire contents of his glass in one swallow. "You want my help courting Lucy?" Blast, he'd just made a mistake hadn't he? He shouldn't be calling her Lucy in front of Berkeley.

"Y . . . yes, Y . . . Your Grace."

Derek eyed the younger man carefully. Seemed Berkeley had a bit of a speech impediment. It must have been difficult for him to come here and ask for his help.

"What exactly do you think I can do to help you?" Derek asked.

"Lady L . . . Lucy, she seems quite taken w . . . with your p . . . penchant for w . . . wit, Your Grace."

Derek furrowed his brow. "She does?"

"Y . . . yes, Y . . . Your Grace. She's mentioned it to me m . . . more than once. H . . . how you and s . . . she banter."

Derek arched a brow. "She has?"

"Y . . . yes, Y . . . Your Grace."

The man was going to have to stop calling him "Your Grace"; it was just too excruciating to listen to, poor devil.

"That still doesn't answer how you think I may be of help to you, Berkeley."

Lord Berkeley pulled his hands back into his lap and stared down at them. "I was h . . . hoping, Y . . . Your Grace, that y . . . you w . . . would h . . . help me say the things I cannot say. That y . . . you w . . . would agree to write a letter to Lady Lucy. As if it were from me."

# ❧ CHAPTER THIRTY-SIX ❧

Derek took a deep breath before he knocked on the door of Upton's town house the next morning. His meeting with Berkeley continued to play through his head. In the end he'd agreed to help the man. Perhaps he felt sorry for the poor bloke, perhaps he was in a good mood, or perhaps he'd decided that encouraging Lucy's courtship by another man was exactly the sort of thing he should do to rid himself of his constant thoughts of her.

If Lucy married Berkeley, this entire twisted mess he'd got himself into might resolve itself and everyone would be happy. At least that's what he'd told himself when he'd heard himself say yes and then plucked out a piece of parchment and scribbled down notes based on the things Berkeley told him he would like to say. The man may have attended Oxford, but apparently he couldn't string together a witty line when it came to wooing a lady of his choosing. Poor bastard.

Regardless of why he'd agreed to it, Derek had finished the letter while Berkeley waited and sent the man off with the thing, all the while calling himself seven kinds of fool. And now he was standing here, with a fistful of flowers for Lady Cassandra, ready to knock on the door and get his own courtship back to rights.

*Rap. Rap. Rap.*

The door swung open. Upton's butler ushered him into the drawing room. Derek presented the flowers, asking the man to deliver them to Lady Cassandra's sickroom.

The butler showed him into the nearest drawing room where Derek paced, waiting for a note of reply. Flowers had been a good idea, hadn't they? Ladies were in favor of flowers, were they not? His mother had always smiled brightly on the few occasions his father had presented her with a bouquet.

Lucy came tripping into the room, a wide smile on her face, intently reading a letter she held in her hands.

She glanced up and jumped. "Der . . . Your Grace?" The letter dropped from her fingers. She quickly bent down to retrieve the sheets of parchment that had scattered across the floor. Derek strode over to assist her.

He picked up one of the pages. Just as he'd suspected, it was the letter he'd written for Berkeley. Hmm. It had made her smile. That was something. Better than flowers?

She'd gathered the rest of the papers and he handed her the other. "Am I interrupting anything?" she asked in a shaky voice he'd never heard from her before.

"No. Not at all. I just sent some flowers up to Lady Cassandra and I was hoping—"

The butler returned just then and presented Derek with a folded crisp white note sitting upon a silver tray. "From Lady Cassandra," the butler intoned.

Derek plucked the note from the tray, unfolded it, and read it while the butler took his leave.

"What does Cass say?" Lucy asked, hugging her letter to her chest and biting her lip in a most fetching display.

"She says the flowers are lovely and she regrets being unable to accompany me today. We'd planned a picnic."

"Oh, yes. That's really too bad." Lucy buried her face back in her letter and turned as if to leave, but Derek's next words stopped her.

"She also says she's asked *you* to keep me company while she is ill."

Lucy froze. She slowly turned around, the hand that held the letter falling to her side. "Yes. Yes. That's right. She did."

He gave her a sidewise smile. "She says that you agreed. Though I must say I find it difficult to believe."

Lucy barely met his eyes. "I'd do anything for Cass."

"Anything like going on a picnic with me?"

Lucy blinked. She pointed at herself with her free hand. "You want *me* to go on the picnic with *you*?"

Derek folded his hands behind his back and braced his booted feet apart. "The food has all been prepared and the basket packed. It would be a shame for it to go to waste."

Lucy nodded. "I am a bit peckish."

He grinned. "So, what do you say?"

She winced a bit as if the words pained her. "Very well, Your Grace. I'll go on a picnic with you."

❧

They assembled their little feast near a garden just south of the Upper Crescent. It was an idyllic scene, with sweeping views of the hillsides beyond town and the sweet smell of summer flowers wafting toward them. Two of the duke's footmen readily rolled out blankets, unpacked the meal, and poured two glasses of sweet red wine before taking themselves off a considerable distance to allow the pair their privacy.

Lucy took a deep breath. After a bit of a rocky start in the drawing room, it was surprisingly not awkward between them today. It was almost as if nothing untoward had happened. Almost. For when she closed her eyes, she pictured Derek on top of her, making her feel things she'd never felt before. She closed her eyes and shook her head. No reason in the world to remember all that. She must act as if that had never happened.

In the end, she'd decided to go with him. A picnic was quite safe and public. There was little chance of them repeating their licentious behavior on a grassy knoll in the middle of town. What harm was there in filling in for Cass today?

"Thank you for agreeing to accompany me." Derek took a sip of wine. He'd leaned back, bracing himself on one wrist. He looked so charming and boyish. She longed to reach out and brush away the bit of dark hair that had fallen across his forehead.

She smiled at his words. He was being nice and accommodating. Most out of character. Why? "Thank you for asking. And I believe that's the most pleasant thing you've ever said to me."

He laughed. "That makes two of us. I think that's the most pleasant thing you've ever said to me."

Lucy busied herself arranging the plates of bread, fruit, and cheese on the blanket in front of them.

Derek cleared his throat. "I couldn't help but notice you were reading a letter earlier, when you came into the drawing room."

A wide smile spread across Lucy's face. "Yes. Yes. I was."

"And the letter pleased you?"

She glanced up at him, wrinkling her nose. What did he care? In fact the letter had been from Lord Berkeley and had been the nicest, sweetest, kindest, funniest, most clever letter she'd ever received. Not too overly solicitous, not too sentimental, not too sweet. It had been exactly what she'd known Lord Berkeley was capable of. He'd told her how much he enjoyed spending time with her and mentioned a variety of topics, all of which kept her thoroughly entertained. Obviously Lord Berkeley was a man of letters, not words. He was the sort who had a penchant for writing. Of course he was. He was an intellectual. Something Derek knew nothing about. "Yes, it did please me."

"Who was it from?"

She smiled at him sweetly. "None of your business."

Derek took another slow sip of wine. "Let me guess. Berkeley?"

She widened her eyes. "How did you—? Oh very well, it was from Lord Berkeley." If Derek was going to be jealous over Christian—ooh, the thought of his given name sent a little thrill through her—then he may as well know the man was quite interested in her. Quite.

"Why can't I picture Berkeley sitting down to write a letter?" Derek said, setting his wine glass aside and leaning forward to pop a grape into his mouth.

Lucy put her hands on her hips. "That just shows how much you know. His letter was beautifully written."

"Beautifully?" he asked, a sardonic expression on his handsome face.

Lucy longed to wipe it off. "Yes, beautifully. He's obviously extremely well educated, not to mention humorous, wise, and witty."

"Witty?" Derek's eyebrows shot up. "Wise *and* witty?"

She nodded. "Yes. Extremely witty."

"I may have to read this letter." He popped another grape into his mouth.

"You most certainly may not." She cut two pieces off the end of the loaf of bread, placing one slice onto a plate for herself and the other on Derek's plate.

His grin was unrepentant. "Careful, Lucy, you don't want your sharp tongue to scare this one off."

Lucy narrowed her eyes on him. "I've been doing an excellent job of keeping my tongue in check around Lord Berkeley, Your Grace. It's *you* I have trouble being cordial to."

"Don't I know it?"

Did he just wink at her?

"I can't help it," Lucy replied. "Some of the things I say . . . I've always been blunt. It's been a curse since birth. Well, since childhood at least."

His intense green eyes narrowed on her. "Why since childhood? What happened?"

"It doesn't matter." She shook her head and reached for a cluster of dark purple grapes.

"I'd like to know," he answered softly.

Something about the tender way he said it made Lucy want to answer him. She pushed a grape into her mouth and chewed and swallowed thoughtfully. "I . . . my brother died when we were children."

A small spark of surprise flashed through his eyes. "I'm sorry," he replied, still looking at her intently. "Is that who you were speaking of, who you'd lost, that day we went riding in Hyde Park?"

Lucy nodded.

"What happened to him?" Derek's voice was solemn.

Lucy looked away. It made her a bit uneasy. For the

first time in her life, she felt as if someone was actually listening to her. Truly listening. The way Derek looked at her, kept his attention focused on her, asked her these difficult questions. No one had ever seemed to truly care before. It was a bit disconcerting.

She took a deep breath. She hadn't shared this story with anyone. Well, Garrett, and Cass, and Jane knew of course, but she hadn't told anyone else. Not ever. "We both got the fever. We were sick for months. Ralph died. I survived."

Derek nodded solemnly. "I'm sorry, Lucy," he murmured again.

Lucy took a sip of her wine. "Yes, well. The wrong child died. At least as far as my parents were concerned."

Derek cursed softly under his breath. His gaze captured hers. "You can't mean that."

She glanced away, unable to meet his eyes. "It's all right. I knew they wanted my brother to live. And believe me, I would have traded places with him if I could have."

"How old were you?" His eyes still watched her intently. He was listening to her answers as if he truly cared.

She swallowed. "Seven."

He reached lightly across the blanket and touched the top of her hand. "That's awfully young to take on such guilt."

She pulled her hand away slowly, self-consciously. "I had no choice."

He watched her again with those intense, knowing eyes. "Were your parents bad to you?"

She smiled a humorless smile. "No. In some ways I wish they would have been. It would have made it easier to bear, I think. Instead they just ignored me. It was as if I didn't exist. As if they had no children after that."

"That's wrong," Derek said softly. "Ignoring a child is the worst sort of cruelty."

Lucy sucked in her breath. For the first time in her life she'd actually had someone say those words to her. She'd felt it in her heart her entire life, that her parents' treatment of her after her brother's death had been wrong, but she'd never had another person, another living being, acknowledge it. It felt good. It finally felt freeing. She gave him a wan smile. "Thank you for that."

"It is. It's wrong. I'm sorry that happened to you. I cannot imagine how difficult your childhood must have been."

She shrugged. "I did what any ignorant child would have and went about trying to get my parents' attention any way I could, by performing acts of bravery and defiance. I tried to be the boy they no longer had."

His brow creased. "How did you do that?"

"I challenged boys to duels. I rode horses astride. I fished. I shot. I even asked my father if I could go to Eton." She nibbled on a bit of cheese.

Derek smothered a smile. "You did not."

She sighed. "I'm afraid I did."

He propped up his knee and rested his wrist atop it. "What did your father say to that?"

"He called the governess and told her to remove me from his study immediately." Lucy took another small bite of cheese.

Derek shook his head. "And so you grew up and developed a penchant for bluntness?"

"Yes. I had few females to learn from really. My mother

completely ignored me, my aunt allowed me to do anything I pleased, and my governess barely paid attention. I was entirely preoccupied with attempting to turn myself into a boy. I became far too blunt."

"How did you become friendly with Lady Cassandra?" He looked genuinely curious.

The question about Cass reminded Lucy why they were there. Derek was not her beau. He was Cass's. And she would do well to remember that. She leaned back, bracing her hands behind her against the soft grass under the blanket, and sighed. "Cass is an angel. She lived at the neighboring estate. I'd ride my horse over and spend time with her. She's the only girl of my age who didn't scorn me and think I was far too crass in my manners and appearance."

He grinned. "How did her mother react to that?"

Lucy snorted softly. "Oh, Cass's mother has never cared a bit for me, I'm afraid. In fact, my original intention in going over to their estate was to attempt to get Owen to play with me."

"Owen?"

"Cass's older brother."

"And did he?"

"No. He was always perfectly nice but Lady Moreland insisted I stay away from him."

"And not her daughter?"

"Cass took one look at me and thought she might help me be more ladylike, I presume, because we did become fast friends. She sees the best in everyone. Especially me. I've always been a mess. Other young ladies' mamas wouldn't even let them consort with me. But Cass has always been loyal to me."

"And you're loyal to her?"

Lucy swallowed. "Forever."

Derek nodded. "I see. That's why you've stood up for her so vehemently when I began coming around?"

Lucy straightened up and traced the edge of the blanket with her fingertip. "Yes. That's why. I love Cass. As I said, I would do anything for her."

He drew his wrist away from his knee. "What about your other friend? Jane, is it?"

Lucy smiled brightly. "Ah, Janie joined our merry band a bit later. She was a societal outcast like me, so we became friends at our debut ball."

Derek raised both brows. "An outcast?"

Lucy sighed. "Yes. It's a little-known fact, but I was escorted out of the queen's chambers when I made my bow."

Derek's eyebrows shot up. "You were?"

"Indeed. I didn't take kindly to the simpering and fawning. I ripped the feathers out of my insanely elaborate coiffure and tossed them on the floor at the queen's feet."

"You did not." His wide smile belied the surprised look on his face.

"Yes. I did. Mama said she refused to have anything more to do with my come-out after that. She went back to the country and left me with Aunt Mary."

"And was Jane escorted from the queen's chambers as well?"

"No. No. Jane did as she was told. Though she later informed me that she thought I'd been brilliant. She's simply much more interested in studying and learning than becoming someone's wife."

"And Lady Cassandra, she accepted both of you the way you are?"

Lucy tossed another bit of cheese into her mouth and nodded. "Unconditionally, that's why we're both devoted to her. Cass could be friends with absolutely anyone. Her connections and manners are impeccable. Everyone adores her. But she chooses to spend her time with the two of us and we love her for that."

"I can understand that," Derek replied. "Loyalty cannot be overvalued."

Lucy glanced away, staring at the rolling hills beyond the town. "That's why you're so set on courting Cass? Because you promised Julian and you're loyal to him?"

He nodded. "Yes. Swift was extremely agitated to think she wouldn't be taken care of. He knew she hadn't yet accepted a suitor."

Lucy expelled her breath. "And Julian never guessed why?"

Derek shrugged. "If he did, he didn't mention it to me. Though Julian is an honorable man. If he's pledged to another, he will make good on that pledge regardless of his feelings for Cassandra."

Lucy nodded. "I suppose that's to be commended, but I think it's awfully sad."

"Why's that?"

"Because what if Julian loves Cass, too? What if they are meant to be together? I've met Cass's cousin Penelope. The girl doesn't have a brain in her head. She's much more interested in fripperies and fashion than Julian. She's more concerned with gathering her trousseau than worrying whom she'll actually be spending the rest of her life with. When she wrote Cass to tell her that Julian was dying, she was devastated, not by news of his impending death, but by the prospect of having to find a new bridegroom."

Derek nodded grimly. "That may be so, but Swift's made his decision."

Lucy crossed her arms over her chest. "And so that's it, decisions cannot be changed?"

"No."

The answer surprised her, but the vehemence in his voice surprised her more. The man put a great deal of stake on never changing one's mind, obviously.

Lucy shrugged. "Well, I, for one, hope Julian lives, returns to England, and marries Cass."

Derek smiled at that. "Why, Lucy, do I detect a bit of a romantic in you?"

She popped a grape into her mouth and smiled. "I cannot help it. I detest stupidity. And it just seems stupid to become engaged to someone whom you don't love or care about merely because your parents believed it would be a good match when you were young."

He pointed a finger in the air. "Ah, but that is how the *ton* works, does it not?"

"Yes. It does. But it ought not. I understand that not all marriages are based on love. But they ought to be based on more than just an old promise and handshake. Especially if Julian and Cass might be truly happy together."

Derek leaned back, bracing both elbows on the blanket. "To your knowledge has Julian ever indicated that he has feelings for Cassandra?"

Lucy studied the blanket. "No, I don't think so."

"Then perhaps you're assuming too much."

She plucked at the grass next to her feet. "Perhaps. Or perhaps I just wish the best for my friend." She shook her head. "At any rate, it hardly matters when it sounds as if Julian won't be returning. My heart is broken for Cass."

A grim nod. "Julian was . . . is a good man."

Lucy nodded solemnly, too. She cleared her throat,

needing to say something to return the conversation to its earlier pleasantness. "Thank you very much for the picnic, Your Grace. It's too bad Cass was ill and you were forced to suffer my company."

He popped a grape into his mouth. "I'm not having such a bad time with you."

## ❧ CHAPTER THIRTY-SEVEN ❧

"Another letter?" Garrett asked, strolling into the break-fast room the next morning. Jane had been nowhere to be found all morning, and Cass was still in her sickbed. Lucy had been eating alone, since Aunt Mary usually took her breakfast much earlier. But this morning Lucy hadn't minded being alone. She'd just received another wonder-ful letter from Lord Berkeley.

"Yes." Lucy nodded happily.

Garrett made his way to the sideboard and loaded ham, eggs, cheese, and toast onto a plate. Then he came to sit next to Lucy. "Ah, young love. It's a wonderful thing."

Lucy slapped at his shoulder. "Stop it. I'm not in love."

"Aren't you?"

"No. I've only barely met him. Though he does seem rather nice. And his letters are"—she sighed—"amazing."

Garrett furrowed his brow. "Never knew Berkeley had it in him, to be honest. He wasn't much of a writer at uni-versity."

"I cannot believe that," Lucy replied, rereading one of her particularly favorite passages. "Just listen to this part—" She opened her mouth to speak, but Garrett dropped his fork and clapped both hands over his ears. "No. No. I cannot listen to a love note written by one of my closest friends to my own cousin. Please do not attempt to subject me to such torture."

Lucy laughed and set the letter aside. "Very well, but suffice it to say he is quite a good writer."

Garrett shrugged. "If you say so. Seems odd that he isn't visiting as much as he's sending letters, however."

Lucy took a sip from her teacup. "Not at all. He's been preoccupied with his cousin's wedding. Besides, between you and me, I believe he expresses himself a bit better in written word."

"Ah, now *that* I do believe." Garrett took healthy bite of eggs.

"It's quite extraordinary, really. When he's here, we barely speak two words to each other. But when he sends these letters, it's as if an entire other world has opened up inside him and he can express who he truly is."

"That's a bit too poetic for me. I'm trying to eat."

Lucy laughed again. "Oh, stop. You're the one who introduced us, remember? I have you to thank for this pleasant acquaintance."

Garrett waggled his eyebrows at her. "Sounds like more than an acquaintance to me. And speaking of acquaintances, I hear you've been spending time with Cassandra's duke lately."

Lucy shrugged and set the letter aside. "Only because Cass can't. But I must say he's been surprisingly pleasant."

Another eyebrow waggle. "Pleasant? That is a surprise."

Lucy took another sip. "Isn't it?"

"Have anything planned for today?" Garrett asked.

"Yes, actually. The duke will be here at half two."

# ❧ CHAPTER THIRTY-EIGHT ❧

"So what did you and Cass have on the agenda for to-day?" Lucy asked with a saucy smile when Derek appeared at the town house that afternoon.

Derek returned her smile and bowed over her hand. "I was hoping to tour the ruins. The bathhouses."

Lucy sat on a settee in the drawing room. As soon as she saw Derek, her plan to get out of the day's activity somehow vanished into ash. What harm did it do, really, for her to spend time with him? He wanted to get to know more about Cass, didn't he? She could help.

Very well. Perhaps the harm it did was that in the last few days while she'd been busily romping with Derek, she hadn't spent any time whatsoever with Lord Berkeley. Oh, the entire thing was so backward and awful. And to make matters worse, soon Lord Berkeley would be returning to London for a bit before retiring to the country for the autumn and winter. She might not see him again for quite a long while. All of these arguments and more raced through Lucy's head. Guilt, it seemed, was her constant companion.

But it didn't keep her from looking up at the handsome duke standing in front of her and saying, "Visit the bathhouses? Now, that is something I'd very much like to do."

He bowed to her gallantly and offered his arm. "I'm assuming Lady Cassandra continues to be waylaid with a cold."

"Yes, poor girl," Lucy replied. More guilt. The truth was she hadn't even checked to see how Cass was doing today. Just assumed—no, hoped—that her friend was still stricken with her cold so that she, awful person she was, might enjoy more time with her beau.

Derek smiled at Lucy. "By all means, then, let's go."

They strolled together out of the drawing room just as Garrett walked past. "Good afternoon." Garrett gave Lucy a raised brow. "Claringdon." He nodded toward the duke.

"Upton." Derek inclined his head in Garrett's direction.

"Here to see Cass, I assume?" Garrett asked.

"Yes, and since she remains ill, Lady Lucy and I have decided to go see the bathhouses together."

To his credit, Garrett's face remained completely blank. "Ah, I see. Enjoy yourselves."

Lucy wrinkled her nose at her cousin but continued through the foyer with Derek.

"Oh, Lucy," Garrett called out when they'd nearly reached the door.

She turned. "Yes?"

"Berkeley says he hopes to have the chance to see you again before he leaves town."

Lucy dropped her gaze to her shoes. Guilt, guilt, and more guilt. "Yes. That would be . . . nice."

Garrett gave her a funny look and strode away.

Derek frowned but helped Lucy retrieve her bonnet and cloak. Then he escorted her out of the town house and assisted her into his carriage. Lucy nearly gasped when she stepped inside. The conveyance was smartly appointed with squabs of deep claret velvet and polished brass fixtures. A carriage fit for a duke. She couldn't help but think that the next time she rode in this carriage it might be as the friend of the Duchess of Claringdon, Cass.

A footman and a groom accompanied them as the coach rumbled over the mud through town to the bathhouses. When they came to a stop in front of the imposing stone structure, Derek helped Lucy to alight from the coach. She tried to ignore the pulse of heat that shot up her arm when he touched her. *This is for Cass*, she reminded herself as he placed his hand at the small of her back to guide her along to the ruins.

They entered the large building. The high gothic arches and stonework made Lucy turn in a circle, examining everything, her mouth a wide O.

"You've never seen this before?" Derek asked, watching her fascination.

"Oh, I've seen it before, more than once," she replied. "But it never fails to amaze me."

For some reason, he smiled at that.

"I've never seen it before." He looked up and turned in a circle, too. "What do you think we should explore first?"

Lucy nearly clapped her hands. "Oh, the pool. The pool."

"What's the pool?"

She gestured with her hand. "Follow me."

Derek followed her down a corridor and through a dank, dark tunnel that smelled like copper. They came out in a cool, shadowed room that had a green pool in the center.

"See." Lucy gestured toward the water.

They made their way over to the edge.

"I would have never known this was here," Derek said. Shadows played off the wall, and the light from the pool made rings around the room. They glowed brightly and then faded depending on the movement of the water.

Lucy took a deep breath. Removing her gloves, she bent down and skimmed her fingers over the surface of the pool. "No one knew it was here for so long. It's amazing to think how long it went undiscovered."

Derek slid his hands into his pockets. "Yes, hundreds of years."

Lucy stood and tilted up her chin to look at him. "Do you have a coin?"

"A coin? Why?"

She smiled. "They say if you toss a coin in this pool, your wish shall come true."

"Do they?" Derek's look could only be described as skeptical.

"Yes. But you cannot tell anyone what you wish for or it may not come true."

He poked his cheek out with his tongue. "You believe that?"

She shrugged. "No use tempting fate."

He pulled a small pouch from an interior pocket of his coat and fished out a coin. He handed it to her. "Here you are, my lady."

"Thank you, kind sir." Lucy took the coin from his hand, trying to ignore the warmth of his bare skin. She squeezed the coin in her fist, closed her eyes, and whispered her wish to herself. *Let everything work out the way it is meant to with Cass and Julian and Derek and Lord Berkeley. Oh, and myself. And Jane and Garrett, too.* Was that too much to wish for? Too late. She tossed the coin in the pool, watching as the little piece of metal slipped beneath the surface. Ripples spread out from the spot where it had vanished.

Lucy turned to Derek. "Now it's your turn," she announced.

"I'll keep my coins, I think." He stuffed the little pouch back into his coat.

Lucy crossed her arms over her middle. "Not a believer, Your Grace?"

"On the contrary, I believe in many things, my lady. For instance, I believe that sound decision-making causes better results than tossing coins into a pool." The way he looked at her made Lucy very aware of the fact that they were alone together in the hushed little room. The footman and the groom had stayed outside with the coach.

She pushed a wayward curl behind her ear, intent upon changing the subject. "Do you believe the waters truly have curative effects?"

Derek smiled. He slipped his hands back into his pockets. "I've no idea, but I cannot think it would hurt to try them. I've heard that people bathe in the hot springs."

Lucy gulped. She nodded. An image flashed through her mind, one of herself in a wet, clingy bit of fabric in the hot water of the springs with Derek, his lips at her neck, his hands on her thighs, his . . .

"The Romans were truly amazing," he said, snapping Lucy from her wayward thoughts. She pressed a hand against her throat and shook her head. "Y . . . yes," she managed to choke out, still actively picturing him without his shirt.

"I studied their battles extensively at university," he added.

Lucy's head snapped to the side to face him. "You attended university?" The words were out of her mouth before she had a chance to examine them. Oh, God. She wanted to kick herself for the rudeness of her question, not to mention the awful tone in which she'd asked it. As if there was no possible way it could be true. She briefly considered jumping into the pool to hide. No. Too idiotic. Plus, it would ruin her clothing. On the other hand, Derek might jump in to save her. And that presented a tempting possibility.

"Does it surprise you that I went to university?" The hint of a smile played upon his distracting lips.

"No. No. No. Of course not." But there was no going back. Her babbling denial was useless.

He arched a brow, telling her without a word that he thought she was protesting a bit too much. "There is much to learn from history books and the armies of the past. I wasn't only trained as a soldier. I studied all the greats, Charlemagne, Hadrian, Genghis Khan."

Lucy stared unblinking into the pool. She nodded slowly. It had been unfair of her, truly unfair, to believe he was merely a brute soldier, not a gentleman. She hadn't known anything about him really. She'd judged him entirely on his status of not having been born into the aristocracy. She swallowed, unable to peel her gaze from the brownish stone of the floor of the bathhouse. The guilt was really beginning to compound today, wasn't it?

"Cass should be here," Lucy blurted out, thinking for some reason that inserting Cass back into the conversation was the right thing to do.

A frown marred his forehead for the barest hint of a second. "Do you think Lady Cassandra would like this?" He gestured to the temple walls, the pool.

"The ruins?" Lucy wrinkled her nose. "Not particularly. Cass is more interested in painting and playing the pianoforte than history or reading. Jane and I are the ones who adore things like this."

"We'll have to bring Jane with us next time then," he said with a smile.

Lucy glanced away. Would there be a next time for them, coming here? That was an odd thought, wasn't it? "I think Jane and Aunt Mary already visited the ruins. Though I'm certain Jane would be eager to return. She always prefers to learn as much as she can about everything."

Derek strode around the room, his boots crunching along the gravel near the pool's edge. "Are she and Upton courting?"

Lucy nearly tripped. Her laughter echoed off the great stone walls. "Garrett and Jane? They can barely tolerate each other. Though I do think much of it is for show. They sort of engage in a merry war of words and have for years. It all began when I brought Jane to the theater with me and she met Garrett for the first time. They both vehemently disagreed about the premise of the play we'd gone to see and it seems they have been continuing the argument ever since."

Derek turned to face her, another smile on his lips. "What was the play?"

"*Much Ado About Nothing.*"

This time his laughter echoed off the walls. "That's ironic."

Lucy smothered her smile. "I suppose it is, isn't it?"

"If they can barely tolerate each other, why did they come to the ruins together?"

Lucy shrugged. "Jane likes to pretend that Garrett needs to be educated in such things, and Garrett likes to tease Jane about being a pedantic bluestocking. It's just their way. They actually enjoy each other's company, I suspect, though neither of them would ever admit it."

"And Cassandra and Julian? You said they've never indicated that they have feelings for each other?"

"Not that I know of. Cass has known Julian since she was a girl. He's distantly related to her cousin. Penelope's parents and Julian's parents have had their betrothal planned for years. Cass had a schoolgirl infatuation with him that she never outgrew. Then Julian went off to the army and she hasn't seen him in . . . probably seven years. She's written to him every day, far more than Penelope ever has."

"Yes, Swift mentioned her letters. They kept him sane, I believe."

Lucy searched Derek's face. "Did Julian ever mention that he had deeper feelings for Cass?"

Derek scuffed at the stone floor with his boot. "I've thought about that a lot over the last few days. I don't remember him indicating anything other than she was the cousin of his soon-to-be betrothed and a good friend to him. If I'd thought he loved her, I never would have promised to marry her."

Lucy glanced away. "Even though he was dying."

"It would have been quite awkward," Derek said.

"But now you feel . . . obligated?"

He nodded.

Lucy swallowed the lump in her throat and twined her fingers together. "Cass has been so worried about him. So frightened. Her worst fears came true when she learned he'd been gravely injured."

Derek braced his foot against a large rock on the side of the pool. "I wish I could have stayed with him. Until"—his voice nearly cracked—"the end."

Lucy nodded solemnly. She walked over to Derek and put her hand on his sleeve. "I'm certain you did everything you could."

He clenched his fist. "The surgeons told me there was nothing I could do, and my orders were to return to London immediately to debrief the War Office about my involvement in the battle."

"Julian must have known you couldn't stay."

Derek's face was grim. He cursed under his breath. "War is hell."

Lucy bit her lip and pulled her hand away from his sleeve. The quiet of the room, the pool, the words they'd just shared. She had to say something probably neither of them wanted to think about. "Derek, when Cass gets better, what shall we do?"

Silently, Derek pulled out the pouch again, extracted a coin, and tossed it into the pool.

Lucy blinked. "What did you wish for?"

"I can't tell you, Lucy, or it might not come true."

# ❧ CHAPTER THIRTY-NINE ❧

The next day, they went riding out into the hillsides surrounding Bath. Two grooms accompanied them, and Derek brought a horse for Lucy. A beautiful little filly with brown and white markings named Delilah.

Lucy stroked the horse's neck and offered her an apple she'd swiped from the kitchens. They hadn't even mentioned Cass. Was it possible Derek was as afraid as Lucy that Cass was recovered? She remained an awful friend. She hadn't even checked on Cass this morning to see how she was feeling.

Lucy had also received another letter from Christian just as clever and charming as the last. But ever since Garrett had mentioned that it was odd that Christian was sending letters more often than he was coming around, she couldn't help but be preoccupied with that thought. Why was it that he sent letters every morning but she hadn't seen him since before she'd received the first one? Why was he so painfully shy and quiet in her company when his letters were so expressive and eloquent?

She shook herself. This was exactly why she'd been on

the shelf for so long. She questioned everything about anyone and, if he was found lacking, chased him away. Sometimes she didn't even wait for a reason to chase him away.
She needed to find a husband eventually. She wanted a
family, children . . . Love? Perhaps that was too much to
ask for, but children would do for a start and a husband
precipitated children. It was time for her to finally begin to
be serious about courtship and finding a willing and worthy gentleman. Meeting Christian had been fortuitous indeed. She had merely to keep from chasing him away.

It was probably best for both of them that Christian
hadn't come around. Less chance for her to stick her foot
solidly in her throat. Besides, she did so enjoy his letters.
What sort of a contrary person was she that she assumed
the worst? She was being courted by a handsome, eligible
viscount who obviously liked her a great deal. Why couldn't
she just accept it and enjoy it?

In the meantime, she was spending time with a handsome, mouthy duke who drove her mad and whom she—
ahem—may or may not have done questionable things
with in the past. Things she couldn't forget, even when she
was reading Christian's letters. Derek's voice snapped her
from her thoughts.

"I thought we'd go for a race." He flashed his famous
devilish grin.

"A race?"

"Yes. Do you race, Miss Upton?"

"Of course I do," she answered with a returning smile.
She was getting quite used to him calling her Miss Upton.
Quite used to it indeed.

"I thought so," he replied. "Any young lady who prided
herself on her boyish pursuits as a child is bound to race."

"Not only do I race, I just might beat you, Your Grace,"
she replied with a laugh.

"No you won't." He winked at her.

Her stomach did that funny little flip it always did when he looked at her that way. And arguing with him about racing was ever so much more enjoyable than arguing with him about Cass's marital aspirations. It was fun, this competition with him. Derek didn't give any quarter, and he didn't back down. When was the last time she'd met a man who treated her this way? Garrett, of course, had always treated her as an equal, but Garrett had known her since she was born. Derek was the first man she'd known who'd ever stood up to her, challenged her, teased her, and did so without the slightest bit of fear that he'd anger her. In fact, he seemed to look forward to angering her. Relished it, actually. And that's what intrigued her about him.

They rode leisurely through town and into the surrounding hillside. There they found a long, clear meadow, the perfect spot for racing.

"Do you require a head start, Miss Upton?" Derek called to her.

Lucy tossed a challenging stare back at him. "It's Lady Lucy, Your Grace, and no, I do not, but if that's your indication that *you* need one, by all means."

He shook his head, the grin still resting on his handsome face. "From that first tree then? To the end of the meadow, near the barn?" He pointed and Lucy turned to look.

She nodded. "Yes. That should give me plenty of time to beat you soundly."

He laughed at that and then they were off. Lucy slapped Delilah's flanks with her crop and leaned low over the horse's head, whispering to the girl to go faster, faster, faster. "I'll give you a bucket of apples if we win,

Delilah," she promised with a giant grin on her face as she maneuvered alongside the duke.

From the moment they'd taken off, Derek hadn't looked back. When Lucy and her horse came galloping alongside, his face registered his chagrin for all of a moment before he leaned farther down over his own horse and slapped his flank with his crop. Apparently, the duke realized he was in for a bit of true competition. His grin was unrepentant.

They raced like that, past the tree, through the meadow, up the hill, and to the top where a small red barn sat, leaning slightly to one side.

Lucy hunkered over the horse, several lengths behind Derek. During a race, it was always in one's best interest to allow one's opponent to believe he would win. But in the last stretch, she slapped Delilah's flank again and the horse took off with a bolt of speed.

Derek's neck snapped up the moment he realized he'd been passed. He leaned low and let out the reins on his gelding. "Yah, yah," he shouted to his horse.

Lucy breathed heavily, laughing. The wind had pulled some of the pins from her hair, and the strands covered her eyes momentarily. She looked back to see Derek's face and wiped at the strands of hair in her eyes.

"No!" she called as Derek's larger, faster mount pulled astride and ahead of her just as they passed the barn.

"I win!" he shouted.

Lucy couldn't stop her laughter. "You cheated!" she breathed, pressing her hand to her belly.

"I did not."

"I know, but I am a very ungraceful loser, Your Grace." She laughed and laughed. "I cannot believe you bested me."

He was laughing, too. As he maneuvered the horse

around to face her, their eyes met. They both were panting and laughing and Lucy self-consciously put her hand to her hair to push the unruly strands back under her bonnet.

"It's been a while since I've had such a close call," he admitted. "Thank you for a most enjoyable ride."

Lucy finished tucking her hair behind her ears and into her hat. She nodded. "Don't worry, Delilah," she whispered to the horse, patting her neck. "I'll get you a bucket of apples yet."

They both walked their horses to a stop and dismounted. When the grooms caught up, Derek motioned for them to take the mounts. The servants grabbed the reins to continue to walk the horses after their hard ride. They trailed off in the opposite direction.

"Would you care to go for a walk?" Derek asked Lucy.

Her stomach did a little somersault. She nodded. "I'd like that."

Derek removed his hat, and they took off down a trail through the meadow past the barn. The wind still whipped through Lucy's hair. She had to hold her bonnet to the top of her head with one gloved hand.

"You're quite an accomplished horsewoman, my lady."

She laughed. "Would you please tell that to my father if ever you should meet? He refuses to believe it still. He won't let me ride astride and refuses to allow me to go on the steeplechases outside the village."

"You cannot go?"

"Oh, I go, all right. Father just doesn't know about it. I'd rather do it with his blessing, of course." She grinned unrepentantly.

Derek grinned back at her. "Why does it not surprise me that you defy your father?"

"It shouldn't surprise anyone who knows me at all,"

she replied. "Least of all Father, yet he continues to be baffled by my behavior."

"I'll tell him how accomplished you are," Derek said.

Lucy nearly stopped short. What was he implying? That he did intend to meet her father one day? The thought made her a little giddy.

Derek led the way over a fallen log. He helped Lucy over it by taking her hand. "Does your father get along with your cousin?"

"Garrett? Oh, they tolerate each other, and Father's resigned to the fact that Garrett will inherit the estate and the title one day, but I wouldn't say they 'get along.'"

Derek nodded. "Yet you're close with your cousin?"

"Garrett loves to tease me and say I'll be an old maid living under his roof forever. And I tease him back and say he'll need me to be his maiden cousin to run his household because he'll never find a lady willing to put up with him."

Derek's face went sober for a moment. "You don't think you'll marry?"

Lucy swallowed. How had the conversation turned to her marriage all of a sudden? She shook her head. "Oh, Cass says she'll help me find a husband. We have an agreement of sorts." She looked away self-consciously. "But truthfully, no. I doubt I'll marry. I've yet to find a man who isn't"—she cleared her throat—"intimidated by me." She needed to change the conversation and change it immediately. It had all become much too serious and much too about her.

"What about Berkeley?" Derek asked, his voice low.

And there was the question Lucy had been dreading. "What about him?"

They walked beneath a willow tree and Lucy pushed her slippered foot against the trunk, hoping against hope that Derek would drop the subject. No such luck.

"I thought you two were—"

"Enough about me," she said, shaking her head. "Tell me, how did you become a lieutenant general? Especially at such a young age?"

He smiled at that. "Am I so young? Sometimes I feel as if I'm one hundred years old."

"You certainly don't look one hundred." Now, why had she gone and said that? She blushed and looked away. Oh perfect. Now she *was* a blusher. He'd turned her into a blusher.

He grinned at that. "Why, thank you, Miss Upton."

She brushed at his sleeve in a playful manner before gulping and snatching her hand away. His arm was solidly muscled. A vision of the muscled abdomen she'd seen the night he climbed up to her window flashed before her eyes. She shook her head. "I'm serious. How did you go about becoming a lieutenant general?"

He scrubbed a hand across his face and looked off into the meadow as if contemplating the matter for a moment. "I was raised in a military family."

She picked her way along the base of the tree, holding up her pale yellow skirts. "You were?"

"Yes, my father was a solider. He fought in the revolution."

She glanced up at him, eyes wide. "Was he a general?"

He pushed his hands into his pockets and shook his head. "No, actually. He never advanced far."

"But you did. Quite far."

He leaned his head back, looking up into the branches of the tree. "I was trained for the military from the time I was a babe. I began military drills when I was three years old."

Lucy stopped and let her skirts drop. She turned to face him. "Surely you're jesting."

"No. I'm afraid I'm not." He smiled at her, and her heart skipped a beat.

"Why so young?" She began walking, much safer than looking directly at him.

He stared off across the meadow again with a faraway look in his eye. "My father intended me to be a great military leader since the day I was born. He ensured that I was prepared for it."

"Is it what you wanted?"

He kicked at a tuft of grass with his boot. "It's all I know, Lucy."

The tenderness with which he said her name made her breath catch in her throat. "You had no choice?"

He shrugged. "We were not of the privileged class. I had few options open to me. The army seemed as good a choice as any."

She bit her lip. "Well, you're obviously quite good at it."

Another shrug. "When you train for something your entire life, it's easy to be good at it."

"I can't believe that. Surely you also have a natural talent for it."

"I suppose I do."

"Do you have any brothers or sisters?"

"Two brothers," he said.

"Are they also in the military?"

"You could say that."

Lucy wrinkled her nose at that answer but let it pass.

"It must have been difficult for your mother to see all of her children go to war."

"It has been." Derek held back the long branches of the willow tree, and Lucy preceded him into the meadow where they resumed their stroll.

Lucy twined her fingers together and watched her feet. "Your father must be exceedingly proud of you."

A wan smile passed his lips. "My father is dead."

Lucy pressed a hand to her throat. "Oh, I'm so sorry."

"It's all right. It's been several years. He knew I'd been promoted. But he never knew I was a lieutenant general, or a duke," Derek finished with a humorless laugh.

Lucy stopped and faced him. "He'd be proud of you, Derek. I'm certain of it."

A look passed between them. One that was intense and real.

Derek glanced away. "No, he'd say he expected no less."

Lucy swallowed the lump that had formed in her throat. "He sounds as if he was quite demanding."

He expelled his breath. "You don't know the half of it."

"More than demanding?" she ventured.

"My father's favorite word was *decisive*. He ensured I was decisive."

*The Duke of Decisive.* The memory of the moniker shot through her mind. She furrowed her brow. "What do you mean?"

He pulled on his lapels, looked down his nose at her, and affected a deeper voice. "A man is decisive, always."

Lucy watched him carefully, suddenly fascinated by the idea that a father would demand that his son be decisive. If Ralph had lived, would her father have demanded that of him? "What did he do? To ensure you were decisive?"

Derek shook his head. "It doesn't matter. Suffice it to say, it worked."

She stopped, put her hand on his sleeve, and looked him in the eye. "I'd truly like to know."

He blew a deep breath through his nostrils and, taking off his hat, ran his hand through his hair. "Very well. But don't say I didn't warn you."

She nodded and swallowed again.

Derek leaned his shoulder against another tree and took a long, deep breath. "When I was six years old, my father taught me how to swim. After I got the right of it, he brought out two of my favorite things."

Lucy eyed him carefully. "What things?"

"One was my favorite toy. A tin soldier. I'd had it as long as I could remember. I took it everywhere with me."

Lucy put her hand to her throat. A chill suddenly came over her. "What was the other thing?"

"My eight-week-old puppy."

Lucy gasped. "What did he do?"

Derek shook his head. Looking down at his boots, he scuffed the tip of one of them in the dirt. "Before I knew what he intended, he tossed both of them in the creek several yards apart."

Lucy grasped her throat. "No."

"He threw them in opposite directions at the same time. Choose," he shouted. "Decide! Now!"

"What did you do?" Lucy bit the back of her knuckles.

"I did the only thing I could. I picked the puppy. I dove in the creek and saved him from drowning."

Lucy's throat clogged with tears. "And your toy soldier?"

"It sank. I never saw it again. Though I used to dive in that spot looking for it. I never found it."

Lucy clenched her fist. "What an awful man."

Derek shrugged. "Perhaps, but he taught me the value of being decisive. There were other drills, other tests, but none as memorable as that one. I've never hesitated a moment since, despite my father's unorthodox method."

Lucy swallowed. That was why Derek was so bent on having Cass. He'd already decided. It all made sense.

She stepped toward him. They were close, barely a hairbreath apart. "The Duke of Decisive," she said quietly.

He nodded. "Yes. That's exactly right."

Lucy looked up at him and blinked. He was so handsome, so handsome and strong. Her heart wrenched at the thought of a little boy who had to choose between his favorite toy and his pet.

Derek reached down and tugged on one of the black curls that had managed to wrangle itself free from her bonnet. "Do you know how pretty you are?"

She inhaled sharply but couldn't take her eyes off his face. "I'm not pretty. Cass is pretty."

"You are. So pretty." He ran the back of his hand lightly over her cheekbone.

Lucy shuddered.

"And your eyes are so . . ."

"Strange?" she finished for him.

"I was going to say unusual. Mysterious."

She smiled lightly. "I suppose those are nicer words for it. Someone once told my mother I was a witch."

"That's preposterous." Derek's jaw clenched. "They said that in front of you?"

"No, but Mother told me."

He cursed under his breath. "Why would she do that?"

"It was always clear that Mother and Father blamed me for . . . not being a boy."

Derek didn't say a word. He just rubbed his knuckle along her cheek again and traced the outline of her ear with his rough thumb. "I'm glad you're not a boy."

Lucy drew in a deep breath.

He leaned down, toward her. She held her breath. He was going to kiss her. She wanted him to. She wanted him to badly. She tilted her head back and closed her eyes.

"Damn it, Lucy. I'm supposed to be decisive in everything."

She opened her eyes and stared at him, blinking.

"That's why it's so difficult for me to know how much I want you."

Lucy glanced down at the soft green grass. Tears sprang unbidden to her eyes. She'd been mistaken. He wasn't going to kiss her.

She turned away. That was for the best.

## ❧ CHAPTER FORTY ❧

Christian sat on the settee across from Lucy, his back ramrod-straight. He sipped his tea and didn't say a word. Had not said a word, in fact, the entire time they'd been visiting. It was terribly disappointing. After all of his lovely letters and the ones she'd written back, Lucy had been certain things would be different between them now. How could they not? After all the witticisms they'd exchanged, the stories, the opinions, the jests.

She eyed him carefully, expecting that at any moment he would open up and become the clever man she knew from the letters. It was just a matter of time, wasn't it? Perhaps he needed more tea. Unlike Derek, Christian drank tea. In large quantities.

He certainly was handsome. That much she'd give him. A more beautiful type of handsome than Derek. Derek was all rugged and muscled where Christian looked more like an archangel carved into stone. Oh, why was she comparing him to Derek? Why was she even *thinking* about Derek?

Derek. Derek hadn't kissed her yesterday. It was for

the best. And if she just kept repeating that to herself, perhaps she'd eventually believe it. Cass was sure to be better any day now. She and Derek would finally begin their courtship. Lucy should be concentrating on her own courtship . . . with Christian. She glanced at Christian. He was still merely smiling at her from behind his empty teacup.

That was it. If he wasn't going to begin the conversation, she would. She cleared her throat. "I found it so interesting, what you said about the state of the East India Company in your last letter. I've often had the same thought myself, but of course, with you being privy to the House of Lords, you must know much more about it than I."

A fleeting look of terror flickered in his eyes before he resumed the study of his teacup. "Y . . . yes," was all he said.

Lucy furrowed her brow. He certainly wasn't making this easy for her. "What do you think the lord chancellor's next decision will be? In regard to the company?" She blinked at him inquiringly.

Christian shakily set his cup on the side table next to him and pulled a handkerchief from the pocket of his waistcoat. He wiped his forehead and let out a deep breath. "I . . . I don't know."

Lucy frowned. She took another sip of tea. He certainly seemed nervous. Oh, perhaps he wasn't in the mood to talk about Parliament and the East India Company. It could be rather boring, couldn't it? That suited her just fine. She actually had another goal today.

She wanted Christian to kiss her.

Frankly, she'd only ever kissed Derek Hunt before. Well, aside from a few overly handsy young men who'd barely been able to locate her lips, let alone use their tongue to any advantage, when she'd first made her debut.

No. Derek was the only one who'd ever truly kissed her, and she couldn't allow that to remain the case. If she and Christian were to have a proper courtship, she might as well get the kissing bit out of the way and erase the duke from her memory altogether. The sooner the better.

She set her tea aside, stood, and moved over to the settee where she boldly plopped down right next to Christian. They were not touching but were barely a pace away from each other. If Cass came in she'd probably scream. If Jane came in she'd probably clap.

"What would you like to discuss, my lord?" She turned her head to face him and leaned in a bit. For convenience's sake.

Christian rubbed his hands down the legs of his breeches and blew out a deep breath. He would not look at her. Why not? "I . . . I d . . . don't kn . . . know."

There was that phrase again. Not particularly varied in his responses, was he? If she didn't know better, she'd think he might have trouble speaking. He'd certainly stumbled over the words.

She inched a bit closer. He twisted his handkerchief and wiped at his profusely sweating brow. "Is . . . is . . . is it h . . . hot in h . . . here?"

It was, but so what? She was about to kiss him. Did she need to tell him as much?

"W . . . would y . . . you l . . . like to go f . . . for a w . . . walk?" He pressed the handkerchief against his upper lip this time.

Lucy looked up at the ceiling and bit her lip. Very well. Apparently she *was* going to have to tell him as much. She leaned even closer toward him and whispered, "I was hoping you would kiss me."

A look of supreme relief crossed Christian's face and

he let out a big sigh. "Oh, I th . . . thought y . . . you w . . . wanted to talk."

Lucy barely had a moment to contemplate that odd statement before he pulled her into his arms. His mouth came crushing down on hers. Just like Derek, the kiss was bold. Just like Derek, he used his tongue. And just like Derek, he did, indeed, know what he was doing. Christian did all the right things actually, every single one. And that's why Lucy was so completely baffled when, moments later, when he released her, she realized that she felt absolutely . . . nothing. She might as well have been kissing a statue.

Blast it. This was not good. It was not good at all.

# ❧ CHAPTER FORTY-ONE ❧

Lucy rubbed her clammy palms down her skirts and practiced her speech in her head for the tenth time. It was now or never. "Cass, there's something I must tell you."

Cass lay snuggled in her bed, her nose pink, her handkerchief clutched in her hand. She looked up at her friend and nodded solemnly. "And there's something I must tell you, Lucy."

Lucy shook her head. "Please let me go first." She'd been planning this all morning. She had to tell Cass what had happened between her and Derek. It was time. The unholy guilt nagged at her, rode her, tortured her. She must tell Cass the truth. Then Cass would understand why she could no longer be her stand-in while she was ill. Lucy mustn't see Derek again. It was for the best. For all of them. Cass would understand, wouldn't she? Or would Cass be angry? She couldn't imagine Cass, pure, sweet, friendly Cass, yelling at her. The image just would not render itself in Lucy's mind. But she supposed there was a first time for everything and regardless of the consequences, Lucy had to tell her friend the truth. Today. Now.

Cass nodded. "All right, Lucy. You go first."

Lucy swallowed the lump in her throat and paced in front of Cass's bed. "It's about Derek."

"What I wanted to say is about Derek, too," Cass answered, sneezing daintily into the handkerchief.

Lucy stopped pacing and furrowed her brow. "What about him?"

Cass leaned back against her pillows. "Well, not Derek specifically, but what Julian said about him."

Lucy searched Cass's face. Her entire speech had flown from her mind. Julian said something about Derek? How was that possible? "What do you mean?"

"Oh, Lucy," Cass said, a sad smile on her face. "I received a letter from Julian this morning. Probably his last." She pulled the tearstained sheets of paper from underneath her coverlet and clutched them to her chest.

Lucy's eyes went wide. She gestured to the letter. "When did you get that?"

"This morning. He's still alive Lucy. He's alive." A shadow fell over her face. "At least for now."

Lucy leaned forward to look at the letter. "What did he say?"

Cass's voice was so soft Lucy could barely hear it. "He said good-bye to me."

Lucy bit the back of her hand, tears welling in her eyes and running down her cheeks. "No, Cass."

Cass swallowed hard. Lucy could tell she was fighting a losing battle to keep from sobbing. "But that wasn't all," she added.

Lucy grasped her friend's hand. "What else?"

"He told me," she swallowed, "he told me to marry Derek."

Lucy's heart clenched. She squeezed her eyes closed. "He . . . he did?"

Cass nodded. "Yes. He says Derek will be good to me and he's a fine man. He said I could do no better.

"He asked me to promise him that I'll marry Derek."

Lucy pressed her hand to her belly to still the roiling there. She was going to vomit. She was certain of it. She took a deep breath. "What about the letter you wrote to him? Did Julian mention it?"

Cass glanced down and scraped at the coverlet with her fingernail. "No."

Lucy furrowed her brow. "I don't understand. He just ignored it?"

The tears started down Cass's cheeks then. "Does it matter? He's dying and he says he's asked Derek to take care of me. Oh, Lucy, I'm so confused. I don't know what to do."

Lucy couldn't breathe. She braced her hands against her knees and concentrated on moving air in and out of her lungs. "Julian is right. Derek will take excellent care of you. You must marry him."

## ❧ CHAPTER FORTY-TWO ❧

This time Lucy didn't take a footman with her. It was wrong and she could ruin her reputation if she was found out but she didn't care. She pulled on her bonnet and her gloves, but it was too warm for a pelisse. She nearly raced through the streets to Derek's house. When she got there she stood waiting, holding her breath, all the interminable minutes it took for the butler to open the door. Haughty she called him secretly in her head. His actual name was Hughes.

Haughty Hughes escorted her into the blue drawing room and informed her that His Grace would join her momentarily. He'd already raised a brow when he'd realized she was alone but Lucy was beyond caring.

She paced the room, replaying over and over again in her mind exactly what she would say when Derek entered the room.

She did not have long to wait.

The door opened and Derek strolled in, looking as handsome as ever. He made her knees weak.

The moment he saw her, he frowned. "Lucy? What's

wrong?" Could he tell? Could he guess by the way she trembled a bit and her shoulders shook? She had to get this over with quickly.

She turned, standing with her back to him, tears filling her eyes. Tears she didn't want him to see. "I've come to . . ."

She heard him step closer.

She squared her shoulders, forcing the words from her lips. "Cass received a letter from Julian this morning."

"Julian? He's still alive." Derek expelled his breath. His voice was heavy with relief. "Any word on his condition?"

Lucy took another deep breath. The deep breaths were helping—or so she told herself. "I don't think he's improved. But that's not what the letter was about."

Derek stood to her right. She saw him from the corner of her eye. She smelled his wonderfully familiar scent, a mixture of soap and spice.

"What did it say?" he asked.

She swallowed and braced her hand against the mantelpiece in front of her. "Julian said good-bye to Cass in the letter. He said good-bye and he told Cass to marry you. He said you'd take care of her."

Derek swore under his breath.

"He asked Cass to promise him that she would marry you," Lucy finished, nearly gasping for breath now.

Derek swore again. "What did Lady Cassandra say?"

"She's confused. She doesn't know what to do."

"Understandable," Derek answered. He paced away from Lucy. Running a hand through his hair, he cursed again. "This is all my damn fault."

"Derek, I . . ." Her voice trailed off. Oh, how was she ever going to say this to him?

He swung around, took two steps toward her, grabbed

her shoulders, and spun her to face him. "What is it, Lucy? What's wrong?"

She lifted her chin and stared him in the eye. "I told Cass she must marry you."

❧

After Lucy left, Derek nearly plowed his fist through the bloody wall. At the moment he wished he had a Frenchman to beat into a senseless pulp. Run through with a bayonet. Shoot through the eyes from fifty paces away.

This was torture, that's what it was. He was tortured by his promise to Swift. He'd squeezed his dying friend's shoulder on the battlefield and promised, sworn, that he would come back and marry Cassandra, if she'd have him. And it seemed she would . . . now. He'd been contemplating going back on his word if Julian lived. But now. Now it was clear. Swift would not be returning. What sort of a man would Derek be if he broke that promise after all? Especially now that Swift had written to Cassandra and told her that Derek had promised to marry her? Would he truly let his friend go to his grave not knowing that the girl who had secretly loved him for years wasn't well taken care of? Derek couldn't live with himself if he did that.

But then there was Lucy. Lucy who drove him mad. Lucy who he couldn't keep his hands off. Lucy who stoked in him the kind of passion he'd never found in the arms of another woman. Lucy was his equal, his match. That's why he was so inexorably drawn to her. Lady Cassandra would be a willing and obedient wife. She would give him peace and understanding. But Lucy would keep him on his toes for eternity, make him crazy and make him mad with lust, too. And now that he'd touched her, felt her silken softness, he couldn't forget. Couldn't turn back. What would he do? Pretend forever that nothing had ever happened between them? Be in the company of his wife's closest friend for the rest of his life and act as if he didn't want her with every bit of himself? Was that even possible? If he married Cassandra he would never be unfaithful to her. He had too much honor for that. And he knew Lucy would never betray her friend, either, but now, now while everything was gray and undecided, it was pure torture.

He'd received another short letter from Collin this week, only informing him that nothing had changed in regards to Swifdon and Rafe. Collin and Adam were on their way back to London. That was all.

And all Derek could do was write a lot of impotent letters from Bath to the War Office, to his mother, and to Lucy pretending to be blasted Berkeley. He bloody well had to stop writing those damn letters for Berkeley. It had been amusing at first. A harmless game. Or so Derek had thought, until he'd realized the harm being done was to himself. Sitting there each day, writing to Lucy, expressing his feelings. At some point, early on, he'd realized that he was writing to her as himself, not Berkeley. He didn't give a damn about Berkeley. In those letters, he'd told Lucy everything he'd ever wanted to say to her. And he'd meant every last word.

They'd worked too, damn it. Berkeley had come sauntering over yesterday to inform him that the letters had earned him a kiss. Derek had wanted to toss him out of his study, but instead he sat there and listened to the torturous account of how Lucy had told the viscount how much she cherished his letters and then proceeded to kiss him. And wasn't Berkeley the scoundrel for telling him? Though in his defense no doubt Berkeley no longer knew where to draw the boundaries with a man who was secretly writing love letters to the woman he was pretending to court.

Derek slammed his fist onto the top of the desk with such force the papers and quills and inkpot bounced. God damn it. What in the bloody hell was he going to do? How would he ever get himself out of this unholy mess?

Undecided. Indecisive. His father's taunting voice echoed in his skull. There was absolutely nothing worse in the world of men than to be indecisive. His father had taught him that from a young age. He'd taught him that well. And Derek had learned the lesson. At a price. He'd grown into a man who was never indecisive. On the battlefield, leading men, in anything in his life. But now, blindly staring at the wall, thinking about Lucy and Cassandra and his promise to his closest friend, he'd never been more indecisive in his life.

And he detested himself for it.

# ❧ CHAPTER FORTY-THREE ❧

There she was. Finally! Jane sat lounging on a stone bench in the garden behind Garrett's house reading a book, of course, and unconsciously twisting a brown curl around her finger.

"Do you have a moment, or perhaps an hour, to talk?" Lucy asked, scooting onto the bench beside her.

Jane looked up and promptly snapped shut her book. "Of course, Luce. I'm sorry we haven't had the opportunity before now. What's wrong?" She pushed up her spectacles.

"It's me, and Cass, and Derek." Lucy dropped her face into her hands. "Oh, Jane. I've gone and made a mess of everything."

Jane pushed her book aside on the bench and put her arm around Lucy. "Don't worry. We'll sort it out. Tell me what's happened."

"As you know, at first I detested the Duke of Claringdon," she cleared her throat, "Derek . . ."

Jane arched a brow. "Yes, and I noticed you're calling him Derek now."

"Oh, that's not the half of it. Let me finish."

"By all means."

"At first I detested him, then he kissed me. Then I detested him more, then he kissed me again, ahem, among other things. And now, since Cass has been ill, we've been spending time together and I . . . I . . . I think I may have feelings for him."

Jane, being Jane, didn't look particularly shocked. "Let's be clear: When you say, 'Ahem, other things,' do you mean the types of things that might necessitate an immediate wedding?"

Lucy looked up into the tree branches hovering above them wishing she could somehow turn into a bird and fly far away. "Not exactly. But let's just say it's nothing I'd want to explain in detail to my mother, either."

Jane nodded sympathetically. "Few things are, dear. Few things are."

"Oh, Janie, what am I going to do?" Lucy let her face drop into her hands again.

Jane tapped her fingertips along the edge of the bench. "I must tell you the truth, Luce. It is a pickle. An astonishing pickle, to be sure. But it's not insurmountable. You know, Lucy, Cass isn't particularly interested in the duke, in fact, she's been acting as if—"

Lucy winced. "Oh, wait. There's more."

Jane's eyebrows shot up. "More?"

"Yes." Lucy nodded. "Cass has decided to give Derek a chance, and today she received a letter from Julian saying good-bye and telling her to marry him."

"Marry Julian?"

"No, marry Derek."

"What?"

"Exactly!" Lucy blew out a long breath. "Julian asked Cass to promise him that she would marry Derek."

"Ooooh," Jane said. "And what about Lord Berkeley? You haven't even mentioned him."

"Oh, I kissed him, too."

"What?"

"That's right."

"How was it?"

"It was . . . nice," Lucy answered glumly. "Oh, Janie. Tell me there's some way out of this. Tell me there's something I can do to make this right."

Jane stood up and paced in front of the bench. "First of all, what's the duke doing kissing you if he's supposed to be courting Cass?"

Lucy nodded. "Yes, there is that to consider. The first time it was quite unexpected and we both agreed never to speak of it again. The second time was a . . ." Oh, she *knew* she was flushed bright red. "A bit more deliberate and bit more involved and I—"

Jane covered her ears with both hands. "Please spare me the details."

"Don't worry. I wasn't going to tell you *that*. It's just that it's been since Cass has taken ill and he hasn't seen her since. I think he's as confused about what to do as I am."

Jane pulled her hands away from her ears. "It does sound like a mess. Have you told Garrett?"

"I can't tell Garrett. I kissed the man! And I . . . did other things."

Jane nodded. "I understand. He's your cousin." She resumed her pacing. "What is it that you *want* to do?"

Lucy blinked. "I don't understand."

Jane laughed. "It's a simple question, Lucy. What do you want?"

"What does that matter? Cass and Derek are meant to be married."

Jane stopped pacing and faced her, her hands on her

hips. "That doesn't answer my question," she replied in a singsong voice.

Lucy twisted her hands together. "I can't even think about being with Derek. It feels like a betrayal of Cass. I'm the worst friend in the world for what I've already done."

"No, you're not. You're merely human, and this entire situation has been complicated to say the least. Cass isn't certain she cares for the duke. You cannot be blamed for being confused as well. Though I must say it complicates things even more that he kissed you. More than once. And, ahem, did other things."

Lucy slapped her palm onto her forehead. "Oh, Jane, what am I to do?"

"You're quite certain you think nothing about Lord Berkeley other than he's . . . nice?"

Lucy sighed and nodded. "Yes. He wrote me these wondrous letters but when we're together, we have nothing to talk about. It's quite awkward. I think I intimidate him."

"And the kissing?"

Lucy squeezed her eyes shut. "All I could think about was Derek when I was kissing Christian."

"Oh, that's telling." Jane leaned down and squeezed Lucy's shoulder. "Let me share some advice that someone quite wise once shared with me."

Lucy glanced up and gave her a hopeful look. "Yes?"

Jane plopped back down onto the bench next to her and grasped her hand. "You can never go wrong if you're honest and follow your heart."

Lucy wrinkled her nose. "Wollstonecraft?"

Jane gave her an exasperated look. "No, silly, *you*."

"Me?" Lucy blinked.

"Yes. You're always saying that to Cass about Julian. You've said it for years."

"I have?"

"You don't remember?"

Lucy shook her head. "Oh, why is it so much easier to offer others counsel than to heed it myself?"

Jane laughed at that. "Now, there's a good question."

Lucy took a deep breath. "Very well. I think I know what I must do."

"What?" Jane asked, leaning forward on the bench toward Lucy.

"I'll tell you as soon as I have it all settled." Lucy stood, scooped up Jane's book, and handed it back to her.

Jane plunked her free hand on her hip. "Not fair. I give you this wonderful advice and you won't tell me what you're planning to do?"

"I thought it was my advice," Lucy said with a laugh.

"That's hardly the point." Jane pushed her nose in the air and opened her book again.

"Thank you, Jane, for everything."

"You're quite welcome. Now run off and do whatever it is you're going to do, so that you may inform me of what it is that much sooner." She smiled at her friend.

Lucy raced out of the garden, into the house, and up to her bedchamber. She hurried over to her writing desk, pulled out a quill and a piece of parchment, and quickly scribbled a note. She sanded it, sealed it, and rang for a footman to deliver it to Derek's address.

She could only hope he would heed its contents.

## ❧ CHAPTER FORTY-FOUR ❧

Lucy glanced both ways to ensure she wouldn't be seen before she ducked under the white trellis and entered the secluded garden near the Upper Crescent. The intimate space smelled like roses and freshly cut grass. She pressed her hand against her middle and let out her pent-up breath. She was alone. Derek had not yet arrived. Perhaps he would not come. Her letter had begged him to meet her here at two o'clock. It was a bit past the hour already. Perhaps he hadn't been home to receive her missive. Would that be a good thing or a bad one?

She paced back and forth across the grass, biting the tip of one finger and replaying the whole of the last few days in her mind. She had to make things right. Had to. Janie had told her to follow her heart, but as soon as she'd heard her own advice she'd realized the truth. Some things were more important than following your heart. In fact, many things were. Things like friendships and honor and doing the right thing. This certainly was. Ensuring that her friend made the right match. That was the right thing to do. She was certain of it. Blast her stupid heart for being foolish and complicating things. But she was about to rectify that.

"Good afternoon," a deep male voice intoned.

Lucy swung around.

Derek stood in the shade near the clethra bush, wearing a light gray coat, black trousers, and black boots with a starkly white cravat. He looked like a dream as usual.

She swallowed. "Thank you for coming."

"How could I resist such an assignation? 'Meet me in the secluded garden'?" The hint of a smile touched his lips. He moved toward her.

She tentatively returned his smile. "I . . . I wanted us to have privacy."

He nodded, his face taking on a serious hardness. "I'm glad you wrote, Lucy. There's something I want to say to you."

She released her breath slowly. "I think I should tell you what I came to say first."

"No, let me."

She pressed her lips together, unable to keep from smiling at that. It was always like this between the two of them. Both so stubborn. "Very well."

Derek clasped his hands behind his back and squared his shoulders. "I intend to write to Julian, today, and tell him I cannot marry Cassandra."

A little gasp escaped Lucy's lips. She raced over to him and splayed her hands wide. "Derek, think what you're saying. You can't do that."

"I can and I will." He scrubbed a hand across his face.

Lucy lifted her chin and looked up into his green eyes. They were bright from the reflection of the grass that surrounded them. "But you promised him. You promised Cass."

He turned on his heel. "That was before. Everything's changed now."

Lucy wildly shook her head. "No. I can't let you do it."

"You're not *letting* me do anything."

She dropped her hands and paced away from him, desperately trying to think of something to say that would convince him. "Think about this, Derek. Julian may be dead already for all you know. The letter may never reach him."

Derek nodded grimly. "That's a chance I must take."

Lucy strode to the opening of the clearing, frantically biting her knuckle. "No. This is wrong. I won't let you do it. I won't be with you. I won't betray my friend that way. And you won't betray yours. That's what I came to tell you. We must stop this. Forget anything ever happened between us. We're going back to London tomorrow, all of us. This is the end."

Derek tried to follow her but she backed away. "Damn it, Lucy. You're being unreasonable. Cassandra and Swift, if he lives, will understand this."

Lucy couldn't stop shaking her head. It was as if the entire thing were a bad dream. If she shook her head hard enough, perhaps she would wake up from it. "But who will Cass marry? She doesn't have Julian and she won't have you."

"There are other men," Derek said simply.

Lucy paced again. "But you know as well as I do that Cass needs someone to take care of her. Someone who'll cherish her, treat her well. Julian chose you for her. That means everything to Cass."

Derek's chin dropped to his chest. "I can't do it, Lucy."

"You must," she nearly shouted.

"I won't," he nearly shouted back.

Lucy's entire body shook with grief, rage, confusion. She squeezed her hands together tightly. How could she get through to him? How could she make him understand? She lowered her voice and spoke softly. "If you make that decision, so be it. But you won't have me."

Derek clenched his fist and pressed it against the bridge of his nose. "Think about it yourself, Lucy. How will it be, me married to Cassandra? Having to see you regularly? It will be torturous. Or do you intend to forsake your friendship with her for the sake of her marriage?"

Lucy squeezed her eyes shut. She would not cry. She *would* not. "We can do it. Be friends. Pretend as if nothing ever happened. And if it's too difficult, then yes, I'll leave you both alone. But I won't be a part of ruining Cass's life and chance at happiness."

"I'm telling you that I cannot do it. I cannot marry Cassandra and remain your friend."

Lucy's shoulders slumped. "So be it."

"What does that mean?"

"We'll never see each other again."

Derek turned on his heel, a savage look in his eye. "Is this about Berkeley, God damn it?"

"What? No!"

A muscle ticked in Derek's jaw. "Blast it, Lucy. Don't do this."

Lucy ran from the clearing. She stopped at the trellis that led outside and turned back to face him, desperately struggling to hold back her tears. She tilted her head to the sky. "It's the only way. Derek, I refuse to see you again. Ever. Do the right thing, marry Cass."

## ❧ CHAPTER FORTY-FIVE ❧

Derek had been back in London for exactly twenty-four hours before his brothers arrived. He'd barely had time to contemplate the mess he'd left with Lucy and Cassandra in Bath. Lucy was scared. She was scared and she was under the mistaken impression that she was doing the right thing. But by God, if Derek had an inkling that it was really because of Berkeley, he'd hunt the viscount down and—

"The Misters Hunt," Hughes announced, snapping Derek from his thoughts. Derek glanced up to see Collin following a bedraggled Adam through the door to the study. The two men fell into a heap on the sofa.

Derek crossed over to the sideboard to pour them both stiff drinks. "You must be exhausted I'm having Hughes make up rooms for you immediately. You'll stay with me until you're rested."

"We have an appointment at the War Office," Collin said.

Derek splashed liberal amounts of brandy into two

glasses. "No. You'll wait until tomorrow. They'll understand."

Adam was silent. Derek turned, a glass in each hand, and ran a watchful eye over his youngest brother. The remnants of a black eye and bruising elsewhere upon his face bespoke the torment he'd no doubt endured. Their mother would be coming as soon as she heard her boys were safe. Derek could only hope Adam healed a bit more quickly so she wouldn't have to know what he'd suffered.

Adam must have known what he was thinking because his split lip cracked into a smile and he said, "Believe me, the broken ribs are much more painful than the blow to my ego resulting from the damage to my face."

Derek strode over to stand in front of the sofa. He handed each man a drink. Crossing his booted feet at the ankles, Derek leaned back against a solid oak table and braced his hands behind him. "Adam—"

Adam took a long swig from his glass, scrubbed a hand through his hair, dropped his head back against the sofa, and closed his eyes. "Don't say it, Derek."

Derek arched a brow. "I find it interesting that you know what I was about to say when I don't."

Collin smiled at that and took a long drink.

Adam glanced up at Derek. "You're going to say I shouldn't have been there. Put myself in danger. Put the mission in danger. But I—"

"You're damn right you shouldn't have been there," Derek replied.

"Blast it. They needed me." Adam groaned when his movement jostled his midsection. The broken ribs were still healing, apparently.

Derek uncrossed his ankles, stood up straight, and folded his arms tightly across his chest. "Why don't we begin with exactly what happened?"

Collin shifted in his own seat and watched his younger brother, too.

Adam took a deep breath. "We made camp outside Charleroi. We each took turns serving as lookout."

"Whose turn was it?" Derek asked.

Adam's eyes narrowed. "You think it was mine, don't you?"

"I didn't say that," Derek answered.

"It was Swifdon's actually. He must have fallen asleep. I don't know. All I do know is that I woke up with a pistol to my head." Adam absently rubbed his jaw.

"And Swifdon and Rafe?" Derek asked.

"They tied our hands behind our backs and made us march."

"Let me guess. They soon found out that you knew nothing and Swifdon and Rafe were the two they wanted to interrogate, didn't they?"

Adam took another long drink. "Damn it, Derek. Don't be smug."

"Is that what happened?" Derek demanded.

"Let him finish," Collin interjected.

Derek nodded tersely.

"They took Swifdon and Rafe. They interrogated them for hours, days. Once when they'd thrown Rafe back in the tent with me, he told me to run if I had the opportunity."

Derek swallowed.

"I told him they'd kill me for sure if they saw me run." Adam had a faraway look in his eyes.

"What did Rafe say?" Derek asked.

This time, Adam swallowed. " 'We're already dead.' "

Derek sucked in air sharply through his nostrils. "And you were able to run?"

Adam nodded, the haunted look still in his eye. "Yes, the next day. I waited till dark. When they untied my hands so I could relieve myself, I told them I was sick. They left me alone a bit longer than usual. I ran as fast as I could for the forest."

Derek expelled his breath slowly. "And you made it?"

"Yes. I still don't know how. I don't think they cared that I'd left."

Derek paced across the rug in front of the sofa. "They probably wanted you to be their messenger. How else would we know for sure that Swifdon and Rafe were taken?"

"I'd already told him that," Collin interjected.

Adam nodded grimly. "Yes. I think that's why."

"And you never discovered Swifdon and Rafe's fate?" Derek asked.

Adam's jaw was tightly clenched. "No. I spent the next day hiking north and then ran into a battalion from Brighton. They took me to headquarters at Ostend."

"Which is where I eventually found him," Collin said.

"Derek, General Markham approved of my—"

"Markham is a fool," Derek ground out. "As soon as Wellington is debriefed on this—"

"You know you don't have to tell the general," Adam said quietly, staring at the floor, shifting his glass in his hands.

"Of course I must," Derek shot back.

"Must you?" Collin asked.

Derek stopped pacing. He eyed Collin carefully. "Look, you're both exhausted and no doubt in need of a good meal and a hot bath. I'll have both of those things sent to your rooms immediately. We'll talk about this again in the morning."

Adam, looking somewhat relieved, set his glass on the table in front of him and stood and made his way to the door of the study.

"Hughes will see you to your rooms."

Adam nodded.

"I'm damn glad you're alive, Adam," Derek bit out, just before his youngest brother quit the room.

Collin stood and drained his glass before setting it aside. "I'm damn glad he's alive also."

Derek nodded. "You weren't able to learn anything more about Swifdon and Rafe?"

Collin glanced down, regret etched on his face. "Nothing."

Derek clenched his fist and braced it against the nearby wall. "I'll talk to Wellington. And this time I refuse to take no for an answer. We're going back there. For them."

## ❧ CHAPTER FORTY-SIX ❧

September in London. The air had turned cooler. The days had become shorter. They would be off to the country soon. And Lucy detested the country. Not the land itself but the company. Being shut up in a house, however grand, with her parents for months was far from her idea of a pleasant way to pass the time. Thank goodness Cass and Garrett lived nearby.

Lucy traced the raindrops on the windowpane of the drawing room. She hadn't seen or spoken to Derek since she'd left Bath. She'd dodged all of her friends' attempts to visit her as well, either claiming she was out or indisposed. Every day she checked the Society pages of the *Times* for the news of Derek and Cass's impending nuptials. It was never there, but surely it was only a matter of time. As the days passed, she became increasingly nervous, certain she would see it soon.

But something else was missing from the pages of the newspaper. News of Captain Julian Swift's death in Brussels. Had it happened and not been reported? Was Cass grieving—and bad friend that she was, Lucy was ignoring her? Oh, she had been convinced that she had to give the entire affair time and space. But it felt as if she was hurting everyone who was important to her.

When Janie came bustling into the drawing room, hands on her hips and no book in sight, Lucy knew it was serious.

"I don't care what your latest excuse is, you're coming to the theater with me tonight," Jane declared, shaking her head so hard her spectacles nearly popped off her prim little nose. She fumbled for them and set them back in place, then crossed her arms over her chest and eyed Lucy sternly.

"I don't want to." As excuses went, it was particularly weak, but at the moment it was all Lucy had.

Jane gave her a long-suffering stare. "I don't care."

"I can't, Jane. What if, what if . . . ?" Lucy couldn't bring herself to say, *What if I see Derek?* It was insane and useless and she didn't want to have to explain herself. "I refuse to go to the theater. That's all there is to it." She nodded resolutely.

"It's *Much Ado About Nothing*," Jane added in a singsong voice. "One of my very favorites."

Lucy winced. Blast it. She couldn't miss *Much Ado About Nothing*. It was one of her very favorites as well. And Jane knew it. Knew it and had come here armed with that information.

"Besides, Upton and Lord Berkeley have agreed to accompany us," Jane added, taking a seat on the settee and removing her gloves. "Do you have any teacakes?"

Lucy gulped. "Lord Berkeley?"

"Yes."

"Is coming?"

"Yes. He's in town for a few more days and he indicated that he's quite eager to see you."

Lucy twisted her hands together. "He did?"

"Yes."

Lucy winced. "I find that surprising given that I haven't received a letter from him since I left Bath. I barely said good-bye."

"Nevertheless, he expressed his intent interest in seeing you again. That must have been some kiss you gave him," Jane said with a laugh. "Oh, come on, Luce, you know it's serious if I'm conspiring with Upton to get you out of the house."

"Where is Garrett, anyway? I haven't seen him in days. How were you two able to conspire without me finding out?"

"Upton paid me a call. We discussed it all at my parents' town house. He invited Berkeley, too. The chap seems quite smitten with you, I must say. I've no idea why you've been hiding in this house for so long."

Lucy set her jaw. "I shall throttle Garrett the next time I see him."

"No you won't. You'll be charming and sweet, at least while Lord Berkeley's around." Jane laughed again. "Now ring for tea. I'm in desperate need of a cake."

"No one *needs* a cake."

Jane gave her a withering stare. "That is hardly relevant."

Lucy shook her head and rang for tea. Jane was not to be dissuaded once she'd set her sights on a teacake. "You and Garrett at another performance of *Much Ado*? That's sure to be a disaster."

Jane tossed a hand in the air. "Yes, exactly! Take it seriously. It truly is. Only for you would I do such a thing as agree to accompany Upton to the theater again. And only for you would I go see *Much Ado About Nothing* with your infuriatingly wrongheaded cousin."

"You may call him Garrett, you know. You two have known each other long enough."

Jane rolled her eyes. "I wouldn't give him the satisfaction."

Lucy turned back to face her friend, a stern and resolute look on her face. "Janie, I appreciate your efforts, truly I do, but there's absolutely no way in the entire world that I'm leaving this house tonight."

❧

Never let it be said that Miss Jane Lowndes was anything other than a bullheaded tyrant when she wanted to be. That was the thought that coursed through Lucy's mind as she stood outside the Royal Theater Company's production of *Much Ado About Nothing*. The play had been thoroughly enjoyed by all. Lucy couldn't remember the last time she'd laughed so heartily. Very well, perhaps Jane had been right, forcing her out of her house. She'd asked Jane a variety of questions about Cass and Julian, carefully avoiding the subject of Derek. Jane had also carefully bypassed each of her inquiries, insisting that if Lucy wanted to know what was going on with Cass, she should stop acting like such a ninny and pay her friend a call to find out for herself.

Lucy, of course, had no intention of doing so, but regardless of the little bit of information she'd been able to wheedle out of Jane, she'd had a wonderful time this evening.

It was lovely to see Christian again. He was as handsome and solicitous as ever. So what if he didn't make her stomach leap the way Derek did? Stomach leaping was quite overrated. It made one far too anxious. It was far too closely related to nausea. Yes, who wanted all that nonsense? Much better to have a sensibly well-settled stomach. Better for the digestion no doubt. And if the man was not the best conversationalist in the kingdom, so be it.

He did try. He smiled at her and asked her halting questions about her health, her parents, her time in Bath. And she only thought of Derek a little when answering them. Well, only when Christian asked about where she'd been, what she'd done, and whom she'd done it with. A bit distracting, to be sure. But then she'd asked him about his own time in Bath, his stay in London, and his plans to go back to Northumbria. It was all quite interesting, if not stomach-leap inducing.

"Amazing that those two couldn't see they were meant for each other all along," Christian said about the performance as they were all leaving the theater together.

"I think it's an awful trick their friends played on them," Jane added. "But it was a pleasure to watch, I must admit."

"Bah. It's preposterous," Garrett said, throwing a hand in the air. "You cannot possibly convince me that a man as intelligent as Benedick wouldn't have known he was being tricked."

Jane tossed her own hand in the air. "Oh, and Beatrice would have?"

"Both of them ought to have figured it out, frankly," Garrett replied, a look of disgust on his face.

"That is why it's a romp play, Upton," Jane shot back, speaking slowly as if she were addressing a child or an imbecile. "It's not a history lesson. It's just meant to be fun."

"It makes no sense. It's silly," Garrett replied.

"And what is wrong with being silly?" Jane asked sweetly.

They'd made their way to the front of the theater and were standing in a long queue waiting for the carriages to come around.

Lucy batted her eyelashes at her friends. "I hate to be indelicate and point it out, but is this not the exact same argument you two had five years ago?"

Jane and Garrett exchanged cantankerous looks.

Garrett shrugged. "Perhaps."

"Yes, and amazingly, he's still wrong, five years later." Jane crossed her arms over her chest and glanced away.

"I'm wrong?" Garrett began. "I think you couldn't be more wrong. And another thing—"

"Oh, here comes the carriage," Lucy interjected, pointing. She glanced over to another line of waiting theatergoers.

She sucked in her breath.

"Lucy? Are you all right? You just went completely pale." Jane's gaze followed hers to the other group. Cassandra and Derek were there, along with Cassandra's mother. They were waiting for a carriage, too.

"Oh, Luce, look. It's Cass and the duke. Let's go greet them." Jane tried to pull her toward the others, but Lucy snatched her hand away.

"No. No. I couldn't." She backed away, unable to drag her eyes from Derek but also hoping against hope that he would not turn and see her. She couldn't breathe. Her heart felt as if it were in a vise. Derek had told her he didn't want to marry Cass. He'd told her he couldn't do it, wouldn't do it. And Lucy had told him he must. Had even been willing to sacrifice her own friendship with Cass for the sake of seeing her happily settled. But the lack of the announcement in the paper had lulled Lucy into a false hope. Perhaps Derek had meant what he'd said after all, that he did not intend to marry Cass, that he wouldn't and truly couldn't.

But now, here was the stark evidence, standing before her in the queue for the carriages. Cass and Derek were courting. They were. Lucy might have said she wanted this, but she couldn't take it. Not now. Not yet. Perhaps not ever, but she certainly wasn't strong enough now. Oh, why had she allowed Jane to needle her into coming to the theater tonight?

She whirled around in a panic to enter their coach, which had just pulled up, and nearly knocked poor Christian over. "May we go immediately, please?" she begged, looking up into the viscount's angelic blue eyes.

Christian nodded. "Of course. Immediately." He snapped his fingers and the footmen attending his coach came to help. Christian himself handed Lucy into the carriage. Jane and Garrett soon followed and the carriage took off quickly, rattling down the muddy street.

Derek helped Cassandra and her mother into the interior of his coach, but his mind kept replaying the moment he'd seen Berkeley's hand on Lucy's back. Derek clenched his jaw. He wanted to tear Berkeley limb from limb.

Derek had hoped coming to the theater tonight with Lady Cassandra would help him learn something about Lucy, but Cassandra had been surprisingly tight-lipped about her friend. Every question he'd attempted to ask about Lucy had been met with the unwelcome news that Cassandra and Lucy apparently hadn't spoken since they'd returned from Bath.

"Every time I've tried to pay a call or send a missive, Lucy's said she wasn't feeling well or made some other excuse. I'm not certain what's wrong with her. I've been worried, Your Grace," Cassandra told him.

Cassandra's mother, however, seemed positively delighted to have the opportunity to accompany her daughter and the duke to the theater, despite his constant inquiries about Lucy.

"Oh, Your Grace. Why, I don't know when Cassandra and I have had a better time."

Derek winced. Perhaps he'd made a mistake in asking Cassandra to the theater tonight. The way Lady Moreland was staring at him like a soldier presented with his ration of rum, he got the distinct impression that the woman was raising her hopes quite high that an offer from a duke was forthcoming for her daughter. Very well. He must face it. It had been wrong of him to ask Cassandra to accompany him tonight, but how else was he to learn anything about Lucy? She'd made it quite clear she didn't want to see him again.

While he waited for word from Wellington in France, telling him whether he'd be allowed to return to the Continent to help search for Swifdon and Rafe, Derek had taken up his issues with Lucy again full force. He'd paid a call to Cass that afternoon, intending that to be the extent of their interaction. When Lady Moreland had come in carrying the tea tray herself and joining the conversation, Derek had been forced to abandon his questioning about Lucy. Instead, they'd had a perfectly boring conversation about the weather and a small variety of other socially acceptable topics before Lady Moreland had asked after his plans this evening. When he'd mentioned he intended to attend the theater, she'd practically leaped across the settee at him in her extremely ill-concealed attempts to invite herself along. "Oh, Cassandra and I love Shakespeare's comedies, Your Grace. We think our butler may be related to him, you know? We've so wanted to attend the theater. We would simply adore it."

Derek had expelled his breath, resigned to his fate. He remembered his own rude behavior weeks earlier when Cass had told him about her trip to Bath. He'd invited himself along then. Surely Lady Moreland's self-invitation to the theater wasn't as egregious as following someone to another town. Accompanying the lady and her daughter to a play would be a pleasant enough way to spend an evening.

He'd been wrong. At least on the last count. Lady Moreland had dropped unsubtle hints the entire night about her desire to see her daughter marry well. For her part, poor Cassandra had mentioned Swift more times than Derek could count, and the entire evening had been beyond awkward. To make matters worse, he'd learned practically nothing about Lucy.

Lucy.

When she'd seen him tonight, she'd gone as white as a sheet and turned away. Derek clenched his fist against the velvet squabs in his coach. Then he'd noticed Berkeley. White-hot anger had flashed before Derek's eyes. Why did he have to see her with Berkeley of all people? Berkeley? Fine. Berkeley and her cousin Garrett were mates, but it didn't make it any easier to watch the viscount touch Lucy. It fact, it incensed Derek. Had Berkeley got some other poor sop to agree to write her letters in his stead?

Derek pressed the side of his fist against the coach's window. Everything about the way things had been left with Lucy incensed him. First, he'd finally decided exactly what he must do to make everything right and she'd refused to cooperate, telling him he must marry Cass. He couldn't marry Cass. How could Lucy not understand that? And second, she'd unilaterally decided exactly how their entire future would go without consulting him. It couldn't be that easy for her, could it? She'd felt something when she'd been in his arms. He knew it. There had to be something more going on. Lucy was scared. Scared of her feelings, scared enough to run away from him and use Cassandra as an excuse to ignore the budding relationship they'd obviously begun together. Damn it. It wasn't fair of her.

And why had she been with Berkeley? She'd told Derek once she had no intention of marrying. Or didn't think she would. He'd tried to ask about Berkeley then but she'd abruptly changed the subject. Was she using Berkeley to try to erase Derek from her mind? Berkeley. A simpering fool who couldn't even write his own letters? By God, the next time he saw the viscount, Derek would pound him into pulp.

# ❧ CHAPTER FORTY-SEVEN ❧

When the door to her bedchamber flew open the next afternoon, Lucy blinked in surprise. She'd been sitting at her desk, writing her obligatory weekly letter to her mother. She assured her mother that she was in good health—not that her mother cared—well chaperoned—not that her mother cared—and still entirely without the prospect of a husband—not that her mother cared, much. But still, Lucy wrote. Hoping one day her mother might show some interest.

At the loud crack of the door against the wall, Lucy dropped the quill and snapped up her head.

"There you are!" Cass stood in the doorway with her hands on her hips looking like a beautiful, angry, blond virago.

Lucy half rose from her writing desk. "Why . . . What? Cass, what are you doing here?"

Cass's breath came in deep pants, and she pressed her hands against her belly. "As usual, the butler tried to tell me that you were indisposed but I raced up here. He tried to chase me, poor fellow. I find I'm actually quite fast. I had no idea." She proudly lifted her chin in the air.

As if on cue, the butler arrived just then in the doorway. He was panting as well, and he looked to Lucy with a guilty countenance. "My lady, I do apologize, but . . ."

"It's all right, Milhaven," Lucy said. "It seems Lady Cassandra has found me."

Cass aimed a triumphant smile at the butler. Milhaven bowed to them both and took his leave.

"That'll teach him to try to outrun me again." Cass trotted over, pulled off her gloves, and took a seat next to the window. "I must say, I believe Shakespierre would have caught me, however."

Lucy couldn't help but laugh at that. "Oh, no, I wouldn't try to outrun Shakespierre. Not on a dare. But I cannot help but think your association with me has taught you bad manners, Cass. Outrunning the butler? That's more like something I would do."

Cass slapped her gloves onto the writing desk and braced her elbows atop it, still working her breathing back to rights. "Enough about running from the butler. Now do you deny hiding from me the last three sennights?"

Wincing, Lucy twirled the quill around the parchment and forced herself to look at her friend. "No. I've been awful. Can you forgive me? I have no excuse."

Cass smiled. "Thank you for that. I do forgive you. Though you left me no choice but to hunt you down like a fox because I have some news for you."

Lucy furrowed her brow. "News?"

"Yes." There was no hint in the tone of Cass's voice.

Lucy's heart jumped to her throat. Her fingers rhythmically clenched and unclenched the quill. "You and Derek are betrothed." The words didn't hurt as much leaving her lips as she'd expected them to. She was numb. She raised her gaze to meet Cass's face.

Cass shook her head. "What? No."

Lucy widened her eyes. "You're not?"

"No."

"If that's not your news, then what—?" She pressed both hands to her cheeks. "Oh, God. Cass, it's not. Is it Julian? I'll never forgive myself if he died while I was being such an awful friend. It's just that—"

"No. No. Julian's not dead."

Lucy closed her eyes and breathed a deep sigh of relief. "Oh, I'm so glad. Have you heard from him? How is he?"

"My news is about Derek *and* Julian actually." A small smile rested on Cass's lips. And if she had a smile on her face when mentioning Julian . . .

Lucy grabbed her hand and squeezed it. "What is it, Cass? Tell me."

Cass couldn't control her laughter. "He's coming home, Lucy! Julian is coming home!"

Lucy raised herself halfway from the writing desk then fell to her knees in front of Cass, clasping both her hands. "Oh, Cass, that's wonderful news. He's recovered?"

Tears of joy shone in Cass's eyes. "Yes. He began to take a turn for the better a fortnight ago and he's healing nicely according to his doctors in Brussels."

Tears sprang to Lucy's eyes, too. "I cannot imagine how happy you must be. This is wonderful news."

"It is, isn't it? I'm so happy, Lucy. I cannot wait to see him."

A shadow crossed over Lucy's mind. "But what about Penelope? Does he still intend to marry Penelope?"

Cass nodded. "Nothing has changed. But that's what I wanted to say about Derek."

Lucy's spine went straight. She let go of her friend's hands. She couldn't stand to hear anything about Derek. She pulled herself back into her chair. "I don't think—"

"I wanted to tell you that I ended things with His Grace. I told him I could not marry him."

Lucy blinked. "You did?"

"Yes. I did.

"When?"

"Before we left Bath, actually. And to his credit, he's made it exceedingly easy for me. Until yesterday, I hadn't seen him since we returned to London."

Lucy's mouth fell open. "Truly?"

"Yes, truly. And you'd know that already if you hadn't been hiding from me."

Lucy bit her lip. "I'm so sorry."

Cass continued in the happiest voice Lucy had heard out of her friend in weeks. "The duke and I went to the theater with Mother last night. We had a lovely time, but you know what I think?" Her small smile was back.

Lucy gulped. "What?"

"I think he only asked Mother and me to the theater so that he could inquire after *you*."

Lucy couldn't help the little smile that popped to her own lips. "I don't believe that. He hasn't been in contact with me since we left Bath."

"What happened between the two of you there?" Cass asked carefully.

Lucy bit her lip. What a complicated question.

"Did you do anything? Say anything? To make him think you didn't want to see him again," Cass prodded.

Lucy nodded. "Yes. I'm afraid I did. But none of that matters. Tell me, why? Why did you break things off with Derek if Julian still plans to marry Penelope?"

Cass patted Lucy's hand. "Oh, Lucy, everyone deserves

to find love the way I love Julian. And just because I can't have him, doesn't mean the duke doesn't deserve to find love with someone of his choosing. Derek doesn't love me and I don't love him. We both know that. He deserves to find someone with whom he can truly be happy."

Lucy's heart nearly beat out of her chest. "But what about you?"

Cass smoothed her hands over her skirts, but the hint of a smile still played around her lips. "I expect it will take a bit for me to become accustomed to Pen and Julian's marriage. But eventually, I may find someone who loves me, who cannot live without me. Either that or I'll run off to the convent." She giggled. "I just need a bit of time."

Cass nodded resolutely but Lucy didn't believe it. This time she patted her friend's hand. "You're brave. Brave to make the decision and brave to face Penelope and Julian's wedding. But I still think that we can—"

"No," Cass said in the firmest voice Lucy had ever heard from her. "No more of your mischiefs. I refuse to attempt to break up my cousin's engagement. I'm just happy Julian is recovering and that I shall see him again. Nothing else matters." Tears shone in her blue eyes again.

Lucy blew out a deep breath. "Very well. I'll let it be. For now." She didn't wait for Cass to protest that last bit. "It's wonderful that Julian is coming home, but what about the letter you wrote to him? Did he mention it? Do you think that will make a difference in his feelings?"

Cass took a deep breath and looked her straight in the eye. "I never sent that letter."

Lucy felt as if she were eight years old and had just fallen out of the apple tree. The breath had been completely knocked from her body. She'd been momentarily paralyzed. "You didn't?"

"No. I didn't."

Lucy shook her head. "I don't understand. I saw you write it. Watched you sand it. Waited while you heated the wax to seal it."

"I know. I did all of that. But I never posted it, Lucy. I just"—Cass glanced down at her hands—"couldn't. And now I realize it was the right thing to do."

"The right thing to do," Lucy echoed.

"Yes. Haven't you been the one encouraging me to stand up for myself, not do everything I'm told? I'm relieved that I didn't send that letter."

Lucy grabbed her friend's hand again and rested her forehead against it. "I'm sorry I tried to convince you to. I thought it was the right thing, at the time. Can you forgive me for that, too?"

Cass squeezed Lucy's fingers. "Of course you thought it was the right thing. And I love you for it, Lucy, truly I do. There's nothing to forgive."

Pulling her hand from Lucy's grasp, Cass clapped. "Now. Enough moping about things we cannot change. Let's discuss something infinitely more delightful."

Lucy stared at her with wide eyes. "Better than Julian coming home?"

"Well, perhaps not for *me*," Cass replied with a small smile.

"What then?"

"When the duke accompanied Mama and me to the theater last night, all he could talk about was *you*."

Lucy counted five. It was finally time to set things right with her friend. "There's something I must tell you, Cass."

She smiled at Lucy. "That you're madly in love with the duke?"

Lucy looked twice. Cass's face was perfectly serene. "How did you know?"

"Oh, Luce, it's been obvious for ages."

Lucy pressed her fingertips to her lips. "Ages? It has?"

"Yes. Janie and I have been waiting for you to finally admit it."

Lucy slapped her hand to her forehead. "You have?"

"Absolutely. It's been clear since we went to Bath that you and Derek were ever so much more suited to each other than he and I. In fact, I'd been pretending to be far more helpless than I really felt in an effort to allow you two to spend more time in each other's company since the Chamberses' ball."

"The Chamberses' ball!" Lucy's mouth was a wide O. "But what about Lady Hoppington's Venetian breakfast? You told Derek he could court you."

Cass shook her head. "It wasn't quite straightforward of me, I know, but I thought it was a way to keep you and Derek in proximity of each other. If I told him to leave, I think he would have then. And the two of you might never have seen each other again."

Lucy covered her friend's hand with her own and squeezed. "You did that for me?"

"I'd do anything for you, Lucy." She went on, "I admit when I got the letter from Julian, it confused and upset me. I had no idea Julian felt so strongly about me marrying Derek."

"It's understandable, Cass."

Cass nodded. "But if Julian were here, and he could see the two of you, he'd know it was for the best. He'd want his friend to be happy. As I do you."

"Oh, Cass, you're so lovely. I'm so proud to call you my friend," Lucy said.

"The feeling is entirely mutual," Cass replied with a smile.

Lucy sighed. "How will I tell everyone else? Does Garrett know?"

Cass shook her head. "About you and the duke? I don't think so."

"But you and Janie do?"

"Of course. Why do you think I faked a head cold and asked you to spend time with him? Not to mention acting like such a spineless ninny the entire time he was attempting to court me. I am a ninny. But I hope I am not quite so spineless."

Lucy's mouth fell open. "You are *not* a ninny, Cass." She plunked her hands on her hips. "You faked your head cold?"

"I absolutely did. Janie helped me put rouge on my nose, but the false sneezing was all me. I did an admirable job of it, did I not? And I can tell you, it wasn't much fun having to be cooped up in bed all those days in a row whenever you were about."

Lucy snorted. "I cannot believe it. You detest lying."

"Oh, it was lying for the very best reason, though, wasn't it? That's why Janie was hiding from you. She thought if she got alone with you to talk, you'd ask her too many questions and she'd be forced to admit to her duplicity."

Lucy shook her head. "You two. I should have known you were up to something, especially when I overheard you saying what a ninny you were being. But I truly believed you needed my help dissuading Derek."

Cass smiled back. "I know how stubborn you are, Lucy. You'd never have discovered what a match you were without a little nudge from me."

Lucy shook her head. "I cannot believe it. And Janie knew about this?"

Cass nodded. "Can you ever forgive us?"

Lucy gave her a sidewise glance accompanied by a wide grin. "I think perhaps I can."

"If you truly have feelings for the duke, I'm happy for you." Cass leaned forward and whispered conspiratorially. "And do you know what I think you should do?"

"No. What?"

"I think you should go to him and tell him how you feel."

Lucy winced. "I don't know that that's such a good idea. I'm not certain how he'll react."

"Why?"

Lucy rubbed her hand across her forehead. "When we were in Bath, I told Derek to marry you. I also told him I didn't want to see him again."

"What? How does that make any sense?" Cass asked with a laugh. "If we'd married, you'd be certain to see him again."

Lucy shook her head. "I wasn't exactly thinking clearly. I only knew I had to get away from him. I felt so guilty knowing how my feelings for him were growing when he was meant for you. I told him I'd forsake my friendship with you to allow you two to marry happily."

Cass's hand dropped to the desktop. "Oh, Lucy. That's the most ludicrous thing I've ever heard. Is that why you've been hiding from me? How could I ever be happily married if I lost my closest friend as a result?"

The two women leaned over the desk and hugged, tears streaming down both of their faces. "I love you, Cass."

"I love you, too, Luce."

They finally let go and wiped their tears away with their handkerchiefs. Dabbing away the remaining wetness from her eyes, Lucy allowed an enormous smile to cover her face. "You know, I think I may do just what you suggested, tell Derek how I feel."

Cass's face turned somber. "Wait, Lucy, there's one more thing I must tell you first."

Lucy searched her friend's face. "What is it?"

"Mama seems convinced that Derek still intends to offer for me. She and Papa have been discussing it. I told her not to hold out hope. I told her that I'd informed the duke I wouldn't marry him. But she won't listen."

Lucy furrowed her brow. "What do you mean she won't listen?"

"Apparently your aunt Mary wrote to her and told her how pleased she was that the duke had been courting me in Bath."

Lucy winced. "Oh, no."

Cass bit her lip. "Yes. And after the duke escorted Mama and me to the theater last night, she's even more convinced he intends to offer for me. I'm quite worried that she and Papa won't let it go. They've even written to Owen."

Lucy stood up and paced over to the window to look outside. "What do you think your mother intends to do?"

"I don't know. But I think I should warn the duke. I don't want him to be caught off-guard if Papa attempts to speak with him."

Lucy bit the end of her fingernail and turned back to look at her friend. "Do you think he'll do that?"

Cass shook her head. "I don't know. I wrote Derek a letter." She pulled an envelope from her reticule and laid it onto Lucy's writing desk. "I intend to have a maid bring it around in the morning. Other than that I'm not certain what else I can do. Besides trying to reason with Mama and Papa again."

Lucy crossed her arms over her chest but forced a smile

to her lips. No sense worrying about something that may not happen. Was there? "Let's just hope it doesn't come to that."

Cass returned her smile. "Yes. Let's."

Lucy scooped up the letter. She gave her friend a sly smile. "You know. I could bring the letter around to Derek tonight if you'd like."

## ❧ CHAPTER FORTY-EIGHT ❧

When Lucy alighted from her cousin's coach, she raced over the stone walkway and took the stairs to Derek's London town house two at a time. She rapped upon the door and fidgeted with her hands, waiting for the blasted butler to open it. "Is His Grace in residence?"

"Yes, my lady, but—"

Lucy didn't wait to be invited. She hurtled herself inside. The minute she'd heard that Cass and Derek hadn't seen each other, that Cass had told him she couldn't marry him, and that they were not, in fact, betrothed, Lucy couldn't get to him fast enough. It was late at night. She'd had to wait for Garrett and Aunt Mary to retire for the evening before she snuck out of the house. She'd bribed the grooms to put the coach to and promise not to mention it to her cousin. She'd arrived at the duke's residence far past the proper time for callers, but she couldn't have cared any less.

"Where is he?" The butler had better not give her any trouble. In her present state of mind, she could fight him with knives and win. Not that she was in possession of a knife, but that was not the point.

Haughty Hughes looked down his nose at her. "His Grace has retired to his bedchamber for the evening. I'll be happy to take your card and—"

"No!" She made her way determinedly to the staircase. Retired to his bedchamber? That sounded perfect to her. Oh, this was going to be the scandal of the year, but Lucy didn't give a fig what Hughes thought. She raced up the stairs, frantically opening the doors to several bedchambers to no avail, before coming to the final one at the end of the corridor.

She grabbed the handle with both hands and swung it open to find Derek sitting across the room, in bed, his hair gorgeously ruffled, a dark green silk robe mostly open showing his muscled chest. A book in his hands. He was reading and wore a pair of silver spectacles that made him look even more handsome. He also obviously hadn't shaved since morning, and the dark stubble on his face made Lucy nearly swoon. She came to a panting halt as soon as she saw him. The door she'd burst through cracked against the opposite wall.

Derek's eyebrow immediately arched. "Well, now, *this* is entirely unexpected."

Lucy slowly retrieved the door, closed it, locked it, and forced herself to walk calmly to his side. "I have a tendency to be a bit unexpected, Your Grace."

A smile hovered over his firmly molded lips. "I'll say. To what do I owe the pleasure of your visit to my bedchamber, Miss Upton?"

Lucy pressed her lips together to keep from smiling. Miss Upton. She'd missed being called that. She took a deep breath. "Why didn't you tell me you were no longer courting Cass?"

He settled himself back against the pillows, removing his spectacles and placing them on the table next to him. "For one thing, I assumed Cassandra would have told you, and for another, you made it quite clear the last time we spoke that you wanted nothing to do with me."

She ran her hand along the blanket next to his thigh. "I only wanted nothing to do with you if you were courting Cass."

He groaned. "You *told* me to court Cass. You demanded I marry her, if I remember correctly."

She touched his hand, lightly. "I thought that's what Julian and Cass wanted."

He tilted his head to the side. His grin was crooked. "Who gives a damn what Julian and Cass want? Besides, what about you and Berkeley?"

"I don't care about Christian."

"You looked as if you cared about him at the theater last night."

She shrugged. "That meant nothing. We cannot even hold a conversation."

"Yes, well, it didn't bode well for the chap given that he had to have another man write letters for him."

Her gaze locked with his. "What do you mean?"

"Meet the author of the letters from your beloved Lord Berkeley." Even though he was sitting, Derek did a semblance of a bow at the waist.

Lucy's mouth dropped open. "*You* wrote those letters?"

"Yes, and you kissed Berkeley."

Lucy snapped her mouth shut. "I might have kissed him, but I was thinking about you the entire time." She didn't stop to acknowledge the mollified look on his face at that news. "How could you? Pretending to be someone else?"

He blinked at her innocently. "I seem to remember

someone once hiding behind a hedgerow and speaking for someone else from atop a balcony. I'd say we're quite even, my love."

The words "my love" made her stop. Stop and stare at him. Then she began to laugh. Lucy laughed and laughed until tears rolled down her cheeks. It was all just too ridiculous. "Oh, Derek. If I didn't know any better, I'd feel as if we'd all been trapped inside the script of a romp play."

He laughed, too, and when their laughter died away, they were silent, looking at each other cautiously, shyly.

Lucy pushed a curl away from her forehead, searching for something new to say to make it less awkward. "Did you know Julian's recovered? He'll be coming home soon."

His fingertips glanced over hers, causing a wave of heat to undulate through her body. "Yes, my brothers just returned from the Continent and told me so. I've never been so damned glad to hear such news. For more reasons than one."

"What other reason?" she asked.

Derek reached out and stroked the side of her bare arm. She shivered. "As soon as Julian comes home, I can explain to him how thoroughly Lady Cassandra has rejected me. Then I can get to the business of marrying the woman I bloody well want to."

Despite his curse word, Lucy couldn't help her tiny smile. She widened her eyes. "Me?"

"Yes, you." He crooked a finger indicating that she should come closer.

Lucy leaned forward.

Another quirk of his finger. "Closer," he said.

She moved a bit more.

"Closer," he coaxed.

"How close?" Her breath fanned across his face.

"Close enough to kiss me," he whispered hotly.

Her lips hovered just over his. "Like this," she murmured just before she brushed her lips against his.

Their lips met again. Once. Twice. Then he tugged her to him, her breasts pressing against his bare chest. His hot mouth opened her hers, his tongue plunging inside.

The kiss was electric, jolting her to the core. Joy sang through Lucy's veins. They were going to make love, the two of them. Here, tonight, in Derek's bedchamber, and Lucy wanted it so badly.

Hastily shoving his book aside, he pulled her on top of him. "I cannot wait to make you mine," he whispered against her mouth. Their lips came together again. Their kiss was hot, fiery. Lucy was sure she would crumple into a messy pile of lust on his expensive duvet.

His mouth owned hers, shaped it, controlled it. She couldn't get enough. She met his tongue thrust for thrust, her hands traveling over his strong shoulders still encased in a robe. His strong possessive hands made short work of ripping off her gloves, and then began unbuttoning the back of her gown. Soon, she was wearing only her shift and stays, panting, still not letting her mouth leave his. She'd known it would be this way between them. Hot, unstoppable. They both were fighting for control. But Lucy soon realized that in bed, Derek would be completely in charge. A shudder of lust worked its way up her body. *Own me.* The thought shimmied its way through her. She surrendered to his deft hands. Derek tugged her against him hard and rolled atop Lucy. She breathed deeply. To be doing this with a man as handsome and wonderful as Derek—it was beyond her wildest dream.

Derek leaned over her and kissed her again, once, twice. She tried to pull him fully atop her but he braced his elbows on either side of her head and held himself away. "Just a moment, love," he said and then rolled to the edge of the bed, stood, and made his way over to the mantel where he doused the candles. The room plunged into shadowed darkness. She could still make out his form from the one remaining candle near the bed. She smiled. He must have done that in deference to her modesty. She pressed her fingertips to her lips. While it was true that she was a bit shy anticipating Derek taking off every last shred of her clothing, she was much more interested in seeing him completely nude than she ought to admit and the candles being out didn't help. Ah, well, she would have a lifetime to learn his body. She sucked in her breath. A lifetime. They were going to be married.

Derek quickly made his way back to the bed and pulled his robe from his shoulders. He tossed the garment on the floor. Lucy got only a quick peek at the magnificence of his body. He was all angled planes and solid muscles. A scar on his shoulder, another near his waist, and, oh, she'd only got a glimpse down there and from what she could tell he was quite well endowed indeed. Derek slid atop her and quickly covered Lucy's body with his own. Her stays were gone in an instant. Derek propped himself up on one elbow and traced the edge of the décolletage of her shift. He was a bit shaky, on the verge of losing control, and Lucy loved it. She could sense it and because he was a man who was usually so self-possessed and in control, she reveled in it.

"Do you know how badly I want to rip this thing off you?" he asked huskily.

A thrill shot through her. "How badly?"

He clenched his jaw. "Very, very badly."

She kissed his ear. He shuddered. "Why don't you?"

"Don't tempt me." His voice was still a bit uneven.

"What's the harm?" she asked.

He nudged his nose against hers and kissed the tip. "What will you wear when you go back home?"

"My gown's still intact, is it not?" She wrapped her arms around his neck and kissed him deeply.

It took a moment for Derek to recover from the kiss before he managed to say, "I don't want the future Duchess of Claringdon to be involved in a huge scandal." He grinned against her lips.

"It's far too late." A kiss on the tip of his nose this time. "Besides, what's the harm if it's with her own husband?"

"I like the sound of that." He nuzzled her ear.

"I have an idea," Lucy said.

He kissed her neck and groaned. He gestured to her shift. "It had better involve the removal of this garment as quickly as possible."

"Half right," she replied coyly. She pulled away from him and shimmied off the bed. She stood and turned back to face him. Derek watched her with intense darkened eyes. "What are you doing?"

"I'm going to take off my shift and you're going to watch."

His green eyes flared.

Lucy took a deep breath. What had come over her? Some impish hoyden's spirit. She had no idea what she was doing. She knew only that she wanted to please him. Well, please him and tease him a little, but judging from the look in his eyes, he liked her idea. Very much.

He'd asked her to do it quickly. She intended to do just the opposite.

She started out by pulling the garment up above her knees with both hands. "How should I do it?" she asked him. "Should I pull it up over my head or down over my hips?" The fabric was tantalizingly bunched at the juncture between her thighs. She held it just there.

Derek scrubbed a hand over his face. "Lord have mercy."

She pulled it up just enough for him to see the sleek side of her bare hip before dropping the fabric. Derek groaned. "Changed your mind?"

She smiled coyly. "I haven't decided yet."

She leaned down, bracing both hands on the mattress and affording him a view of her heaving breasts pushing anxiously against the fabric of her shift. Derek's eyes riveted to that spot. Lucy put a hand to one of the sleeves, caressing her shoulder. "Perhaps this is the better choice."

She slowly pushed the sleeve over her shoulder with the tip of one finger. Derek closed his eyes and groaned again, but only briefly. "I do like where you're going with this."

She stood up and ever so slowly pushed the other sleeve over the other shoulder. Then she pulled out both arms, still holding up the décolletage to cover her breasts.

Derek scrubbed a hand over his face again. "I survived Waterloo, but this is going to be the death of me."

She wagged a finger at him. "Ah, ah, ah, Your Grace. Don't be impatient."

She undid the ribbons with one hand and stepped out of the garment, still holding it up in front of her where it covered her breasts and hung in a tantalizing drape between her legs. She gave him a sultry look and watched with fascinated pride as his eyes flared with lust.

"I can't stand it anymore," he groaned, just before he reached out and grabbed Lucy's hand, tugging her into the bed with him with one solid movement. He grabbed her shift in both hands and ripped the garment out of her hands, tearing it apart. He tossed it on the floor in an ignominious heap. Lucy gasped against his mouth.

"I'll buy you another. I'll buy you a hundred others. But I have to have you *now*."

She wrapped her arms around his neck. "As you wish, Your Grace."

Derek leaned up on an elbow to get an unimpeded view of Lucy's lush, ripe body. She was perfect, gorgeous, a man's dream. Her breasts were round and full. He cupped them both in his hand, weighing them, feeling them, savoring them. Her hips were narrow and straight. Her thighs had the perfect bit of plumpness. Her legs creamy and long.

"God, you are gorgeous," he breathed against her ear.

"So are you," she said as his lips descended again to own hers.

He smiled against her mouth. Then he stopped, pulled back, stared deeply into her soul. "Your eyes, they're so unique. I love them."

"I've always thought they made me different. I didn't like them."

"They do make you different. But that's what's fascinating about them. They're like you. Like mirrors into you. You're different and depending on your mood, your eyes change colors. Did you know that?"

She shook her head. "No."

"When you're happy, they're light."

"And when I'm angry?" she asked with a smile.

"They turn dark and stormy."

"Stormy?"

"Maybe not stormy."

"Which way do you like best?"

He kissed her again. "I like the way they look right now."

"How's that?" she barely whispered.

"Beautiful and staring up at me. They're luminous."

Lucy wrapped her arms tighter around his neck and kissed him.

Derek pulled back and looked into her eyes again. Searching for any sign of fear or unhappiness. "Lucy, you've never . . ."

Lucy blinked at him. Was he truly asking her if she was a virgin? "No. I've never."

The look on his face was half relief and half pain. He pulled one of her hands from behind his neck and kissed her knuckles. "I don't want to hurt you, love."

She reached out and traced the line of his dark eyebrow with her fingertip. "You could never hurt me."

His mouth found hers again, stroked her tongue, stoked the fire that was a roiling mass below her belly. All she could think about was wanting his hand *there* at that private spot between her legs. The spot that ached for him.

"I'm going to make this good for you," he promised, just before he slipped his head under the covers and began to descend her naked body. First, he stopped at her breasts, a hand kneading one while his tongue found the soft pink tip of the other. He tugged gently with his lips, letting his teeth scrape lightly against the sensitive peak.

Lucy couldn't help herself. She arched her back off the bed. Whatever he was doing, she didn't want him to stop. Her fingers tangled in his dark hair and she held him to her. "Derek."

His hand came up to pluck at her other nipple. He scraped his short nail across it. The roughness combined with the heady sensation of his mouth still tugging at her other breast made her groan. "Derek," she called again, her fingers still tangling in his dark hair.

His breath was a puff of hot air against her sensitive breast. "I could make you come like this, do you know that?"

Lucy was mindless with wanting. She didn't know exactly what he meant but she desperately wanted to find out. She murmured her belief. "Mmm. Hmm. Is that a promise?"

He nipped at the sensitive peak of her breast. "Don't challenge me."

"But I love to challenge you," she gasped, her head thrown back.

She felt his smile against her belly. "Let's do twenty ways to make you feel good. Shall we? I'll start with one of the best."

Lucy shivered. The scrape of his stubbled chin against the soft skin of her abdomen made her jump. Oh God, where was he going?

"I could make you come just like this," he repeated, still torturing her nipple between his thumb and forefinger. "But I'm going to do something even better."

Lucy didn't have long to contemplate what something even better was before Derek's hot breath hovered just above the juncture of her thighs. Oh, God. He was going to . . . *Oh God, yes!* The tip of his tongue dipped into the cleft between her legs, and Lucy shuddered. Her entire body clamped together and trembled. His hands moved down to cup her hips, holding her steady, mastering her.

Derek knew when the tension left her legs. It was around the third deep lick. The feel, the heat, the taste of her made him insane. His hips moved unconsciously against the mattress, mimicking the movement of thrusting into her. He wanted her so badly, couldn't remember the last time he'd been this consumed with lust. But this was Lucy's first time. She might be a hellcat outside bed, might tease him, tempt him, and torment him, but she was a virgin, still, and he couldn't just take her with the swiftness with which he longed to. No, he had to make this completely unforgettable for her. After all, he wanted her to come back for more. He smiled at his own thought.

His tongue traced the soft pink edges of her. And he nudged her most sensitive spot with the tip of his tongue, again, again. Lucy's hips nearly bucked off the bed. His mouth followed her, claimed her, refused to retreat. He was holding her wrists now, had them pinned at her sides next to her hips. She struggled to pull her hands away from his strong grasp, but he didn't allow it. "Easy," he murmured against her intoxicating curls.

"I want to touch you," she moaned, trying again to free her wrists from his grasp.

"Love, if you touched me right now, I'd explode."

She bit her lip and shuddered again. "I want to make you explode."

He smiled against the warm flesh of her thigh. "You first." His tongue plunged back into her cleft, mercilessly swiping against the hot wet flesh. Once, twice. He swirled his tongue against the little nub of sensation that he knew would take her where he wanted her to go. Her breasts were heaving against the sheets, the sensitized nipples being rubbed raw by the soft linen. Everything that touched her skin was a torture, a torture leading to that apex between her legs where all sensation was concentrated at the moment. Her hips tensed. She lightly squeezed his head with her knees while her hips moved in an unconscious rhythm along with his torturous licks. He kept up the stroking with his tongue again, again, again, until Lucy's feet arched off the bed. Her hips bucked, and the most powerful sensation of her life rocketed through her. She let out a keening cry while the feeling burst through her in an explosive moment that left her shimmering and shivering, hot waves of lust and amazement rolling through her entire satisfied body.

Derek held her while the rhythmic shudders coursed through her. Then he wiped the tears away from her eyes and pushed the sweaty bits of hair off her forehead. He nudged his nose against hers and kissed her full on the mouth. "How was it?" He stared into her dazed eyes.

A catlike smile spread across her gorgeous face. "I've never felt anything like that, ever."

He kissed her smooth shoulder. "I'm glad to hear that."

She playfully slapped at his shoulder. She was still breathing heavily, panting. "I'm serious, Derek. I never knew that existed. If I'd had any idea that you were capable of . . . that, I'd have kissed you instead of arguing with you the first night I met you."

He let out a sharp crack of laughter. "Now, that I highly doubt."

"Truly," she said, wiping the back of her hand across her forehead. "That was simply amazing."

He grinned from ear to ear.

Lucy widened her eyes at him. "Oh, no. Now I've fed your arrogance."

"What? A man can't bask in the glow of admiration for his lovemaking?"

She bit her lip, already preoccupied with something else. "Derek, would you . . . do you want me to do that to you?" she asked a bit shyly. She ducked her head under the covers, revealing only her eyes, and blinked at him.

Derek shuddered. "Oh, God, Lucy. I don't think I could live through it if you did that to me, now. Someday? Hell yes. But tonight I just want to make it special for you."

He rolled atop her and she threaded her arms around his neck. "I want you to make me yours, Derek. In every way."

He kissed her again, deeply. He pushed his knee between her legs, his probing heat slid between her thighs searching for her wet warmth. He kissed her eyelids, her cheekbones, her ear, her neck. "I'm sorry, love," he mur-mured just before he slipped into her, burying himself to the hilt.

Lucy gasped lightly at the invasion, but the sharp pinch was over quickly. The pained look on Derek's face was much worse than the discomfort she'd felt. "Don't look so upset," she said, kissing his cheek.

"Did I hurt you?" he panted.

"I'm fine."

Somehow Derek knew she wouldn't be dramatic about it. She might have a rapier for a tongue, but she was hon-est and forthright and simple in so many ways. Ways he greatly admired.

He kissed the tip of her nose. "I love you," he breathed, just before he began a slow steady rhythm with his hips that had Lucy wet and wanting all over again.

"I love you," he whispered against her ear many min-utes later just before he exploded inside of her and col-lapsed on top of her, satisfied and happy.

"I love you, too, Derek," she whispered into his ear.

# ❧ CHAPTER FORTY-NINE ❧

Lucy rolled over and stared at the gorgeous man sleeping beside her in the early-morning sunlight. The truth was, she'd tiptoed over and opened the curtains to get a good look at him. Then she'd scurried back to bed and slipped under the sheets, a bit self-conscious of her own nakedness. Derek, however, had nothing to be self-conscious about. The man was an Adonis. She could stare at him all day.

He stretched his arms above his head and rolled over in his sleep to face her. Lucy watched him carefully. She was discovering all sorts of new and wonderful things about him, in addition to the fact that he was an absolute dream in bed. For instance, she noticed for the first time that his dark hair was slightly curly at the ends. She snuggled into her pillow and watched him, his perfectly straight nose, his sensuous mouth, his strong rigid shoulders so muscled and . . . ooh. She took a closer look at the scar on his right shoulder. No doubt a result of one of many battles.

This man was a survivor. The thought hit her out of nowhere. He had been born into an unextraordinary family and made himself extraordinary. And he was that. Extraordinary. Extraordinarily handsome. She covered her smile with her fingers and then reached out and traced a fingertip along the ridge of hair that trailed down his belly.

There'd been a time when she thought he didn't belong in the aristocracy. But now she realized how noble he really was. The man had survived the hell of war, led his troops through battle, and won. He was noble. The best sort of noble. More noble, certainly, than many of the pampered members of the *ton* who had done nothing more extraordinary than be born into their particular family.

Derek had told her he loved her last night. Told her so while he'd been deep inside of her, making her feel things she'd never felt before. Could it be true? Could this extraordinary man really love her? How long would it take to get used to that thought? She'd told him she loved him, too. And she did. She did. She loved everything about him. His loyalty to his friends. His refusal to back down. His humor in the face of her rudeness. His handsome face and his prowess in his role in the army. Not to mention the things he knew how to do in bed. She breathed deeply, a wicked smile on her lips.

Derek rolled over a bit more and opened one bright eye. "Good morning."

"Good morning," Lucy replied, snuggling back down next to him.

He put an arm around her waist and pulled her close. She turned in his embrace so that her back was to him. She fit perfectly in that space, his arms wrapped around her.

"How did you sleep?" he asked.

She nearly choked. "Ahem, we didn't sleep much, did we?"

"Hmm. You're right." He kissed the back of her head. "I wonder what time it is."

She sighed. "A bit after dawn."

"The damage is most likely done to your reputation. Therefore, I see no sense in leaving the bed until morning. I'll have a tray brought up for breakfast."

Lucy half turned to face him. "No! I cannot be here and have a servant bring us food."

He gave her a slow, sensual smile. "Why not?"

"Why not? I'm probably already the scandal of the year given the fact that I've visited you alone at your house in the middle of the night and have yet to come out."

He pulled the hair away from her cheek and stroked her face. "My servants would never disparage the name or reputation of the future Duchess of Claringdon."

Lucy stopped short. The future Duchess of Claringdon? Her. She was the future Duchess of Claringdon. It was an amazing thought, but true. She grinned. "I am a bit hungry."

He laughed and rolled over atop her and kissed her full on the lips. "You are beautiful."

"You mentioned that earlier. I don't quite believe you."

He looked sober. "Lucy, what are you talking about?

"I know I'm not Cass. She's so . . . perfect and I just wonder if . . ." She trailed off into confused embarrassment. What had she wanted to say? *I just wonder if you'll still love me in the future? If you'll take your love away from me if I displease you? Like my parents did when Ralph died.*

He stared into her soul. "Cass is beautiful, that's true, but she's not more beautiful than you are. You're absolutely breathtaking. I thought that the first night I met you."

She widened her eyes. "At the Chamberses' ball?"

"Yes."

She gave him an incredulous look. "No, you did not."

"I most certainly did. I thought how it was really too bad that such a beautiful lady was so set on hating me."

Her smile faded. "I didn't hate you, Derek, truly. I only wanted to help Cass."

Derek nodded and kissed her cheek. "I know."

Lucy cleared her throat, her face turning pink. She rolled over and slid her arm around his side. "Didn't you say something about twenty ways to make me feel good?"

He gave her a roguish grin. "Ah, yes. I believe we still have nineteen more to go."

Lucy laughed and nipped at his corded neck. "By all means, Your Grace. Let's begin."

# ❧ CHAPTER FIFTY ❧

Later that morning, Lucy stood in front of her open wardrobe, hands on her hips, staring at the contents. Which items of clothing might she retain as the new Duchess of Claringdon and which had to go? Oh, she needed Cass's help. Lucy didn't give a fig about fashions, and neither did Jane. Jane had on more than one occasion remarked that she'd become a nun for the simplicity of dressing and never having to buy fripperies if it weren't for all that religious nonsense she just couldn't get past.

Thankfully, Lucy had managed to slip back into the house early this morning with Garret and Aunt Mary being none the wiser. Lucy was just about to give up on the clothing and go in search of Cass when a sharp knock sounded on her door.

"Who is it?" she called.

"It's me" came Cass's sweet voice.

Lucy hurried over to the door and opened it. Excellent timing. "Come in, dear. I was just looking at—"

Lucy snapped her mouth shut. Cass stood in the corridor

looking quite pale and wringing her hands. "Oh, Lucy, you must come quickly."

Lucy's heart leaped to her throat. "What is it, Cass?"

"Mama and Papa have gone to the duke's town house to demand that he offer for me." The words rushed out of Cass's mouth like water through a dam.

Lucy's hand flew to her throat. "No."

"Yes." Cass nodded, her blond curls bobbing at her temples. "It's awful. I'm mortified. I'm afraid that if the two of us don't go and try to explain what's happened, Papa will end up with a forced offer from Derek and I couldn't stand it. You must come with me, Lucy. You must help."

Lucy nodded rapidly and pointed down the corridor. "By all means, let's go."

The two hurried downstairs where Lucy took a moment to hastily throw on a pelisse and a bonnet. Then they were off in the coach Cass had come in.

Their insistent knocks at Derek's door were met with Hughes's monotonous tone. "Yes?"

"We must speak with His Grace immediately," Lucy said.

Thankfully, the butler acted as if he'd never seen Lucy before. "His Grace is already occupied with callers at the moment."

"We know!" Cass brushed past the large man. Lucy was impressed by her forcefulness.

Hughes looked at them both as if they were street urchins forcing their way into the kitchens and demanding scraps. Clearly under duress, he showed them to the drawing room where Lord and Lady Moreland were already having words with the duke. Lucy and Cass rushed inside. But the other occupants of the room didn't seem to notice them.

Derek stood next to the mantelpiece, his hand braced against it, his face a mask of stone.

Lady Moreland, her nose high in the air, sat on the settee. Lord Moreland paced across the expensive carpet nearly shouting at the duke. "I will not have my daughter treated so cavalierly."

A muscle ticked in Derek's jaw. "My lord, if you'll just be reasonable—"

Lord Monroe pulled on his lapels. "I've been reasonable, Claringdon. More than reasonable waiting for you to make my daughter an offer. I demand you make things right."

"Yes, we were quite convinced an offer was forthcoming," Lady Moreland said, dabbing at her brow with her handkerchief.

"I'm certain if we all just discuss this rationally . . . ," Derek continued.

"The time for being rational is over," Cass's father nearly shouted.

Cass took a deep breath and stepped forward. "Mother, Father, I know you both think you're doing the right thing for me, but you're making a terrible mistake."

The Monroes turned to stare at their daughter. "That's enough from you, Cassandra. You haven't been thinking properly in weeks," her mother said.

Cass raised her hand in a pleading gesture. "Mother, please. I will not marry the duke."

Her father clamped his jaw so tightly his jowls shook. "Young lady, you do not know what you're saying."

Cass raised her chin. "Yes, I do. I'm telling you that I refuse to marry him."

"You *will* marry him and that's an end to it," her mother insisted. "Captain Swift plans to marry your cousin when he returns. Do not hold out false hope on that score. Besides, he's a second son. He'll never hold a title."

That last comment caused Derek to raise his brows.

Cass pushed up her chin. "I do not hold out false hope, Mama. Believe me. But that does not mean I should ruin another man's life by dragging him into a loveless marriage."

"Who says it's loveless?" her mother snapped. "You could well learn to have feelings for each other someday."

Cass smiled and crossed over the thick carpet to lean down and pat her mother's cheek. "Oh, Mama. I do know you want the best for me. Truly, I do. But the duke is madly in love with Lucy and I cannot blame him." She turned to her two friends and gave them a warm smile. Lucy smiled back and Derek nodded and shifted on his booted feet, his hands folded behind his back.

"Lucy!" Lady Moreland wailed. "Lucy's the biggest wallflower in the *ton*."

Lucy wrinkled her nose and clapped her hand over her mouth. Somehow she didn't think pointing out to Lady Moreland that Janie was a bigger wallflower than she was a prudent idea at the moment.

Cass's father slapped his leather gloves against his thigh. He pointed at Cass. "I don't care who he's in love with. He's led you on and if he's a true *gentleman*, he'll do the right thing and marry you, by God."

None of them missed the emphasis the man placed on the word "gentleman." He was questioning Derek's honor. Derek's fist was tightly clenched.

Lady Moreland shot up from the settee. "Tell me, Claringdon, do you still refuse to marry my daughter?"

Derek nodded. "Inasmuch as she refuses to marry me as well, my lady. Yes."

Cass nodded. "Mama, if I marry someday, I want it to be to a man who loves me as well as the duke loves Lucy."

Lady Moreland turned a mottled shade of purple. "Lucy? Lucy Upton will never be a duchess!"

Derek clenched his jaw. "I've done my best to be civil, Lady Moreland, but now I must ask that you leave my home. I won't have you disparage my future wife."

Lucy gasped softly. Derek stood up for her. No one had ever done that before. Cass tugged on her mother's hand. "Let's go, Mama, before you say something you'll regret."

Cass's father pulled on his gloves so hard, Lucy wondered if the leather would shred. He stalked to the door and opened it, turning to wait for his wife to follow.

Lady Moreland turned in a swirl of orange silk, savagely clutching her reticule. She faced Derek and Lucy, who stood together near the fireplace.

"You mark my words, Claringdon," Lady Moreland seethed. "You may refuse to marry Cassandra but it'll be a cold day in hell before a duke marries the likes of Lucy Upton. I'll go to the queen herself and inform her of this travesty. I happen to know that the conditions of your investiture require that the Crown approves of your wife. The queen will never allow it."

Lucy swallowed and glanced away. Derek, the muscle still ticking furiously in his jaw, nodded at Lady Moreland. "You do what you must, my lady, as will I."

Two minutes later, all three of the Monroes had left Derek's town house. Cass had given Lucy a hug and said her good-byes to Derek, offering them both her best wishes. Lord and Lady Moreland had resignedly trotted out to their carriage with their daughter. Lady Moreland paused only long enough to give Lucy another simmering narrowed-eyed glare.

As soon as the door closed behind them, Lucy sank to the sofa. Shaking, she dropped her head into her hands. Derek crossed over to her and sat next to her. He pulled her tight against him. "It's an idle threat. She's angry, that's all."

Lucy tugged herself out of his arms and looked at him. "No, Derek, you don't understand. The queen, she . . . She doesn't approve of me. She won't approve of me. Why didn't I think of this before? It will never work."

A thunderous expression moved across his face. "What do you mean?"

"The queen won't say yes. I know it."

"There's no guarantee Lady Moreland will even bring it to her attention. She was probably only bluffing."

Lucy shook her head. "You don't think the queen will notice when one of her dukes marries?"

"I don't give a damn what the queen thinks. We can get a special license and be married before anyone can object."

She put a hand on his sleeve. "Is what Lady Moreland said true? Is it a condition of your investiture that the Crown approve of your wife?"

He swore under his breath. "Yes."

Lucy squeezed her eyes closed. "They won't accept me."

"That makes no sense. You're the daughter of an earl."

"The unwanted daughter of an earl who disgraced herself at her come-out. There's more than one reason I've remained unmarried all these years, Derek."

He scrubbed both hands through his hair. "Your debut was five years ago. Not to mention we've already—"

She looked away, couldn't face him. "I trust you won't tell anyone about that. And you must ask Hughes to be discreet as well."

"Damn it, Lucy, of course I won't tell anyone, and

Hughes will be out on the street if he dares breathe a word about it, but—"

Her head snapped back to face him. "You don't understand the ways of the *ton* as I do, Derek."

"I don't care about the bloody *ton*," he growled.

Lucy searched his face. "You say you don't care, but what if you were forced to give up your title?"

He grabbed her by the upper arms and stared into her eyes, his words coming through clenched teeth. "It won't come to that. Say yes. Marry me, Lucy."

Lucy pulled away from him, stood, and crossed over to the door. She placed her hand on the cool brass handle and faced the dark wood. "I cannot say yes to you, Derek. Not knowing it may cost you everything you've earned. My answer is no."

## ❧ CHAPTER FIFTY-ONE ❧

A summons from Queen Charlotte. No matter how many times Lucy stared at the odious bit of costly vellum, wishing it to perdition, it lurked on the edge of the writing desk, haunting her.

The queen, the prince regent's mother, had been the bane of Lucy's young life five years ago. She and her mother had gathered the requisite fripperies and frills: huge old-fashioned hooped skirts, feathered headdresses, and high-heeled boots with too many ribbons to trip over. They had dutifully trotted to the palace to make Lucy's requisite debut in the queen's chambers. It was the one time Lucy could remember her mother paying the slightest bit of attention to her since before Ralph died. And Lucy had tried, truly. As hard as she could. But Mother wanted her to pretend to be someone she was not. Someone like . . . Cass. And Lucy had failed, again. She would never be a son. She was an inadequate daughter.

They'd traveled to the palace that day, only to be escorted out after Lucy's antics had garnered the censure of the queen and the derision of the princesses. Lucy had never been so glad to leave a place in all her life. The only good thing was that she'd never have to return.

Never, that was, until Her Majesty summoned her.

It seemed Lady Moreland had made good on her threat to bring the nation's newest duke's marital plans to the attention of her monarch. Because Derek had been granted his title with stipulations, without Their Majesties' approval, he could not marry. It was unthinkable but it was true. The royal approval must be had. And Derek had chosen the most unsuitable candidate in Society. Her.

Never in her life had Lucy wished more that she was respectable and proper and knew how to do and say the right things. But the queen already hated her. If she remembered her, that is, and how could she not? A young lady who started a scandal in the chambers? One who essentially had a tantrum and didn't show her sovereign the proper respect? An abomination. Yes, that was her. Lady Lucy Upton, abomination.

And she'd already made the biggest mistake of them all. When she'd spent the night with Derek, it had never occurred to her that Lady Moreland might try to upend her marriage plans, but it seemed Cass's mother was so thwarted in her dreams for her daughter, she was set on revenge no matter the cost.

Cass had snuck over to visit Lucy, despite her mother's insistence that they end their friendship. Cass had cried and told Lucy how utterly ashamed and sorry she was for her mother's behavior. "I've tried to reason with her, Lucy. She refuses to listen."

In the end, it seemed, there was nothing anyone could do. Lady Moreland was well connected at court and set about making it her business to bend the ear of the queen. She couldn't force a duke to marry her daughter, but she certainly could set about trying to ruin said duke's plans to marry an inappropriate duchess. And now the summons from the queen sat on the desk, like an awful little papery recrimination, reminding Lucy of how utterly unladylike and unworthy she was and always would be.

Lucy had just decided to toss the summons into the fireplace when Cass and Jane floated into the drawing room.

"We've come to help. A plan is in order," Jane declared, hands on her hips, already searching about for the tea tray on which she would inevitably find her favorite cakes.

"Plan?" Lucy echoed, turning to face her friends. "Am I to have a plan?"

"Of course you must have a plan," Jane replied, taking a seat on a rosewood chair next to her friend. "This situation isn't about to resolve itself, is it?"

Lucy frowned. "What situation?"

Cass crossed over to the writing desk and scooped up the summons. "Just as we suspected, the queen wishes to see you."

Lucy blinked. "How did you—?"

Cass shrugged. "I did some investigating. Seems when a duke decides to take a bride, the potential bride must be officially summoned by the queen."

Lucy rolled her eyes. "I suppose I should be honored that she's bothering to take the time to meet with me."

Cass stamped her foot. "See, right there. That is the attitude you must change if we're to help you."

"Have you told His Grace?" Jane, having found the tea tray, popped a piece of cake into her mouth.

Lucy sighed. "No. What's the use? She will never approve of me. Oh, Cass, why did I ruin your potential engagement for this? You and Derek might have been happy together."

Cass slapped at Lucy's sleeve. "Are you completely daft? We would have made each other miserable and you know it. Not to mention, he happens to be madly in love with you and you with him."

"Tell her the other part," Jane prompted.

Cass turned back to face Lucy. "Oh, yes. I also discovered that the duke received a similar summons."

Lucy frowned. "To see the queen?"

Cass shook her head. "No, the prince regent."

"Derek detests the prince regent," Lucy replied.

"It doesn't matter. If he's to get his approval, he'll need to be convincing. Which is why we're here to help you with your plan."

Lucy glanced between her two friends. "You keep using that word. What exactly do you expect me to do?"

Jane set her plate aside and wiped her mouth with her napkin. "We expect you to put on a show, of course. It'll be just like a play."

Lucy tossed a hand in the air. "A play? What are you talking about?"

Cass took a deep breath. "Lucy, listen to me. You must go to court and be demure and presentable—and most of all, quiet."

Lucy narrowed her eyes on her friend. "You say that as if it's something I could actually accomplish."

"Of course you can, Luce," Jane added. "Pretend you're an actress."

Cass nodded. "We're serious, Lucy. You must speak only when spoken to, you must keep your eyes downcast, and you must be the picture of a reformed fine lady. You must convince the queen you've changed since your—ahem—unfortunate incident five years ago."

Lucy groaned. "Do you have any idea how difficult that will be for me?"

Jane grinned widely. "Of course we do. That's why we're here to help."

Cass leaned over and squeezed her shoulder. "You must do it, Lucy . . . for Derek."

"Does Derek know about this?"

Jane and Cass exchanged uneasy looks. "Not yet. We decided we would see how it goes before—"

"Getting his hopes up?" Lucy provided.

"He has enough to worry about what with impressing the prince," Cass said.

Lucy glanced between them again. "Fine. What exactly do you suggest?"

Cass's smile widened. "We're going to turn you into a lady. Well, a lady of court."

Lucy shook her head vigorously. "Oh, no. My mother tried that once and I—"

"With all due respect," Cass replied, clearing her throat, a determined gleam in her eye, "your mother is not *me*."

Lucy's gaze swung to Jane, who shrugged. "Don't look at me. I'm merely here to cheer you on. This ladylike business is entirely Cass's domain."

Lucy whimpered. Could she do this? For Derek? She didn't know but she had to try. She took a deep breath and let it out slowly. Then she reached out and squeezed her friends' hands. "By all means, then, let the plan begin."

## ❧ CHAPTER FIFTY-TWO ❧

By the time Lucy arrived at the royal palace a sennight later, she'd been schooled in absolutely every single bit of decorum—and for lack of a better term, girlishness—than she had in her prior twenty-three years of life. What Cass knew about being a lady could fill volumes. It was quite extraordinary. For example, who knew there was a proper way to laugh at a gentleman's jest? A proper way to ensure your gait was not too hurried? A proper way to raise your skirts when walking through mud? And a proper way to address certain members of the queen's household? Oh, Lucy had probably heard these rules before, naturally, but she hadn't been paying a whit of attention five years ago. It had bored her to distraction, actually. But now, with her future with Derek in jeopardy, Lucy studied these asinine bits of decorum as if she were the most zealous and ambitious young lady on the verge of making a debut.

The rules had all been repeated ad nauseam, drilled into her head, and practiced over endless rounds of rehearsals attended by Cass as the devoted and strict instructor, Jane as the audience and general jeerer, and Garrett upon occasion when the subject matter called for a male to be present, such as dancing.

But most surprising of all was that Lucy actually enjoyed some of it. She kept Derek in her thoughts. Doing these things with Derek, spending time with him. It all seemed like a small price to pay for a future with him. And by the end of it she'd had the thought more than once that if she hadn't spent so long vehemently protesting the general concept of participating in lady-like pursuits, she might very well have enjoyed them all along.

But still, as Lucy approached the great doors to the queen's chambers, her insides quaked. No matter how many hours Cass had spent teaching her, did she truly have it in her to be a proper lady? The smell of lemon polish reminded her of the last time she'd been here. She gulped. At least her mother wasn't with her this time to see her shame. Oh, she'd written to her mother, and casually mentioned that she would be going to see the queen, but she'd steadfastly refrained from adding the bit about a possible engagement to a duke. No sense getting Mama's hopes up too high if nothing were to come of it. Of course, the rumor mill might well make it to her mother's ear before she had a chance to explain. But that was a risk Lucy was willing to take. Aunt Mary, at least, had promised to keep quiet until after everything was settled one way or another. Lucy could always count on Aunt Mary to take her side over her mother's.

Two handsome footmen sporting royal livery pulled open the great doors to the chamber. Lucy sucked air through her nostrils and then slowly began her march toward the throne. Her footsteps echoed against the marble floors. The closer she came, the more she recognized the details from the scene of five years ago. The princesses were lined up in chairs on either side of their mother, the servants stood at rapt attention along the walls, the ladies-in-waiting and the rest of the court milled about, laughing and— Oh wait, they weren't laughing. They were silent. All silent. Watching her approach.

Lucy concentrated on putting one foot in front of the next. Balance, Cass had said, was the key to mastering the formal dress of the court. The hoops that had nearly upended Lucy five years ago were tamely mastered this time. At least she could claim that small victory.

She glanced around. Aunt Mary had escorted her and Cass was there, just as she'd said she would be. She'd begged her mother to allow her to come today. Lucy suspected Lady Moreland had allowed it so that the queen might see how much better a duchess Cass would make, but Lucy appreciated her friend's presence nonetheless.

Cass and Aunt Mary both gave Lucy encouraging smiles just before she came to a halt several paces in front of the queen's throne.

"Lady Lucy Upton, Your Majesty," some regally dressed servant announced.

The queen looked down her nose at Lucy. She seemed to study her from top to toe. No doubt the princesses were doing the same. She couldn't look at them.

"Lady Lucy," the queen intoned.

Lucy held her breath. If she remembered correctly this was one of the most difficult parts. A throne room bow wearing hoop skirts was something from which one might well never recover. But she and Cass had practiced until Lucy felt as if her ribs might crack. She was prepared. Gulp. She hoped.

She lowered herself into the sweeping bow, hoping against hope that she did not tip over and fall flat upon her face. "Your Majesty."

"You may stand," the queen offered shortly thereafter.

Lucy slowly and carefully righted herself. One exceedingly awful part finished. How many more remained?

The queen folded her hands in her lap and glared at Lucy. "Lady Moreland tells me she questions whether you are a suitable wife for Claringdon."

Lucy kept her gaze trained on the floor. She wanted to slap Lady Moreland, or at least deliver a crushing set-down to the matron. How had lovable, wonderful Cass come from such a hideous woman? Lucy shook her head. Must concentrate. *Demure. Demure. Demure.* "I understand, Your Majesty."

"And do you agree?" the queen asked, her voice pitched high.

"I do not, Your Majesty." If demure called for lying, Lucy just couldn't do it. She could nearly hear Cass wince.

"I see." The queen held out her hand, and a footman rushed forward with a sheet of parchment. Another footman hurried forth and presented the queen with a pair of golden spectacles. She perched them upon her nose and unfolded the parchment. "It says here that you've been known to do tricks on horseback."

Lucy gulped. Oh, no. The queen had a list? This could not end well. "Yes, Your Majesty."

"You learned to hunt and fish as a child?"

Eyes still riveted to the floor, Lucy nodded. "Yes, Your Majesty."

"You make poultices for horses?"

Lucy swallowed. "And hounds. And sometimes people, Your Majesty."

"You once challenged a boy to duel?" The royal voice went up in pitch again at that one.

"Yes, Your Majesty."

"Hrmph."

Sweat trickled down Lucy's brow. Oh, this was not going well. Not going well at all.

"You." The queen stopped, and Lucy dared a glance. The queen removed her spectacles and rubbed her eyes before placing the frames back upon her regal nose. "You asked your father if you could attend Eton?" The queen's eyebrow arched and she looked around at the princesses. "That cannot be right."

"It is, Your Majesty," Lucy replied. That was it. If she heard a thud it would be Cass fainting.

The princesses giggled at Lucy's confession. Lucy winced. She remembered that tittering sound from five years ago. It had been etched in her brain.

The queen narrowed her eyes and stared at her. Lucy contemplated her monarch. This woman had fifteen children and a mad husband. She'd seen her share of oddities no doubt. But she was looking at Lucy as if she were a creature from another world.

"Turn around, Lady Lucy," the queen demanded.

Lucy gritted her teeth and did as she was asked.

"I'm told you have a sharp tongue," the queen said next. *Demure. Demure.* "Also true, Your Majesty."

The queen pulled the spectacles from her nose. The footman rushed back to retrieve them. "And are you curbing it today for my sake?"

"Absolutely!" Perhaps that had been a bit too vehement.

More giggling from the princesses. Lucy wanted to sink through the floor.

"I see," the queen intoned. "Lady Moreland also informs me that when you made your bow, you caused quite a scene."

Lucy let her shoulders relax for the first time since she'd entered the chambers. Oh, thank heavens. The queen didn't remember it herself.

"I . . . may have, Your Majesty."

"Did you or didn't you, Lady Lucy?"

She could hear Cass's voice in her head. *Say you didn't. Say you didn't.*

Lucy took a deep breath. "Yes. I made an awful scene, Your Majesty. One that I am extremely regretful of at present."

The queen's eyebrow shot up again. "And did you regret it at the time?"

Lucy squared her shoulders and pushed up her chin. This was it, the final strike against her. "No, Your Majesty. I only regret it now because I hope it will not affect your decision as to my worthiness to marry the Duke of Claringdon."

A gasp went round the room. All eyes were on the queen's face. What would the royal lady possibly say to that?

From the corner of her eye, Lucy spied Cass standing next to Aunt Mary rapidly fanning herself. Aunt Mary seemed to have a permanent wince burned onto her features, and Lady Moreland had her arms crossed over her chest and a satisfied smirk on her face. She knew she'd won.

Lucy picked up her skirts. Cass had been adamant. She must back out of the room as soon as the queen dismissed her. One never turned one's back to a monarch, and Lucy's retreat was about to be the most humiliating in history.

"I have one more question for you, Lady Lucy," the queen said.

Lucy gulped. "Yes, Your Majesty?"

"*Why* do you wish to marry the Duke of Claringdon?"

Lucy took a deep breath. "The truth is, Your Majesty, I regret that he is a duke. I want to marry him because he is the best man I've ever known. More loyal and loving and kind than anyone knows. I love him, Your Majesty, and I would do anything for him. Including coming here today and wearing this ridiculous gown with the equivalent of a bird in my hair and stays that may end my life, and simper and scrape and act proper for the chance to spend the rest of my life with him."

That had done it. She'd rendered the poor princesses speechless. Their royal mouths had all dropped open simultaneously.

Lucy glanced about the chamber. Cass's mother was practically rubbing her hands together with glee. And Cass had gone so pale, Lucy was certain she would faint—which might be just the distraction Lucy needed to back out of the room without as many people watching. *Faint, Cass. Faint.*

The queen narrowed her eyes on Lucy and drummed her fingers along the arms of her ornate chair. "I remember you, Lady Lucy. You told me you didn't enjoy being forced into uncomfortable clothing for the sake of propriety and you kicked off your shoes after declaring that they pinched your feet hideously."

Lucy closed her eyes. Oh, yes, that had been her, all right. She bowed her head. "Yes, Your Majesty."

"Then you pulled the feathers out of your hair and asked your mother if the 'blasted thing' was over yet."

Lucy pressed two fingertips to the throbbing pain in her skull. "Yes, Your Majesty."

The queen leaned forward just a bit. "You are your parents' only child, are you not?"

That was a surprising question. "Yes, Your Majesty. My brother Ralph died at the age of nine."

The queen glanced around at the princesses. "Can you imagine, girls, not having any sisters?"

The princesses' sympathetic murmurs filled the state room. With such a robust family, no indeed, they could not imagine any such thing.

The queen looked down her nose at Lucy once again. "I shall leave it to you to inform Claringdon that you're to be his bride."

Lucy's heart stopped. If anyone was going to faint now, it just might be her. "Did I hear you correctly, Your Majesty? I thought you said—"

The queen nodded. "You're of good family. I see no reason to object. Seems to me you're both a bit unconventional and will be the perfect match for each other. Not to mention there is hardly enough true love in this world."

The princesses collectively sighed.

The squeal Lucy heard next must have been her own but she didn't stop to examine its origin. "Thank you, Your Majesty. Thank you very much." She began to back away. Oh, it was taking far too long. About halfway across the room, she turned, picked up her skirts, and ran full tilt.

Lady Moreland's vehement protests echoed through the chamber. Lucy's eyes briefly met Cass's. Cass's mouth was as wide as an O.

"Lucy, you're running," Cass called, an undercurrent of disapproval and warning in her voice.

"I know," she called back.

"Why?" Cass's voice was filled with nerves. Then, "Where are you going?"

Without breaking her stride, Lucy yanked off her feathered headdress and tossed it in the air. "I'm going to be bold!"

# ❧ CHAPTER FIFTY-THREE ❧

It took more than a bit of cajoling on Lucy's part to convince Hughes to inform her of his master's whereabouts that evening. Apparently, Derek had been at the club all afternoon and had only returned home briefly to change his clothing and leave again for a dinner party.

The prince regent's dinner party.

Lucy sighed. Two royal visits in one day. What she wouldn't do for that man.

When Garrett's coach pulled up in front of Carlton House, Lucy was shaking with nerves.

"Are you quite certain you don't want me to come with you?" Garrett asked. Her cousin was such a dear. He'd insisted upon accompanying her.

"I must do this myself."

"Very well, but I shall wait here for you."

Lucy nodded. A backup plan. Yes. Good.

The royal butler eyed her up and down but appeared to take her word for the fact that she was indeed named Lady Lucy Upton and had urgent business to discuss with the Duke of Claringdon. She was soon ushered into the dinner party.

Lucy had heard tales of the prince regent's infamous dinner parties, but of course she'd never been invited to one. The reality was beyond her imagination.

An enormous table had been set with the finest of china, linens, and crystals. The table was lined with huge platters of meats and cheeses, sweets and puddings, vegetables and birds, and roasts, and gravies. All sorts of wines and chocolates. Everywhere she looked there was something more delectable than the last. The prince himself was perched in the center of the ostentatious display; two gorgeous ladies sat on either side of him. Next to one of them was Derek.

Without taking her eyes from him, Lucy slowly made her way into the center of the room. She knew the moment Derek spotted her. His gaze focused on her and he stopped talking to his dinner companions.

Lucy continued on trembling legs. She stopped on the other side of the table from Derek and called out in a clear, sure voice, "Your Grace?"

All conversation ceased. The clatter of utensils, the laughing, the music. Complete silence descended upon the room as all eyes riveted on her.

"And who might you be?" the prince regent asked, guzzling a cup of wine.

Lucy answered him without taking her eyes from Derek. "I'm Lady Lucy Upton," she said. "And I've come to see the Duke of Claringdon."

The prince set down his cup and wiped his bulbous lips with his napkin. "Ah, your future wife, eh, Claringdon?"

Derek's jaw was tight, but his eyes remained locked with hers. "I'm not certain, Your Majesty. She said no the last time I asked."

"Does anyone have a pack of cards?" Lucy called out.

The prince regent scoffed. "Do I have a pack of cards? Surely you are jesting." He clapped his hands and a footman materialized with the cards within seconds. The servant handed them to Lucy.

Derek watched her carefully. "Lucy, what are you doing?"

She stepped forward until she stood in front of Derek. She held out the cards to him. "Pick a card, Your Grace. Just one."

He swallowed. "What for?"

"As you said, you asked me to marry you once and I said no. But I'm here tonight to change that, to fix it."

"What do you mean?" Derek's eyes were hooded.

"The number on the card shall represent the number of better responses than 'No' to the question 'Will you marry me?'"

"Lucy, you don't have to—"

"Pick," she murmured achingly.

Derek's gaze dropped to the cards. He pulled out one and flipped it over.

"Ten of clubs," the prince announced, rubbing his chubby little hands together with glee.

Lucy raised her voice loud enough to be heard by the entire room. If she was going to humiliate herself in front of the *ton* today, she might as well make a real show of it.

"'Yes, because you lived through the war,'" she said.

Derek held up a hand to stop her. "Don't—"

She spoke even louder the next time. "'Yes, because of the beautiful letters you wrote to me.'"

His eyes never left hers.

"'Yes, because you never backed down to me.'"

Derek's face softened.

" 'Yes, because you punched a tree.' "

The prince regent nearly spit out his wine. "Punched a tree, Claringdon?"

"Don't ask," Derek growled.

Tears tumbled down Lucy's cheeks. " 'Yes, because you chose the puppy.' "

"I won't even ask," the prince said, one royal eyebrow raised.

" 'Yes, because you once challenged me to a word duel and won.' "

Derek's mouth quirked up in the barest hint of a smile.

" 'Yes, because you hate to drink tea.' "

"So do I." The prince guzzled more wine.

" 'Yes, because you're loyal to your friends.' "

"That's eight!" someone called from the far end of the table.

Lucy swiped at her tears with the back of her hand. " 'Yes, because you learned to change your decisions.' "

"Nine!" another voice called.

" 'Yes, because I love you desperately and cannot live my life without you.' "

Derek dropped his napkin onto the table, pushed back his chair, and stood. "Lucy, wait."

"No. You got to do all the talking last time we had a wager. It's my turn."

He pulled his handkerchief from his pocket and handed it to her. "You don't need to say any more. You had me at 'Your Grace.' "

She couldn't help but smile at that.

"I meant what I said," Derek continued. "I don't care if the queen doesn't approve of you. Or the prince here, either. I'll renounce my title if I must."

The prince's eyes went wide, but he happily slurped more wine.

Wiping the tears from her eyes, Lucy gave Derek a sidewise smile. "Completely unnecessary, Your Grace."

Derek furrowed his brow. "What?"

"The queen gave us her blessing."

"And I do, too, for what it's apparently worth," the prince regent added on a hiccup. "This is downright bloody romantic."

Derek leaped over the table, scooped Lucy into his arms, and spun her around. "Really?"

"Really." Lucy laughed through her tears.

"Really," the prince added.

Derek fell to one knee. "You'll marry me?"

Lucy fell to her knees, too, and hugged him. "Yes. Yes. Yes!"

The prince regent leaned back and elbowed the Marquis of Colton. "Well, if that wasn't *The Taming of the Shrew* in the flesh. I daresay this is one of the most diverting dinner parties I've held in an age, eh?"

Derek stood and pulled Lucy up into his embrace. "Now, my love, let's see about getting a special license. For I cannot wait to make you my bride."

## ❧ CHAPTER FIFTY-FOUR ❧

Twenty minutes later, they were at Derek's town house. They'd quickly said their good-byes to the prince regent and the other esteemed guests at the dinner party and hastily taken their leave, dismissing Garrett—who merely raised his eyebrows and said, "I do hope the wedding is imminent," before ordering his coach back home. No doubt everyone in attendance knew exactly what they were up to.

Thankfully, Haughty Hughes had already retired for the evening. The moment they entered the foyer and divested themselves of their cloaks, Derek pulled Lucy into the nearest drawing room.

"Shouldn't we go to your bedchamber?" she asked, a shaky smile on her lips.

"No. I can't wait. I have to have you now. I've been thinking about taking you in a drawing room ever since Bath."

Derek shut the door behind them and locked it. Then he turned to Lucy with a dark, passionate look in his eyes. He stalked toward her and captured her lips, moving his hand behind her neck to grasp her head and move it in rhythm to his kiss. Lucy gasped against his mouth.

Heedlessly knocking over furniture, he dragged her to the side of the room and pushed her up against the wall, roughly but not enough to hurt her. "Spread your legs for me," he demanded. "Now."

Lust, hot and powerful, shot through her. She did exactly as he said. He lifted her against the wall, fumbled for the buttons on his trousers with one deft hand, then gathered up her skirts, pushed her shift up to her hips, and entered her in one sure, solid thrust.

Lucy's head snapped to the side against the wall. Her mouth was open, her breasts heavy, hot. She moaned. She'd never felt anything like it. She'd been ready for him in just those brief moments. The instant his hands had touched her she'd been hot and wet and wanting. Derek's eyes were closed and his jaw tightly clenched. "You. Feel. So. Damn. Good." He punctuated each word with a thrust.

Lucy's head tossed back and forth. "So do you."

She thought this was all there would be, that they'd stay like this until that amazing feeling only he could make her feel washed over her in hot, welcome waves, but instead he pulled out of her and set her down. She wanted to sob. Her wobbly feet found the wood floorboards and she braced herself against him, one hand on his shoulder, still breathing so heavily she thought her heart would beat from her chest.

Derek spun her around and made quick work of the buttons on her gown. Soon the entire mass of fabric swooshed down around her feet. His body heat was gone for a moment while he pulled a padded stepstool over. "Kneel here," he commanded.

A rush of heat and longing spread to Lucy's limbs. She turned and faced the wall, kneeling on the soft stool wearing only her shift. She braced her hands against the windowsill in front of her. Even though it was dark, she was thankful the curtains were drawn. Derek undid her stays, pulled them over her head, and discarded them. Then he pulled the pins out of her coiffure quickly, messily, tugging at her hair a bit, causing a bit of pain. She didn't care. The entire mass of her shiny dark hair fell over her shoulders and Derek splayed it over her back. "You're gorgeous," he whispered in her ear.

Lucy could tell by the shuffling of fabric behind her that he was removing his trousers this time. "Spread your legs," he demanded again. She did. "Wider."

She pushed her knees farther apart. A thrill shot through her.

Then he was there, behind her, tugging her shift up over her hips, probing at her softness. Lucy was bent over on the stool, braced against the windowsill. She was more than wet and ready for him. Hard and smooth, he slid inside of her with one sure thrust. Lucy gasped. Derek groaned. "Damn it. I thought about this all night. I can never have enough of you." He hadn't yet begun to move, and Lucy was completely at his mercy. She tried to rock her hips back and forth, but his large, strong hands grabbed her around the waist, owning her.

He leaned over her body and bit her earlobe. "I want you, Lucy." One sure thrust. "I want you." Another thrust.

Lucy moaned. She turned her head to the side. Wanting to kiss him, to feel his mouth on hers. She leaned back against him and wrapped her arms behind his neck, forcing her breasts to jut out. His hands moved up and caressed them, flicking the sensitive peaks and making Lucy moan again.

"You're mine," he groaned. Another hard thrust. "Mine."

She tried to grab him, her arms grappling behind her head. "I'm yours," she echoed on a groan.

"I didn't want this," Derek whispered into her ear. "I didn't want to fall in love and become a slave to a woman's body."

She shuddered. "You're my slave?"

Another deep thrust that made her whimper. "Yes. You make me so hard." Another thrust.

She gasped. "Derek, I want you. So much."

Another deep thrust made Lucy close her eyes and moan. He moved his hand around to lightly caress the nub between her legs. He bit her neck softly.

Lucy cried out. His fingers drove her mad, circling her again and again, softly, so softly, bringing her to the brink of a ecstasy and then . . . stopping.

"No!" she cried out as his finger fell away from the place she wanted it the most. She nearly sobbed.

He withdrew from her then and pulled her up from the stool. He leaned down and drew up her shift and pulled it over her head. He threw it into the corner and stared at her body like it was a priceless painting. "You're so beautiful," he whispered. "So damn beautiful."

Tears pricked behind Lucy's eyes.

He lifted her tenderly, easily, and carried her over to the sofa. He laid her down so reverently. "Lucy," he whispered as he covered her with his huge hot body. "I love you."

He thrust into her again in one sure solid movement and she arched her back off the sofa. He leaned down and sucked her breast into his mouth, playing with her, toying with her. He thrust again. "I want you." He thrust again. "So. Damn. Badly."

Lucy was completely mindless. Her fingers tangled in his dark hair, her mouth open and red and raw from his fierce kisses. She'd been a bit tender when he'd first entered her but that was long forgotten now with all the overwhelming feelings he was stoking in her body. He plowed into her again and again and that, combined with the force of his hot wet mouth sucking on her nipple, made her groan. She was so close, so close. And he knew it.

He gave her a devilish grin and pulled out of her. "No!" she cried this time reaching for him, tugging on him, trying to force him back inside her by wrapping her leg around his back. Instead he let his wicked hand slide down to the juncture of her thighs, where he slipped one hot finger inside of her. Lucy's head rolled back on the cushion. "Are you trying to kill me?"

"Never, my love. I just want to give you the most amazing feeling of your life."

"You already have," she breathed.

"To date," he said wickedly, just before he slipped his finger back inside her. His dark head moved back to her breast, tugging relentlessly with his teeth. Once, twice, matching the rhythm of his finger. He stroked her again, again, while his tormenting mouth kept up its pressure on her helpless breast. Then his thumb found that perfect spot between her legs and he rubbed it in a circle just as his mouth tugged for a final time on her swollen, aching breast.

"Oh, God, Derek!" she cried as the wave of her orgasm crashed over her with a force that tore a scream from her chest. He rolled onto her quickly and slid inside her, her internal muscles climaxing, flexing. He thrust into her one, two, three times, gritting his teeth as her hot wet warmth milked him and he exploded in the most intense release of his entire life.

※

They snuck out of the drawing room. Derek had put his clothing back on and been on the lookout for servants. Lucy had tossed on her shift and said a little prayer that they'd make it up the staircase and down the long corridor to Derek's bedchamber without being caught. But truthfully she didn't care. All she cared about was this man, her love, the way he made her feel, the way she hoped she made him feel, and the amazing fact that they'd found each other and were going to be married. Married. She still couldn't believe that. Even though she said it over and over in her head, it started to sound made up, as if it had no meaning. But she repeated it nonetheless.

They made it safely to his bedchamber. Derek quickly locked the door behind them, then scooped Lucy into his arms and carried her over to the bed where he laid her gently. She pushed up onto her knees and pulled her shift over her head. Derek quickly shucked all of his clothing again and soon they were rolling around, giggling and laughing and kissing and then, seriously, making love.

"I'll never get enough of you," Derek whispered into her hair after they finished.

Lucy propped herself up against the pillows, the sheet pulled up under her arms. Derek situated himself next to her.

"So tell me, Duke of Decisive, when did you know for certain you loved me?"

Derek braced both hands behind his head and stared at the ceiling, a grin on his handsome face. "Let's see. I believe it was right around the time when I realized that thinking of another man's hands touching you made me want to tear the chap limb from limb."

Lucy widened her eyes. "Truly?"

"Yes, when I saw Berkeley helping you into your coach at the theater, I wanted to kill him."

Lucy shook her head. "Like the time you punched the tree?"

"Yes," he growled. "Exactly like the time I punched the tree."

She laughed. "And your murderous thoughts translated into love?"

Derek turned to brace himself up on one elbow and stare at her. He pushed a curl behind her ear. "I knew it because I remember thinking that if I married Cassandra, I wouldn't mind who she consorted with."

"You did?"

"Yes."

Lucy's eyes filled with tears. "It's amazing to me that you love me."

He traced her cheekbone with the tip of his finger. "Why would you say that?"

She pulled up the covers to her neck. "You could have had Cass. Cass is so perfect and pretty and well put together. She's demure and sweet and never says anything rude or cross or offensive. Me? I'm quirky. My eyes are two different colors and my hair is too curly and completely unmanageable and when I blow my nose I sound like a goose."

"A goose?"

"Yes. Did you know when Cass blows her nose, you can barely tell?"

He pulled her into his arms. "Apparently, I like ladies who are rude and cross and offensive." He smiled at her. "Until I met you, I'd never met anyone, let alone a female, who stood up to me the way you did, who challenged me. It was quite a new experience for me, I have to say."

She smiled against his shoulder. "It was?"

"Yes. Your eyes are unique and your curly hair is beautiful and you do not blow your nose like a goose and even if you did, I wouldn't mind. Being demure is highly overrated."

She smiled at that. "It is?"

He nodded. "Yes."

"Will you please tell my mother that?"

He pulled her into his arms and kissed her. "Absolutely."

"I never met anyone like you before, either, Derek. All the men I'd known were so easily scared off when I opened my mouth. They never stood up to me like you did."

He half laughed, half snorted. "I know. You'd been waiting for someone to challenge you for a long time."

She sighed. "I suppose this means we're perfect for each other."

He grinned at her. "My thoughts exactly."

They lay snuggled together for a few minutes before Lucy ventured, "Derek?"

"Yes, my love?"

She traced a fingertip down his bare chest. "There is one bad thing about our wedding."

He frowned. "What's that?"

She sighed. "You won't be able to call me Miss Upton any longer."

He pulled her into his arms. "No, but I'll be able to call you Her Grace, the Duchess of Claringdon. My wife."

She wrapped her arms around his neck and kissed him. "I like that last one the very best."

## ❦ CHAPTER FIFTY-FIVE ❦

It was the day of their wedding. With the prince's help, they'd got a special license from the archbishop. Derek jested that it seemed being a duke was good for something after all. And while the ceremony had been short and fast, Cass, Garrett, and Jane had all been there. Along with Derek's mother, who was perfectly lovely, and Aunt Mary and Mrs. and Mr. Lowndes. Derek's brothers came, too. They were both as handsome as their older brother. But even though they'd been invited for Cass's sake, the Monroes had decided not to attend. Duchess or no, Lucy would be *persona non grata* with Cass's parents for quite a while to come. That much was clear. Apparently, they couldn't bring themselves to watch as a duke slipped through their fingers, especially since Cass had no other impending offers of marriage. "Mother said if I end up an unmarried spinster, it will not be her fault," Cass reported.

Lucy had even invited—

"There's my daughter, the Duchess of Claringdon!"

Lucy glanced up. Her mother stood in the foyer of Derek's town house.

As soon as they'd received Lucy's hastily written letter, her parents had rushed to town to wish the new couple well. Their blessing was more than granted. In fact, they were absolutely delighted with the prospect of their daughter, the duchess. They'd stood in the church this morning and beamed at Lucy.

Lucy's mother held out both gloved hands to her. Lucy made her way over and allowed her to pull her into a hug but not without a sharp pulling together of her brows.

"Mother?" Was this truly the same woman who'd essentially washed her hands of Lucy? Now she was here, in London, dressed as if she were about to take dinner with the queen, and acting as if they'd always had the best of relationships.

"Aren't you going to introduce me to your new husband?" her mother asked.

Lucy nodded. "Where's Father?"

"He's out dealing with the man who's taking care of the coach. I'm not entirely certain what he's up to."

Derek strolled over to them.

"Mother, I'd like you to meet Derek Hunt, the Duke of Claringdon."

Her mother executed a perfect curtsy. "Your Grace."

Derek bowed over his mother-in-law's hand. "Lady Upbridge, a pleasure to meet you."

"Believe me, the pleasure is entirely mine, Your Grace," her mother replied.

Lucy's father came bustling in just then, the same uncharacteristically happy look on his face. "My darling," he said, hurrying up to Lucy and hugging her as if they'd ever been the hugging sorts.

"Good morning, Father," Lucy said, still baffled by her parents' new demeanors.

Garrett strolled up. "Uncle Theodore. Aunt Frederica." The two gave him blank stares as if he didn't exist. But, Lucy noted, when they realized that the duke was narrowing his eyes on them for their behavior, they both reluctantly greeted their detested nephew. "Garrett. Uh, g . . . good to see you," her father managed to choke out.

Her mother merely said, "Garrett," in her most perfectly condescending tone.

Garrett was obviously attempting to hide his smile. "Always a pleasure," he said in a voice that implied it was, in fact, never a pleasure.

Garrett shook Derek's hand then turned to Lucy while Derek spoke with Lucy's parents. "The ceremony was lovely," Garrett said.

Lucy had tears in her eyes. She hugged her cousin. "Thank you, Garrett."

"For what?"

"For being willing to take care of me even when you thought I would be an old spinster."

Garrett threw back his head and laughed. "How do you know I didn't just pay Claringdon here to take you off my hands?" He bowed to Lucy. "Well, *Your Grace*, you truly are a duchess now. The first Duchess of Claringdon. Berkeley's heartbroken of course, but I'm certain he'll survive. He's already back in Northumbria."

"I wish Lord Berkeley the very best." Then Lucy leaned up and whispered, "And you, my cousin, may very well have your chance with Cass now."

Garrett's forehead wrinkled into a frown and he opened his mouth to speak, but just then Jane and Cass came up to them. Derek and Lucy's parents went over to speak with Derek's mother and the Lowndeses.

Jane hugged Lucy. "I cannot say I envy you being leg-shackled, but for a wedding it wasn't half bad."

Cass had tears in her eyes. "Oh, Lucy, it was so pretty. I'm so happy for you. You're a duchess. A real and true duchess."

Lucy laughed. "Yes, an unexpected duchess to be sure, but a duchess nonetheless."

"A duchess with a formidable tongue and penchant for bluntness," Garrett added.

"Guilty," Lucy agreed.

"When you wear a turban in your old age and stare at younger folk through your quizzing glass you'll be positively frightening, Lucy," Jane said. "I should know because I intend to be there with you, doing the exact same thing. With great aplomb, I might add."

Lucy laughed again. "Ooh, I'm quite looking forward to that, actually."

Lucy heard Derek speaking to her parents. "You know Lucy is an excellent rider." He addressed that comment to her father. "And being demure is highly overrated," he told her mother. She could just picture her mother's reaction to *that* statement. When he was done talking to her parents, Derek strolled over to their little group and put his hand around his wife's waist. He dropped his head and kissed her shoulder. Jane and Cass sighed.

"The only thing that would make this day more perfect would be if Swift were back to see it," Derek said to Lucy. He'd also mentioned something about how two of their other friends were apparently still missing on the Continent, but he hadn't wanted to spoil the day by explaining the details.

Lucy smiled and patted Derek's hand. "He'll be here soon, my love." She glanced over at Cass. Her friend wasn't speaking; she had turned away from the group and was tellingly tugging on the end of her glove. "Cass, are you all right?"

Cass nodded, wiping away a tear with a handkerchief.

"Dear, what is it?"

"It's nothing, I'm just . . . I'm so happy for you, Lucy. Truly I am. You've fallen in love and got married. A dream come true."

Lucy hugged Cass's shoulder and pulled her tight. "Don't worry, dear. You deserve the very same. And I've every confidence that you'll find it."

Cass nodded.

Jane came up to the two of them, and the three friends separated themselves from the others. "Well, Lucy. We started out trying to help Cass, and so we did."

"And in the meantime, Cass helped me, too. She helped me find love, just like you promised, Cass."

Cass smiled at Lucy. "Oh, Lucy, it was so obvious that you and the duke belonged together."

Jane nodded. She put her arms around her friends' shoulders. "So, what shall we turn our considerable talents to next, ladies?"

"Next is you, Janie," Cass said with a bright smile. "Lucy's going to help convince your mother to leave you alone when it comes to getting married."

They all glanced over to where Lucy's and Jane's parents were conversing. "Perfect," Jane said. "You'd better stop them from talking to Lucy's parents then. Their daughter just unexpectedly married a duke. They're never going to let me forget it. Up till now, I've been able to point at Luce and say, 'See, she's a wallflower, too.'"

Lucy laughed. "Don't worry, Janie. I'll make certain you're all right. I'll rescue you."

"I like the idea of a lady rescuing me instead of a man.

As it should be." Jane gave a resolute nod. "Mary Woll-stonecraft would be proud."

Cass laughed. "We must think of a way to keep Janie away from the marriage mart for good."

Lucy nodded. "Agreed."

"I agree, too," said Jane. "But for some reason, I think that you, my dear Cass, may be the next recipient of our collective help."

Cass blinked. "What do you mean? Lately I've been considering the convent."

"I do envy the nuns their simple clothing," Jane continued. "But what do you think I mean? Julian is on his way home."

"Oh, no, no, no. I've given up that hope. I intend to do nothing more than wish Julian and Penelope well."

"And hopelessly pine for him?" Jane asked.

Cass shrugged. "That part, I may well be unable to help."

Lucy and Jane patted Cass's shoulders.

Derek strolled up then and pulled his wife away from the little group and into a corner. He slipped a giant ring on her finger. Lucy looked down. The ring had three stones: a large square diamond in the center with a small, square sapphire on one side and a matching emerald on the other.

Lucy gasped. "What's this?"

"It's your ring. I picked it out this morning especially for you. It reminds me of your beautiful eyes."

Lucy reached up, threw her arms around his neck, and kissed him. "Oh, Derek, I love you so much. Thank you." She held out her hand and stared at the ring contentedly.

"You're welcome, my love. And I'm hoping it will make you more forgiving when I tell you that I must leave soon on a trip to the Continent."

Lucy furrowed her brow. "The Continent?"

"Yes. A bit of unfinished business from the war."

Fear gripped her heart. "Will you be safe, Derek?"

"I promise."

Her shoulders relaxed a bit. "Then I suppose I can spare you for a bit. I'll be busy learning how to be a duchess, no doubt."

He pulled her against him and whispered in her ear. "Do you want to know a secret?"

She turned her face to look up at him. "Yes. What?"

"This is what I wished for, when I threw that coin in the pool at the bathhouses."

She smiled wide but slapped playfully at his shoulder. "You're not supposed to tell what you wished for."

He pulled up her hand and kissed her knuckles. "It already came true."

COMING SOON...

# The Accidental Countess

## AVAILABLE IN OCTOBER 2014 FROM
## ST. MARTIN'S PAPERBACKS

And look for these novels in Valerie Bowman's
Secret Brides series

"Too delightful to miss!"—Lisa Kleypas

*Secrets of a Wedding Night*
*Secrets of a Runaway Bride*
*Secrets of a Scandalous Marriage*

From St. Martin's Paperbacks